Timebound:

A Steampunk Time-Travel Adventure

Book 3 of the Keeping Time Trilogy

by Heather Albano

Stillpoint/Prometheus

Stillpoint/Prometheus
Stillpoint Digital Press
Mill Valley California USA

FIRST EDITION

Special Hardcover ISBN 978-1-938808-52-4
Paperback ISBN 978-1-938808-50-0
Ebook ISBN 978-1-938808-51-7
version 1.0
The dingbat font used throughout is Nymphette, designed by Lauren Thompson, and the decorative fonts are Steampunk, designed by Marta von Eck, and Octant by Catharsis Fonts. All are used with permission.

❦

BY HEATHER ALBANO
Fiction:
Timepiece
Timekeeper
Timebound

Games (Choice of Games):
A Study in Steampunk
Choice of Broadsides (with Adam Strong-Morse and Dan Fabulich)
Choice of Zombies (with Richard Jackson)
Affairs of the Court trilogy (with Adam Strong-Morse and Dan Fabulich)

❦

INTERESTED IN SPECULATIVE FICTION?
SIGN UP FOR NEWS, GIVEAWAYS, AND MORE AT
stillpointdigital.com/prometheus/news

MANY THANKS TO:

Rocco and Claire Albano
Jennifer Regan
and
Ron Streeper
"Mary Shelley"-level Kickstarter backers
and godparents of
Stanislaus Lis
Rosamund Holborn
and
Arcturus Bastion

Timebound

Part One: Then

"Shall we never, never get rid of this Past?" cried he, keeping up the earnest tone of his preceding conversation. — "It lies upon the Present like a giant's dead body!"
—Nathaniel Hawthorne, *The House of the Seven Gables*

Chapter 1

The letter arrived on a day when nothing much else was occupying Maxwell's attention—no evening entertainment to prepare for, no headache from a previous evening's entertainment to recover from, no tailor appointments, nothing but a visit to a boxing salon or a drive in the park to occupy a gentleman of independent means until the gaming-hells opened.

Or the paying of calls, but Maxwell avoided those whenever he could. To the oft-stated envy of his friends, he had no mother or sister—or aunt, any longer—to compel him to so much as make a pretense of interest in the Season's young ladies. Most of Maxwell's set stood upon the threshold of thirty, an age when one's youthful foibles tended to prompt exasperation rather than indulgence on the part of one's parents. But Maxwell had no parents. Nor did he have any other compelling reason to marry—no title or estate for which he must procure an heir, no debts to be settled. The inheritance he had received upon the attainment of his majority, combined with some skill in the Exchange, was more than sufficient for his wants. He therefore had no reason to peruse the marriage-mart.

The day was rainy, ill-suited for the grays. The papers contained nothing of interest—with Wellington's monsters ferociously keeping the peace in all corners of the Empire, there were few suspenseful military conflicts to follow. Maxwell had nearly decided that the hours before dinner would be best spent at the boxing salon when the library door opened. His manservant entered, bearing a letter and his customary distant expression. From what Maxwell could see at this short distance, there was nothing particularly unusual about the letter—except its presence, for he did not cultivate the sort of friendships that prompted letter-writing. Indeed, those of his set who might, for lack of a better word, be termed friends—those boon companions with whom he drank and diced and hunted—were not the sort who ever willingly picked up a pen. And letters from his solicitors or other men of business would surely have been delivered first thing, by the morning post.

A prick of curiosity managed to reach his skin through the indifference that customarily swathed him from the outside world. He reached out and took the letter.

It was addressed in a prim, feminine hand, an occurrence sufficiently rare that a spark of alarm collapsed his indifference altogether. He ran a quick mental reckoning of his after-hours entertainments in the past three months. Surely none of them could be writing to make a claim upon him? He had so far been careful to not litter his life with encumbrances.

He tore open the envelope.

"Dear Cousin Maxwell," the letter began, and Maxwell, over the sharp flood of relief, cursed himself for a fool. His cousin's wife. Of course. No doubt, as the rest of his set married and settled down, he would have to become accustomed to receiving dinner or Christmas invitations from their wives. A circumstance that would need to be carefully managed, as no doubt many of those wives would have sisters on the hunt for husbands.

"Dear Cousin Maxwell," Priscilla had written, "I hope this letter finds you in good health. It was such a pleasure to meet you in August, though of course regrettable that it had to be under such sad circumstances. A thousand pities that your busy schedule did not allow you to make the journey for our wedding."

Maxwell pursed his lips. It seemed his cousin by marriage was a mistress of the art of delicate disapproval, like her mother-in-law before her. Maxwell had attended his aunt's funeral, and more recently his uncle's, being not quite willing to endure the round social condemnation that would surely occur if he did otherwise. But he had not felt himself similarly compelled to attend Georgie's wedding, and it seemed Georgie's wife intended to punish him for the slight. She had been full of sugar-coated barbs at his uncle's funeral, and apparently her quiver was not yet empty.

"George and I are finding the Hartwich estate quite comfortable. A great many alterations will be necessary, of course..."

Maxwell's eyes skipped a sentence, then two, then a paragraph. He avoided social functions and family obligations in order to avoid being bored by this sort of nonsense; was it now his fate to have it follow him by letter? He flipped to the second sheet.

"...which brings me to my reason for writing."

Finally.

"Whilst supervising a thorough cleaning of the garret, I discovered a trunk embossed with your father's initials. By its weight, it appears to contain a great deal of memorabilia, perhaps from his Army days. Unfortunately, the key is long since lost. The clasp could be forced, of course, but George is unwilling to do so, as the trunk, though residing in our garret, is not properly speaking our property. He instructed me to write and inquire whether you might wish to come to Hartwich and sort through its contents for yourself, or whether you would prefer we take on the chore of disposal." She signed herself his "affectionate cousin."

It was like missing a step in the dark, like lowering one's guard and receiving a punch to the gut at the boxing salon.

William Carrington's memorabilia. Likely from his Army days.

In other words, from the days before he fled to the Continent in disgrace, taking his wife but abandoning his infant son.

Maxwell stood still, then calmly put the letter on his desk and calmly walked to the sideboard to pour himself a brandy.

"Will there be any reply, sir?" his manservant murmured tonelessly.

"No—" All at once Maxwell changed his mind. "Yes. Send a telegram to my cousin George in Hartwich. 'Arrive tomorrow afternoon. MC.' Then pack my valise."

"Not bad news, I hope, sir?"

"No." Maxwell tossed back the brandy. "A matter of business, nothing more."

W hen he had left the Hartwich estate at the age of twenty-one, it had been with the firm intention of never returning. Such a pledge had been impossible entirely to keep, as it had been necessary to return for his aunt's funeral and then for his uncle's. Each time the place had seemed to loom over him as the coachman drew up before the front doors. It loomed now as he disembarked.

His cousin's wife was stiffly and correctly welcoming. She was displeased, Maxwell inferred, and after a moment's thought identified why. Perhaps there might have been more courteous ways to phrase the telegram than announcing his imminent arrival. Well, too late now.

"Is Georgie not about?" he asked her.

"George had business to see to on the estate," Priscilla answered, managing to impart the flavor of correction into her tone without actually over-emphasizing her husband's name—neatly done, Maxwell had to admit. He grinned a little to himself behind her back. George Carrington the younger had been "George" to all and sundry for years before his father's death. Only Maxwell persisted in using the diminutive. One took one's revenge wherever possible. It was not as though Georgie had the advantage of height, weight, or training any longer.

"He will join us at dinner," Priscilla added.

"Fashionable hours or country hours?" Maxwell asked, for the fun of seeing her bristle.

She did not disappoint. "We dine," she said frostily, "at seven."

"In that case, there is plenty of time for me to get through my business here," Maxwell said. "If you could have the chest brought to my room, I'll force the lock with a fireplace-poker and sort through the contents at once. I'll be out from under your feet before breakfast."

He fancied he saw her thaw a degree or two. Well, and why wouldn't she be pleased to be rid of the interloper?

He had been an interloper in this house since the moment he had arrived as an infant.

"I asked George which was your old room, and directed the maids to make it up for you," Priscilla added. She turned to ring the bell, giving Maxwell a chance to set his jaw.

"How delightful," he said. "Very considerate of you."

"I'll have the footmen bring your valise and the trunk. Is there anything else you might require? Tea, or other refreshment?"

"A decanter of brandy wouldn't go amiss," Maxwell said. "Very wet out there today."

⟨⟩

The chamber had been so thoroughly redecorated that it provoked no memories, unpleasant or otherwise. Which was something, at least. Maxwell sat before the fire, nursing Georgie's excellent brandy and eying the broken chest at his feet, its lock still intact and its hinges forced open.

There was surely nothing inside for him to care about. A matter of business, no more. Sort the papers, give instructions for disposing of whatever else was in there, endure Georgie's conversation for one meal, make tracks back to his life first thing in the morning.

No mysteries were about to be solved by the opening of this chest.

But for some reason it felt as though the universe was holding its breath as he reached for the lid.

The universe must have exhaled in disappointment, for there was nothing within worth the anticipation. A leather-bound tome whose gold embossing proved it to be volume three of David Hume's *History of England*. Two cloth-bound books of the sort typically used to keep journals and household accounts. A red velveteen bag, its drawstring pulled loosely closed. And atop them all, a letter. Addressed to him. By his full name, which he never used, in a hand he had never before seen.

A confession? Some mysteries were preferable unsolved. If one did not break the seal, one did not have to know precisely what scandal had prompted one's father to flee to the Continent. One did not have to know for certain wheth-er one's mother had abandoned her child to run away with her husband—or whether she had left her baby behind to run off with some other man altogether. He knew the latter was a possibility; his cousins had taken care that he know it. She'd been of easy virtue enough to climb down bedsheets once in her life, fleeing to Gretna Green with his father before she was of age to marry under English law—and if once, why not twice? But if one did not break the seal, one did not have to know, and the fire crackled invitingly against the November damp. A flick of the wrist would send the letter into the flames, set it burning like the rubbish it was.

Maxwell sighed. If he meant to do that, he would have done better to save himself the train fare. And this was nothing but a matter of business. He picked up the letter.

Or he attempted to, but the wax sealing it closed had melted and re-hard-ened over the twenty-nine summers and winters the chest had sat unremem-bered in the Carringtons' garret. The paper now adhered firmly to the red velveteen bag. Exasperated, Maxwell picked up letter and bag together, and the loose drawstring mouth opened, dumping the contents literally into his lap.

He had time to think, *The last damned thing I want is my father's watch—* Then he got a good look at it.

And nothing was ever the same again.

One could not be indifferent when one held in one's hands an object that could not possibly exist. Instead of one face, it had four, two crowded on one side and two on another. One of these looked like it might actually tell time, though it was not doing so at present. The second had both an inner and outer dial, with numbers running all around it. The third was even more complicated, comprised of eight dials nesting within each other. These had numbers as well, ones significant enough that they immediately jumped to his attention: 0, 2, 1, 1, 1, 8, 1, 9. The second of November, 1819. The day his parents had vanished.

And the fourth face simply could not exist.

The fourth face displayed moving images. Tiny ones, but perfectly distinct, a scene aboard a sailing ship that lurched over waves even as he watched it. And then dissolved, to be replaced by knights in plate mail competing in a joust.

The dry and logical voice he kept within had no chance to offer any opinions about coincidence, or to speculate with what Georgie might be lacing his brandy. The situation was too real, too immediate, to be considered sardonically at one remove. Maxwell's heart beat fast and his palms sweated as he held the timepiece. With his other hand he fumbled to pick up the second object the red velvet bag had deposited into his lap.

A locket. Of the sort a man rather than a woman would wear, and so the contents came as no particular surprise. This was William Carrington's memorabilia, after all. Of course he had a locket containing a picture of Elizabeth Barton.

Maxwell had only ever seen one portrait of her, the one painted on her sixteenth birthday, a year before she had run off to Gretna Green and her family had disowned her. It had hung in a disused bedchamber in the house of his Barton grandparents, but he had managed to carve out a little time to creep away and stare at it upon each childhood visit. She looked to be a few years older in this little locket miniature, or perhaps it was only the matron's cap confining her curls that granted the illusion.

The letter. The letter would explain all this. He had never in his life opened a letter so eagerly.

My dear son, it began. *We need your help.*

And for the second time in two days, Maxwell felt as though he had been punched in the gut.

Chapter 2

He wore the locket that held her picture hidden beneath the collar of his shirt, and he carried volume three of Hume's *History of England* everywhere he went. He kept hoping the book would crumble to dust in his hands, or he would open it to find it no longer contained the engraving of the fainting Elizabeth Barton, or he would wake with memories of a childhood in which he was welcomed home from school by a mother's warmth instead of an aunt's thinly-veiled dislike. Surely some attempt would work, and he would emerge into a happily-ever-after that had always been.

He did not know what on earth had possessed her to cap her time-traveling career by posing as a prophetess in Henry VIII's court. Even for the reckless, impetuous, adventurous girl he had come to know from the pages of her journal, it seemed an unnecessary, not to say a suicidal, risk. Yet she had done exactly that: Hume's *History of England* confirmed William's letter.

Elizabeth Barton, variously known as the Holy Maid of Kent and the Mad Maid of Kent, had claimed to be born in 1506, but nothing could be substantiated about her early life. She might have suddenly appeared, full-grown, at the age of nineteen—which was, Maxwell had cause to know, exactly what she had indeed done. She took a job as a servant girl in Thomas Cobb's household and was working there when she fell seriously ill on Easter Sunday of 1525 and began to speak in rhyming prophecies. St. Sepulchre's in Canterbury had opened its doors to her, and thereafter Sister Elizabeth rubbed shoulders with some of the most influential men of the day—Wolsey, More, even Cramner. Cramner said she had, by the power of the Holy Ghost, told him of many things done and said in other places—places where she could never have gone herself, places from which she could have received no word.

Of course she had.

At first Sister Elizabeth confined her prophecies to general warnings against sin and vice, but when King Henry declared his intention to have his marriage to Katherine of Aragon annulled in order to marry Anne Boleyn, she suddenly became specific. Elizabeth Barton spoke openly against His Majesty, gathered about her a group of important supporters, and went so far as to force herself into the King's presence. She publicly warned him that if he divorced Katherine and married Anne, he would no longer be king of the realm, would reign a mere seven months after his second marriage, and would die a villain's death.

Of *course* she had.

Given the personality revealed in her journal, given William's clue that she had died by the hand of Henry VIII, Maxwell could have picked her out of Hume's *History* even if she hadn't called herself by her real name.

What he could not infer from the pages they had left behind was *why*. William had not explicitly said in his letter. Elizabeth's last journal entry said only something cryptic about "one last journey, to rescue a friend in need"—though she had scribbled rather than carefully written the words, and the word "friend" might have been "fool."

William's last entry definitely used the word "fool." In a deliberate parody of his wife's phrasing, he had written, "One last journey, to rescue two fools in need." Elizabeth and who else? No one else in Hume's *History* immediately leapt to Maxwell's eye as a time traveler.

Confronting a king rarely ends well for the person who forces herself into His Majesty's presence, and it had not ended well for Elizabeth Barton. She and her supporters had been arrested on charges of treason. The "Mad Maid of Kent" confessed, probably under torture, that she was a "poor wench without learning" who had invented all of her "visions," and she and all her supporters except Thomas More were sentenced to death. Elizabeth Barton's head was struck off, parboiled, and impaled upon a pole of London Bridge—the only woman in British history to be accorded such an honor.

And William Carrington had spent the next forty years trying to rewrite the timeline and bring her home.

It's too late for me, he had written in the letter that had changed Maxwell's life one gloomy November afternoon. *I am about to die as an old man in 1819. There's nothing you can do for me. All I'm asking you to do is rescue her.*

But Maxwell, who after all had studied logic in some of the most privileged classrooms in the Empire, was able to work out that rescuing Elizabeth, if it could be done early enough, would have the side effect of preventing William ever starting his doomed quest. It was *not* too late for William. It was not too late for either of them. For any of the three of them.

It was never too late if one had a timepiece.

Sitting on the floor of Georgie's guest room, frantically flipping the pages of his father's journal until golden candlelight faded into dawning day, Maxwell had seemed to see the universe smoothing itself into an orderly pattern. For the first time in his life, he had known what to do. For the first time in his life, something other than a moment's pleasure compelled him forward. When he reached the last page, he had snapped the journal shut, risen from the floor, straightened his ruffled hair in a gesture that looked, in the mirror, like a knight pulling down the visor of his helm, and set off to right this wrong.

He was not certain now how many years ago that had been. It was still November of 1848—it was eternally November of 1848—but Maxwell was aging in leaps and bounds as his father had.

The timepiece would not take him to Henry's court, no matter how hard he tried, but at first that had not troubled him. He could go other places. With all of time to play with, surely there was some thread he could pull free and thereby unmake the whole tapestry. He wrote letters, appeared as a heavenly messenger, tried to ingratiate himself with an earlier generation of the Cobb family that would someday employ Elizabeth Barton...but no attempt had any effect.

The picture in Hume's *History* never changed. His memories of hiding in the window-seat, exiled from the fire lit family circle of aunt and cousins, remained fixed. On the other side of history, his mother's head still rotted on the pike on London Bridge.

William had not died trying to bring Elizabeth home, not exactly. Maxwell, piecing together the wording of the letter and an old tale of a monk's body found hanging in a wood near the house his parents had been renting in 1819, had recognized early on what William had done instead. Back then, he had been outraged at his father for giving up. Maxwell had vowed that he would surrender to no such weakness, that he would never be stopped until he succeeded. But tonight—the twenty-third of November 1848—how long had it been the twenty-third of November?—tonight he stared at the image of the Mad Maid of Kent reflected in the glass of the brandy bottle and understood the lure of the rope.

The image wavered and distorted as though the glass of the bottle had been harbor water disturbed by a ship's wake—reasonable enough, given it was the second brandy-bottle he had opened tonight. If Priscilla had never written that damned letter, if he had never surrendered to that moment's impulse, he would have never known there was anything to be missed. He might have gone about his hollow pleasurable life, the round of grays and boxing-salon and gaming-hells, with an acceptable degree of contentment. But now there were twin aching holes in his chest, one of angry pity for the boy in the window-seat who should have had a family fireside of his own, and the other a growing, grinding self-loathing as failure piled atop failure.

What the hell was the point of a timepiece, if it could not be used to mend what mattered? What the hell was the point of William bequeathing it to him, if he could not effect a rescue? He remembered now with bitterness that moment of crystal clarity in Georgie's house. He had seen himself as a knight-errant, sent by a wise man on a quest to undo the unspeakable harm that had befallen the world. Befallen the world of the boy in the window-seat, at least. And that had been illusion. Indulgence. There was no pattern, no grand and glorious obligation, no knowledgeable sage behind the scenes—just himself and the pocket watch and his failure to do anything worthwhile with it. His life was not a facet in some grand plan; there was no meaning to his life at all. No point in forward motion. Nowhere to move to.

He wondered how long he would decide to keep moving, in that case.

There was a way to check, of course. One could not cross one's own timeline.

His fingers felt as though they had doubled in size. He fumbled at the catch of the pocket watch for long minutes before he forced it open, and it took more than one try to spin the tiny dials. *If it takes me to tomorrow, I'm not there to-*

morrow. But if it won't take me to tomorrow, at least I'll know I didn't kill myself tonight.

Even in his own head, the grammar sounded suspect, but he knew what he meant.

If it won't take me to New Year's Day, I'll know I'll find reasons for making it through another six weeks.

He could not imagine what those reasons might be, but it would be reassuring to know his older self would discover some.

If it won't take me to 1858...or 1868...or 1878...or 1888...I'll know I am to live to a ripe old age. He supposed that would mean he had found a way to accept his failure, though such acceptance seemed impossible now.

If it won't take me to...to...to 1948, or 2048, or 3048...then I suppose that means...then I'll know I'm to carry on time traveling.

He guffawed suddenly at the absurdity of it and reached for the brandy, and the unsteady sweep of his arm knocked the bottle to the floor. It touched the soft carpet with hardly a thud, and the amber liquid soaked noiselessly into the embroidery. Maxwell lurched to grab his satchel out of the way of the flood, lest the liquor ruin William's journal within.

He found himself standing, the room dipping and swimming around him. Going forward to discover what choice he would make seemed, in that moment, a perfectly reasonable thing to do. It only took him four tries to shove the *History* back in the satchel.

He had set the watch to...something in the future. He couldn't remember what. 3048, he thought. He squinted, but now could make no sense of the numbers—they bled into each other as the room whirled. He shrugged and depressed the side button twice and the top once. That took several tries as well.

3048, he thought.

The world around him went white, then black, then every color of the rainbow.

⁂

For a moment, Maxwell thought he was in a thunderstorm, though no rain fell. Lightning lit up the sky in a flash of blue-white, then was gone. It was followed by a crash of thunder, deafening, just overhead. A sudden cold wind sprang up and tugged at him, and he stumbled forward two or three steps.

He had seen brick walls in that lightning flash. Even through the brain-deadening fog of the brandy, that seemed wrong. He would not have expected the London of 3048 to look quite so prosaically similar to the London of 1848.

There was a second flash of lightning...and hard on its heels, a burst of thunder. It shook the ground under Maxwell's feet.

And it shook the ground again.

He understood with unconcern that something enormous was advancing upon him. It took another stomping, earsplitting step. It did not occur to him to run; he awaited its arrival with no more than vague curiosity, still puzzling over the longevity of brick buildings.

Something grabbed his arm and jerked him to one side.

Even night-blind and six or seven sheets to the wind, Maxwell's reflexes knew what to do with an attack like that. He put all the strength of his arm behind an uppercut...but somehow it did not work as expected. He seemed to drive forward very slowly, and his opponent was simply not there when his fist reached its goal.

Lightning lit up the sky, and Maxwell saw that he was facing opponents, plural, all ragged- looking men like the first. They circled him, closing in. He stumbled to engage with one, then another, in a drunken ballet. Somehow he lost the satchel. Then his nose exploded with blood and a distant, muted pain, and he collided with slow inevitability into one of those perplexing brick walls.

It was very difficult to keep upright. He slithered down onto the cobblestones, then found himself unable to rise. A heavy weight pinned him down and a leathery hand slapped itself with indecent haste over his mouth. "Shut the bloody hell up!" the owner of the hand hissed in Maxwell's ear.

Maxwell realized distantly that the ground had been shaking all this time, and the lightning flashing with increasing regularity. Another blue flash seared his eyes...and this time, did not fade.

Now he could see that he was lying in an alleyway, one strewn with broken things and filth. Over his captor's shoulder, he could see a bit of the intersecting street, wider and more evenly cobblestoned, but no cleaner. The surrounding buildings rose four or five stories, and higher still, a distant wall blotted out the horizon.

A foot the size of a boulder stomped down onto the cobblestones. Under the blue light, it glinted copper-red. Maxwell's captor shrank back from it, but his hand did not leave Maxwell's mouth and his weight did not leave Maxwell's back.

The boulder-sized foot was attached to a tree-trunk-sized leg, also copper. Maxwell's eyes traveled slowly upward, annoyed at the way the leaning buildings interrupted his view of the torso, until his eyes rested on the head. It was level with the top of the distant wall. Without mouth or nose or ears, it put him in mind of a Tudor knight's helm, except for the blue-white light that poured from its eyes and lit up the entire street. It tilted its head this way and that, shining light into shadowed corners, and Maxwell had time to wonder if it would be able to see his little group crouched in the alleyway. It occurred to him that perhaps it would not be such a good thing to be caught.

But the giant passed on. Lighting flashed in the direction it had gone, and tremors ran faintly through the cobblestones for quite a long time after. Only when they were completely gone did the weight atop Maxwell fractionally relax.

This seemed like important information, but Maxwell could not remember what to do with it. He was musing over the presence of the copper giant. And, more distantly, still puzzling over the presence of brick walls in a London sufficiently far in the future to be inhabited by copper giants. And finally, he was wondering how he could be this dizzy when lying prone. The last few shreds of consciousness were slipping from his grasp.

"What the hell is wrong with you?" his captor demanded in an Irish brogue. "Don't you know enough to get out of their way?"

"I don't think he knows much of anything," another voice pointed out. "He's drunk as a lord."

"Spider," said the man holding him down, inexplicably.

"The Spider'll have to know," the other agreed. "We better take him in."

And that was the last Maxwell heard before unconsciousness claimed him.

❧

Someone was coughing.

The sound splintered through his aching head, and his stomach lurched upward in response. He rolled to his side with an effort. He did not actually vomit, but perhaps that was only because—judging by the smell—he had already emptied his stomach. He fell back with a groan.

"There, there, sir," a voice murmured soothingly. It was a woman's voice, old and rough and raspy, heavily Cockney, one he was sure he had never heard before. "You're in good hands."

He barely managed a word of response. "What...?"

"You were knocked down in the street by runaway horses," the woman said. He didn't remember being anywhere near horses, but certainly it felt as though something had pummeled him. "It seems you took a drop too much first." That he did remember. He could see his own hands opening the second bottle of brandy. "So no doubt you feel quite wretched, but I don't think you took any real damage." She broke off, coughing again. "Ah, forgive me, it's the damp gets into my throat. Can you tell me your name, then?"

He slitted his eyes open. The room was mercifully dim, lit only by a flickering candle near his face and a smoldering fire a little further off. In between the two, a woman sat in a rocking chair. With the candle positioned as it was, he could see very little of her face. He discerned the outlines of her cap clearly, but would have been hard-pressed to tell the color of the hair that straggled from it. From the way she hunched over the knitting in her lap, he guessed the hair must be gray.

"What's your name, lad?" she persisted.

It was a kindly voice, for all its roughness. Maxwell let his eyes close. "Carrington."

"There we are, and that's just what the card in your pocket said. My lads would have it you'd been killed, but I told them you weren't much hurt, a strong man like you. And the date, sir, do you know that?"

Sometime in the future, was all he could think. And, *If I can get to the future, I didn't kill myself tonight.*

He must have said some of that aloud, for she agreed. "No, you didn't get yourself killed tonight, though near enough to it. Can't you tell me the date?"

He tried to open his eyes again. There was something wrong about the room. How had he come to be here? The last thing he remembered was opening a second brandy bottle. He supposed he might have gone walking while several sheets to the wind, and it would have been easy enough to fall under a cart's wheel in such a condition, but how would he have managed to get so far from home? The room, what little he could see of it in the uncertain light, was the poorest of poor hovels.

He remembered something about unexpected brick walls. And an enormous metal foot. And spiders.

"There was a spider," he said. No, that wasn't right. The old woman coughed again, and when the spasm had ended, he tried to rephrase. "Men set upon me, out in the alleyway."

"No, no, sir," she soothed. The knitting needles clicked. "'Twas a cart near ran you down. And you'd had more than enough to drink, no doubt you're remembering dreams."

"No," he said from a great distance, shutting his eyes against the pain. "They attacked me. And said they were taking me to see the Spider. Who's the Spider?"

"That's a funny thing to hear. I shouldn't wonder if that knock on your head is to blame. You'd a card in your pocket, so my lad went to your house to fetch your servants, but have you other family? We could send for them. Write to them, maybe."

"I've no family. My mother's dead, and my father with her. I keep trying, but I can't..." Abruptly, Maxwell remembered he shouldn't speak of that. He dragged his eyes open completely. "Wait, *where* am I?"

"My kitchen," the old woman said, pausing in the rhythmic clicking of knitting needles to look at him with serious dark eyes. "The lads brought you here, where you'd be safe. Tell me the date."

"Who are you?"

"What's the year?" she countered.

Every muscle in Maxwell's body had tensed. "Why do you want to know?"

"What year was it when you awoke this morning?" she said, and for the first time, Maxwell caught sight of what she had half-hidden beneath the half-complete blanket.

He lunged upright, but far too slowly. His head felt as though it would split open, his sense of balance was gone, and she moved faster than he would have thought possible for a woman that age. She eluded his grasp, then hard hands seized him from behind and shoved him back down.

He hadn't even realized there was another person in the room, let alone a man practically standing over him. When he could see clearly again, the old woman stood straight behind the rocking chair, aiming with a dead steady hand the smallest pistol he had ever seen. Her knitting had dropped from her lap and lay abandoned on the floor with the rest of her pretenses.

The hand that did not hold the pistol held his pocket watch. "Fascinating trinket you have here," she said—and her voice was different now, still raspy, but cool and clear and not in the least kindly. "Fascinating suit of clothing. What year was it when you awoke this morning?"

If he had not actually seen her jump from the chair, he would have sworn she was a different woman. Decades younger.

"Age is all in how you move," she said, sounding amused. The Cockney accent was gone from her voice. "I was an actress for many years. Well, I'm an actress still, in every way that matters. So I should say, I performed upon the stage for many years. When you've a voice like mine, you're often cast as old women even when you're still quite young. And I...have chosen to take advantage of the freedom such a role provides. I'm the Widow Ramsey, no danger to anyone at all—"

A cough spoiled the last words. For an instant Maxwell assumed it was part of the act. In the next instant, he identified it as an opportunity, but the bodyguard standing behind him pressed a second pistol to his skull while the Widow Ramsey was still groping for her rocking chair.

"Damn," she muttered after a few moments, dabbing at her eyes and mouth. She had laid the pistol beside her on a little table, but still had hold of the watch. She leaned back in the chair—confidence, or had the coughing fit tired her? Maxwell forgot to wonder as she drew his father's little journal from her apron pocket. "Fascinating trinket," she said. "Fascinating suit of clothes. Fascinating—" She flipped the pages with one finger. "—tale. I'd take it for a fairy story, except here's the watch."

"You had no right to go through my things—"

"Excuse me," she cut him off, "you burst onto *my* street, half an inch from being captured by the Prime Minister's patrols and giving them all this. I shudder to think what could be done with it in the wrong hands."

"What's happened to England?" he whispered.

"What year was it when you awoke this morning?"

He surrendered. If she had read his father's journal, she already knew most of the story anyhow. "The year of our Lord eighteen hundred and forty-eight. Now tell me, what has happened to England?"

She nodded, apparently accepting the bargain: an answer for an answer. "The Empire is a divided entity. The very rich live high above in their dirigibles. The rest of us live below, kept in check by their constructs. Are you the William Carrington who wrote this account?"

"No. His son. William Maxwell. I go by my second name."

She nodded, and went back to flipping pages. After a moment or two, she looked back at him inquiringly.

He realized she was granting him a turn to ask a question. Floundering at the unexpected courtesy, he managed, "Is it—is it—what year is it now?"

"The year of our Lord nineteen hundred and ten." She looked at him thoughtfully. "Would you like some water?"

There was still a pistol clapped to his skull. The dichotomy of threat and courtesy together staggered him more than almost anything else about this night. "I—uh—yes. If you please."

The Widow Ramsey gestured, and a second man Maxwell had not noticed in the shadows left his place long enough to thrust a chipped cup of warm and odd-tasting water into his hand. The man with the pistol did not move.

The Widow Ramsey gestured again, putting Maxwell in mind of a queen upon a throne, and the second man set an additional candle on the table at her side. She looked over at Maxwell, more of her features perceptible now. She was indeed younger than she had initially appeared, though her heavily-lined face made it hard to tell by how much. "Your turn."

"My—? I—" She might as well give him free turns, he thought furiously, given how little he was doing with them. He made a vicious effort to think through the headache. "How—how did this happen?"

She understood his "this" to mean the state of affairs in England. "A little at a time," she said. "We were in danger, and the constructs were built to protect us. Do you know how the Battle of Waterloo was won?"

"Everyone knows that," Maxwell said. "Wellington's monsters. Now they protect all parts of the Empire."

"In your 'now,'" she agreed. "Four years after your 'now,' in 1852, they rebelled, throwing off their yoke and using Britain's own strategies and tactics against her human soldiers. These constructs were built to protect us from them. Now we are the danger protected against."

"By whom? Who has caged you here like rats? Why do you not fight?"

"How did your mother die?"

After a stunned moment, Maxwell gestured at the book. "Two-thirds of the way through. There's a letter from my father tucked between the last two pages with ink." The Widow Ramsey turned the pages one-handed, without letting go of the timepiece. "Why do you bother asking me any of this?" Maxwell demanded. "You have the whole story right there."

"I didn't have time to read your father's novel-length saga. You weren't unconscious that long." She found the letter, unfolded it, and studied it a moment. "The Mad Maid of Kent? Truly?" She looked up and seemed to judge the truth from his face. "I suppose it would make sense, a prophetess being actually a time traveler."

"You're unusually well-read."

"For a woman of my class? I'm not of that class, though, not originally. I had the run of a baronet's library when I was a child. I've always liked Tudor history, and I think I would remember that story either way. She was a most outspoken young woman, the Mad Maid of Kent. Courageous, to defy a King to his face. Even braver to continue her defiance when she was warned by so many to stop."

"Yes," Maxwell said. "From all I hear, that was my mother through and through. Fearless and outspoken."

"From all you hear?"

"From what I have read in my father's journal. My other relations spoke less kindly of her."

"You never had the opportunity to judge for yourself?"

"No."

"But you have this timepiece. Why do you not travel to the past and rescue her?"

His eyes wanted to close against the headache and the weight of it all. "I've tried. I've spent…years trying. The watch won't let you be in two places at once. All my chances are closed to me."

The Widow thought that over. "So you likewise cannot go to your own past."

"Or future." He realized he was several questions behind and tried to rally. "Why do you not fight those who oppress you?"

"We did." The Widow Ramsey leaned back in her chair with a sigh. "'The 95,' people say. Like the Jacobite rebellions, back two centuries ago in Scotland— they're called the 15 and the 45, and we picked up the same pet name. We lost, just like them. And Whitehall destroyed us afterwards—just like them." He must have looked puzzled, for she went on, "Did you ever learn what happened in the Scottish Highlands, after the 45? It's worth discovering. We were razed to the ground in exactly the same way." She was silent a moment. "We started too late. Our inventor had his stroke of brilliance too late. By the time we were positioned to fight, it was too late."

"'We,'" Maxwell said. "You were one of them?"

"Indeed I was." She looked speculatively down at the watch. "I know *exactly* what mistakes led to our defeat and to their deaths. Which has been a useless piece of hindsight. Until now." She looked back up. "What in God's flaming hell are you doing walking around drunk with treasure like this, Maxwell Carrington? You were two steps from arrest, and if they'd taken you, the Prime Minister would have this weapon to use against us in addition to all the rest. We can't let it fall into their hands."

"I'm not part of your 'we,'" Maxwell said, "and the watch is mine. I'd rather it not fall into *anyone* else's hands."

She cocked an amused eyebrow at him. "Bit late."

"Fine, very well." It was only sense to surrender for the moment. He would find some other chance to take it back. "It's fallen into your hands, but at least keep it from the Prime Minister—and from the Spider I heard your men speaking of. Who is he, anyway? The, the, Bandit King or some such, is that it?"

"Not much else to do down here in the stews but crime," she said, in a tone of agreement. "The Spider keeps it civilized."

"I don't want it in his hands even if he *is* civilized." The Widow Ramsey smiled again, and Maxwell groaned. "A bit late for that too? You work for him, then?"

"No," she answered in a tone of great precision, tucked the pocket watch and the journal back into her apron, and took up her knitting. The candlelight threw her shadow against the wall, so large it overwhelmed the rest of the hovel. In the guttering light, she seemed to have more than the two arms, and the knitting spilling from her lap looked like a fisherman's net. Or a giant web.

His head was swimming and his mouth tasted foul. He feared he might be on the verge of unconsciousness once more. "What did you put in that water?"

"Nothing." She did not look up from the web she spun. "You're suffering from a knock to the head on top of too much liquor. You did this entirely to yourself."

"Why were you not executed with your co-conspirators in 1895?"

Despite the enormity of her shadow on the wall, she had somehow managed to shrink again into the chair, back bent, fingers working the knitting. She looked once more decades older. "I'm nobody important," she said. "Just the Widow Ramsey. In years past I was a music hall girl, now I take in the sewing, before long I'll be dead of the black lung, why would anyone give me a second glance? I'm nobody."

"'Nobody,'" Maxwell snorted. "I see. And I work for the Spider now, is that it?"

She did not look up from her knitting. "Very perceptive of you, Maxwell Carrington. But you had better get some rest first. We'll begin in the morning."

Chapter 3

Maxwell woke with a blinding pain behind his eyes, painfully loud church bell chimes clanging in his ears, and the sense that he had been having a long, convoluted nightmare. He lay very still with his eyes closed, trying to remember where he was.

Not on his silken sheets in his St. James Square house, that was certain. The fabric rubbing against his bare skin—bare skin?—was far too rough. But it wasn't his cell in the priory of Tudor-era St. Bartholomew's the Great, either. The smell was all wrong. So were the church bells.

The church bells ought to be telling him something, but he couldn't think what.

"He awake yet?" a gruff voice asked from the doorway.

"Still sleeping it off," another voice replied in an Irish brogue. Maxwell identified that voice as belonging to one of the men who had attacked him in the alleyway on the previous—

Oh.

It came flooding back in a rush of unwelcome images. Before he could acclimate to them, a foot poked his side, none too gently. Maxwell blinked up into the unfriendly face of the larger of the two who had stood guard over his interrogation by the Widow Ramsey.

By the Spider. She's the Spider.

"Get up," the Irishman said. "Get washed and put this on." He dumped an armful of cloth on the pallet next to Maxwell. "She wants you."

"The Spider?"

The big man looked at him in silence for a moment. "The Widow Ramsey. We do not use the other name."

"I'll use whatever name I like," Maxwell said. "How do you intend to stop me?"

The big man smiled a little in a manner Maxwell did not care for at all. "She wants you alive, for some reason, but there are enough other ways to dissuade you."

Maxwell struggled up onto one elbow, noting first that his pallet appeared to be on the floor of a garret of some sort, nearly bare of furniture and icy cold, and second, that he was clad only in undergarments. He raised an eyebrow at the bundle on the floor beside him. "I would prefer my own clothing, if you please."

The Irishman barked a laugh and stepped back with folded arms.

The water in the cracked basin was freezing cold, and so dirty Maxwell did not feel as though the transaction worked out to his advantage. The shirt and trousers were, oddly enough, a decent fit, and he'd worn clothing that smelled worse. The Widow Ramsey received him in the same kitchen in which she had interrogated him the night before.

Her age was as hard to decipher in the wan daylight as it had been the night before. The hair peeping out from her cap was indeed iron-gray, her face was lined and worn, and she bent over, supporting her weight with a stick—but he could not forget how fast she had moved the night before. She glanced up at him and spoke with the Cockney accent she had assumed when they first spoke.

"Sleep well, Mr. Carrington?"

He ignored that. "If you'll return my belongings, I'll be on my way."

"No, I don't think you will," she said. "If I understand your father's journal, you're unable to leave for another sixteen hours whether I return your timepiece or not. Don't you want to learn a bit about where you've landed?"

"Not especially."

"Well," said the Widow Ramsey, "I'm afraid you've no choice in the matter. You'll be coming for a walk with me."

"For what purpose?"

She smiled at him. "I told you, I take in the sewing. I have mending to deliver."

The big Irishman shouldered past Maxwell, grasped a sack sitting in the corner of the kitchen, and swung it to his shoulder. "One or another of Mrs. Ramsey's boarders generally goes with her, to carry what she cannot," he explained. "But she'd be well able to walk the streets alone and fear nothing."

"I'm nobody important," the Widow Ramsey said, smiling serenely. "But all three of my boarders are known to work for the Spider, and they're fond of me, so I'm under the Spider's protection too. Not that anyone knows who the Spider is—but everyone knows better than to trouble someone the Spider protects."

The kitchen door opened, and Maxwell turned to see a slim, fair-haired girl enter. She wore the most extraordinary costume—tight trousers, tall boots, a bodice that made him think of Tudor peasant women, and a blouse tugged down low to expose her shoulders and the slight swell of her breasts. Strapped across her narrow hips was a belt. In the belt rode the largest knife Maxwell had ever seen a woman carry, and the smallest pistol he had ever seen in any context.

The girl looked him over, unimpressed.

"Maxwell Carrington," the Widow said in introduction, "Meg Drew. Connor O'Sullivan—" She nodded to the big man carrying the sack and amusement vibrated in her voice. "—you, ah, met last evening. Along with Ernie Clay, who isn't about just now, but whom I shall formally introduce later."

Maxwell eyed his three opponents as they left the dilapidated kitchen for the street. After last night, he knew better than to underestimate the Widow Ramsey, but at the moment she was confined by the role she had chosen to play and weakened by whatever illness caused her cough, and Maxwell was no longer drunk. He *was* unfortunately half-blind with headache, but he might never get a better chance. O'Sullivan was weighted down by the sack, and the girl was a tiny thing—

"Don't even think it," O'Sullivan advised in a low voice. Maxwell started. Looking up, he found the big Irishman regarding him sardonically. "And a word of friendly advice: don't underestimate Miss Drew."

The air outside was as thick and acrid as though a fire had broken out somewhere near. The Widow Ramsey was not the only one who coughed as it struck her throat; Maxwell could not help the reflex. Between his stinging eyes and the yellowish-gray cloud they seemed to have stepped into, it was hard to see, but after a moment's ferocious blinking, he made out buildings rising far, far overhead. Seven or eight stories they must be, piled haphazardly atop each other, looking ready to crumble at the slightest touch. Higher even than that, a great wooden wall rose, bisecting the sky. What weak sunlight there was filtered through a tiny gap in the wood and brick, nearly overhead. It felt like a Tudor prison cell.

It did not, however, *sound* like a Tudor prison cell. The yellow fog seemed to vibrate with a muted rattling—insistent, insidious, and burrowing into Maxwell's skull to worsen his headache. The others did not seem troubled by it. Indeed, they did not seem to notice it at all. Nor did they react when the ground shook under their feet, but Maxwell tensed, his inner vision suddenly presenting him with an image of an enormous looming copper giant, one foot raised to crush any careless mortal that crossed its path.

"It's all right," the Widow Ramsey said. "It's on the other side of the Wall. We're in no danger from it unless we venture out."

"We'd be its fair game then," O'Sullivan remarked, "seeing as none of us have work permits."

"You must have the proper papers to lawfully leave Spitalfields," the Widow Ramsey explained to Maxwell, though he had not asked. "A permit saying you've a job in the outer City."

"Not so many of those as there used to be," O'Sullivan said. "I remember when a Spitalfields lad could at least win a billet as a groom. But lately the toffs have been moving their London houses to the balloons above, where there's no need for either horses or men to look after horses. I'm not saying I regret the loss of the workhouse—"

"Then suppose you don't say it?" Meg suggested from Maxwell's other side.

"—but at least there was work then."

"We do all right inside the Wall," Meg said. "At least, the half that's the Spider's territory does."

The Widow Ramsey gave her a sidelong smile.

Meg returned it. "Where are we off to first, Auntie?"

They spent all morning touring the most extraordinary collection of tumbled-down buildings, delivering packets of mended cloth to ragged denizens who identified themselves variously as carpenters, weavers, bakers, potters, and apothecaries. All greeted the Widow Ramsey courteously, without any hint that they knew of her other identity, and they paid for her services with scraps of metal unlike any other coin Maxwell had ever seen.

The Widow Ramsey saw him looking and handed him one of the scraps to examine. "No Bank of England branch this side of the Wall," she explained, in a tone that was good-humored enough. "But a civilization functions more smoothly when tokens are used in place of outright barter, and it so happened there was a forger of no mean skill in search of employment. The Spider set him up as a coin-smith. What you're holding there is a talon. Ten talons to a raven. It has never been decided whether ten ravens would be a flock, an unkindness, or a conspiracy, because there's nothing here priced that high. A talon buys a loaf of bread."

Maxwell silently handed the coin back, not having to feign indifference to her explanation. He truly did not care.

But afterward, he could not help noticing that the amounts being handed to the Widow Ramsey in exchange for mended garments seemed rather excessive, if a talon bought a loaf of bread. He noted further that she did not tuck the coins into her apron pocket, but rather made a show of handing them to O'Sullivan, who added each new offering to a pouch hung round his neck. They appeared to be enacting this pantomime not for Maxwell's benefit but for that of the customers. Was this motley collection of humanity paying protection money to the Spider's tax collector, in the guise of paying the Widow Ramsey for doing the sewing, not knowing she herself was the Spider? Layers and layers; conspiracies within conspiracies.

Shortly thereafter, Maxwell could not help observing that the description "layers within layers" applied to the conversations too. The customers spoke naturally enough to the Widow, but when they turned to Meg, their words became stilted. They spoke of the weather, but awkwardly, and she answered in reassuring rote phrases. Apparently the river was in no danger of rising, despite the recent unexpected rain, but the locals should stay inside and bar their doors tonight, just to be safe. Maxwell remembered Meg speaking of "the territory behind the Wall that belonged to the Spider," and wondered briefly who controlled the other half, and what "rain" and "rising water" might signify. Then he reminded himself that it was no business of his and that he did not care.

The day droned on. The streets twisted like a knotted rope, walls of black-smeared brick and weather-worn wood pressing close on either side, yellow fog thickening and the rattling drone growing louder. Sometimes figures appeared suddenly from the fog and as suddenly vanished. It was a nightmarish reality, perfectly in keeping with Maxwell's pounding head.

What proved to be the last stop of the day was a cobbler's shop, at first glance no different than any of the other places of business they had visited—a rundown room on the ground floor of a ramshackle house. But a second look showed a sparseness to the furnishings, an unnatural lack of clutter in the corners. The cobbler himself, a thin man whose eyes kept flicking from side to side, was far more nervous in his manner and speech than any of the other tradesmen who had paid the Widow Ramsey for doing their mending. He seemed surprised to see her at first, and then abruptly remembered and rummaged in a strongbox for a few of the metal scraps. He uncurled a sweating palm and handed the Widow Ramsey its contents without any pretense of receiving mended clothing in exchange.

The Widow handed the coins ceremoniously to O'Sullivan.

"How are you finding your new premises?" Meg asked the cobbler.

The cobbler looked at her. "Quiet," he said in a tone of great care. "Thankfully." Then he glanced fearfully at Maxwell. "That's to say, it's given me time to set up a bit, you see. No doubt I'll have customers soon enough, once word gets about."

"Indeed you will," Meg said. "Just as the Spider promised. You're safe here and you'll be part of the village soon enough."

"You don't need to worry about Lord Bastion," the Widow Ramsey assured him. "You've made your mark on the Spider's enrollment list and you've moved your shop to the Spider's territory. You're protected now." She indicated Meg and O'Sullivan. "Just as I am."

The cobbler twisted his hands together. "I did hear—that's to say, I mean no disrespect, I don't mean to question, but—there is a rumor—"

"About rising water?" Meg interrupted. "That's got nothing to do with you or your shop, you know. It just rains sometimes. There won't be a flood, the Spider won't allow it. By tomorrow all should be...dry enough." For the first time, she seemed to be getting tangled in the metaphor. The Widow Ramsey glanced at her, and Meg colored a little before recovering. "You just might want to stay inside tonight. Bar your doors. Just in case."

The cobbler did not appear to find this reassuring, and after a few more such exchanges, Meg gave up on trying to allay his fear. The Spider's unofficial tax collection party departed the shop soon after.

They were most of the way back to the boarding house when the Widow Ramsey said, as though continuing a conversation begun much earlier, "They've walled us up alive in here. It's become almost impossible to get work permits, now that the factories are staffed by constructs."

"The metal man that almost killed you last night was a construct," O'Sullivan put in for Maxwell's edification.

The Widow nodded confirmation. "First they were controlled by men piloting them, then they were controlled by clockwork. The large ones have replaced men in the Army and the police force, and the smaller ones have replaced men and women in the factories."

"A disturbing pattern," O'Sullivan commented. "The toffs still need human servants to cook and clean—for now. But it's said in a few years there will be still smaller clockwork constructs that can do that work as well. And then they won't need us at all. No employment, no education, no room for advancement, no food, and no way to leave. They'll just hover high above and wait for the problem to take care of itself. It worked in Ireland."

There was silence for a few moments.

"During the *potato famine*," O'Sullivan clarified in a tone of exasperation. Maxwell's confusion must have been evident on his face. "Christ, aren't you from exactly then? You are…but you've no idea what I'm speaking of. Whole villages starved and to this day are left deserted, and you have *no idea*." He looked over at the Widow Ramsey and rolled his eyes.

"It's bad," Meg said, taking up the conversational reins, "but not so bad as it could be. The Spider sees to it enough goods are smuggled in, and we've got our own little village here. The Spider's territory does, at least. Lord Bastion still bleeds his vassals dry, but still it's better than when all the little crime lords scrapped for their own gain."

"It was bad, after the 95," the Widow Ramsey agreed. "Before that, Robert Locksley and Arcturus Bastion held the Underworld balanced between them. Locksley died in the uprising, and Adolphus Bastion took advantage of the chaos to oust his father and take over that empire. I believe he had thoughts of claiming the entire Underworld, but he couldn't manage it. He was never the man his father was.

"He did have a decent advisor for a time, though," she added after a moment, as though determined to speak justly of her enemies. "The Spider and the man behind the Bastion throne worked together to defeat all the little crime lords, and the two of them balanced the world behind the Wall between Bastion and the Spider as once it had been balanced between Bastion and Locksley. Unfortunately, Ellis is dead now, and without him standing behind the throne, Adolphus Bastion is a predatory menace. The Spider's the only one who can keep him in check."

"Someday it will be more than in check," Meg said. "More of Bastion's vassals change allegiance every day."

"Now, Meg," the Widow drawled, "you know very well the Spider doesn't court defectors. What an idea."

"I didn't say that." Meg dimpled. Now they were playacting for Maxwell's benefit, he was sure of it. "The defectors come because they wish to."

The Widow Ramsey allowed that. "Because where the Spider has power, the rules of civilized society are enforced. Which seems like a good use of power to me." Maxwell had still not responded, with voice or with expression. She gave him a good long opening, and when he did not take it, finally prompted, "And what might you think of that, Mr. Carrington?"

Maxwell glared at her sidelong. "Nothing in particular, Mrs. Ramsey."

The boarding house appeared abruptly out of the fog, its three stories making it seem very nearly cozy in comparison with some of the other eight-story towering monstrosities. The Widow Ramsey did not speak again until all four of them stood within its walls and the doors were shut.

"That's a shame," she said then, letting the Cockney trickle out of her speech once more. "I was hoping you'd see the value, and perhaps find within yourself an interest in staying. You said your own quest had failed, after all, and it doesn't sound as though much awaits you at home. The Spider could use another strong man to help keep the *pax araneae*."

"For what imaginable reason," Maxwell said tightly, "would I want to do that?"

Her lips thinned. "Because it is a problem in need of solving."

"Perhaps so, but it's nothing to do with me."

"And that," said the Spider, "is why I'm keeping your timepiece. From all I've read of your parents, a tour through my city would have been enough to buy their help."

I'm keeping your timepiece. He had been nearly certain of it since their conversation last night, of course. The confirmation still turned him cold—so instantly numb that the taunt about his parents barely registered. "You do not mean to return it."

"Indeed I do not," the Spider said, turning her back with ostentatious indifference. While Maxwell was still in the split second of deciding whether he could bring himself to strike an old woman, Connor O'Sullivan and Meg Drew moved easily into position, robbing him of the opportunity. "I can make better use of it than you ever have."

Chapter 4

Locked in the icy upstairs garret while afternoon turned to black night and the Spider decided what to do with him, Maxwell Carrington weighed his options.

The raw cold bit through the thin fabric of the shirt they had given him. He wished for his frock coat, or for some warming brandy. He was aware that he might as well wish for the moon. Or wings. Or a time machine.

With no other options, he wrapped himself up in the smelly, scratchy, threadbare blanket while he took stock of the situation. He had neither the skill nor the tools necessary to pick the lock. The building's construction did not seem overly solid, and he thought he might be able to break the door down with a sufficient application of force—but Clay and O'Sullivan were still in the kitchen with Meg Drew and the Spider, and all four of them were armed with those wicked-looking little pistols. Maxwell had no weapon but his fists, so any escape that began with a loud noise was doomed to failure. Besides, he did not know where the old woman had hidden his timepiece or his father's journal, and he could hardly escape in any permanent manner without retrieving at least the first—

But as the thought occurred to him, he saw the counterargument. Indeed, he must retrieve the watch to permanently depart, but that retrieval might be attempted after an initial escape. He still had something like six or eight hours before anyone could use the thing. If he could get away from here now, he might be able to later return before the Spider could abscond to some other time period with his timepiece. He would not be able to raid the boarding house alone, but it sounded as though this "Lord" Adolphus Bastion had a force of men equal to the Spider's. An alliance with his enemy's enemy was the best chance Maxwell would have of retrieving his property and escaping back home.

Which still left him with the problem of leaving this room.

As neither picking the lock of the door nor battering it down was an option, Maxwell turned his attention to the window.

He was still examining it when he heard footsteps on the stairs. The door jerked open to reveal Clay and O'Sullivan, both armed. Unlike the morning's encounter, Clay took the lead and did the talking. Otherwise, the script was the same. "Come downstairs. She wants you."

Maxwell descended the rickety stairway in front of Clay, Clay's pistol pressed to his back. They were taking no chances. As the blackness of the stairway began to give way to the glimmer of light and marginal increase of warmth of the kitchen, he caught scraps of a conversation—surely not an argument?—between Meg and the Widow Ramsey.

"I heard you," the older woman was saying. "But you don't run things, Meg, not yet."

"There's no sense to it, Auntie! It's an insane risk."

"I know it looks so," said the Widow Ramsey, "but I need you to trust my judgment. I'm—"

"Playing a hunch?" Meg sighed.

"Gambling on a long shot," the Widow said. "It isn't quite the same thing." She looked up as Maxwell and his guards entered the kitchen. "Ah, good. We are attending a meeting tonight, Mr. Carrington. You'll be coming with us."

"For what purpose?"

"There is more of my city I wish you to see." The Widow Ramsey smiled at him as though she could read his mind and divine his plan for escape and vengeance. "And if you accompany us under guard, I at least know where you are."

∽

The Spider conducted her operations from a rocking chair in the kitchen of a ramshackle but still comparatively cozy boarding house. Lord Bastion conducted his from an underground sewer.

Or what had once been an underground sewer, or perhaps several layers of collapsed sewer. Maxwell could not tell precisely; the ceiling disappeared into the shadows far above. The hall surrounding him was so large it might have held the throngs that had once crowded the Bath Assembly Rooms—but it presently stood empty, save for Lord Bastion, two Lord-Bastions-to-be, the Spider, and her two companions.

Lord Adolphus Bastion sat high above them, upon a literal as well as a figurative throne. Reachable only by a set of steps, his seat had been obviously and ostentatiously designed to tower over those on the ground. The throne was a fine piece of workmanship, all things considered—hewn out of some white stone, polished until it gleamed, disconcertingly bright against all the dimness and dirt. Perhaps, as the Spider employed a coin-forger, Lord Bastion employed a sculptor. It would not be the oddest part of this situation.

The old man sitting upon the high seat had skin as white as his hair and the bloated, bulging contours of a garden slug. Perhaps he never left this place, or perhaps not enough light filtered past the Wall to tan anyone's skin. By his side stood an equally pasty man of middle age—presumably his son, though it was hard to trace family resemblance between the pinched rat-like face of the one and the pallid double chins of the other. At the foot of the throne sat a narrow-faced child with the pale skin of his father and grandfather, and hair so light a shade of tow-blond it might as well have been prematurely white. He was watching everything closely, learning the family trade.

For a long moment, Lord Bastion and the Spider regarded each other. Then the Spider turned to the long wooden table that sat so incongruously in the middle of the sewer, pulled out a chair at one end, and seated herself.

It looked for a moment like deliberate insult. Maxwell tensed. But Adolphus Bastion only pulled himself to his feet and oozed his way down the steps, his son and grandson falling in behind him.

Bastion's son pulled out the chair at the other end of the table. Lord Bastion lowered himself into it, and the son took up a protective stance behind him. Meg Drew arranged herself in a similar stance behind the Spider.

"I thought," Lord Bastion said, flicking one hand in Maxwell's direction, "we agreed upon one bodyguard apiece. Not two."

"Your grandson is here," the Spider said.

"To observe. To learn. He can hardly be counted as a combatant."

"The parallel is remarkably apt, in that case. I assure you this new member of my organization is no one who should concern you." Lord Bastion looked unconvinced, and the Spider sighed. "Adolphus, we are on *your ground*. You have many more people than Alexander and Alistair to ensure your safety. This posturing serves no purpose. Suppose we move on to the purpose of this meeting?"

Adolphus Bastion chuckled. "As you wish, Katarina."

During the journey from the Widow Ramsey's boarding house to Lord Bastion's sewer, Maxwell had learned more about the social mores of Underworld crime lords than he had ever wanted to know. From his captors' conversation, he had gleaned that a sit-down such as this would traditionally be held on neutral ground, but that the Spider preferred to enter Bastion's stronghold and speak privately to him there. She did not feel she risked her safety in thus preserving her anonymity, for Bastion knew exactly what sort of backlash would result if he killed the Spider, and he did not dare unleash that chaos.

Over the course of the next few hours in the sewer, Maxwell learned more. His guess at the meanings of "rain" and "flood" had been correct; there was indeed a small-scale conflict being waged in the stews. Minor incursions had been made by Bastion's people into the Spider's territory. Contraband stolen by her people from the city outside the Wall had been hijacked by Bastion's vassals. Some of the lower members of the Spider's organization had retaliated in kind. No one had been killed—yet—but the two crime lords were meeting now to defuse tensions before an all-out turf war could begin. It was to no one's advantage if the city behind the Wall burned.

During those three hours, Maxwell additionally learned one especially valuable, if unwelcome, piece of information: that Adolphus Bastion would be a worthless ally.

Perhaps that was why the Spider had wished Maxwell to come along—to demonstrate how foolhardy would be any attempt to join the opposition. Maxwell had of course never met Arcturus Bastion, but it did not take knowledge of the long-dead father to see that the son was not half his equal. With every word, Adolphus Bastion betrayed himself as petty, greedy, and incapable of taking the long view. His son Alexander likewise betrayed himself as foul-mouthed and cruel. Of the child Alistair, Maxwell had no opportunity to judge, but with two such role models, it could hardly be hoped he would grow up to be anything better.

"House Bastion breeds true," Meg muttered as the Widow Ramsey's party walked back to the boarding house, the sit-down concluded and new treaty amendments in place. "For as long as anyone in Spitalfields can remember, there's been one Bastion bastard on the throne, one lurking in the wings, and one learning the trade."

"For longer than that," the Spider confirmed. "They were legendary when I was young, when Locksley controlled the other half of the Underworld. Of course, most of them were more impressive specimens than Adolphus."

"Every time I see that man," Meg said, "I wonder how he can possibly wield the power he does."

The Spider shrugged. "He presides over an empire that was assembled by the wits and strength of others, and so far his contribution to the dynasty is that he's managed not to lose it."

"Yet," Meg murmured with a little smile.

"Well," said the Spider, "at least he's managed to be losing it only one vassal at a time, so slowly it's not noticeable."

"How did he ever take it from the great Lord Arcturus in the first place, though?" Meg wanted to know. "No one's ever said."

"He couldn't have done it without Bill Ellis helping him," said the Spider. "Ellis hoped for great things and lived to regret who he put in power. Adolphus and Ellis chose precisely the right moment to strike, in the chaos after the 95. That is, *Ellis* chose to strike in the chaos; Adolphus, left to himself, would have struck about then anyhow, no matter the strategic situation. He spent all his life cowering like a cur before his father, and it was in 1895 that his patience suddenly broke. If there hadn't been a war on right then, he would have attempted to oust his father anyhow, and he would have lost. And we'd be dealing with Lord Arcturus now." The Spider considered this hypothetical state of affairs. "While that would not be pleasant, it might in some ways be preferable. Lord Arcturus was both vicious and ruthless, but he wasn't stupid. He understood the power balance between himself and Robert Locksley; he understood how both could work within it to the benefit of each one's vassals; he understood that even the stronger of two parties derives no benefit from a turf war, and that wars are therefore to be avoided. He didn't dabble in nonsense beneath his notice. Whereas Lord Adolphus—" She sighed. "—amuses himself by hijacking my shipments of grain."

Meg stopped. "You think he ordered that?"

"Of course he ordered it, dear. He's a short-sighted bully who enjoys tugging other people's strings. We've done this dance many times before, he and I. It hasn't escalated to war because I won't allow it to. Which means, I suppose—" The old woman smiled. "—the power is really mine."

Indeed. Adolphus Bastion might be the enemy of Maxwell's enemy, but he was demonstrably valueless as an ally. Maxwell considered the strategic situation as the Spider's boarding house came once more into view. Very well, the great white leech on the high white throne would not be directly useful. Perhaps he could still be leveraged indirectly. Perhaps there was a bribe that would work or a weakness to be exploited. Or perhaps an appeal to a more legitimate form of authority would be the correct risk to take? Maxwell had been stripped—literally—of the outer markings of a person of gentle birth, but he still had his stance and his accent. If he could manage to escape the Spider's custody even briefly, perhaps he could summon allies from among the legitimate authorities of this London.

Meg, engrossed in the history lesson the Spider was imparting, had ceased to pay Maxwell close attention. The Widow Ramsey was leaning heavily on her stick now, stifling coughs between her words. They were nearly at the boarding house.

He would never have a better chance.

Maxwell took one deep breath, shoved the girl into the old woman, and ran.

He had barely made it ten paces before Ernie Clay loomed up out of the shadows and clubbed him to the cobblestones.

*

For the third time since arriving in 1910, Maxwell woke with a pounding headache and no clear idea of where he was. He groaned, tried to turn over, and discovered he could not. A web-work of rope held him fast to the cot.

"There, now," the Widow Ramsey's voice soothed him. "Are you feeling any better?" She moved closer, and he had time to reflect that the very last damned thing he wanted was someone's motherly caress.

He needn't have worried. She drew only close enough to set down a candle. She positioned it just where the light of the flame hurt his eyes, nowhere near the proximity required for either of them to touch the other. Then she stepped back.

"Leave the revolver," she said, speaking over his head to someone else. "And close the door behind you."

There was a startled silence. "But—" Meg's voice protested.

"You and Ernie did your job with the knots," the Spider said. "I'll be safe, you needn't worry. And I require some private conversation with Mr. Carrington. Go."

Meg went without another word. The Spider returned to her rocking chair, which Maxwell could only halfway see through the dazzle of the candlelight. He heard her ostentatiously cock the pistol but couldn't see what she did with it. He had no intention of beginning the conversation.

Her first words were not at all what he expected.

"Do you play chess, Mr. Carrington?"

"Yes," Maxwell said warily.

"I assume by that you mean you have been taught, but not much more? Because you do not play it well." The Spider broke off, coughing. "Perhaps," she resumed a few moment later, "you are a man who prefers games of chance. I expect you spend time in the—gambling-hells, I think they were called?"

"They were," Maxwell said, "are, and they're well enough for a night's amusement, but I prefer to make my fortune in the Exchange."

"Ah, yes, of course. That makes perfect sense. The Exchange is a matter of numbers. Facts. A bit of what the Germans call psychology, but only a bit, only on a large scale. *True* gambling requires you to read your opponent's face—and you're not terribly skilled at matters involving people, are you?"

She paused. It might have been to invite him to answer; it might have been to smother a cough.

He didn't answer.

"*I* gamble," she said. "And I play chess. I'm quite good at it. My mentor taught me many years ago, back before the 95, when we were still planning our rising. He was known as Robert Locksley in the stews, but his real name was Frederick Kent. Frederick, Lord Seward. He knew chess and strategy and all the rest that's taught to young men by their tutors while young women learn watercolors and embroidery.

"And he taught me. He was always teaching. He didn't come to the warehouse often—he should never have come at all, of course; it's a wonder we weren't all unmasked long before 1895—but sometimes he would slip through the stews and spend an evening playing chess with Trevelyan or with me." She coughed. "He never fit there, of course. Though I think he would have stood out anywhere, even if he hadn't been born a lord. He was a great lion of a man, handsome and confident, with enough energy for any three people. Trevelyan was more the sort that faded into sh—shadows—" That coughing fit was longer. She let it have its way with her, then continued as though there had been no interruption. "Physically, I mean. He drew notice soon enough once he opened his mouth. Caustic as acid and brilliant as flame. But still nowhere near Seward's equal at chess. I wonder if there wasn't something a bit relaxing in knowing he couldn't win and need not try? I'd come home and Seward would be grinning across the chessboard and Gavin would be frowning, and I'd know it hadn't been a good day, but I'd also know the next day would be. Seward was very good indeed at determining what we all needed and seeing that we had it.

"And he knew I had the aptitude for strategy that Trevelyan lacked. He knew it before I did. I didn't realize then how deliberately he was teaching me. I wish I could thank him now. By the time the world came crashing down around our heads I could beat him at the chessboard.

"I play for higher stakes these days," she went on. "On a larger board. And something I've learned is that the placement of each piece is important. They must be set where they can play to their strengths. It takes time for a novice player to learn what those strengths are. Knights, in particular, can take one by surprise."

After that, she fell silent for so long that finally Maxwell gritted his teeth and asked the question she seemed to be waiting for. "How so?"

"In a world where a good day is two paces forward and one back," the Spider said, "a knight moves two paces forward and one sideways." He could hear again the brief smile in her voice. "The knight's abilities force the player to look at the board in new ways, consider new dimensions."

"You're in a chess game with Bastion," Maxwell sighed, in an attempt to move the conversation on.

"Bastion is the least of my concerns." The Widow Ramsey sounded impatient. "I want you to understand that it would have been easier for me to have one of my people slit your throat while you lay drunk than to risk my safety by sparing your life."

"And so?" Maxwell said. "Why didn't you?"

"Because in addition to being good at chess, I do quite well at whist. And any other game of chance which requires the player to read her opponent's face. For a great variety of reasons, I'm rather good at embodying other people's perspectives. Which is something…you have no experience doing and no idea how to do, isn't that right? I've never met a man so firmly locked inside his own head—except Adolphus Bastion, but there's nothing in there with him but whistling air, so he can only do so much damage. You're different." She sighed. "Very well, let me put it this way. Mr. Carrington, you owe me your life."

"And you've *stolen my timepiece*," Maxwell snarled. "Suppose we call it even."

There was a pause.

"That's *my mother's* life you hold in your hands," he added—and immediately wished he had not. It was a good argument, and true besides, but he would have retained more dignity staying silent.

The Spider sighed again. "I hold a great many lives in my hands, Mr. Carrington. I'm evaluating the strengths of more than one piece on the board just now." She coughed, swallowed it by sheer impatient force of will, and rose. Now he could see her face in the candlelight. "I will say it again, Maxwell Carrington: You owe me. It is due solely to my order that you're not lying at the bottom of the river with your throat slit and due solely to my protection that you're not being tortured for information in the Prime Minister's Tower or Bastion's cellars. So I have a proposal for you. Serve me faithfully a year and a day, and we will call your debt paid. Upon that day I'll return your timepiece, and you can go where and when you will."

Serve me faithfully? She said it as though it were a reasonable offer, rather than words that would have belonged better to the days of Arthur's knights or the fairies of a German fable than to anyone modern.

"A year and a day," Maxwell repeated.

The Spider inclined her head in assent and waited.

What could not be achieved by a frontal assault might possibly be achieved by patience. Maxwell's mother might not have approved, but his father would have. Maxwell had all of time to play with—or would once he had his time-piece back—so what was a year and a day to him?

And there was a decent chance he wouldn't have to wait that long. Achieve the Spider's trust and he might learn enough of her secrets to steal it back sooner. Not skilled at matters involving people? Nonsense. She would shortly learn better.

"I accept," he said, and the Spider's dark eyes glinted triumph.

Chapter 5

Someday, all food would be transported by dirigible, direct from the few green farms that remained on the British Isles to the fine folk who lived in the City Above, and on that day those in the City Below would be without recourse indeed. Every member of the Spider's smuggling organization could see the writing on the wall.

Almost literally. The writing might be metaphorical, but the Wall that enclosed the Spitalfields ghetto was very real indeed.

But for the moment, the River Thames was used as it had been used for centuries to transport food and other goods to Londontown. While ships still traversed the river, they could be boarded, and while warehouses still dotted the riverbank, they could be robbed. Not too much at one time, not enough to alert the warehouse owners or prompt the ship captains to take more organized precautions against piracy—just enough to keep the City Below from starving. The Spider played a delicate and dangerous game.

Connor O'Sullivan foresaw a future where the Wall surrounded buildings as empty as the Irish villages' huts, and Maxwell saw no reason to doubt his prediction. But for the moment, *for today,* food was still delivered by ship, and so there was still some action the Spider's organization could take. "All we've got is today," the Spider was fond of saying, "one brief span between dawn and dusk." The younger members of her organization talked eagerly of taking arms against the City Above, and Maxwell was certain his parents would have been part of a brilliant grand vision to remake the world—but all *he* could see his way clear to doing was to help the Spider and her people fight each day's battle, from dawn to dusk.

Or on occasion, from dusk to dawn. Tonight it was a matter of sneaking through the sewers that provided a secret way out from behind the Wall, dodging the construct patrols, and liberating some newly-stacked sacks of flour from a warehouse. Maxwell's fingers were not yet clever enough to work the warehouse lock, and he had too much the look of a gentleman to pass for a Spitalfields native, but his well-nourished childhood meant he was sufficiently strong to be of great assistance with the hauling of sacks.

He therefore waited near at hand, ready to step inside the warehouse the instant the Spider's primary burglar had the rear door forced open. Once inside, he grasped the nearest sack, swung to his shoulder, and stepped into the alleyway. As he left the warehouse, Clay entered it. As usual, Clay's lip curled at a little at the sight of Maxwell.

Maxwell brought the sack down the alleyway to where Meg waited, guarding the entrance to their tunnel. When he was three steps away, she tapped her heel against the wall behind her. A stone shifted aside, and hands reached up out of the darkness to take Maxwell's burden from him. He had scarcely needed to break stride. He knew the sack was now being passed from hand to hand, all along the length of the tunnel, and as he turned back to the warehouse for another load, Clay made the last few steps of his own journey. Maxwell, already partway back to the warehouse, could clearly envision Clay's hands lowering the second sack to the waiting stretched-out arms.

Maxwell almost fancied he could hear the rhythm to which they all moved, as though an actual drum beat an actual cadence over the ever-present hum—not fast, but unfaltering. Four of the Spider's men walked the circuit between the tunnel and the warehouse. Whenever a sack reached the tunnel mouth, hands were ready to receive it. No one hurried. No one missed a beat. The Spider's empire worked like a well-oiled machine. He had once heard Katarina comment dryly that she had learned such choreography in her youth—an ironical comment, obviously, though Maxwell could not perceive where the irony lay.

It was odd to think of her as "Katarina." He had only recently been invited to call her by her first name, a mark of favor that had both surprised and pleased him. He rather thought Meg Drew and Connor O'Sullivan were also pleased by it on his behalf. Ernie Clay, of course, could not have been more displeased. Clay still persisted in seeing Maxwell as an incipient traitor in search of an opportunity, a perspective Maxwell could not reasonably consider a personal insult under the circumstances. Clay had, after all, been entirely correct for the first few months they had worked together. Maxwell had spent those months scheming countless ways to retrieve his mother's watch and his father's journal, by trickery or by force. Neither ever worked—Katarina Rasmirovna could out-scheme anyone and kept at least one bodyguard always by her side, so none of Maxwell's offensives got very far. She always knew they were coming, knew the shape of them almost before he knew it himself, and disrupted them with an air of amusement rather than anger.

The offensives grew increasingly halfhearted as time went by. The more he saw of the grim gray world he had landed in, the more he agreed with her than those at its helm should not be given any further power. He did not, in point of fact, want this Prime Minister to have his watch. He did not want Bastion to have it either. The fourth or fifth time O'Sullivan dragged him along on some expedition on the Spider's orders, Maxwell's participation owed less to the hostage status of his timepiece than to his honest considered opinion that these actions were the morally correct ones to take. He admitted to himself that he might have chosen to do just this, had the choice been his to make. He still resented having the choice taken from him.

After another four or five expeditions, even that resentment had faded. No matter who had chosen it, he was fighting on the right side. It had taken him a while to become comfortable with his own change of heart; it had taken the Spider's other operatives much longer. Clay was the last remaining holdout, but again, Maxwell could hardly fault his caution.

Maxwell frowned, jolted from his musing back to the here-and-now, aware he had seen something disturbing without being able to consciously identify what it was.

A shadow. A shadow had shifted, down at the end of the alleyway. Shadows did not shift without something to shift them. Might it be a cat or dog or some such, one of the strays that haunted the warehouse district? Possibly a large dog—but on balance, Maxwell thought it had been too big. A child, then. The Spider had sent no children on this expedition, and street children did not tend to congregate on this side of the Wall. Could be nothing, could be some recently orphaned brat or perhaps someone from the Spider's territory who had followed the adults out of a sense of adventure—

All the time he was thinking, Maxwell's feet kept walking. He picked up a sack, hefted it to his shoulder, turned his back on the end of the alleyway where the shadow had flickered, trudged his way down to where Meg stood guard, waited while she tapped the code that opened the tunnel, handed his sack down to the waiting hands.

But he did not immediately return to his job, instead touching her on the shoulder to get her attention. He pointed to his eyes, then down to the alleyway's other end, then gestured to indicate the height of the unknown moving shadow. Meg frowned, peering past him into the dimness.

Both of them jerked when blue light flooded the alleyway from behind them. Maxwell had an instant to see the scene it illuminated, frozen as though in a painting: A cluster of armored man-sized shapes, the newest generation of police coppers, able to move far more silently than their larger brethren; Clay, halfway between the coppers and the tunnel that led to safety, a sack of flour upon his shoulder; Franklin, returning to the warehouse for another load; Strachan, caught in the very act of exiting with a sack. And the face of the child whose shadow Maxwell had seen a few moments before. A pale sniveling rat face. Lord Adolphus Bastion's grandson Alistair.

Well, that was one way to win territory from one's rival: arrange for her best operatives to be taken into custody by the police.

Meg's heel had already drummed upon the tunnel door. It opened, and she ducked inside. Maxwell hesitated for an instant, but no frontal assault would help Clay and the others now. He swung down into the tunnel after her. The last thing he saw was Ernie's face, displaying curled-lip disgust and sour satisfaction in about equal measure.

They slammed the hatch closed, the Spider's operatives started running to safety, and Meg stayed just long enough to touch the match to the fuse rigged for this purpose. The tunnel would collapse behind them. The Spider's folk would use a different tunnel next time.

✺

"Goddamned Bastion," Meg spat as they banged open the door of the Widow Ramsey's boarding house. Connor O'Sullivan looked up in surprised alarm from his seat outside Katarina's bedroom door, and Meg started to explain.

"Never mind," Maxwell cut her off. "Go and change your clothing, and I'll do the same. We can beat the prison wagon if we're quick about it."

Meg looked taken aback, then nodded once. She ran for her bedroom as Maxwell ran for his. Katarina would have to be told of the night's events and of the Bastions' involvement—but that could wait for morning, when she woke. He and Meg did not need Katarina's orders to know what to do next, and their Spider suffered more from the raw autumn weather than did any of her people. This wouldn't be the first time her boarders silently colluded to grant her more sleep.

Where a frontal attack could not succeed, a flanking maneuver might. There were ways to free comrades in arms from the grip of the law if one stayed free oneself. Maxwell tore off his laborer's shirt and trousers, and started to don the various pieces of what his associates had christened his "toff's garb." Katarina had laid out a considerable sum—considerable by the standards of the organization, at least—to acquire a proper gentleman's suit of clothing, right down to the underclothes, meant to be used in exactly situations such as this. Dressed like a member of the respectable class, with the accent and bearing to match, Maxwell could manage transactions the others could not in the City outside the Wall. Someday those in power would move the prisons up to the balloons that comprised the City Above and he would not be able to manage this sort of subterfuge—but for now, *for today,* there was something he could do. He gave the situation a moment's more thought, then swapped his good coat for one slightly shabbier and added his parson's collar. Meg joined him in the kitchen, dressed like a street urchin, and the two of them hastened their way to one of the other secret exits under the Wall.

The sky was brightening into a rare fog-less dawn as he and Meg caught up with the prison wagon outside Bridewell. It had gathered up assorted other miscreants since capturing Strachan, Franklin, and Clay, and the entire collection now awaited decanting into the prison yard. Maxwell stayed out of sight until the coppers, large and small, stomped off to their patrols, and only human guards were left to oversee the prisoners. Human guards were possible to distract. Someday, perhaps, it would all be done with clockwork, and then this maneuver would no longer work, but *for today*—

Maxwell selected a drunkard wearing more-or-less respectable clothing who slumped against the prison wall about halfway up the yard. Then he emerged from the shadows, straightened his coat collar in a fussy manner, and ambled his way over to the guard in charge. Peering as if nearsightedly at the man, he asked in a quavering voice the procedure for bailing his neighbor over there out of his present trouble. Age, as Katarina always said, was all in how one moved. And spoke.

"He's a good man, to be sure," Maxwell prattled on, "but recently beset by troubles, and perhaps not possessed of the fortitude that might be wished in meeting them…"

While the guard's attention was divided between the presumed parson and the man he sought to intercede for, Meg Drew's clever fingers were filching keys and unlocking prison wagons and manacles. Maxwell could play out every move behind him as his voice went on rambling in the character of the old parson. Noting a charm on the guard's watch chain that identified him as a member of a particularly intolerant temperance organization, he added a bit about the evils of liquor. One tailored one's disguise to the needs of the moment and the weakness of the adversary.

Katarina had instructed her people well in the art of assuming pleasing shapes, had taught them how to spot the indications that told a person's habits and characteristics, and how to strike the right note to manipulate each individual. Maxwell had learned the lessons painstakingly, as though memorizing mathematical formulae— *Half-statements are more valuable than whole statements. Pique their interest, keep them off-balance. Grant concessions that do not matter; allow them to feel they have the upper hand.* It was not unlike the mathematical formulae employed in the boxing ring, seeking out weak points and opportunities.

Maxwell was considered a decent enough pupil, but no prodigy. Meg was the prodigy, somewhat disturbingly donning each new persona as easily as she changed her clothing, as easily a boy street urchin now as she had been a distressed and helpless young woman in their last such improvisation. Katarina alone never seemed disturbed by her protégé's ability, saying fondly that Meg reminded her of herself, a great many years ago. "*Nearly* as good, but not quite; keep practicing," Katarina always added. She said it with a wink, but there was truth underlying the teasing. No one, after all, could outscheme Katarina Rasmirovna.

Now Maxwell kept the conversation going while watching, out of the corner of his eye, Meg shepherd the Spider's newly-rescued operatives out of sight. For verisimilitude, he invested a bit of coin in obtaining the release of the still-drunken man—who looked uncertainly at the unknown parson who spoke for him but made no move to dispute the stroke of undeserved good fortune. By the time the emptying of the prison wagon was noticed, the drunkard and his ministerial rescuer had long since ambled out of the jail together into the morning light.

There was no morning dawn yet on Maxwell's side of the Wall, as sunbeams would not clear the high brick edifices for another few hours. There was barely enough dim gray light to see the broken cobblestones and crumbling buildings of the slums. It ought to have been a depressing sight, but Maxwell walked through it with the sense of a good night's work completed. Undressing in his upstairs bedroom, he heard with satisfaction Meg returning with Ernie Clay. All the Spider's people were safe and accounted for.

∞

He descended into the kitchen late that cold winter afternoon to find that it was Clay's turn to sit in the chair that physically blocked the door leading to the Widow Ramsey's bedroom. Ernie glanced up from his rhythmic knife sharpening at the sound of Maxwell's footfalls.

They looked at each for a moment. Then Clay tipped his head toward Katarina's door. "She wants to see you. Said to send you in as soon as you woke."

Maxwell nodded, hoping it was for a commendation, aware it could be for a tongue-lashing, reviewing the night's events in his mind and trying to decide if there was any part of the near-disaster that could be attributed to carelessness on his part. He didn't think so. Nor was it likely she would be annoyed at not being consulted, as prompt action to rescue the prisoners had undeniably been the correct course of action. Very likely it *was* a commendation. He crossed to Katarina's door.

Clay went back to his knife sharpening, but as Maxwell raised his hand to knock, he heard the voice behind him say gruffly, "And thanks."

∞

Katarina received him enthroned in her bed, covered with quilts and propped up with pillows. She scarcely moved from this room now, but her air of authority had not diminished in the slightest. She waved to him to sit in her usual regal fashion.

She had been reading by candlelight, one skeletal hand holding the book close to her eyes, but as he took the chair beside her bed, she closed the little cloth-bound volume and set it aside. She did not mark her place, but her memory was still phenomenal, so no doubt she could remember it. Or perhaps she had read the book so many times that she knew it by heart and it hardly mattered where it fell open. He tilted his head to see the title as she reached for the ever-present gasper burning on a plate on her bedside table.

"Tennyson," she said. "*Idylls of the King.*"

"King Arthur?"

"Yes." She drew a long drag from the gasper, exhaled smoothly, and almost managed to stop the cough that followed. "I was pondering the tale of desperate measures taken to save Britain at her darkest hour. It seemed topical, for some reason."

He smiled a little.

She seemed to be waiting for him to say something. When he did not, she went on, "Nice work last night. And even nicer work early this morning."

So she had called him in for commendation after all. He smiled more genuinely.

She took another drag from the gasper, watching him as though something amused her. Finally she said, "It's a very important day for you, isn't it?"

Maxwell almost struck his forehead as memory slammed into place. "It is. Good Lord, I had…actually forgotten."

"A year and a day tomorrow," Katarina said, and coughed. "I don't suppose you want to go home?"

"No," he heard himself say, wondering when that had become true. But true it was. Contemplating his old life of horses and women and gambling-hells, he found nothing attractive in it. "No, I truly don't."

"I'm pleased to hear it. You've turned into quite the asset to my organization, Mr. Carrington. It's very good to have a man of your caliber fighting at my side."

"Thank you—" he started to say.

"But it doesn't go very far toward solving the overall problem. One more good man fighting by my side here and now doesn't make that much of a difference. Not in the grand scheme. We've already lost this war."

For a moment, it felt like a gut-punch. Then he caught her meaning.

"But there was a time," she said, "back in my youth, when this cause of mine floated on a full sea. When we hadn't lost yet. When one man could have taken the tide at the flood and won."

"You can't mean me?"

"No." She smiled a little. "I mean Gavin Trevelyan." She took a little book from under the topmost of the moth-eaten quilts that covered her, and it took Maxwell a moment to realize it was not his father's journal. "This was Gavin's," Katarina said. "His notes when he was building the rail-gun. It worked in the end, but too late to make a difference. Ten years earlier, it might have changed everything."

"You want me to take him a message. You want me to leave?" He was startled by how much it felt like betrayal.

"For what it's worth," she said, looking up at him with a genuine brief smile, "I actually don't."

The unusual sentiment was spoiled by a convulsive fit of coughing. The fit went on for a long time, and at the end of it, Katarina leaned back, dabbing at her lips. It was no longer possible for her to hide the blood that stained her handkerchief.

"I don't have much time left," she said at last. "Obviously. It wouldn't matter if I did; the future looks to be more rather than less dire. Your arrival here was… fortuitous. One might almost say miraculous, if one had not stopped believing in a benevolent deity some time ago." She bent over coughing again, and this time the cough turned to retching. It seemed hours before she brought up the clot of blood, but Maxwell knew better than to offer aid or sympathy. He waited. When the fit had passed, she slumped exhausted against the pillows.

He stayed where he was.

A long time later, Katarina opened her eyes. She looked around, took note of his presence, relit her gasper, and continued the conversation as though there had been no pause. "I know everything we did wrong," she said. "I know every moment that balanced on a knife's edge. Between you and your father's journal, I know how the timepiece works. No one has ever has such a tactical advantage as I suddenly have. Here." She leaned over and opened the top of her bedside table, took out William's journal and the watch, stacked them atop Trevelyan's notebook, and handed the lot to Maxwell.

He found himself thinking, *She keeps her secrets in an unlocked drawer?* And then, *Why is that the part of this that shocks me?*

"They used to be in a locked one," Katarina said, eyes crinkled at the corners with amusement. "But the solution never really satisfied me. I know so many safe-crackers, after all. Now I hardly ever leave this room—and if someone were to get past my bodyguards, I'd have bigger troubles."

Maxwell sat still, feeling dizzy as the world swirled around him. "When I woke I had no plans further than—than fighting tomorrow's battle."

"I know," she said. "But we need to win the war, and that can't be done from here."

He took a deep breath. "Am I to go now?"

"Not this instant. We should discuss a strategy, take time to plan it, ensure you have everything you need. But soon. While I'm still here to see you off. I think Meg can step into my role as Spider successfully enough—I hope, at least—but if there is a struggle with Bastion after I die, I would hate to see you and your timepiece be causalities of it. I want you safe out of here while I can still guard your escape."

❧

Three days later, Maxwell climbed to his garret bedroom to change into the clothing he had brought from 1848. He had not even realized Katarina had kept it for him, and it felt odd indeed to don it, halfway between preparing for a fancy dress party and resuming a discarded skin. Buttoning the shirt and drawing on the trousers was not so bad, it being a difference in degree only from the modern clothing he had become accustomed to wearing. But it was odd indeed to fasten the buttons of the waistcoat, with its gay stripes and pointed front, the height of fashion a long time ago. A *very* long time ago, as Maxwell had come to measure time. He stood for a while before the little shaving-mirror, trying to coax his fingers into remembering how to tie a cravat, before finally giving up on fashion and just knotting the thing into the best bow he could manage. He intended to arrive in his own damned study, after all, and his manservant would scarcely expect Maxwell to look immaculate after a night of hard drinking. After that he donned the frockcoat—cut in the latest style, or what had been the latest style way back when. It was a style particularly well suited to a man of his build, with its full shoulders, rounded chest, and tightly-cinched waist. He had lost weight over the past year.

The suit would look most odd in Geneva of 1775, the Scottish Highlands of 1800 where the first escaped monster had been captured by the Crown, Wales of 1872, or Devon of 1876, but he was going back to 1848 first. It was not as though Katarina could spare the funds necessary to finance a voyage such as this, and it would be a trivial matter for Maxwell to turn some of his own personal fortune into gold. Gold could then be turned into coin of whatever time he visited, and coin into clothing that would not attract attention.

As a final step, he fastened his mother's timepiece to his waistcoat. As usual, it felt heavier than its size suggested it should. He opened it and watched the fourth face cycle through images of the places he had most recently been. As none of them were in any manner whatsoever good memories, he snapped the watch shut.

Well, his future would be better than his past.

He and Katarina had spent every moment of three days planning, and surely there was nothing left to be said, but he went to formally take leave of her anyway.

Her bedchamber was dim in the autumn twilight, raw and chill from the fog that seeped through every crack in the walls and window. The candle on the bedside table guttered, and the constant gasper smoldered on the plate: a fuzz of gold and a dot of red in the midst of all the colorless gray.

Katarina's spare form seemed even smaller than usual, dwarfed by the pile of thrice-mended quilts that covered her and by the pillows that propped her upright. Her eyes were closed and she did not open them when he cleared his throat, so Maxwell, after a brief hesitation, took the chair beside the bed. He might have gone over his notes one last time, but instead he picked up the *Idylls of the King*.

The name "Tennyson" was vaguely familiar—Maxwell seemed to recall a poet of that appellation who had published a book of verse that had been quite well received, in the winter of 1842 or 1843. It would appear the poet had gone on to greater fame. He flipped through the pages, then turned back to the first one and resolved to peruse them in order, beginning with *The Coming of Arthur*.

"You shouldn't read that," Katarina murmured a long time later, and Maxwell looked up. Her eyes were crinkled at the corners, far more than usual crow's feet. "You don't want your head stuffed full of quotations you can't use."

"I suppose I could use them if I befriended Tennyson," Maxwell suggested.

"And claim credit for some of his best lines?" Katarina smiled a little. "For all we know, you'll do just that. It would explain the ending—Arthur sleeping for centuries in Avalon, to return when Britain faces her darkest hour."

He found himself more pleased and embarrassed than perhaps the offhand comment warranted. "You're casting me as Arthur?"

"Why not? The prince born of famous parents who has inherited a sword and the responsibility for wielding it."

"Which makes you who, the Lady of the Lake? The enchantress Morgan le Fay?"

She raised her eyebrows at him. "Which makes me Merlin, thank you. I know what is to happen, and I'm trapped in a hollow oak by…well, the analogy collapses at that point. There's no Vivien, unless Vivien is who I used to be." She broke down in a coughing fit, a comparatively mild one this time. "Trapped by circumstance," she said at last, "and by the way this magic works. I can't cross my own timeline. Even if I could, I no longer have the stamina to do what must be done. So I send younger folk to fight my wars."

He carried a notebook of dates and places. He intended to acquire an atlas in 1848 and work out latitude and longitude from there. On the other side of history, there was a Genevese student walking down an ever-darkening path, from which he might still be diverted. There was a monster running free in the Highlands, not yet captured by the Crown. There was a Welsh farmer's daughter who could still be saved from death, the successful field-test of a construct that might be sabotaged, and a man with a rail-gun who had not yet fallen to construct fire in an alleyway. Surely Maxwell would be able to stop *one* of them. On the other side of history, the crows that plucked at his mother's eyes mocked his overconfidence, but surely *one* of these moments would yield to his and Katarina's plotting.

"Start at the beginning," Katarina said as she had said before. "If you can change that Genevese idiot's mind, it will surely end there, and all will be well. No monsters means no constructs, after all… If you have no success with Frankenstein, work forward. I keep envisioning you helping the 95," she said, smiling a little, "but I hope you make an end of this long before. If you *are* forced to help the 95, see to it you help them earlier. Trevelyan and I both were working for Seward by the end of 1882."

He nodded. She had said it all before, more than once, but he was too nervous to take exception to the drilling. He thought of a question he had not asked: "Is there anything I should say to you? That is—to her?"

Katarina looked surprised, then interested. She reached over to her bedside table for the gasper. "A personal message, do you mean?" She took a thoughtful drag and blew a smoke ring toward the ceiling. "I suppose you could tell her that Gavin Trevelyan will never…" She cut herself off with something between a laugh and a cough. "Except, of course, she knows that." The cough took over.

When it had passed, Katarina leaned back against the pillows with tears in her eyes, and accepted the water he poured for her. "Actually," she said when she could speak, "what you should tell her is to stop smoking these damned things before they eat her lungs from the inside. Except she knows that too."

Maxwell could find nothing to say to this.

Katarina took a deep breath and managed not to choke on it. "Never mind. Don't worry over either. What you should do is get her the information she needs to *stop this.* Stop this future before it's born. After that, she's perfectly capable of making her own decisions. Some of them no doubt bad ones, but if you're successful I won't be the Katarina who has to live with the consequences." She tried to smile.

He tried to smile back.

It was a miserable failure on both their parts. Katarina pushed aside her pile of handkerchiefs and stretched out a hand to him. He took it uncertainly. He had never been overly comfortable with touch.

The grip of that skeletal hand was stronger than he would have supposed. Katarina's customary irony was gone, her large dark eyes looking straight into his. "You're the only hope for Britain, Prince Arthur," she said, and it ought to have sounded foolish, but it was nothing of the kind. She nodded to the time-piece in his belt. "Fix this. You're the only one who can fix this."

Chapter 6

He arrived in 1883 ten years later.

He had followed Katarina's instructions and tried to change history at one of the earlier junctions, but just as with his various attempts in the Tudor era, he had failed every time. He had worked out each of his deceptions meticulously according to her principles, but they never succeeded. No one could out-scheme Katarina Rasmirovna; so the failures must, he came to realize with familiar self-loathing, be due to his execution rather than to her plans. He tried to distance himself from his emotional response, tried to see his monumental task merely as a puzzle to be solved, but found such detachment increasingly difficult to achieve.

Young Viktor Frankenstein would not be manipulated away from his studies; Maxwell had managed to interest him only briefly in mathematics and the respectable branches of science before the boy returned like an iron filing to the lodestone of Cornelius Agrippa, Albertus Magnus, and that which man was not meant to know. Older Viktor Frankenstein, not recognizing Maxwell as the family friend of his childhood, had accepted Maxwell's invitation to Scotland with pleasure...but then deviated back to his original course and his laboratory in the Orkneys. General Brown had seen through Maxwell's cover story and struck him with a pistol. Brenda Trevelyan had fled from his rescue attempt in fear. Maxwell's attempts to shoot down either the monster captured in 1800 or the men who captured it had likewise met with failure. And just when he thought he had finally succeeded in undermining the Tavisford factory, Sir Charles' men, in some mysterious way alerted to his presence, had blocked his escape and dismantled his explosive. Maxwell had given up on Waterloo as a junction to affect—there were just too many ways the timeline could correct itself—and so he had very few options left. It was time to find Katarina Rasmirovna at an earlier point in her life and tell her what she needed to know.

Her arachnoid older self had described the location of the warehouse-hideaway used by the resistance in those days, but had added a warning against knocking at the front door without introduction. Maxwell therefore intended to spend the evening at the Shoreditch Empire, where he might waylay the young Katarina after her performance.

Now he walked through the rabbit warren of the Shoreditch district's streets, trying for the brisk stride of a man who knows exactly where he is going and is certainly no hustler's mark, mentally consulting the map he had studied over coffee in a hotel earlier in the day and trying to match it to his memories of the place. For the first time, this was a difficult task; for the first time, his ability to recall detail proved more of a distraction than an aid. It must be because he walked through this city during so many different time periods, accumulating memories each time. In the days of Henry VIII, before the King turned on the Church, the area had been dominated by the wealthy Holywell Nunnery. In 1910, Shoreditch had been reduced to a deserted pile of rubble. In 1845, the High Street had boasted fine modern shopfronts and industry of all descriptions, and the Church of St. Leonard's was the first in London to be lit by gas.

The High Street now was nowhere near so elegant now as it had been in 1845. The old bustling storefronts of furniture makers, cobblers, jewelers, and printers had given way to warehouses of unvaried and uninteresting aspect, and to tenement buildings that housed the workers who, in this time period, had not yet been replaced by clockwork constructs as factory laborers. The Shoreditch Empire stood on this street. Maxwell reflected he would have done better to have purchased a much different suit that morning, after converting the last of his gold into currency. The fine three-piece drew attention from quarters whose attention he did not want.

Well, but at least he was not the only one slumming. The night was warm, and pleasant enough if one ignored the yellow-gray smog hanging over everything, and he saw a few other men too well-dressed for their surroundings meandering their way through the filth and broken cobblestones. A few stopped where women in tight trousers or tighter gowns lingered under streetlamps, but most continued onward to the Shoreditch Empire, where the few streetlamps that were not broken guttered in an ominous fashion. Through flashes of spluttering light, Maxwell could see that the sign over the tavern door had, at one point in the distant past, been beautifully carved and bravely painted. Now, its only positive trait was legibility.

The gentlemen in whose company Maxwell found himself dropped their coins into the doorkeeper's outstretched hand without speaking, but Maxwell found he preferred to be certain before he invested any further in this endeavor. "Is Katarina Rasmirovna on the bill tonight?" he asked.

The doorkeeper sighed.

"Of course she is," said an annoyed well-bred voice behind Maxwell. Maxwell turned as well as he could in the inadequate space, to find that the speaker's dress was as rich as his speech. "Why else would we be here? Pay your ninepence and stop blocking the stair."

Grateful he had spent the time that morning studying his new collection of coins so that he might now utilize them without hesitation, Maxwell fished out a ninepence and dropped it into the waiting hat without another word.

Rowdy voices drifted from the other side of the curtain, and Maxwell braced himself as he shouldered it aside. But the crowd packed into the dingy room seemed friendly enough. Most of them were fortifying themselves with mugs of beer, and these sloshed carelessly as their owners exchanged greetings.

The men looked grim, and drawn, and tired—but there was a difference between them and their counterparts of 1910. After a moment, Maxwell identified it. These men had not yet lost hope. They still believed the future might be better than the past.

And so it will be, he vowed to the lot of them.

Maxwell saw the two gentlemen he had followed, and the one behind who shouldered impatiently past, making for a raised platform adorned by a single bench. Since apparently a ninepence entitled one to these premier seats—the only seats in the room—Maxwell seated himself there, and composed himself to wait.

He waited through a clown guiding a troupe of performing poodles, a conjurer whose carelessness made it obvious (to Maxwell, at least) how each trick was done, and a screechy aging singer whose tugged-down bodice attracted more appreciation from her audience than did her voice. He somehow managed to keep the impatience off his face.

Then the two-instrument "orchestra" played a sprightly theme, and the men sharing Maxwell's bench all straightened in expectation. The standing crowd shouted approval. There was a pause—and then onto the stage strutted a young soldier.

Soldier? Maxwell thought in confusion. And then, *Yes, of course, there are still soldiers in 1885. Fewer than there were once, but the military hasn't been entirely automated yet.*

It was Katarina. Had to be. He would have known from the reaction of the crowd, but there were other clues. This soldier's back was almost too straight, the stride almost too precise. And each gesture—the sharp right-angle turns that took the soldier to the center of the stage; the crisp drawing and saluting with the sword—was conducted in rhythm, to a beat not actually present in the "orchestra's" background theme.

As with the conjurer, he could see how the trick was done, but this time it enhanced rather than detracted from the experience. The illusion was deliberately imperfect. At first glance, Katarina looked like an exaggeratedly-ideal soldier, definitely male, a smooth-faced boy just old enough to wear the uniform. If one did not look for the slight curve of waist and hip—though every man in the audience was looking as closely as he could—one might be completely fooled. But the overly-emphasized, overly-correct gestures invited a second look, and the second look introduced doubt. The result was a strange shifting perspective, a reality that altered itself with each blink of the observer's eye.

Then the figure on the stage began to sing, in a low, throaty voice that similarly might have taken a trouser role in an opera, and yet was not flawlessly male—inviting yet another closer look, yet another facet to the constantly shifting perspective. And the sound of her voice banished the last shred of doubt from Maxwell's mind.

He had never heard her sing, of course. He had never so much as heard her speak in a loud clear voice without the clarity devolving at once into a cough. He still knew instantly that the voice was hers. Of course she would have sounded like this in her youth.

Katarina's song narrated the story of her persona—a half-pay officer disastrously in love with an heiress, despairing at the obstacles of family and public opinion rising between him and his true love. Each word and each gesture was correct for the character—as before, exaggeratedly correct. Nearby on the bench, someone who had apparently not seen Madame Rasmirovna's performance before tonight began to chuckle with appreciation. Another newcomer, this one in the standing crowd, shifted from foot to foot in discomfort.

But Katarina was far from done. While the orchestra continued the theme, she deliberately removed her hat and shook loose her long black hair. When the audience's whoops and hollers subsided, she took up a position on the other side of the stage, entered into the character of the soldier's lady love—and executed that illusion with the same deliberate imperfection, singing in a higher register, making her movements those of a girl in long skirts, while all the time wearing the coat of the uniform of Her Majesty's Army. There were more chuckles, more expressions of discomfort, more hoots from the audience.

She sang three more verses, one for the soldier, one for the lady, and the last for the soldier again, narrating how they overcame the obstacles and lived happily ever after. In the pause between each verse, she removed a piece of clothing and therefore relied increasingly on movement and voice rather than costume to carry her performance. By the time she came to the last line, she had discarded the soldier's coat to reveal a tightly-laced bodice on top and slim, trouser-clad legs below. Between the outfit and her long black hair cascading down her back, she looked uncannily like the prostitutes soliciting half a street away, yet she still somehow conveyed the persona of the soldier.

When she reached the end of the—duet? Something in Maxwell's head wanted to call it a duet, as odd as that otherwise sounded—she spread nonexistent skirts and sank to the floor in a curtsey. Then she straightened and bowed deeply from the waist, and the audience whistled and stamped its approval.

"Thank you," Katarina Rasmirovna said, voice carrying easily above the noise. It was and was not the voice Maxwell knew. Young and clear and ringing without the suspicion of a catch in the throat—and yet familiar, bone-deep familiar, as though he were returning home after ten years odysseyan wandering. She thanked the crowd two or three more times, bowing to different sides of the applauding house, before laughingly raising her hands for quiet.

"One more song," she said, and the house broke into applause again. Katarina grinned, quieting them again with raised hands. "One more for luck," she said. "Just as me. What will you have?"

Only a few of the shouted suggestions were lewd. Despite the costume, identical in every point to that of the working girls outside, she retained their respect. She leaned her elbows in a friendly manner upon the back of the chair she had been using in her act, and listened with her head to one side until one shouted suggestion caught her fancy. "Oranges and Lemons," she called back, nodding. The crowd applauded. Katarina straightened, nodded to the orchestra, and began.

"*Gay go up and gay go down*

To ring the bells of London-town.

'*Oranges and lemons—'*"

"Say the bells of St. Clemens'," the room chorused with her, making Maxwell start at the suddenness of it.

The rest of it went that way too, a call and response where she sang the phrase and her audience responded with the name of the church.

He knew the song, as it happened. More accurately, he had known it once. They had sung it with different words in the days of the Tudors.

'*Two sticks and an apple,'*
Say the bells at Whitechapel.

'*Halfpence and farthings,'*
Say the bells of St. Martin's.

'*You owe me ten shillings,'*
Say the bells at St. Helen's.

'*When will you pay me?'*
Say the bells of Old Bailey.

'*When I grow rich,'*
Say the bells of Shoreditch.

'*Pray when will that be?'*
Say the bells of Stepney.

The audience let Katarina have the final lines to herself. She gave it a dramatic pause, spreading her hands out for emphasis. "Says the great bell of Bow—" Maxwell heard the chuckles around the room, hard but not entirely humorless. "'—I am sure I don't know.'"

❧

The alleyway outside the theater's back door was crowded with men, gently born and otherwise, holding mingy-looking bouquets. Maxwell realized belatedly he ought to have provided himself with flowers. Well, if Katarina brushed him off in favor of a man who observed the social niceties, he would consider this reconnaissance, and return tomorrow with something from a decent florist, sure to attract her attention.

But Katarina shook her head with a smile at all the local boys and slumming gentlemen attempting to catch her attention with their offerings, and walked off alone in the direction of her warehouse home. She was wearing the same trousers and bodice she had worn onstage and had added neither hat nor coat—because the night was warm or because she possessed none? There was no way to tell.

Maxwell decided the best course of action was to pace her until they were clear of the crowd. He followed all the lessons in which Meg Drew had once schooled him, but the idea of a gentleman truly hiding here in the stews was a cause lost before it began. He knew from the growing tension in her posture that she had become aware of him. Remembering the disaster with Brenda Trevelyan, he resolved to clear his throat and request her attention the instant they were near a working streetlamp. He would begin by saying her name, and when she turned, he would—

"Stop right there," a voice grated from behind Maxwell, and something cold and ominously pistol-barrel-shaped pressed itself to his back.

Maxwell caught his breath. A dozen scenarios and half-formed plans for escape stampeded through his head before his brain took conscious note of the accent.

Welsh.

Come to Katarina Rasmirovna's defense.

Well, it was worth the gamble.

He raised his hands easily, feigning nonchalance. "Gavin Trevelyan, I presume?"

The figure behind him went completely still for that instant. Then the pistol pushed more firmly against his back and the voice countered, "My name's not all that relevant, is it? It's yours that matters."

Up ahead, Katarina had turned. She was watching this byplay with her arms folded, leaning casually backward with a booted foot braced against a working streetlamp. Her face was in shadow, and Maxwell had never seen the old woman she would become in such a pose, but the attitude conveyed was so uncannily the Spider's that he found a lump in his throat. Taking Maxwell's momentary inability to speak for refusal to do so, Trevelyan grunted impatience and pushed him into the light.

"I knew he was there," Katarina informed Trevelyan, coming to briskly frisk Maxwell for weapons. "I had the situation in hand."

"Of course you did," Trevelyan said impatiently. "It's not as though I feel the need to come see you safely home every night, is it? But when I happen to be out walking and see a stranger at your heels, you can hardly expect me to act as though the matter does not concern me."

Katarina relieved Maxwell of the small revolver he had likewise purchased only that morning, and with which he had not yet had time to achieve proficiency. She glanced at it with surprised approval—so apparently he had at least chosen well—opened it, noted that it was indeed loaded, and spun the cylinder closed before stepping back and lifting it in a businesslike manner to point at Maxwell's chest.

Katarina began, "Now then—" at the same time Maxwell began, "Don't shoot—"

And then they both stopped on a caught breath.

Maxwell's momentary speechlessness, though it did not especially do him credit, was understandable enough. Between his distance from the stage, the tobacco haze that had floated in the air, the layers of costuming she wore, and the distraction of her performance itself, he had not gotten a particularly good look at her in the theater. Now, with both of them standing under a functioning streetlamp, nothing impeded his view. He saw large dark eyes, a beautifully-molded mouth, arched dark brows, and coiled hair so absolutely black that the gaslight found no other buried color to glint against. And the most magnificent figure he had ever, in a lifetime of considerable experience, laid eyes upon.

He should have expected this. Why had he not expected this? Even ravaged by age, war, malnutrition, and the black lung, he had been able to see that the Katarina of 1910 must have once been quite handsome. He should have been able to extrapolate, to reason backward…but the fact was he had been utterly unprepared for the full truth of the matter. The Katarina of 1883 had the sort of beauty that made men's words stutter and stop.

He blinked, trying to regain command of himself. And only then realized the expression on Katarina's face was *recognition*.

"I take it you've met before?" Trevelyan said dryly behind him, keeping Maxwell's arm in a firm grip and his own pistol pressed to Maxwell's back.

"Not to say met," Katarina said slowly. She moistened her lips. "But I know him."

His heart spasmed. She knew him? Not possible. *She* knew *him?*

"I've seen you before," Katarina said, which was also not possible, unless she meant in the theater. For a wild moment he thought of second sight, prophetic dreams, intertwined fates— But she went on, "You tried to sabotage the Tavisford factory."

"You saw me?" was all Maxwell could manage.

"In fact," Katarina said, "I stopped you."

She had stopped him. *She* had stopped him. He wasn't sure whether he wanted to laugh or weep.

"In the years since, I've…rather wished I hadn't," Katarina went on. "But can you blame me telling Sir Charles I saw a strange man in the wood? You appeared out of nowhere and disappeared into nowhere, and…I didn't get a very close look, but as far as I can tell you haven't changed a bit in seven years. Not one bit." She took a deep breath. "Who are you?"

He'd come intending to spin an elaborate tale—*half statements are more valuable than whole statements; pique their interest; keep them off-balance*—something that would hold her attention long enough for him to get inside the hideout. Now that possibility was closed to him. Like her older self, this Katarina had already discovered too much for such a ruse. Head spinning as it had on that long ago day when he'd attempted to resist her interrogation through the effects of drunkenness and concussion, he found himself with no option but the truth. "My name is Maxwell."

"And your other name?" Trevelyan tightened his grip, shifting Maxwell's imprisoned arm slightly upward.

"'Maxwell' is the only name I care to give you," he retorted.

"Oh, I think we'll be needing at least one more," Trevelyan breathed in his ear, compelling his arm upward another fraction.

With two pistols aimed at him, Maxwell did not dare seek the leverage to physically free himself. Fortunately there was another type of leverage to hand. "As you wish." He forced his voice to stay calm despite the pain screaming through his arm. "Seward."

If Trevelyan had not been in physical contact, he would have no doubt been able to hide his reaction. But Maxwell felt the inventor's shock in the sudden tightening of his fingers. Then he felt the pistol clap hard against his skull and knew the forefinger of Trevelyan's other hand had begun to pull back the trigger.

"No. Wait." Katarina spoke intensely rather than loudly. "Not here. Take him home first. We must learn what he knows."

Maxwell had no desire to object. He had cleared the first hurdle. They were taking him to the warehouse.

❧

The hideaway of 1883 was much larger than the building from which Katarina Rasmirovna would one day enforce her *pax aranaea*. The front door opened into a lengthy corridor whose floor was nothing but bare boards, whose walls were whitewashed and had seen better days, and whose only light came from a single wavering candle shoved into an old and battered sconce. Katarina took the candle and by its light relocked the door and fastened two large bolts above and below the lock, while in the shadows Trevelyan used strength and pistol to hold Maxwell fast. Maxwell might have fought free then—he was instinctively feeling out weight and posture and weak points even as the locks snapped shut—but there was no reason for him to try.

Katarina and Trevelyan together manhandled Maxwell down the whitewashed hall. He rather thought he could have found his own way based only on the stories she had told him (her older self would one day tell him) but he forbore to mention this. A cool draft rushed from a passageway to the left, carrying with it a suggestion of a large open space that was almost certainly Trevelyan's workshop. The right-hand turn led to a dim, dusty, overcrowded sitting room that reminded Maxwell, with a sharp tug of homesickness, of the Spider's kitchen.

Although there were some differences visible, once he looked for them. Apparently Katarina had become a more conscientious housekeeper in her old age, or had found it prudent to keep the younger members of her organization busy with housekeeping chores, for the Spider would never have tolerated the dust and grime that lay thick on the floor, or the cobwebs stretching unhindered in the corners of the doorframe.

The Spider hadn't liked cobwebs. He had never thought about it that way before, and it abruptly seemed hilarious, but now would be a terrible time to chuckle.

The only furniture in the room appeared to be a bookshelf—loaded down with tools and crockery and a number of other things that were not books—and four straight-backed chairs surrounding a rickety table. Two of these were occupied by a pair of half-grown boys playing at some card game whose specifics Maxwell could not make out. One glanced up at the sound of footsteps, and then both scrambled to their feet. They were scrawny, underfed lads dressed in charity-bin clothing too large for their frames, but they faced Maxwell defiantly, as though unafraid of the threat he might represent.

"Go home," Trevelyan told them, shoving Maxwell into one of the chairs.

"But Mr. Trevelyan," the smaller of the boys protested. "Won't you need—?"

"We don't know what sort of danger this is," Katarina said, rummaging on the bookshelf and coming up with a length of rope. "And until we know, you're better out of it. This isn't a game, Ernie. Go."

"Ernie?" Maxwell looked down at the undaunted little figure. "Ernest Clay?"

The boy stared back. "What's it to you?"

The other must be Connor O'Sullivan. Ropes were pulled tight around Maxwell's wrists and ankles.

"I said—" Katarina began, and both boys scrambled for the exit. Maxwell was left alone with two loyal vassals of Robert Locksley, both of whom possessed a weapon and a good reason to believe their master under threat from this interloper in toff's garb. He took a deep breath and tried to project the same fearlessness as the boys had.

Adolphus Bastion's people would have begun with interrogation, by preference the sort that utilized the roughest of ready means. Robert Locksley's people at least had the sense to begin with the establishment of objective fact through tangible evidence. Maxwell uttered no protest as Katarina and Trevelyan methodically investigated his clothing, its pockets, and the secret slits of its lining.

He was in the *warehouse.* He was sitting in *Locksley's warehouse,* two feet from *Gavin Trevelyan,* thin and hawk-nosed and caustic and so exactly matching the Spider's description that he paradoxically scarcely seemed real. It was like visiting Camelot.

They had not gagged him, so he might have spoken, but instead he waited quietly and let them get on with it. Once they found the Spider's letter, her words would convince them more effectively than his ever could.

The banknotes in his pocket held Katarina's interest for a speculative moment. The locket containing Elizabeth's portrait occupied her for longer. Maxwell managed to keep the finger-twitching desire to get it back from crossing his face. The timepiece, once opened, captured Trevelyan's attention instantly and completely, and the inventor and the actress sank into matching cross-legged postures on the floor to examine it. Maxwell released a breath he had not completely realized he was holding. Trevelyan at least was most of the way swayed toward accepting his impossible tale, and Maxwell hadn't even begun to relate it yet.

Finally they found the oilskin packet containing Trevelyan's notebook, enclosed as though for protection in what appeared to be several sheets of blank paper. Maxwell cleared his throat then. When his captors looked up, he calmly recited the recipe for the solution that would make the invisible ink appear.

Trevelyan stared at him. Then he got up and went for his laboratory.

Sometime later, Maxwell had the satisfaction of watching the words appear on the blank pages, and the shock concurrently materialize on both Trevelyan's face and Katarina's. The handwriting was hers and the name on the outer sheet was his.

"It's—it's a trick," Katarina said as Trevelyan picked up the pages. "A trap. Some feint of Bastion's. He employs forgers just as we do—"

But Trevelyan's face was changing, the last of the suspicion gone, the color visibly draining even in the inadequate candlelight. "No," he said at last, his voice rough.

Maxwell knew why. Thirty years in the future and ten years in the past, the Spider had allowed him to read the letters before she copied them over in invisible ink. She had in fact instructed him to learn them by heart, and he had done just that in the three days after she told him he must leave and before he left. The matters she wrote of were private; but the message had to reach its recipient even if the paper were destroyed, and the Spider was (had been) (would be) (would never be, if only he could get this right) a practical woman. Maxwell had not forgotten a word in his ten years of journeying. He knew what Trevelyan was reading now.

"No trick," Trevelyan said, lifting haunted eyes from the paper and meeting Katarina's anxious gaze. "There are…" He cleared his throat. "There are things written here I've only ever told you. And some other things I've…never told a living soul. But I suppose if I were to say them aloud to anyone…anyone now living…it would be…" Trevelyan's tongue tripped over the strange new language of time travel. "…will be. Was. Was you."

The room was silent. After a moment, Katarina reached out, and he gave her the letter with the slowness of a dreaming man.

"This letter is written in your hand," Trevelyan said. "This notebook is written in mine. This watch…" He turned back to Maxwell with the sudden sharp attention of a striking falcon. "Right. Who are you?"

"A courier," Maxwell said.

"What's your name?" Trevelyan demanded for the second time that night.

"It truly is Maxwell."

"Your full name."

Maxwell hesitated. "My surname is Carrington," he said at last, "but I don't use it. That's not who I am any longer."

"Mr. Maxwell, then," Katarina said. She laid the pages back down on the table, rested her hands on the back of another of the unstable chairs, and raised her eyebrows at him. "You can't possibly expect us to believe this. Who do you work for? Bastion?"

Maxwell locked eyes with her. "Never."

"Who, then?"

"You."

Katarina shook her head, smiling gently in a way he knew full well betokened danger. "Where did you hear the name Seward?"

"You told me," Maxwell said. "About six streets from here, about twenty-eight years from now."

"Do you know what's in here?" Trevelyan spoke with his head down, dexterous fingers flipping the pages of the notebook.

"If I understood her correctly," Maxwell said, "the puzzle pieces that will, when assembled, enable you to design a rail-gun of sufficient strength to take down a construct." He gave it a beat. *Leverage. Weak points. Opportunities. Keep them off-balance.* He knew where to find the hidden chinks in Trevelyan's armor of indifference. "You can't unmake your mistake, but you can redeem it."

Trevelyan's eyes came sharply up. "So you know about that too."

Maxwell nodded. "I tried to unmake it for you, as you've already heard, at the Tavisford factory in 1876. I was unsuccessful, but that book will teach you how to destroy the mechanical monster you created."

"Gavin," Katarina said.

Trevelyan looked at her and lifted the notebook. "This couldn't be faked."

"*Anything* can be faked. Bastion, or the Prime Minister—"

"Unless you've told Bastion or the Prime Minister things I've whispered to you in the dark—"

"—of *course* I haven't—"

"—then there's only one way they could have gotten into that letter," Trevelyan said. "And you saw him in the factory, and look at the watch! Occam's razor says—"

"Occam's razor tells you he's trustworthy?" Katarina indicated the pages on the table, the pocket watch beside them, the notebook in Trevelyan's hands, and Maxwell tied to the chair.

"Occam's razor tells me he's traveled through time."

Katarina said slowly, "I'm…coming to believe that part. But that doesn't mean he's on our side. It doesn't mean you should trust him."

"I don't," Trevelyan said. He reached for her hand in an overt gesture of affection that seemed, from Katarina's reaction to it, to be unlike him. "I trust you. And this is what you would do, if you had a watch like this. This is exactly the letter you would write."

Chapter 7

Maxwell leaned back from the chessboard, physically tired as he might have been from exiting the boxing ring, but more exhilarated than he would have supposed it possible to be upon losing a chess game. Not only was he visiting Camelot, he was playing chess with King Arthur.

On the other side of the board, Lord Seward contemplated the arrangement of the pieces with approval. His black silk mask lay at his elbow, within easy reach if a stranger should happen to burst into the warehouse. The mask did a reasonable job of concealing his handsome, strong-featured face, but the tawny hair still struck Maxwell as distinctive, and "Robert Locksley" wore a sedate dark coat that nevertheless called attention to itself as being too fine for the stews. Maxwell found himself agreeing with the absent Spider that Seward should never have risked himself (should not now be risking himself) by coming to the warehouse in such an inadequate disguise. He remembered her saying it was a wonder they hadn't all been unmasked long before 1895.

"Not bad," Seward said.

Maxwell was momentarily too pleased by the compliment to remember to deflect it. Then he raised his eyebrows, deliberately ironic. "For a defeat, you mean?"

"A defeat, but a well-played game," Seward said. "That capture of my bishop—that was executed well. I thought you pursuing an entirely different strategy—and a poor one, as I took pawn after pawn and even a knight."

"Ah, well." Maxwell shrugged. "Granting concessions that do not matter can be the correct strategy, especially when facing a stronger opponent. It allows him the upper hand he expects to have. Obviously it didn't work in this case, but—"

Seward barked a laugh. "You sound like me."

Maxwell shook his head. "I sound like her."

Seward's smile softened. "Of course."

At the far end of the corridor, the outer door opened. Seward rose at once, reaching for his mask, and Maxwell rose with him. But Katarina's "hullo" rang against the walls the moment after, and her mentor relaxed. "And there's my star pupil now."

Katarina and Trevelyan entered together, both of them looking disheveled and exhilarated. Seward raised his eyebrows. "What have the pair of you been doing?"

"Nothing that need worry you," Katarina said. "A minor scuffle with some Bastion foot soldiers who strayed into Locksley territory. *Truly,*" she said more firmly, at Seward's sudden scowl, "nothing worth mentioning. Locksley's folk came off best, and it was just enough of a quarrel to get the blood pumping."

"And justify a pint after," Trevelyan said. He took Katarina's shawl from her shoulders and hung it on its peg, then crossed to examine the chess board. "Who won here?"

"Whom do you think?" Seward retorted, feigning offense. "But Maxwell put up an admirable fight. I rather feel like claiming credit even for that. One might call me his grand-mentor, after all. Or something of the sort."

And this, *this* was what made his sojourn in 1883 so unbelievable. Maxwell had expected scenery and set pieces that matched the Spider's tale-telling—and he had found them, precise as though painted to the old woman's specifications. Connor and Ernie played cards and engaged in petty theft; Katarina Rasmirovna held theater-goers spellbound with male impersonation acts; solitary constructs paced streets where the sky was visible rather than blocked by dirigibles and where no building rose above five stories. Gavin Trevelyan and Lord Seward faced each other across chessboards, the former with shoulders hunched and brows drawn but the latter surveying his underling with something like affection, and one knew by those signs that today was not a good day, but tomorrow would be. Maxwell had walked into Camelot, and there were Arthur and the knights.

What struck him speechless were the moments when they broke from the roles in which the Spider's tales had bound them, yawned and stretched and paced about, jested and spoke impatiently, even took a night's leisure from in-venting now and then—because even the most passionate of inventors needed the occasional outing. It appeared Trevelyan and Katarina had both enjoyed this one. Trevelyan would never be a jolly man, but he at least seemed more relaxed than he had been when they departed. And Katarina— Maxwell glanced over and saw Katarina smiling to herself as she tucked her hair back into its knot before the small cracked mirror that hung on the wall. Even in the warped and twisting glass, she had the most beautiful face he had ever seen.

Trevelyan was still looking at the chessboard. "As it happens," he said to Seward, "I've been giving that matter some thought."

Seward settled back down in his chair, still looking amused. "Lines of descent?"

Trevelyan did not seem to notice the mild humor. "Strategy." All at once it was as though the clouds had rolled in, obscuring his rare good temper. He turned away, heading to the bookcase as though in search of something—a tome, perhaps, that would prove whatever point he was about to make—but his right hand did not actually draw any of the few books toward him, and his left tugged at the collar of his shirt as though it were too tight. "Maxwell," Trevelyan said without turning, "why are you here?"

Every nerve in Maxwell's body came to full attention, and he found himself balancing his weight on the balls of his feet and sweeping a glance around the room to be sure of all the obstacles, without consciously deciding to do so. Trevelyan's voice had not sounded precisely threatening, but there was *something* about it— "I believe I require a more specific question," Maxwell said calmly, "if I am to give a useful answer."

"We're building a rail-gun ten years earlier," Trevelyan said. "Well and good, and surely a better tactic than not building one. But as a strategy—given the other strategies a man with a timepiece might be pursuing—it's not what you'd call efficient. Why are you *here*, now?"

His collar seemed to be choking him. Maxwell was at the right angle to see a glint, and remembered the Spider saying something about Trevelyan wearing his dead wife's wedding ring on a chain around his neck.

Oh…hell.

Half statements are more valuable than whole statements. Maxwell said, "The Spider identified a number of weak points, moments in history where properly applied pressure could change—"

"Yes," said Trevelyan, "but this isn't a moment. This is a war. A whole collection of moments and falling tiles. If you want to be seeking a *moment,* I can suggest one." He reached for his collar again, then forced his hand away. Instead he took up some object from the bookshelf and toyed with it. "If you save one life in Wales eleven years ago, you save all the downstream lives trampled under construct feet. Couldn't you try that? Because stop that moment, and I— Without that moment, I would never—" He couldn't seem to say it. "Because without that moment, there'd be nothing for a mad inventor to avenge."

Maxwell couldn't bring himself to say, *I already tried to change that and failed.* How do you tell a man you let his wife die? Behind Trevelyan, the brief pleased flush had faded from Katarina's face. She pulled out her cigarette case.

Trevelyan was still talking. "Maybe it couldn't be done at all, but mightn't you try? You've got the timepiece, you could be my—" He breathed a laugh around the word. "—knight-errant as easily as you're the Spider's, couldn't you slip out to 1872 and just try—and then if it doesn't work, come back here and we'll—"

That, Maxwell at least had an answer for. "I can't leave a time period that isn't mine and be certain of returning. A time traveler only has one chance to affect each junction."

"Ah." Trevelyan seemed to deflate. At least, his shoulders sagged. But he kept his face hidden, so no one could spot any change to his expression. After a moment, he said, "Well then," as though they were speaking of something inconsequential, and pushed himself away from the bookcase. "Well, no matter. Then we'll do all we can here and now."

Katarina extracted a gasper from her little case and returned the case to her pocket.

"It's time I said good night and let you get on with it," Seward said, pushing back his chair once more. "Trevelyan, expect your materials day after tomorrow; Katarina, expect me on the thirteenth of next month; and if you need me sooner, the usual channels will suffice." Trevelyan acknowledged this with a grunt and disappeared into the laboratory. Seward donned his too-fine-for-the-stews coat, fitted his mask over his face, and headed for the outer door. Katarina went to see him out, leaving Maxwell alone and fuming.

Though truthfully, could Trevelyan even be blamed for anything save a want of timing? He might trust Katarina Rasmirovna with his life, enjoy her company and take comfort in her bed, and still would choose to be married to his wife if the choice were his to make. Maxwell wore a locket under his shirt collar also; he knew something about the clinging fingers of the past. But still, the *timing*, what a hell of a way to spoil an otherwise pleasant evening.

"Something you want to say?" Katarina asked behind him.

Maxwell turned, surprised. She had returned from locking the door behind Seward and was lighting her cigarette.

"You've a look on your face I've seen before," she said, shaking out the match. "I think you mean to break gently to me the news that Gavin Trevelyan is still in love with his wife?"

Maxwell was silent.

"I'm aware of the fact," Katarina said. "There's a collection of men waiting for me outside the theater every night, if I decided I wanted something different. I don't…I didn't…at the beginning of all this, I didn't want someone who loved me. Gavin's not my first love any more than I'm his."

She might have turned for the door then, but Maxwell said, "May I ask what happened to your first love?"

Katarina hesitated, then blew smoke at the ceiling. "He was the one who recruited me into Locksley's organization. He's dead now."

"I'm sorry."

Katarina lifted her shoulders. "We're at war. It happens. People lose those whom they love, and then take what comfort they can from companions. In the shadow cast by the funeral pyre, when none of us may live to see tomorrow, one doesn't need more than comfort."

"I see."

She might have turned for the door then, too, but hesitated just a beat too long.

Maxwell fumbled to fill the silence. "Chess?"

Katarina flashed brief genuine smile at that. "I would have thought you'd be tired of losing by now." But she came back toward the table and stabbed out her gasper in a convenient dish.

Maxwell started resetting the board. "What makes you think I mean to lose?" he attempted the sally.

Katarina drew back Seward's chair. "Did you not say I'd taught you? That implies I know everything you—"

"I said you will teach me someday," Maxwell said, settling into the banter with more confidence. "You don't know now all the tricks you'll know by then, and so—" He flashed her the smile back. "—I still have a chance."

"That's what you think," Katarina said, and the game was on.

∽

The chessboard was not the only teaching tool in use among Robert Locksley's people. One learned all sorts of things about one's companions during the casual conversation of late night watches, in celebrations of missions concluded successfully, or while binding wounds acquired in missions less successful. It was through these conversations that Katarina Rasmirovna and Maxwell no-longer-going-by-Carrington became acquainted.

He learned that she was known far and wide, well beyond Spitalfields and into the more respectable parts of town, for her male impersonation acts— "and I could wish otherwise," she said, grimacing. "If I were less famous, I would be able to impersonate a gentleman in the real world, where it might do some good. I did that a bit when I was very young, before I made a name for myself on the stage. I miss being Colin, sometimes."

She learned of his admittedly boast-worthy skill with numbers and probabilities, useful for generating funds quickly at the gambling table, or over a longer time frame on the Exchange. It also somehow netted him the responsibility of keeping Locksley's organization's books—the real ones and the ones that supported one cover story or another—but Maxwell didn't mind that.

He learned that she dressed as she did not because she had ever earned her living working as a prostitute, but because her persona off the Shoreditch stage was as carefully-constructed as the ones she played upon it. The trousers allowed her to slip in and out of whatever role she chose at the moment. "If I manage the posture correctly, they'll half-mistake me for a man, at least long enough to follow my orders," she explained. "If I *want* to be mistaken for a whore, I can manage that too."

"Why would you ever want to?" he wondered.

"Turns me invisible," she said. "No one ever looks at a whore's face."

He learned of her skill in planning operations—or to be more accurate, rediscovered it, for of course it had been the Spider's defining quality. For the first time, she told him where she had acquired it. "Locksley, of course," she said, "but before that, my mother and Sir Charles. Back in the days when the monsters first came from the moors, they held the village together. Whenever there's something I must do that means rallying the troops, I pause for a moment to hear her voice or his, and then I say what they would say."

Not all the revelations were earth-shaking ones. She learned that while he might appreciate music, he was incapable of generating a pleasing melody with his voice or with any other instrument. He learned she was a crack shot with the little pistols known as revolvers, having been taught by her mother's friend Sir Charles during her childhood and coached by "Robert Locksley" in more recent days. She learned he didn't care to celebrate Christmas.

She looked more taken aback than he had expected when that tidbit came up, in not quite casual conversation, on Christmas Eve of 1883. She had come upstairs, a book in one hand and a bottle in the other, to find him hard at work on conspiracy ledgers, which she laughingly ordered him to put away. His blank face, then belated realization of the date, told her something he hadn't realized he should have been concealing. "Ah," Katarina said, wind gone from her sails. "I...take it you're not a particular admirer of the holiday?"

Maxwell shrugged, recognizing he had introduced an awkwardness into the conversation, but not knowing how to mend matters now. "It's never meant much to me."

"Never ever?" Katarina said, and then, "Oh, I see."

She looked enlightened, which meant he had somehow given away more than he had meant to. *Clearly* this was an eccentricity he should have been concealing, but it hadn't occurred to him to consider the holiday anything but an onerous obligation to visit the family he disliked. He supposed, come to think of it, that it would be less onerous for people who enjoyed the company of their families.

Katarina dropped down to sit cross-legged on the floor beside his mattress. "Bah, humbug, is it?"

He let the ledger close. "Please tell me you're not quoting Dickens."

"Oh, you know it? I wasn't sure if it was after your time."

"No, I'm sorry to say that piece of sentimental drivel and I are contemporaries. It's the most cloying morality tale I've ever had the displeasure of encountering."

"Well, *I* like it," Katarina said, as though that settled everything. "In fact—" She held up the book. "Sir Charles gifted me with a copy when I was ten. My mother and I used to read it to each other as a Christmas Eve treat. I even managed to continue the tradition after I came to London, with one friend or another. And since Trevelyan is..." She hesitated. "...downstairs drinking toasts to the dead, as is his custom, I thought I might seek better company in which to carry on *my* custom. But if you dislike the story so greatly, I won't inflict it upon you."

Trevelyan is a fool to ignore what he has in front of him here and now, Maxwell did not say.

"I've plenty of my own dead to toast as well, of course," Katarina went on, as lightly as such words could be said. "But even in wartime, one can't spend every moment in the shadow cast by the funeral pyre, can one? Not *every* moment. So…if you do not care to read aloud, perhaps you would join me in drinking to something else?"

"That," Maxwell said, "I would be pleased to do."

Katarina flashed him a smile. "We even have some halfway decent Scotch whisky with which to do it. A gift from Seward."

Maxwell got up to find two teacups that had not yet made their way from his bedroom to the scullery, but Katarina rolled her eyes at him, took them from his hands, and went downstairs to exchange them for clean ones.

"Where is Seward tonight?" Maxwell asked when she returned. "At some enormous country estate, with all of his extended family?"

"I somehow don't think the duty is as unpleasant as your tone of voice makes it out to be," Katarina said with amusement. "But no, I believe he and Rachel are in fact ensconced in a small discreet hotel." She set the mugs on the floor beside Maxwell's mattress, and nodded that he should take over the role of uncorking and decanting the whiskey.

He fished a multiplex knife from his pocket, used the blade to slit the foil, and plunged the corkscrew into the cork. It came free with a satisfying *plonk*—and perhaps it was a bit odd for him to be so intensely aware of each sensation, given how many times he had opened a bottle without thought back in 1848, but it had in fact been a *very* long time since he had drunk good whisky, or anything else save ale and gin. Even in the ridiculous chipped teacup, even in the bad light, he could see how richly the amber liquid glowed as he poured.

He lifted the cup toward his nostrils, swirling to release the flavor, and the taste of peat smoke seared the back of his throat before he could so much as sip it. Katarina inhaled, then sighed appreciatively. Maxwell was not sure he wanted to know how she had learned to master drink this strong, or who had taught her.

"Very well, then, to what are we drinking?" he asked.

"The Spirit of Christmas Present," Katarina said, suddenly fierce. "One day, right here, right now, ours between midnight and midnight."

She sounded so like the Spider that Maxwell was momentarily unable to speak. He recovered just in time to touch his mug to hers. "The Spirit of Christmas Present, then."

A little later, he could not resist commenting, "Still a toast to the dead, though, isn't it? Or the almost dead? Doesn't the Spirit die at midnight, like a mayfly?"

"I thought," Katarina said, "you didn't know the story."

"I said I didn't like the story," Maxwell corrected. "I read it once."

"You have a remarkable memory, in that case."

Maxwell exhaled a laugh. "And you are a remarkably well-read woman."

"For my class?" she asked with a smile. He couldn't remember when he had heard her say that before—or if it had not been she who uttered the words at all. Perhaps they had been said by the Spider. It occurred to him, as the memory flitted away from his questioning grasp, that he might have swallowed the whisky a little too quickly. It had been a *very* long time since he had indulged himself with strong spirits.

"Whose name aren't we mentioning?" he asked a long time later.

Katarina raised sculpted black eyebrows at him.

"You're drinking a toast to one of your dead after all, aren't you?" He wasn't sure how he knew.

She was silent so long he began to think she would not answer. Finally she said, "His name was Jacob. He worked in the theater. He was a good man and a kind one. He was a survivor of Murchinson's. He recruited me to work for Seward." She cleared her throat. "He died for his beliefs."

"To Jacob, then."

Katarina inclined her head.

Later, she asked, "And you? Who of your dead are you drinking to?"

Maxwell swirled the whiskey in his teacup. "I was raised an orphan," he said. "All I knew of my parents was that my father had fled to the Continent in disgrace when I was an infant, and died there. My mother likewise disappeared, either with him or to the arms of some other man, no one was ever certain. She'd run away to Gretna Greene with my father in the first place, when she was just turned seventeen, and apparently there was an aunt of hers who did worse, so there was…There was precedent."

He had not quite meant to start there, but it had seemed important she understand it all. Now he felt stuck in the mud of the confession, unable to set the wheels turning again.

Katarina watched him in silence.

Finally she offered, "My mother always said she had married my father. She said he was a Russian nobleman who fell in love with her when he saw her perform at La Scala, and that she came home after he died of fever."

Maxwell glanced up, interested. "But?"

Katarina shrugged. "But others in Tavisford said otherwise."

"You didn't ever ask her."

"No." Katarina smiled a little. "If I had, she would have answered honestly. And in lieu of the honest answer, there was…there was at least a chance he had married her. A chance he had loved her. A chance he had actually been a Russian lord, instead of some nameless gypsy stagehand." She took a swallow of whisky. "So there's precedent in my family too, if that makes it easier."

Maxwell grimaced. "It might actually make it harder. Perhaps I shouldn't have started there. It was what I was raised believing, but it turned out to be untrue. When I was thirty, I discovered the timepiece and the journals, and I learned for the first time who they had really been." He pulled the little leather journal out of his breast pocket, and it fell open at the page he wanted. "Look how my father writes of her. She was fearless. She met straight on what had to be met; she never hesitated to do what had to be done. And look what you can see of him, in the way he writes. He cares so greatly about the people they try to help. It matters so much to him. Look at all the people whose lives were bettered by the actions my parents took." He poured himself more whisky. "I started by wanting to save her—to save them—but I can't. I never can. I have a *time machine,* and I can't save them." He tried to smile. "My past is fixed, which is of course true of everyone."

"Well," Katarina said, smiling, "your presence here means it's not true of me. But overall, I take your point."

"That *is* the point," Maxwell said. "I can't save them, I can't ever save them, but perhaps it doesn't matter, if I can save—something else. If their ideals live on, if I'm the sum of their lives, if because of them I fix—all this—" He gestured. "Then that would make sense of it. That would make it come out all right."

Katarina nodded.

"Not," Maxwell added, "that I've done so well by that measurement either. I keep failing. I try to make history change, and I keep failing. I thought I was doing all right under the Spider, helping her hold back the tide, but I haven't managed so well on my own."

"It seems to me you do very well indeed on your own, as long as you're living in a straight line," Katarina said. "You only ever failed to meet your own standards when you're in the act of traveling in time. Living in a straight line, you've stolen grain shipments to feed the hungry, you've ransomed men from workhouses and prisons, you've used your status as a gentleman to protect those who cannot protect themselves." After a moment, she added, "I think they'd be proud, if they knew." He was surprised at how much it meant to hear that. He looked up to find her contemplating her mug. "I know the Spider would be."

Maxwell drained the last droplets from his teacup, rather than reply.

"So what's next, then?" Katarina asked, in the tone of one who deliberately changes the subject. "What will you do after the war?"

Maxwell shook his head. "I can't see that far ahead."

She moved impatiently. "That's what Gavin says. And I understand, but… couldn't we talk of it anyhow? In the future conditional tense, if the future tense proper is too difficult to manage?"

Maxwell had to smile. "What would be next for you, then, if we were to arrive at the end of the war?"

"La Scala. Assuming I haven't irretrievably ruined my throat by then. Seward says he will help with lessons and fees." She poured herself another small measure. "What about you? Would you go home?"

"No reason to," Maxwell said. "There's nothing particularly homelike about 1848. I…might stay, I suppose?" He considered the idea for the first time, and was surprised how attractive he found it. "If we were to arrive at the end of the war, why couldn't I stay?"

Katarina spread her hands—or spread one, at least, and gestured expansively with the mug held in the other. "I see no reason why you couldn't." She smiled. "You should. It'll be good to have you here, for the building part that will succeed the destroying."

She was dreaming if she thought *that* would happen in either of their lifetimes, and he might have chided her for the optimistic non-conditional future tense, but on second thought, perhaps it was all right to talk as if the dream could come true. "Very well, then, it is agreed."

She peered at him. "What is agreed?"

Maxwell poured a final swallow into his own mug. It seemed necessary to toast the bargain. "If we reach 'after the war,'" he said, "I pledge I'll stay long enough to attend your debut performance at La Scala. And then after that... well, then we'll see."

Katarina grinned at him. "It is agreed," she said, and reached to touch her mug to his.

Outside, a cacophony of bells began to tell midnight.

"'Gay go up and gay go down,'" Katarina quoted. "'Happy Christmas' say the bells of Londontown."

Maxwell supposed the Spirit of Christmas Present might have its moments after all, but declined to give her the satisfaction of saying so.

He had the feeling she knew anyway.

Chapter 8

n Tuesday, the twenty-fourth of August, in the year of our Lord eighteen hundred and eighty five, the bottom fell out of Maxwell's world. Again.

Seward had always been less circumspect than he liked to believe himself. He was simply too notable a figure, too strong a personality, to fade into the background as the mastermind of a conspiracy must. Maxwell had warned him of this fact more than once—and Katarina had seemed to agree, no surprise there—but she had too much respect for Seward to openly challenge him, and Maxwell alone had not been able to persuade the nobleman to change his ways. Seward's conspiracy would have been safer if Seward had kept his hands completely off it, but that was perhaps an unreasonable expectation. He had started it in the first place because he could not bear to stand quietly by when action was called for. Besides, no man likes to be told that *he* is the weak point in a defensive fortress.

Seward had at least taken reasonable precautions with regard to ownership of the warehouse, and that was the only reason his arrest did not instantly doom his companions. The warehouse was owned by a third party, with misdirections set up at every financial point. Everything else, Seward had done in his own name, mingling the orders for Trevelyan's supplies in with the legitimate work of the legitimate factories he actually owned. For quite some time, Seward had gotten his people what they needed—be that reinforced steel or the whisper in the ear of an MP—quietly, steadily, without the least suspicion of a suspicion. So long had this state of affairs persisted that the night he failed to arrive for a meeting, no one thought anything of him being tardy by half an hour...or an hour...or a little more. It was not until the chiming clock marked him a full two hours behind his time that Maxwell felt a chill rise inexorably in his chest, and cursed himself for sitting so long unconcerned.

He pushed back his chair—sharply, with the impatience that would better characterize a young buck than the sage advisor to the head of a conspiracy—but Trevelyan stopped him with a grim hand on his shoulder. It was Katarina who went out on reconnaissance to gather what intelligence was to be had.

She returned well after dawn, whey-faced from tension and fatigue, with the news that Frederick, Lord Seward, had been arrested as he rose from his dinner-table.

Maxwell reflected, not for the first time, that he unfortunately did not possess the temperament required to sedately manage a conspiracy. It must be his mother's legacy that caused his mind to turn first to Seward and wonder how he might be freed, might be spirited away… Trevelyan, not distracted by such woolgathering for a moment, said only: "His papers. Is there anything to link him to us?"

"How in hell should I know?" Katarina snapped. "His house is surrounded by bobbies and coppers; I couldn't very well climb through a window with all of them watching. But my guess is not, or they'd be here now. The warehouse isn't in his name, I know that."

"Then we might have a day or two of grace." Trevelyan scowled at the far wall. "Call it two days of grace…and a steadily falling barometer…It can be done. We'll field-test the prototype Thursday night."

"We'll what?" Katarina stared at him. "I thought you couldn't be ready before next week and were waiting for more equipment in any case."

"I've been taking inventory," Trevelyan said, "assuming any chance of that requested equipment had gone up in smoke." He had indeed spent the night so engaged, combing through supplies and paperwork with fingers that never hesitated or quivered. "And I can almost do it. I can scavenge the javelins from the last prototype—they're smaller than I wanted, but they'll work well enough for a single field test. I won't have time to mold and fire another set of ceramic isolators, but I can make new ones from tanned leather—enough layers will do it. I'm still fine-tuning the firing mechanism, but I could have that done before the storm strikes. The glass isn't falling *so* very fast; I've got thirty-six hours, maybe forty-eight; I can do it if we're not raided. The only thing—" He broke off.

"The only thing?" Maxwell prodded. The idea of having only one tangible problem to address was, in comparison to contemplating the overall situation, a stunning relief.

"I must have the gold-plated conductors. The ones Seward contracted out to von Willebrand." Trevelyan blew out his breath. "Or I must have gold bullion enough to melt down in the forge."

Maxwell and Katarina looked at each other. "Make your adjustments," Maxwell said. "We'll get your conductors."

"We've no way of knowing where they are, if the shipment ever arrived or if it was confiscated with Seward's arrest. How do you mean to—?"

"That's not your concern," Katarina interrupted. "Let us worry about that. You worry about getting the prototype working."

Trevelyan closed his mouth and nodded once. "Done." Without a backward glance, he swung for the laboratory.

Maxwell and Katarina looked at each other again.

"So," Maxwell said. "Gold. That's quite a problem. At least it's a single tangible—"

"It's tangible, but it's not the only one." Katarina started to pace, counting the difficulties on her fingers. "One, tanned leather. That's easy; we'll ask him how much and buy it locally. Two, assembling the troops. They think we're a week out at least from another field-test, so we'll have to pass the word as quick as we can. Three." She turned to look at him. "We cannot assume forty-eight hours of grace. We can hope for it, but while we're hoping, we'll burn any papers we want to keep out of Imperial hands and set up an escape route."

"Your friend with the submersible—?"

"Is actually in port this week. Thank heaven for small mercies, I suppose." Katarina rubbed her hands over her face. "Four, gold-plated conductors. All right. Come with me and let's get a proper shopping-list." She led the way down the corridor, calling as she went. "Gavin?"

They stopped at the door of the laboratory, and Trevelyan looked up, scowling, from the prototype he was already pulling to pieces. Katarina held up a hand. "This won't take a moment. We need only two answers from you. First, determine how much leather you need, and any other specifications, and I'll send one of the lads to buy it. And second—" She looked at Maxwell.

"—second, do you have any idea at all how von Willebrand sent the conductors? Which ship, expected when, to which of Seward's factories?"

Trevelyan shook his head. "All I can tell you is the last such parcel was sent to Peterson. I remember the label. And Seward was to bring it perhaps tonight or perhaps not until next week, so it may not even be in the country yet."

"If it's still *en route,* what will do in its place?" Maxwell asked. "You said you could melt gold bullion. How much?"

Trevelyan shrugged helplessly. "Fifty sovereigns?"

At Maxwell's side, Katarina actually choked. Seward might have been able to come up with such a sum, but it was a year's wages for her. "I know," Trevelyan said, but she cut him off again.

"Don't worry about it. Worry about the prototype. And tell me how much leather, as soon as you know. We'll handle this." She drew Maxwell away, shutting the laboratory door firmly behind them. "It needs a gentleman to inquire at shipping offices," she told him, "and someone with my connections to inquire at the docks. We'll meet back here by noon to compare notes."

༄

Maxwell left the warehouse and stepped into a world that seemed to have transformed overnight into something darker and harsher. Surely more constructs than usual walked the patrol route; surely they loomed more ominously over Spitalfields. A departing construct's back looked uncannily like a segment of Wall. The implications made his breath catch hard somewhere below his breastbone. *The future has come.*

No. The hell it has. Not yet. Maxwell pulled himself together. The current path foreshadowed certain ends, but the path could still be departed from. Surely they could still wrest history off this disastrous collision course.

Surely.

He kept his head down and his coat collar turned up, muffling himself despite the heavy August heat, shielding himself until he was out of the stews. At least there was a blanket of yellow fog to hide him. It seemed to vibrate, the clattering of a million gears at once, smoothed by sheer number almost—but maddeningly not quite—into a hum. The closer he got to the factories, the louder and more insistent grew the rhythmic clatter. Maxwell had walked here often in the past two years, and had grown so used to the noise he was scarcely more perturbed by it than a native Londoner—but it seemed louder today.

The library had the last week's editions of *The Times,* which had lists of ships docked from Germany during that time, which led to a list of five shipping offices. Maxwell went to each, and at the third was able to discover that a parcel from von Willebrand's factory had indeed been delivered to Albert Peterson, one of Seward's men of business, on Monday afternoon.

At least it was in the country. But was it at Peterson's home still, or had he transferred it to Seward before his lordship's arrest?

Maxwell had met Peterson only once, some time ago, in Seward's company, back before he had begun insisting on caution and he and Seward therefore spent no time whatsoever publicly in each other's company. Peterson must be at least partially trustworthy, or Seward would not have delegated to him the receipt of items needed for the overthrow of the government...But Maxwell had no way of knowing precisely how much Peterson knew. Or, indeed, whether it might not have been he who betrayed Seward in the first place. For all Maxwell had insisted upon the distance, and would have preferred an even greater divide, there was a definite disadvantage to the right hand not knowing what the left did.

He already knew the police were watching Seward's house. There was no need for him to draw attention to himself by confirming it. He strolled instead past Peterson's. The curtains were drawn and the place looked uninhabited, but there were a few deliberate-looking loungers positioned across the street.

"Possibly in Seward's house," Maxwell told Katarina that afternoon. "Possibly in Peterson's. Possibly in an evidence lock-up at Scotland Yard. Three equally impregnable fortresses. Perhaps we should consider a money-lender."

Katarina grimaced, but didn't argue.

"Do you know any?" Maxwell asked.

"A few. All unsavory types. Though I suppose it's not overly likely we'll have to live with the consequences." In response to his lifted eyebrow, she clarified, "I expect we'll need to flee, so it doesn't matter what bridges we burn in London."

"Right," Maxwell said. "Then we should look into burning this one. I don't know that we have another option. There might be ways to get into each house if we had more time, but as it is, nothing but outright burglary would answer."

"And we of Locksley's empire of crime have a remarkable dearth of experienced criminals in our ranks," Katarina agreed with a sigh.

Maxwell nodded.

"Although—"

Maxwell looked up sharply at her change in tone. She had paused in her pacing, attention arrested by something only she could see, looking as though fascinated at the dingy whitewashed walls of the sitting room.

"Although," Katarina said slowly, "we're hardly the only power in the East End. Oh, that's...that's elegantly symmetrical." She turned to Maxwell, genuinely smiling. "I think I know who could supply us with burglars of the necessary skill. And if all else fails, I do believe he acts as a moneylender too. Come with me to pay a call, won't you? Leave your nice things here and go as shabby as you can."

Was she actually asking *him* to act as bodyguard to *her*? "It's dangerous, then?"

Katarina smiled at him. "Not for the two of us together."

❧

Lord Bastion's sewer had not changed in twenty-five years. *Would* not, Maxwell amended to himself, change in the *next* twenty-five years.

There was, as there would be later, a white-haired ruler sitting on a throne. There was, as there would be later, a middle-aged man standing at his side. There was, as there would be later, a child learning the trade at his grandfather's feet.

Amid all the similarities, the differences stood out starkly. This Lord Bastion was a cadaver rather than a slug. He might have been carved from the same alabaster as his high seat, his skin as white as his hair, his cheekbones sharp enough to cut glass. The manner in which he eyed his visitors brought forcibly to Maxwell's mind the Spider's assessment of him. *Lord Arcturus was vicious and ruthless, but he wasn't stupid.* No, those cold watchful eyes were not stupid at all.

Whereas Lord Adolphus amuses himself by hijacking my shipments of grain. Adolphus, still of vigorous middle age, was not a slug yet either. But something in the stance, the expression, the distracted roaming gaze, suggested an affinity for the appetite of the moment. He had not inherited from his father the sharp cold eyes that saw six strategic moves ahead.

Or perhaps it was only that Maxwell knew what he would become and saw in the man's face what he expected to see.

"My dear young lady," said Lord Arcturus Bastion to Katarina, while his son Adolphus eyed her low-cut bodice without the slightest attempt at decorum. "You represent Robert Locksley, you say? In what way may I be of service to Robert Locksley?"

Katarina lifted her chin. "Robert Locksley requests a seventy-two hour truce, during which time he may be of service to you."

"Robert Locksley cannot be of service even to himself," the old man corrected her pleasantly. "Lord Seward cannot request anything from the Tower of London. Oh yes, I know Locksley's true name. Whatever made you think I didn't know?"

"I never considered the matter one way or the other," Katarina said. "Whatever made you think Robert Locksley was only one person?"

That got Bastion's attention.

It got Maxwell's as well. He stopped wondering how in the hell Bastion had obtained that inconvenient piece of information and instead turned his eyes to Katarina. She looked utterly unimpressed by the company in which she stood, and equally unconcerned over the identity she had just claimed as her own. *Is this how it happens? Was I just privileged to see the beginning? How odd, and how wonderful, to be present at the moment when someone becomes who she is meant to be.*

Lord Arcturus recovered his air of mockery after the slightest of pauses. "And you come running your own errands, Miss Locksley?"

"It's 'Madame Rasmirovna,'" Katarina said, "and I come conducting my own negotiations. You would not leave so important a matter in the hands of a subordinate, either."

Bastion leaned back, looking interested against his will. "What happens in seventy-two hours?"

"A lightning-storm."

One skeletal hand rubbed at the alabaster chin. "Continue."

Katarina drew a breath, exactly in the manner of one placing her last cent on the gambling table. "Lord Seward's arrest comes at an awkward time for us. Locksley's inventor requires a shipment of materials to complete a prototype weapon, and we need a clear field under a lightning-storm to test it. If the test works, we have a weapon capable of taking down a construct. The tiles fall from there."

"A great many tiles," Bastion pointed out.

"Obviously. But fewer than if the test does not go forward."

Bastion considered it. "If those are the stakes, a seventy-two hour truce is the least of what you need. You said a shipment of materials and a clear field? I imagine you desire me to assist with these matters as well."

"Very perceptive of you." Katarina spoke with a little grudging admiration, and the old man softened at the thought of scoring a touch. *Grant concessions that do not matter. Allow them to think they have the upper hand.* "A small parcel addressed to Seward's man of business Albert Peterson currently resides in either Peterson's house or Seward's, both of which are under police guard. Among those who profess allegiance to you are those with the skill to obtain it for us. It must be obtained tonight. Then, on the night of the lightning-storm, we will need as many as you can spare to join us as we engage in ploys to draw the construct-pilots' attention away from our testing-field. Fifty should do it."

"The value of this parcel?" Bastion inquired.

"To the ordinary man? Very little." Katarina spoke as though she had no knowledge of any gold that might coat the conductors. "To our inventor? Irreplaceable. To the man from whom Seward commissioned them? I imagine his lordship paid fifty guineas, or a hundred."

"You want a truce for seventy-two hours," Bastion repeated, "fifty of my men and women to engage in activity that very nearly *ensures* rather than *risks* their arrest, and a burglary of goods valuable enough to count as a hanging offense. And why should I do this? What can you give me in return?"

"I can give you a war." Katarina smiled at him. "A chance to join with us to fight off the boot on all our necks."

Adolphus Bastion took an eager step forward.

His father gave him a disgusted look. "Oh, of course, that excites *you*. It would."

Adolphus' face slowly suffused with a tide of red shame.

Lord Arcturus turned his attention back to Katarina. "Having grown beyond a child's view of the world, I do not consider war a profitable investment of my time."

"Between neighbors? Of course not," Katarina said. *He understood the power balance between himself and Robert Locksley; he understood how both could work within it to the benefit of each one's vassals; he understood that even the stronger of two parties derives no benefit from the ruin of a turf war. He didn't dabble in nonsense beneath his notice.* "But I speak of the sort of war that unites neighbors against an outside force, and that is a very different thing. New fortunes are made as old civilizations crumble."

"You are young and foolish, like my son," said Lord Arcturus. "I rule an empire now, and see no advantage in staking it as a gamble for something different."

"Or perhaps," Katarina said sweetly, "your forces are not so formidable as we've all been led to believe, and the burglary I requested is beyond your powers?"

Adolphus, for all his embarrassment at his father's public rebuke, now surged forward, furious, intent on defending the old man from this slander.

Arcturus rolled his eyes and stopped his son with a lifted hand, too experienced to react to such an obvious jape. He looked down upon Katarina, amused. "Do you propose something else in its stead?"

"Fifty sovereigns would answer my purpose just as well."

Keep them off-balance. Lord Adolphus actually choked as Katarina had done earlier, for the first time provoked into a genuine reaction he could not mask. "My dear young lady, do you imagine if I had that kind of money hidden under my bed I would live like this?"

"No." Katarina smiled at him again, all cheerful charm. "But I imagined it was worth asking."

Lord Arcturus leaned back again, huffing a slight chuckle. "So we're back to the burglary. And again I ask, what do you mean to offer me in exchange for your three-fold ludicrous demand?"

Katarina took a deep breath. "I'd be in your debt."

For the second time the old man on the throne appeared interested. His son appeared very interested indeed, looking ever more speculatively at Katarina's bodice.

She rolled her eyes. *"Professionally,"* she clarified, looking at the elderly Lord Arcturus and not his son. "Not personally."

"By the look of you," Adolphus muttered, "the professional and personal are one."

"Shut up, boy," the old man snapped.

"Is that indeed what you infer from my appearance?" Katarina spoke over him. "Looks can be so very deceiving." She turned slightly, not quite presenting Adolphus her back but very definitely dismissing him as beneath her notice. To Lord Arcturus, she said, "I am speaking seriously. I could be quite useful to you in a professional capacity. I am an actress, on stage and off. I know the art of inhabiting a part, trouser roles as well as skirt. There's very little I can't manage as long as you can get me the costuming for it. Secondly, anyone in the stews who doesn't already owe you fealty owes Robert Locksley a favor. And finally, I've rubbed elbows with more respectable sorts in my time. I think you would find our association very profitable indeed, and I offer it to you for…let us say a year and a day."

Katarina ignored the catch of breath Maxwell could not suppress in time. He wanted to catch hold of her and shake her, wanted to demand if she could possibly mean what she said. Did she truly intend to owe favors to *Lord Arcturus Bastion*?

In the set of her shoulders, in the memory of her offhand comment about the probable need to flee London, he found his answer. She was certain they would need to flee by submersible in two nights' time, so she cared nothing for what bridges she burned now. It was far past the time she was meant to be at the Shoreditch, he suddenly realized, and she was here instead. She had never missed a performance before, not on any account. She therefore did not think Bastion would have any opportunity to collect his debt.

"A year and a day," Katarina said. "In exchange, a seventy-two hour truce; fifty of your best to light up the skies and distract the coppers the next time it storms, probably in the early hours of Friday morning; and two burglaries, to be executed immediately, now, tonight."

Lord Arcturus looked as though he could not decide between amusement and offense. "Do you actually think a year of your time is so valuable?"

Katarina laughed—an absolutely honest sound. "I think it's cheap at twice the price." She met Bastion's eyes and smiled. "But I'm in a hurry. So I'm offering you a discount." More soberly, she said, "I am here because you are one of the forces in this city. Where you throw your weight matters. Throw it behind my people, and we disrupt the balance of power forever. Hold back—and those on top stay there."

"I am among those on top," Bastion pointed out.

Katarina smiled again. "If you truly thought that, you'd be a man of small imagination, and I know you're anything but."

Bastion considered it for a long, silent moment—long enough that Maxwell could feel perspiration oozing out of every separate pore of his skin. "Done," Lord

Arcturus said at last. "Seventy-two hours. Fifty men and women. One parcel. A year and a day."

"A year and a day starting the morning after the lightning-storm," Katarina clarified. "I'm rather occupied between now and then."

"Starting the morning after the storm," Bastion agreed. "You'll present yourself here at nine."

"Of course," Katarina said pleasantly.

Bastion nudged his grandson. "Pass the word for Maude Briggs."

Katarina exhaled, long and exultant. "We'll be all right now," she murmured to Maxwell.

"You'll work with my ringmaster to arrange the circus you need when next it storms," Bastion said to her, "and your associate will work with my son to plan the acquisition of your parcel. Or the other way about, if you prefer."

Maxwell turned to face Katarina, raising his brows in a silent question.

"Circus," Katarina said, touching her own chest. "Parcel," she added, nodding to him. And then, barely moving her lips, "You'll be all right?"

"Oh yes." Maxwell cast a glance at the oily Arcturus, prowling step by confident step toward them like an overfed cat. "I'm ever so much better armed than I was the last time I stood here."

Adolphus reached them in time to hear the comment. He looked Maxwell up and down with disdain. "Have we met, then?"

"Not y—" Maxwell cut himself off. The course would be departed from. A box of gold-plated connectors, an army of foot soldiers, a successful field test, a submersible. For a moment, Katarina's certainty caught him up as well; for a moment, he believed it could be done. He looked Adolphus up and down in his turn, and changed his response. "No, can't say as we have."

☙

atarina departed for home after an exhaustive planning session with Maude Briggs. "If she were not personally loyal to Bastion, I'd try to recruit her," she commented to Maxwell. "But as it is, there's no point. And...Max?"

"Yes?"

"There's no need to distract Gavin with chatter of bargains made today. After it rains is soon enough."

"I understand." He rather thought she planned to delay telling Trevelyan of her promise to Bastion until their submersible was most of the way to Bremerhaven. Or perhaps to keep the secret unless and until necessity drew them back to London.

Katarina looked over at Lord Arcturus and his son. "Do you go with Adolphus' motley crew tonight?"

Maxwell shook his head. "There might be some value in having a gentleman along to distract the guards, but there is also value in me not showing my face. Adolphus doesn't want me there, anyhow. Understandable enough, as we've never worked together."

"Fairly said, but—" Katarina's eyes narrowed. "He had better be planning to actually hand those conductors over to you."

"He is," Maxwell said. "He won't break his father's promise."

"You trust his honor?"

"I do not. But he defers to the wolf in the pack who snarls the loudest, and at the moment, that's Arcturus."

"The cowed don't always stay that way," Katarina pointed out. "Everyone has a breaking point."

"Adolphus's won't come for ten years yet." Maxwell considered. "Well, if the war comes early, his uprising may as well, but even so there's still time."

Katarina smiled a little. "So you did know him."

"Briefly. In 1910 and 1911, when he was an old man."

"When his appetites ran roughshod over the stews, no doubt."

Maxwell looked at her sideways. "When he was kept in check by the Spider, in point of fact."

She spluttered a laugh. "Truly?" She looked over at the three Bastions, then back at Maxwell. "It seems I'm to become a formidable woman."

"You're a formidable woman now," Maxwell said, forgetting to catch back the words.

That startled another laugh out of her. To his surprise, he thought she blushed a little as well. She made him a mock curtsey, ridiculous in trousers. "Why, thank you, sir."

He floundered for an instant, not knowing what to say next. Talking about their mission seemed to be the thing to do; reassurance seemed to be what was appropriate. "We have this in hand," he said, and she looked up at the change in tone.

"Nearly," she agreed.

"Very nearly," Maxwell persisted. "I do believe we'll bring it off."

"I think so too," Katarina said, meeting his eyes. After a pause, she went on, "And speaking of which—as there's a great many folk I must speak with, I ought to see if I can reach any of them before curfew tonight. You'll be all right here?"

"I'll be fine," he said. "I can handle Bastion. I'll see you in a few hours."

"You will." Katarina gave him a nod and turned for the exit, walking with a brisk, confident stride he did not think was in any way an act.

❧

It took more than a few hours. It was in fact *seven* full hours later, with Big Ben poised to strike three, before Adolphus' burglars returned with a small brown-paper-wrapped parcel. It had been in Peterson's house, left possibly as a snare to draw out Seward's supporters. No one volunteered details of how the snare had been avoided, and Maxwell did not ask. He made a show of opening the parcel and examining the contents. Though he had no idea what they were meant to look like, he could at least confirm Adolphus had not substituted pebbles or some such—and he had not; the conductors were shiny gold. Maxwell nodded his approval, turned up the collar of his overcoat, and started for home through the sullen August air.

He knew the rhythm of the constructs' patrol as intimately as he knew the rhythm of the blood in his veins. He could tell right away that something was off-kilter. The thunderous footfalls were faster than usual, the lightning flashes coming from the wrong parts of Spitalfields. Retreating to Bastion's hell-hole was not an option, so he kept moving, but he slowed his pace, staying in the shadows, listening hard, trying to discern a pattern.

At the corner of Brushfield Street, where a gas lamp threw a little fitful light, a pack of six Wellingtons exploded around the corner from the direction of the docks.

Wellingtons? In *London?* In *1885?*

There were no Wellingtons in 1885 London, save the miserable specimen in the Zoo. There had never been Wellingtons running loose even in 1875 London, not the way they had menaced the moors of Devon.

It was as though Seward's arrest had changed the very parameters of the universe. For a panicked ice-cold instant Maxwell was absolutely certain that the timepiece had somehow activated itself in his pocket, that he and Trevelyan's priceless conductors had somehow been thrown back to 1875, to a pocket of history he'd just never heard about when some rogue Wellingtons had infiltrated London after all, and how was he ever to get back—

Then blue-white lightning seared the sky, a construct lumbered around the corner in pursuit of the fleeing monsters, and Maxwell, dodging and scrambling his way into the safety of a dark alley, recognized the staged hunt for what it was.

The morning papers had contained news of Seward's arrest. The evening papers had contained lurid accounts of his empire of crime. And now Wellington monsters, the nation's feared scourge, were seen running loose through the streets Seward had controlled. Set loose, no doubt, by his criminal empire in retaliation for his arrest, and requiring heroic constructs to bring them down and protect all decent Londoners—

Not a bad story. Maxwell pressed himself against the filthy brick wall, watched the blue light flash overhead, and wondered where the designers of the narrative had found six Wellingtons. It suggested some sort of hidden storage facility. He wished he could think such a thing too sinister for the present British government, but he knew the future that government was hurtling toward.

We'll change it. We'll fix it. The course will be departed from.

Blue lightning flashed again over the straggling chimneys and cannon-fire rattled Maxwell's teeth in his head. Blinded by the light as though by an actual lightning-flash, he could not see even the brick wall he huddled against. But he heard, clearly, the screams of Wellingtons in pain.

Not enough distinct screams for all six of them. Two, at most. Which left four at least still running through the stews with constructs at their heels. For the hunt to serve its purpose, the construct pilots would let it play out for a long as possible, to be seen by as many as possible. With no way to predict how long it would last, with no way to predict which way the Wellingtons would flee, how was Maxwell to get home?

The ground-shaking footfalls of the construct at least told him where *it* was, and it seemed to be moving away from him. He would do best to keep to the alleyways where it could not fit. Where was he now? He mapped the route in his head as best he could and fished out the dark lantern Lord Arcturus had loaned him. His lordship had cautioned that it must be returned by Katarina on Saturday morning, promptly at nine, but they'd all be on a submersible by then.

Or possibly they would be dead, the way this day was going.

He kept to the shadows and he kept to the alleyways. Perversely, the Wellingtons and the construct seemed to be following the same route, shifted over two or three streets. When Maxwell's alleyways intersected with main streets, he caught glimpses of their enacted hunt, sometimes just in shadows on the cobblestones, sometimes actual momentary blue-lit images of frightened faces and rags and heavy metal feet. The rest of the time, as he hastened along with the dark lantern mostly shuttered in one hand and his other against the soot-covered brick, he followed their movements in his mind. It made him think of shadow puppets against a silk screen, like Séraphin's *Ombres françaises,* which he had seen during a brief holiday in Paris in 1843. Séraphin too had used clockwork to animate his shadow puppets.

The glimpses grew fewer and further between, and eventually the blue light stopped flashing altogether. Maxwell stilled as well. The construct was immobile, was waiting, and that was *enormously inconvenient,* since he couldn't hear it when it stood still. He saw up ahead a patch of lighter gray, where his alleyway intersected with a larger street. If he were to stand there, he might take a cautious reconnaissance, perhaps catch a glimpse of gaslight shimmering off a giant copper foot, and chart the rest of his journey accordingly. He wondered where the surviving Wellingtons had gone to ground. The confident tactically-trained Wellies that had plagued Katarina's childhood might have been planning a flanking maneuver, but he didn't think these particular ones, with their maddened eyes, were capable of sophisticated strategy. Where in hell had they been kept, all this time?

He reached the mouth of the alleyway and eased around it. His foot lucklessly caught against a crate, tipping it over with a slight but definite thump—

—and scaring the two emaciated Wellingtons that were cowering in a refuse heap just on the other side of the corner. They exploded from their hiding place like a flock of birds driven from cover by a poacher's shot, racing pell-mell into the open, scattering tins and crates and who knew what else with a racket loud enough to wake the dead. Almost directly over Maxwell's head, from a side-street a bare few feet away, the searing blue light flared to life. Maxwell was close enough to hear the gear whine as the heavy foot drew itself up and plunged itself down and the construct resumed its pursuit.

He could have run the other way—back down the alleyway or even along the main street in the opposite direction from the construct. It wasn't looking at him or for him, and it would be distracted for a few moments at least; he would have been able to get most of the way home in a solid sprint before it recovered sufficient leisure to pursue him.

But that first searing lightning-flash had shown him something other than fleeing fear-crazed Wellingtons. There were youngsters standing in the street. A boy and a girl, perhaps twenty or a bit younger, standing near enough to an alleyway that they might have sheltered in it, but not moving toward the shelter. They stood stock still out in the open street, staring up at the oncoming construct as though they had never seen one before, in as much danger as if they stood immobile on a train track.

If they were among Locksley's foot soldiers, if they had any knowledge at all of the field-test plan, the very last thing the conspiracy needed was for them to be arrested. If they were *not* Locksley's foot soldiers, the very last thing *they* needed was to be *mistaken* for such and arrested. Trevelyan would have left the fools to their fate, but Maxwell knew what Katarina would want done, and so he turned left instead of right and ran, keeping to the shadows as much as he could and hoping the sweeping blue light would not catch him, to get the children hidden in an alleyway before the staged battle reached them.

The next lightning flash confirmed the youngsters' location, and he made for it, reaching them as darkness descended once more. He caught hold of the girl's arm to pull her aside.

It was the strangest feeling—

~

A s his hand closed over her sleeve, as his foot hit the ground, the city seemed to shiver around him. He couldn't see at all, he was moving by instinct and touch alone—yet the world still seemed to shimmer before his eyes. In that moment, he seemed to become separate from it.

He was accustomed to feeling separate. He had first learned the feeling in a window seat outside a fire lit family circle. Until the age of thirty, he had often experienced the sensation of watching his life, as though played out on a stage, as though from the box seats. In every time period he had visited before this one, he had always been grafted on, looking in, not really ever one with the people who lived there. In every time period he had visited *except this one*, and he hadn't even realized how seamlessly he fit here until the world lurched all around him in an alleyway and he blinked away momentary dizziness to find himself once again watching from the outside.

~

It was an odd hallucination, but he didn't have time for philosophical contemplation right at the moment. The instant's dizziness had caused him to stumble, and instead of pulling the girl out of danger, he had accidentally pulled her off her feet. They fell together, the boy shouting at him to unhand her, a crack of fear in the young voice not quite masked by the bravado. Then there was an impetuous young fist connecting with Maxwell's mouth, interrupting Maxwell's attempt at soothing explanation, and Maxwell *really* did not have time for this. Seward was rotting in a cell or possibly stretched out upon a rack, a lightning-storm was brewing and Trevelyan was racing to be ready for it, and the construct was no doubt turning down the damned street even now to resume its patrol.

Maxwell reeled back from the punch, lunged forward and caught the cub an elbow to the solar plexus, and once more master of the situation, no longer bothered to restrain himself from giving voice to his exasperation as he fumbled to open the dark lantern. He wasn't trying to injure either of them, though they certainly deserved it for wandering about after curfew, like simpletons from whatever distant land might yet remain that had never seen a construct. The lantern resisted his fingers, and all the time he was listening for the return of the metal beast and the howling Wellingtons it chased, all the time thinking of Seward beyond his help and Katarina awaiting his return and Trevelyan's conductors in his pocket, all the time hampered by this curious distancing feeling, as though he no longer quite belonged to the air and stone surrounding him, as though his fingers fumbled because they did not belong to the same world as the lantern. "Don't you know enough to get out of their way?" he ended his diatribe as he finally got the light unshuttered.

And lifted his lantern to see his mother's face.

Chapter 9

"Y ou all right?" Katarina asked in a whisper, catching hold of his wrist to stop him.

Maxwell leaned against the wall and shut his eyes tight against the dizziness for a moment. At one end of the corridor, huddled in the entryway and no doubt wondering why they had not been invited inside, Ernie and two of his brethren staggered under the weight of the message they bore. Four of Locksley's men arrested, the only charge as yet breaking curfew, but it was not at all clear they would stand up to questioning. At the other end, hidden in the shabby little sitting room, a seventeen-year-old Elizabeth Barton and a twenty-year-old William Carrington gazed with marveling and horrified eyes at the horrific future into which they had somehow stumbled. In the workroom Trevelyan was building a weapon, in the Tower heaven only knew what Seward was enduring—

"Max?"

"Yes." He opened his eyes. "Yes, fine. Do you— You do realize who our guests are?"

"Indeed I do." Katarina's eyes glinted with something like amusement. Horror piling upon horror as it was, he supposed she might as well take some amusement where she could find it. "Even if I didn't remember your real name, I've seen your locket. Their timing is what you might call impeccable."

"They're at the very beginning." He tried again to shake off the dizziness and managed it better this time. "They don't know anything."

"You could warn them."

"But what happens if I do that? Do I—cease? Disappear?" Was that what was already happening, this strange fading feeling?

"Does it matter?" Katarina said. "Go back in there and warn them now, and you can stop all of it before it starts. You can save her."

"I…suppose I can." It was bizarre to contemplate.

"I thought that was what you wanted." Katarina watched him with an expression he couldn't decipher.

"I did," Maxwell said, "I do, I…" He realized the truth as he said it. "I did once. That's where this started, but that was…so long ago. It's been more than a decade since I accepted that failure, and since then I've started wanting other things." He gestured to the chaos outside, including Trevelyan's laboratory with an unsteady wave.

"I think you might be able to have both."

"No." That time the realization was immediate, hitting like a blow to the back of the skull. "No, in fact I cannot. If I tell them, if they act differently, I'll have a different past. I won't follow the same path, I won't end up here. I can't risk that. I don't want to leave you." He realized what he had said and clarified, "You and Trevelyan. What if no one ever brings you the Spider's message, because I'm not there to do it?"

"What if we fail tonight, even though you brought it? You might be casting your lot with the twilight of the world." She shook her head as though in disbelief. "And your other choice is to go *home*. You fool. You have the chance to go home."

"I—" He looked down into her luminous eyes. "I think I'm already there." When had that happened?

Katarina swallowed. "Do you mean that?"

"Yes." He pushed off the wall, making himself square his shoulders and speak with confidence. "The future can still be changed. This is absolutely not the twilight of the world. If this chance fails, there are others, and I will hold this line with you as long as it can be held."

She had to clear her throat before she could speak. "Very well," she said. "Bravely chosen. And...I'm glad of it."

She put out her hand, and he took it.

"But if we mean to proceed—" She gestured for him to accompany her back toward the sitting room, her posture and tone of voice changing, reverting back to business. "In that case, we've got to divide forces. We've got to go and pay four drunk and disorderly fines before the bobbies realize what they've caught. You have to go."

"Under other circumstances, perhaps," Maxwell said, scrambling to keep up with the pivoting conversation. "But as it is—"

"Don't worry about—" Katarina glanced in the direction of the parlor and rephrased. "About this other matter. I can see to it, to them. You *know* that's true, Max. I can keep them safe just as well as you can—better, maybe—but no one can fetch our foot soldiers out of quod except a gentleman, so for all the same reasons you shouldn't have gone to the door just now—"

"A gentleman wouldn't walk the streets for another hour or two. It would be more natural to wait a bit." Moreover, waiting an hour or two would give him a chance to drink some tea, or possibly something stronger, and eat some breakfast with his— with Elizabeth Barton and William Carrington, who were not yet his parents.

Katarina looked as though she knew what he had been thinking, but she said only, "Yes, but you don't want Ernie and that lot coming in to see our guests in their vintage Regency fashions, do you?"

"Well..." Maxwell couldn't think of a good counter-argument. Perhaps it would be just as well to settle his nerves and prepare some neutral topics of conversation before he saw the two of them again. "You're right, of course." He stopped her with a touch on her arm. "Take care of them," he said. "Please. Be very careful with them."

"I understand," Katarina said, holding his eyes. Then she handed him one of Trevelyan's new latch-keys, and he went off to attend to his duties as Locksley's representative while she went off to look after his wayward barely-out-of-childhood not-yet-parents.

❧

He remembered that day forever after as disjointed—playing the part that got four Locksley foot soldiers freed from jail, coming back to find to his horror that Katarina had taken Elizabeth out into the city, then to find that she had taken William, then to learn with relief of Meg Drew's rescue and with horror of Rachel Temple's death. His head gradually felt less dizzy, his fingers less clumsy, his ability to move through the world easier—not as though the feeling of separateness was receding, but as though he was becoming accustomed to it, as one might adapt to thin air on a mountain peak. By the time he caught up with Katarina in the late afternoon, he felt well enough to attribute his strange sense of unreality to sleeplessness. It was getting on for three days since had done more than doze for an hour, so it probably *was* sleeplessness in truth.

Or it might have been only that rage had cleared his head. It had been many years since he had been so angry with anyone. The last time, come to think of it, would have been when he woke immured in the Spider's web.

He had been horrified to hear that Katarina risked Elizabeth's life, safety, and future by taking her for a walk through 1885 London. He had been unable to catch up with them, and his relief at returning to the warehouse to learn Elizabeth had been brought back safely lasted only as long as it took Trevelyan to tell him that Katarina had left again, this time with William in tow. Maxwell growled incoherent fury and swung back for the door.

His foot had barely cleared the threshold when he saw them. His twenty-year-old father could not have been more definitively out of place in the stews of 1885 if he had been wearing a suit of medieval armor. The bright blue coat with its bright brass buttons must surely be visible for miles in any direction, even through yellow fog. Katarina, walking at his side, suited her surroundings well enough, but if anything made William Carrington more noticeable by the contrast. *Why is that lad wearing such an old-fashioned costume?* Maxwell thought sourly, quoting what he was sure were the thoughts of every passerby. *And why is he walking with a prostitute?*

"…not quite Milan, but still singing work of a sort," Katarina was saying. "I meant to take proper lessons, work my way up, end in La Scala eventually, just like my mother. Only perhaps without the Russian nobleman entanglement, as it seemed messy. But—" She shrugged, spreading her hands to indicate the world all around her. "This happened instead. Duty called, I suppose you could say."

William nodded. "So your plan for after the war is to go to La Scala?"

"Indeed it is." Katarina smiled at him. "And you? What are your plans?"

"For after the war?" William exhaled a rueful laugh. "I...never got that far. Since my war has been over for a year, I suppose I ought to come up with something."

"So," Maxwell cut them off. "You're back."

Katarina lifted her eyes to meet his, then raised one eyebrow, completely unimpressed by his anger. "Yes, we are. Good afternoon, Mr. Maxwell."

"Good afternoon." Maxwell glared at William. "Would you excuse us a moment, Mr. Carrington?"

"Er—of course." William edged toward the warehouse. "I'll just go and see about making myself some tea."

"Thank you." Maxwell stepped aside to allow the younger man to pass, refusing to think about the oddness of his father's shoulder brushing his own. He fixed his eyes on Katarina's. "May I have a word with you?"

"Not out here," she said, and walked before him into the warehouse.

Maxwell slammed the door behind them. "Have you gone mad?"

Katarina reached around him to do up the bolts.

"I said—"

"I heard you. Lower your voice, unless you want young Mr. Carrington to be able to eavesdrop from the scullery."

Maxwell followed her down the corridor, lowering his voice. "What the devil is wrong with you?" he demanded. "What were you *thinking*, taking her out into the city?"

"That she was at least as safe under my watchful eye out there as she would have been under Trevelyan's inattentive eye in here," Katarina said. "Especially when you consider that, if I understand the young lady's character correctly, she would have been very likely to sneak off on her own and go exploring. At least under my scheme, someone knew where she was."

"And taking William to Murchinson's? What would have happened if he'd drawn attention?"

"Oh, you sound like Trevelyan. I took him because you weren't here and it couldn't wait. There might not have been another chance."

"We cannot risk losing—" It was unlikely William could hear them, but Maxwell still couldn't bring himself to name, out loud, exactly who they couldn't risk losing and why. "We cannot risk losing people from the past," he said, staring at Katarina meaningfully. "What if they were to perish here? Their deaths could alter—" He gestured helplessly to himself, to her, to Trevelyan in his workshop with a weapon ready to deploy a full decade before 1895. "Their deaths could alter *everything*. Did you *actually* just imperil *the entire rising* to save Meg Drew?"

"No, I was trying to—" Katarina looked at him, considered for a moment whatever she saw on his face, and stopped. She folded her arms. "I apologize," she said. "But there's no harm done."

"I suppose not," Maxwell had to admit. "But none of us should be taking any risks at all. The whole thing is balanced on a knife's edge, and—"

"Max," Katarina said quietly—and then again seemed to change what she was about to say. "Do you think it will work tonight?"

He had been sure when they stood together in Bastion's sewer. But now, all the doubts rose in a dark tide. "I...don't know."

"I think it will," Katarina said. "At least, I hope it will. But while we're hoping, we lay out the next line of defense. If it doesn't work...?" Katarina's voice trailed off into a question.

Maxwell looked at her. "You don't mean only, 'if it doesn't fire.' You mean if—"

"Yes," Katarina said. "I mean, if. You said you wanted to stay here and hold the line, but—but what will you do, if?"

Maxwell sighed. "Orkney, the fifteenth of September, 1790. I'll have another try at stopping it before it starts."

She nodded, approving the strategy. "Did you ever..." It was easily the third time she decided not to say something. He opened his mouth to bluntly demand what words she kept swallowing, but she spoke over him. "Did you ever think of going to Pendoylan, the eighteenth of May, 1872?"

That stole the wind from his sails and the breath from his lungs. "Katarina—" Somehow he had gotten through all this time without having to admit it, and now here it was, the moment when he could not duck the question. "I've already been there. I've already failed there. Katarina..." He thought about the implications, all the implications. "Would you really wish for that to be altered?"

One corner of her mouth twisted wryly. "Yes, I think I would. But there's no chance of it?"

Maxwell shook his head. "I've already been there. And to the University of London the following year. To Geneva in 1788, to Inverness in 1800, to Carron Valley in 1855...to every place she and I could think of where the outcome trembled on a knife's edge and there was a chance I could affect it."

"And now here," Katarina said.

"And now here."

"And if we fail here—?"

"Then to Orkney," Maxwell said grimly. What other options were there? "To induce him to change course if I can, and to shoot him if I cannot. I have grown both brutal and desperate in my old age. We have to stop this. It doesn't matter what tool we use."

Katarina nodded as though he had said something insightful. "That's why I took William to Murchinson's."

Maxwell didn't perceive the connection, but said "Yes, I see," in an effort to turn the conversation. He went on to make his real point again: "We absolutely cannot risk either of them any further. I'll make sure they're back home before the excitement starts here."

"I don't think the storm intends to cooperate with your time-table," Trevelyan's dry voice countered. The inventor appeared from the direction of the laboratory, wiping his hands on a rag and looking almost relaxed, in comparison with the last frantic forty-eight hours. "Their watch won't work until, what, three in the morning? I doubt the lightning will hold off so long."

"You're ready, then?" Katarina asked.

"Indeed I am," Trevelyan said, in the tone of a man setting down a burden that strained his back. He inclined his head toward the laboratory. "Come and see."

∽

The rail-gun glimmered under Trevelyan's electric lighting, crouching defiantly in the center of the laboratory. Too small for a cannon and too big for a rifle, its silvery side twisted all their reflections into monstrosities. Maxwell looked up from running fingertips over the gleaming hide to find that his parents had come to join them. Trevelyan explained to them how the rail-gun was meant to function, and Elizabeth declared herself all impatience to see it working.

"You will be doing no such thing," Maxwell said, straightening sharply from his examination of the trigger. "It is too dangerous to have you two anywhere near this field test. I am sending you home before we begin."

Trevelyan glanced over his shoulder at the barometer pinned to the wall. "No, Max, I'm not thinking you are. The storm won't hold off until three tomorrow morning."

"Good," Elizabeth said, pertly tossing her brown curls. "You dragged me all over this miserable city, then left me trapped in here and incapable of aiding it. At the very least, I want to see what *you* are going to do with this miraculous—"

"*No.*" The word scorched the back of Maxwell's throat. "Absolutely not. Even if I cannot send you back, I will not see you exposed to that danger."

"With all our associates raising hell out there," Trevelyan said, "this is very likely the safest place in the city. Unless you want to take them *completely* elsewhere." He nodded to the watch chain stretched across Maxwell's waistcoat.

Katarina looked over to meet Maxwell's eyes. "You can," she mouthed the words at him.

Maxwell frowned at her. "I don't want to leave…" *You.* "…this junction." He cleared his throat. "Not unless I must."

"Then just keep them by you," Trevelyan said. "If the plan works as it's meant to, there's nothing to worry about. If not, the three of you can pop out of time." Maxwell started to argue further, but Trevelyan raised one imperious hand. "Did you hear that? Thunder, far off. We've no more time for talking. Let's get ourselves ready."

∽

Maxwell crouched with the others on the rooftop—waiting for the storm to break, listening to Big Ben tolling out the hours, and finding these activities insufficient distraction. The decision had seemed—not easy exactly, but obvious, inevitable, the only one possible to consider—when he had made it in the corridor that morning. Throughout the day, he had been so absorbed with one worry or another that he had been able to avoid looking his choice directly in the face. Now he watched Elizabeth Barton fearlessly climb ladders, curiously ask questions, and impatiently dodge his attempts to see to her safety—and had to confront the fact that in an hour's time, he meant to knowingly send her to her death.

It wouldn't happen immediately, of course. She would arrive back safely in 1815. She and William would have adventures by pocket watch. She would climb down a trellis and they would run away to Gretna Greene. They would have more adventures. They would have a child. And then she would go to the court of King Henry VIII to rescue someone else, some fool in need of saving. She would feign visions, discuss theology and philosophy with the most influential men of the age, threaten the King to his face, and wind up with her head struck off and mounted on a spike with crows plucking out its eyes. William would try and fail to rescue her, over and over, until ending his own life in 1819 at an age considerably more advanced than twenty-five.

Maxwell didn't wish any of it upon them. Quite apart from personal considerations, they were nice children. He liked Elizabeth's vivacity and William's deliberate care. They deserved better than the fate they were headed for.

But it's their fate, he rationalized to himself. *It's already happened. It keeps happening, no matter how many times I try to stop it, no matter how many times my father tried before me. And because of it I inherit a time travel device and a desperate quixotic quest, and Katarina Rasmirovna sends me back from her future to stop the end of the world, and Katarina Rasmirovna and Gavin Trevelyan and I will* stop it, our success starts now, here, tonight.

He looked through his field glasses to confirm that was true. Out in the darkened streets, a hundred pinpricks of light—half of them Bastion's and half of them Locksley's—moved together in what was not quite a pattern, playing out a dozen distractions that pulled the constructs' attention away from the warehouse district. All of them nudged into place by Katarina so that Trevelyan might have his chance to strike one hard blow, Seward's plan continuing though Seward was no longer there to oversee it, the Spider's plan continuing though she was dust in the wind, less than that, a person who would never be. Maxwell looked up from his glasses to see Elizabeth Barton, seventeen years old and fearless, smoothing down her skirt as the wind billowed the cloth, eagerly awaiting the night's adventure. And then he looked away from her, to Katarina's intent expression, and from Katarina to the city with all its pinpricks of light shining desperately against the darkness.

Why couldn't I stay? he'd said to Katarina two years ago. *I think I am home,* he'd heard himself say that morning. Why not consider the future, even if only in the conditional tense? Why not plan for after the war?

He turned deliberately away from his parents to watch Katarina the spider and Trevelyan the inventor. They and Seward the chess master were the only people who had ever felt to him like family. *I cannot risk this cause to save one woman's life. And if anything less than absolute disaster befalls us tonight, I will not go to Orkney. I'll stay here and help them hold the line.*

It was the right decision. He knew it from the way he felt the instant after it was made—the muscles of his back relaxed and he could draw a deep breath for the first time in longer than he could remember.

He had time to savor three full inhalations of the rich humid air before the lightning-bolt sizzled down the rod and charged Trevelyan's rail-gun.

Chapter 10

Half an hour later, he watched Katarina Rasmirovna and Gavin Trevelyan die in an alleyway.

"…had it coming…" Trevelyan slurred as Maxwell bent over him. "…poetic…justice…" Because of course Trevelyan would say that. In Trevelyan's arrogant self-absorbed head, this was Trevelyan's story—a Celtic tale of mischance and hubris and sins coming home to roost. And it *was* that, of course it was, Trevelyan was an actor who had pushed the world around him into motion, but Trevelyan was not the only actor here. This rain-soaked moment of despair and loss was a scene in other people's stories as well.

"Never…mind…me," Trevelyan gasped. Maxwell had run to him and not Katarina because Katarina had died instantly, crumpling into the shadows like a marionette with cut strings. He had ripped open Trevelyan's blood-stained shirt on the chance of stemming the welling red tide, but it was plainly a useless notion.

Trevelyan locked eyes with him. "You fool. *Run.*"

Maxwell caught hold of Elizabeth with one hand and William with the other, and ran.

The waterfall of rain cleared his head like a slap to the face. He did not pause by Katarina's body; there was no chance to save her and no time to say goodbye. No time to mourn, no point in mourning the life he had thought for a fanciful half-hour might be his. It could never have been his, for he was the Spider's emissary, not one of Locksley's soldiers. He might have been briefly distracted by the daydream of a life here, but he had never been entitled to it.

The Spider's last words to him had been *"Fix it,"* and so he would fix it. He would go to Orkney after all. First he must get William and Elizabeth home safe, or Lord only knew what would happen to the timeline and the Spider's last best hope… He managed to send them home two heartbeats before a construct captured them. He departed himself one heartbeat before it captured *him*.

He arrived at Orkney too late—of course he did. Elizabeth and William showed up as well—of course *they* did. He was somewhat touched to be considered one of those fools in need of saving. That night was a blur, but he did remember drinking, quite a lot in point of fact, and he thought he remembered breaking down sobbing more or less in his father's arms. *They were my friends. They were my friends.*

The following day, Elizabeth grabbed his arm and forced him to take her and William along to his last ditch effort at Waterloo, breaking one of the two priceless timepieces in consequence and displaying the kind of recklessness that would, in Tudor times, get a woman's head struck off and mounted for birds to eat.

Twenty-four hours after that, the three of them gave Britain into Napoleon's hands.

❧

He did not know immediately that they had done so, of course. For a brief period of time, in fact, it appeared as though they had achieved success. Maxwell even had the discomfort of witnessing his parents' first kiss—or a version of it, at least, because surely it couldn't have happened this way originally.

He began to cautiously fancy, one again, that perhaps this could all work out. With Waterloo fixed and the Spider's charge accomplished, perhaps he could warn Elizabeth and William to keep clear of Henry VIII's court. Perhaps the boy in the window seat could have a normal childhood after all—perhaps Maxwell would even remember it. Katarina Rasmirovna would grow up in a world menaced by neither Wellingtons nor constructs, would never go to London, and would never become either a freedom fighter or a criminal mastermind. She would become a singer at La Scala instead, and Maxwell would be an old man by that time, but perhaps he would never know what he had missed. A Maxwell with a normal childhood would most likely marry some nice girl and have a normal adulthood, and perhaps that would be enough. Or perhaps he might choose something less conventional, might go adventuring across land and sea. There might be other women like Katarina to be found, out there beyond the boundaries of proper society.

But he and his parents landed in an 1885 that was too dark, too quiet. A Gavin Trevelyan who somehow knew them and somehow was still a freedom fighter discovered them before anyone less savory could do so, and conducted them to a hideously familiar warehouse hideaway, peopled by almost-familiar *doppelgangers*.

Which was when Maxwell realized that time travel did not work the way he'd thought it did.

Because the past in which he had been born had never happened, and here he stood. Because in this timeline, Elizabeth Barton and William Carrington had vanished in 1815, leaving behind no child, and *here he still stood*. In this nightmare world where Napoleon's grandson ruled Britain, Robert Locksley's freedom fighters struggled against him, Brenda Trevelyan was alive, and Katarina Rasmirovna was the worst possible version of herself.

It didn't bear thinking of, but there wasn't brandy enough in occupied Britain to drown it.

〜

"**I**'ll have her hide for a drum skin," Seward said, his face white. His name was Frederick Kent in this timeline, but Maxwell still thought of him as Seward. In this timeline as in the other, he commanded the resistance. His underling, the young Prussian Emil Schwieger, had just completed his report on the disaster that was their venture north.

Christopher Palmer's cottage had been set afire—either by a mysterious enemy or by Katarina Rasmirovna. The Frankenstein papers had been stolen—either by a mysterious enemy or by Katarina Rasmirovna. There was no question who had stolen the damaged pocket watch. William had witnessed Katarina do it.

Seward turned away, shaking his head, taking abbreviated steps as though the ruin of their plans were a physical thing that blocked his path. He put a hand out toward one of the straight-backed chairs, seeking support.

Maxwell understood his dizziness. Katarina, a thief and a traitor? Even days later, Maxwell could hardly believe it.

Seward gave his orders, but Maxwell barely heard them. Elizabeth went to bed, Schwieger went off to hunt for Katarina, and Seward likewise disappeared into the night. William, tasked with guarding the working pocket watch, sat down with it and Frankenstein's journal. Maxwell established himself at the dining table with the brandy bottle.

Disillusionment was truly the order of the day. He knew the others had grown more and more disgusted as he daily numbed himself with drink, but he really could not care. Every time he closed his eyes, he could see Katarina fall into the shadows of an alleyway.

He had been too far away to stop it, burdened as he had been with the children from the past. He knew it was unfair—irrational—to lay any of the blame for Katarina's death at his parents' door, but the thought kept intruding. If he had not been distracted by protecting Elizabeth and William, might he have been able to save her? Could he have stopped her running into the street, tackled her away from the hail of bullets, taken her with him when he escaped to Orkney? Perhaps together they might even have achieved success where he alone had failed? An image rose in his mind—the two of them traveling through time, following the river upstream and down, finding the junction points, working together to fix it…

And then it broke like a pricked bubble. An alternative not even worth thinking about, a circumstance that could never come to be.

Instead, how *fortunate* for him, he had as comrades-in-arms his wayward parents and their genius for disaster. And together, he and they had *indeed* succeeded where he alone had failed. They had succeeded in changing the timeline. Into this. Into *this*.

Into a world where no English child born in 1818 could possibly have grown up in a big echoing empty house, where there could not possibly have been fash-

ionable parties to peer at through bannisters or a fire lit family circle to be exclud-
ed from—and yet his memories had not changed. He could still feel the chill of
the window seat. The locket still pressed against his skin under his collar. Had he
been able to consult Hume's *History of England,* he was sure he would have found
it still contained the engraving of the condemned Holy Maid of Kent.

He had spent so many years trying to save her. From herself, her choices, her
misfortunes, her fate—nothing, he realized anew, that he had ever had leverage
to change. And now he could not escape the fact that he had spent years trying
to save not paragons, but flawed human beings (very flawed) much like himself
(more like himself than he wanted to think about, in point of fact). An impossible
quest toward an unworthy goal.

He stared at the brandy bottle. He stared full in the face the realization that
he could never save her. Not her, not the father who had followed her into destruction, not the boy in the window seat. Rewrite the timeline, and all three still
remained. He would always be the boy in the window seat and her head would
always be mounted on the spike of London Bridge. Perhaps that was why his
future self would send her the watch, a surrender to the inevitability of time, acknowledgment that they were all trapped in its cogs. That they were fated to turn
the world into this horror—Britain cowering under the Eagle's talons, Katarina
a traitor and a thief, Trevelyan poised to make *yet again* the mistake that had
doomed one timeline already to hell—and so they might as well get on with it.

"I think I've found you," William said.

Maxwell looked up in automatic reflex, his train of thought broken, but
found within himself no great interest in discovering what William meant.

"In the Genevese's journal," William went on. He got up and joined Maxwell
at the table, a thumb between the notebook leaves to keep his place. "You said
you had tried to stop him by trying to redirect his youthful studies? I have just
read of a mysterious stranger doing precisely that." William looked back at the
notebook and read,

> *On this occasion a man of great research in natural philosophy was with
> us, and…all that he said threw greatly into the shade Cornelius Agrippa,
> Albertus Magnus, and Paracelsus, the lords of my imagination…All that
> had so long engaged my attention suddenly grew despicable. By one of
> those caprices of the mind, which we are perhaps most subject to in early
> youth, I at once gave up my former occupations; set down natural history
> and all its progeny as a deformed and abortive creation; and entertained
> the greatest disdain for a would-be science, which could never even step
> within the threshold of real knowledge. In this mood of mind I betook
> myself to the mathematics, and the branches of study appertaining to
> that science, as being built upon secure foundations, and so worthy of my
> consideration. Thus strangely are our souls constructed, and by such slight
> ligaments are we bound to prosperity or ruin. When I look back, it seems
> to me as if this almost miraculous change in inclination and will was the*

*immediate suggestion of the guardian angel of my life—the last effort
made by the spirit of preservation to avert the storm that was even then
hanging in the stars and ready to envelope me…It was a strong effort of
the spirit of good, but it was ineffectual.*

The account of their interaction was somewhat more grandiosely phrased
than Maxwell remembered, but the facts were correct enough. William looked
up from the page. "That was you, sir, was it not?"

"That was I," Maxwell agreed. "Ineffectual. As usual."

"I wouldn't say that. You changed his mind for a time."

"Ineffectually," Maxwell said. "Equally ineffectual were my attempt to remove books from his purview and my attempt to distract him from his Orkney
pilgrimage by inviting him to stay with me in Scotland. Not to mention my attempt to lure Brenda Trevelyan from the Wellingtons' path. And my attempt to
drive the first monster away from capture by British regulars. And my attempt
to change the monster war in 1852." He tipped the last of the brandy into his
glass. "One spectacular disaster after another."

"No," William said. "One failed attempt after another, perhaps, but none
were disasters until Waterloo. You needed our help for that."

It was so exactly what Maxwell had just been thinking that he snorted half
a laugh despite himself.

"The coincidence of the names is curious, don't you think?" William went
on. "His young brother William and his betrothed Elizabeth. He goes on at
some length about them both. They were paragons of perfection, it would appear, Elizabeth in particular." He flipped back a few pages.

*Her hair was the brightest living gold…a crown of distinction upon her
head. Her brow was clear and ample, her blue eyes cloudless, and her lips
and the molding of her face so expressive of sensibility and sweetness, that
none could behold her without looking on her as of a distinct species, a
being heaven-sent, and bearing a celestial stamp to all her features.*

William looked up. "Not much like our Elizabeth, eh?"

"No," Maxwell said with some emphasis. But after a moment's reflection, he
was forced to add, "But his Elizabeth wasn't…exactly like that either. I met her,
and she was a sweet girl, but not…" Not whatever fulsome words Frankenstein
had chosen. "I suppose," he said slowly, discovering the thought as he said it,
"no one ever is what they seem to be in the pages of a journal."

"Do you know what became of them? Of Viktor's sweetheart and brother?"

"If you read far enough," Maxwell said, annoyed at being distracted from
pursuing this new line of thought, "you'll find out what happened to William.
You're not very far in, are you?"

"It's slow going," William defended himself. "The man has the most over-
wrought style of prose I've ever had to pick through."

"The child William was the first to be killed by Viktor's monster. I don't
know what happened to Elizabeth. The monster killed Frankenstein once he

had what he wanted, but I can't imagine he would have cared about the girl. Perhaps she married someone else."

"I'd have thought you'd say, 'Perhaps she took the veil.' Her 'saintly soul shining like a shrine-dedicated lamp' in the Frankensteins' peaceful home, and all."

"She really wasn't like that." Maxwell peered down into his glass. The brandy weighed him down like a heavy blanket, and it was hard to give the idea the focused attention it deserved. "Not so—exaggerated, not so perfect, as Viktor's writings would have you believe. Journals..." How interesting it was to realize this. No one was a paragon, not really. So a journal that made it seem as though someone was... "Journals lie."

He woke the following morning with a pounding headache and no clear memory of the end of the conversation. But the realization stayed with him, and there was a surprising sense of calm to be found in it. Journals lie. No one is the way they tell their own story—or the story of someone they love. No one is a paragon. It had always been unfair of him to expect his parents to be such.

First they had been paragons to be rescued, then they had been paragons to emulate, then he had seen them fall from the pedestal and reveal themselves as worthless smashed shards.

And they were not in truth worthless, any more than they had been perfect.

So what was to be found on the other side of disillusion?

∽

Maxwell washed, dressed himself neatly, combed his hair, and descended the stairs. It was the first day in quite a few he spent completely sober. Seward seemed warily impressed when he came home in the evening to find Maxwell sitting at the table, drinking tea instead of brandy, and reading through Frankenstein's journal. He asked if Maxwell would look after the sleeping Elizabeth while Seward took William along to assist in his latest search for Katarina—among the third-class theaters likely to be hiring. Maxwell agreed. There was a dangerous moment when Elizabeth awoke before they left, but William was able to persuade her back to bed without telling her what he was about to do. It was really the only solution; one could not take an innocent young lady such as Elizabeth to the sorts of theaters in which Katarina would be singing. Maxwell sat down to while away the time until she awoke properly, thinking perhaps they might even be able to talk a bit. It was far past time he started viewing Elizabeth in her own right, not who her vanished-timeline counterpart had been, nor yet who she might grow into becoming someday.

He was pleased with the decision—the sense of generosity it brought with it made him feel quite virtuous—and therefore considerably less than pleased when she turned on him.

She came downstairs in her Regency-style frock, curls brushed in a sketchy sort of way, and like Seward, seemed initially pleasantly surprised to see him sober. It was hardly a compliment, but Maxwell could not very well take offense.

"Good morning," she greeted him. "Evening, I should say." She looked around the silent warehouse. "Where is everyone?"

"William went with Kent to look for Katarina," Maxwell said. "Schwieger is—"

Elizabeth stopped cold. "Gone to find Katarina? But I asked him and he said—William lied to me?"

"He didn't *lie*," Maxwell countered. "He said what was needful to keep you safely here. You must see that those theaters are no place for—"

"He lied," Elizabeth repeated. "So did you. So did Frederick Kent. How dare you?"

How dared *he*? "I believe Kent phrased it as not wishing to have a loose cannon aboard his ship," Maxwell snapped back. "Clever turn of phrase, that. If you had known, you would have wanted to come. If he had denied you permission, you would have taken matters into your own hands." The fury of the last few days rose up in an irresistible tide. "And we really can't afford to hand any more victories to the French."

"I've done nothing you have not," Elizabeth shot back, "except to succeed where you failed. You don't know better than I what is best to be done. Your judgment is not more valuable than mine—"

"I am three times your age," Maxwell retorted. "I have been traveling for longer than you have been alive."

"—fine, then perhaps it is now, but it certainly wasn't when you first began traveling. You think you know better than everyone. You thought you did even at the beginning. I'm not a pawn in your chess game, Mr. Maxwell, or don't you understand that? You can't move me into position, assume I'll stay there, and declare your aim achieved! I've as much soul and mind and heart as you, as much right to move myself about the board!"

"Because that worked so well at Waterloo?"

"You were the one who insisted on handling Waterloo in a twenty-four-hour scramble! William and I both wanted to arrive earlier, find a way to talk with the Duke, and explain to him what actions of his would lead to the future we had seen! But you assumed—implied—you said we could not trust him to act as he ought. And by that you meant, we could not trust him to act as you wanted him to. As though the Duke of Wellington were a pawn on a chessboard too, to be coaxed into position with a carrot or bludgeoned from behind with a whip. Have you *ever* dealt straightly with anyone? You sent me a pocket watch but chose not to share your knowledge of its power. You chloroformed John Freemantle rather than sharing knowledge with the man who commanded him. You tried to kidnap Brenda Trevelyan instead of delivering a plain warning—"

Maxwell slammed closed Frankenstein's journal and stood up, knocking his chair to the floor.

"—you blindfold all of us and tie our hands and push us into place, and then you're surprised when we react by fighting for freedom!"

He turned away because it was better than saying what was on the tip of his tongue, banging his way upstairs to sleep in Seward's bed.

∽

He dreamed he was watching Katarina Rasmirovna waste away from the black lung.

He dreamed he was watching Katarina Rasmirovna fall to a hailstorm of bullets in an alleyway.

He dreamed he was standing under Elizabeth Barton's head mounted on London Bridge. A big black crow wrenched one eye from its socket, and the head screamed his name.

He was awake, breathing hard, staring wildly around Seward's Spartan warehouse bedchamber. No crows here, no bridge, no rotting woman's head, but this scream had been real. She had screamed, downstairs. She had called his name.

He scrambled to his feet and ran.

Elizabeth Barton and Emil Schwieger were in the center of the sitting room, struggling over a golden pocket watch. Maxwell instinctively clapped his hand to his pocket—because he frankly wouldn't have put theft past either of them—but his timepiece was there.

The second timepiece had vanished with Katarina Rasmirovna into the night.

So this must be a third.

A third timepiece. A third time-traveler. Emil Schwieger was the joker in the deck.

Elizabeth was bent almost double, both hands wrapped around the watch, squirming and straining against Schwieger's grip on her arms. Schwieger got an arm around Elizabeth's chest and forced her upright, trying to use his other hand to pry apart her fingers. Elizabeth jerked and wrenched and managed one instant's freedom of movement. She launched the watch into the air—not well and not far, but it skittered across the floorboards in Maxwell's direction, and he lunged forward and caught it up. "Get away from her," he started to snap, but the words froze in his throat when he saw the knife blade under Elizabeth's chin.

"I don't want to hurt you," Schwieger whispered to her, his voice all the more menacing for its lack of volume. "Don't make me hurt her," he repeated, looking over her head at Maxwell. "Put it down."

There was not a doubt in Maxwell's mind that Schwieger would do anything to regain his timepiece. He hesitated—but there was never any doubt what he would do, either. He tossed the pocket watch onto the table.

"Step back," Schwieger ordered.

Maxwell took a step back toward the doorway, holding his arms slightly open and his hands away from his body. The muscles of Seward's arms were clenched tight, tension in every lineament, eyes looking everywhere. A nervous opponent, and therefore an unpredictable opponent. "You have what you want," Maxwell said calmly. He calculated the distance between himself and Schwieger. The table was partially in his way, the chairs possible obstacles or possible tools. "Now let her go."

Schwieger leaned forward, quick as a striking bird, and caught the timepiece by its chain. Elizabeth fought him for one instant before his grip closed around her arm again.

"Stop it," Schwieger said to her. "I don't want to hurt you. I didn't come here to hurt anyone." He held her against him with one arm, knife in the other, watch dangling from its chain in his knife hand. "I came for the monster notes. I never wanted anything more, and you locals were never meant to be involved." Elizabeth was an unpredictable factor in this conflict as well. If she put all her strength into breaking Schwieger's grip at the same time Maxwell lunged— "You have no idea what horrific a future this world is hurtling toward! It hasn't happened yet, I can still stop it, you have no idea what we'll start doing to each other twenty-nine years from right now unless someone stops it!"

1914, Maxwell's mind supplied the date without his conscious calculation. Schwieger was therefore from a timeline where 1914 was measurably worse than 1911—and Maxwell had found 1911 sufficiently objectionable. "In that case, you have what you came for," he said. "So let her go."

Schwieger shook his head. "One thing more," he said. "Your watch too."

Absolutely not. If there was one thing he was *absolutely not* about to do, that would be spend his life—and his parents' lives—in this hell-hole mistake of a timeline. "That's not yours to take."

Schwieger pressed the knife harder against Elizabeth's skin, glaring at Maxwell. "It very much is. You must be mad if you think I'll leave it in your hands and you free to do more damage. Put it on the table, or she comes home with me as hostage for your good behavior." Maxwell licked his lips for another attempt at distracting him, but Schwieger barked over him. "Now!"

Nothing for it, then. Now.

He made sure to let Schwieger see his shoulders sag as his hand moved toward the pocket watch threaded through his waistcoat, as he rebalanced his weight on the balls of his feet. *Grant concessions that do not matter, let them think they have the upper hand.* He met Elizabeth's eyes. Schwieger's muscles relaxed just fractionally, the blade shifting just slightly from Elizabeth's skin.

Her boot heel connected with Schwieger's knee at the same moment Maxwell launched himself through the space that separated them. Schwieger staggered, Maxwell crashed into them, the knife and pocket watch struck the floorboards with a clatter, and the three of them fell in a tangle of limbs. Maxwell got hold of his mother and pushed her free of Schwieger's reaching hands. He pinned the young Prussian to the floor, drawing breath to demand surrender—but Schwieger's hands came up at the same moment and fastened around Maxwell's throat.

The need to breathe was overwhelming, terrifying and primal and absolute. The world was black and flashing with color, and he was making the sorts of noises the Widow Ramsey had once made as she lay dying in her kitchen bedroom at the end of the world. Maxwell's left hand, then his right, released Schwieger almost of their own volition to pry the clutching fingers from his windpipe. He managed to grab one Prussian wrist and jerk it free. He felt the chain of his locket snap.

Too late, he realized the trap. Still with one thumb on Maxwell's windpipe, still making the world dim around him, Schwieger jerked his other hand from Maxwell's grip—and grabbed not for the knife that had fallen to the floor nearby, but the timepiece that had fallen beside it. Maxwell saw Schwieger's hand close into a fist over the watch with the slow inevitability of a nightmare. Choking desperately for air, Maxwell tried to free his own timepiece from his waistcoat or his collar from Schwieger's grip, but—

—they fell, through blinding light and swirling darkness and rainbows.

Part Two: Now

The elimination of German heavy-water production in Norway…was the main factor in our failure to achieve a self-sustaining atomic reactor before the war ended.
— Dr. Kurt Diebner, German scientist
quoted in *Assault in Norway* by Thomas Gallagher

Chapter 11

Knut Haukelid felt the repetitive thud of the turbine as a dull throb in his breastbone. At first it had been hard to distinguish the sound over the swirl of the wind and the roar of the waterfall, but now it filled the air, overwhelming, inescapable, signaling the journey's end.

Coming smoothly to a stop with barely a whisper of ski against snow, he turned to look back at his comrades. Eight bulky silhouettes on skis stretched out in a line under the light of the quarter-moon, bending their heads against the wind of the frigid Norwegian night. Haukelid was in front, serving as an advance scout. He was always the man in front.

He and his fellow saboteurs had grown closer than brothers in the three horrific years since the Nazi conquest of Norway. He knew them all intimately, knew about their childhoods and families and favorite foods and cherished memories. It was odd to contemplate that this was very likely the last night on earth for them all. Not that such considerations mattered any longer; their lives would be well-spent if only they could achieve their goal.

Haukelid turned from regarding his comrades to survey their destination. Vermok lay before him, shining in the moonlight, on the other side of a seventy-five-foot-long suspension bridge swaying over a six-hundred-foot drop. It looked like a fairytale castle, like a fortress on an ice floe, as remote and inaccessible as something constructed by a medieval king or the fabled Danish Snow Queen. One might almost expect to find a guardian troll hulking under the bridge.

In reality, it belonged neither to history nor to fairytale. Vermok was an eight-story hydroelectric plant, the only place in the world producing something called "heavy water." None of the saboteurs had been told precisely what heavy water was or what it did, but the stakes of their mission had been made crystal clear: Unless the plant's heavy water creation capability was destroyed, the Nazis would use the heavy water to develop a weapon capable of wiping out entire cities and turning them to smoking craters in the earth. And they, the team of saboteurs codenamed "Operation Gunnerside," represented the Allies' last hope for Vermok's destruction.

Movement flickered out of the corner of Haukelid's eye, and he turned his head under its hood to see Rønneberg join him. In the rucksack on Rønneberg's shoulders, Haukelid knew, there resided one of the two sets of charges to be used tonight. Also on Rønneberg's shoulders rested the responsibility for this night's success.

Haukelid was always the man in front—the advance scout. That did not mean he was the leader. Joachim Rønneberg commanded this sabotage mission, with Haukelid as his second, and it was better so. Rønneberg was the most extraordinary natural leader Haukelid had ever met, not in a dramatic way that drew attention, but by quietly and consistently giving his best to every task set to him, and thereby inspiring everyone else to do the same. Even had the fate of Norway and the war not been riding on tonight's work, no one on the team would ever be able to bring himself to disappoint Rønneberg.

Rønneberg did not speak. Neither did Haukelid. Everything had already been said during the endless planning sessions. Haukelid only gestured, as though presenting Vermok for inspection, and Rønneberg nodded slightly, moving forward to examine it on the off-chance of some difference between the reality and what had been captured in the maps and photographs he had spent months studying.

Haukelid already knew there was no such discrepancy. Their intelligence had proven admirably accurate, and he could have wished it otherwise. The problem facing the saboteurs was exactly as bad as the intelligence had predicted.

The hydroelectric plant was guarded closely, as befitted the source of a war-ending, world-changing weapon. The natural protections alone would have made it a formidable fortress to breach, the shelf upon which Vermok sat being the only protrusion from an otherwise vertical mountainside. Above the plant, the mountain face rose to a height of three thousand feet; below the plant, the sheer six-hundred-foot drop ended in the unforgiving Mana River. These natural obstacles meant there were only three ways to reach hydroelectric plant on its the rock shelf: a treacherous series of steps snaking down from the top of the mountain, a one-track railway line that ran from the village of Rjukan straight into Vermok's yard, and the single-lane footbridge leading across the gorge to the valley's north side.

And to these natural protections the Nazis had added many others. They had blacked Vermok's windows to hide it from nighttime Allied bomber raids. They had mined the area around the feed waters on the top of the mountain and installed trip wires on the steps leading downward. They had mounted machine guns and floodlights on the main building. Two guards patrolled the bridge at all times, and a third soldier manned the guardhouse on the Vermok side of the bridge, where he could sound the alarm at the least sign of trouble. Once the alarm was sounded, the floodlights would turn night into day, the soldiers in Vermok's barracks would rush to defend their comrades with automatic weapons and savage dogs, and the German garrison in nearby Rjukan would be alerted.

Security had not always been so fanatical—but Gunnerside was not the first team of saboteurs to try to take out Vermok. This time, the Nazis were ready for them.

Rønneberg gestured, and Haukelid accompanied him back to where the men had taken refuge behind a screen of evergreen brush. The sound of rushing water and the throbbing of Vermok's enormous turbine made conversation a not unreasonable risk. Rønneberg motioned the saboteurs to cluster around him and painstakingly went through the plan step by step, one final time. The men could have all recited the plan with him, but they listened intently anyway.

Behind them, Vermok waited.

It had been, for all of them, a long and twisting road that had started with the fall of Norway and culminated in this moment. Haukelid had fled by plane when the Nazis took control of his home country; some of the others had escaped across the North Sea to the Shetland Islands in fishing boats like their Viking ancestors. Jens-Anton Poulsson had endured the longest and most circuitous of the journeys—forced by circumstance to take the long way around, he had left Norway for Sweden, then Sweden for Finland, then traveled through Russia, Turkey, Egypt, India, South Africa, and Canada before presenting himself to the Allied commanders in London.

The Norwegian expatriates had trained together in Scotland, learning how to shoot Tommy guns and pistols, how to force locks and set booby traps, how to handle explosives and parachute from airplanes, how to fight hand to hand and with knives—all of this with the expectation that eventually they would be parachuted back into Norway to organize resistance cells. And in October of 1942, Poulsson and three of the others had indeed been parachuted into Norway as part of "Operation Grouse"—but not to organize a Norwegian resistance. Poulsson's team had instead been tasked with reconnoitering the area, then leading to Vermok a subsequently arriving team of British sappers. Together, the British and the Norwegian soldiers would sabotage the heavy water plant and destroy the Nazi Empire's chance of creating their city-annihilating weapon.

But the plan had gone horrifically awry.

"Operation Freshman," a team of British sappers, were to be brought to Norway by plane-towed gliders instead of being dropped by parachute—and the British had never before used plane-towed gliders. The glider pilots had been given little time to practice their new skill, and the terrain and climate of Norway made glider operations particularly hazardous, but the mission went ahead despite these risks.

The night Freshman arrived in Norway had been a night of heavy cloud cover, and both the gliders and one of their tow-planes crash-landed in the mountains. At the first crash site, all four men aboard the plane and three of the seventeen aboard the glider were killed instantly. The survivors were found by German troops early the following morning, and in accordance with the Furher's Commando Order, were led in front of a firing squad that same evening and shot.

They were the lucky ones.

The other glider crashed into a different mountain. Its survivors were tortured for information by the Gestapo before being allowed to die. Whatever secrets the Britons managed not to reveal were betrayed by the gear that had been found with them: snowshoes, tents, radios, explosives—and a silk map with a planned escape route. On this map, the location of Vermok was circled in blue ink.

It was the worst of all possible situations. Not only had Freshman failed—but now the Nazis knew what they had been trying to do.

In response, the Gestapo had arrived in Rjukan.

For the first fifteen hours of their arrival, the village had been under what was described later as a state of siege. Every single house was searched for signs of collaboration with the British saboteurs. The spot where the gliders had been intended to land was cordoned off and combed for clues. General Nikolaus von Falkenhorst, the German commander-in-chief in Norway, personally inspected the defenses of the Vermok plant.

He ordered the hillside to be mined, installed electric searchlights, and assigned German-born troops to augment the Austrians who had been guarding Vermok, tripling the size of its guard. Von Falkenhorst increased the size of the Lake Moss garrison as well, and stationed two hundred soldiers in Rjukan itself. The suspension bridge was now guarded twenty-four hours a day by a rotating three-man patrol, one of whom had access at all times to an alarm. Rumor had it that the Gestapo had never left Rjukan, but was running operations from its best hotel, waiting for the next Allied sabotage effort.

And now here the next Allied sabotage effort stood—or rather, crouched out of the wind, behind the screen of evergreen—poised for its moment, knowing the Nazis were waiting for them to come.

"You have your set of charges?" Rønneberg said to Strømsheim—calmly, as though discussing theater tickets. "Good, and I have mine."

Tonight Rønneberg would be in command of the demolition team, while Haukelid led the covering party. Haukelid had absolutely no doubt of the demolition party's ability to execute its mission; they had been training for months. Every single one of them could have found his way around the plant blindfolded, and could have planted the explosives and set the charges nearly in his sleep. Rønneberg and the demolition party would have no difficulty in doing their part once inside.

The problem was getting them there.

In his mind's eye, Haukelid again examined the fortress and its three blocked entry points. The German mines on the mountainside had made it impossible to use that route. Two choices were left—kill the guards patrolling the suspension bridge and cross that way, or try to descend into the gorge, cross beneath the bridge, climb the cliffs to the railway tracks on the other side, and follow the tracks into the plant. Their intelligence on the railway line was sketchy. The tracks *might* not be guarded. They *might* not be mined.

But everyone knew the gorge was too steep to climb.

And if the gorge was impossible, the only path left to them was the bridge.

The orders from London were clear. Rønneberg was even now repeating these orders, point by point. *As quietly as possible, kill the guards on the bridge. Enter the plant. Destroy, in order of priority, the machinery and the existing stocks of heavy water. Then split into small groups of not more than three men and proceed to Sweden via—*

But Haukelid privately thought there was no point in considering escape routes. He really did not think any of them were going to make it out.

If only they could make it in— But in his heart of hearts, he was worried about that too. In their planning sessions, he and Poulsson had maintained it would be impossible to get across the bridge without alerting the Nazis, and argued that the last thing Gunnerside wanted to do was attempt the sabotage in the middle of a firefight. Poulsson had pointed to the photographs they had of Vermok, to the small trees growing on the side of the gorge. Where trees could grow, a man could climb.

But those photographs had been taken in summer, and now it was the dead of winter, so the photographs proved nothing, and everyone knew that gorge was too steep for a human to ascend.

It was in any case too late to be thinking about this. Poulsson and Haukelid had not carried their point. A course of action had been decided upon in a democratic fashion, each man voting for his preferred approach. Gunnerside would follow the orders London had sent.

Haukelid had never particularly seen the value in following other people's rules—not at school, not in his straight-laced parents' household, not in the sequence of jobs he had held after school. But the matter had been decided.

"Once the guards are down, the covering team will lead the way," Rønneberg was saying. "The demolition team must prioritize its own survival long enough to get into the plant. However." He had not raised his voice, but he held everyone's attention. "If the demolition party is killed before the plant is reached, everyone is to act on his own initiative to complete the operation." He looked at each man in turn. "One of us at least *must* arrive at the objective to do the job. Do you all understand?"

Everyone understood.

"Very well, then." Rønneberg looked at his watch. "Half past twelve. Remember—what we do in the next hour will be a chapter in history for a hundred years to come. Together we will make it a worthy one." He nodded to Haukelid.

Haukelid stepped out into the snow, the man in front.

t midnight, the guard shift had changed. Haukelid had watched it happen, noting unhappily the crisp alertness of the new guards, despite the hour and the cold. Even the men they had relieved, retiring to their barracks after a long shift in the cold, walked with brisk steps and looked warily from side to side. They knew the importance of what they guarded.

Rønneberg's planned half hour delay had been intended to allow the guards time to relax and become complacent. Unfortunately, these particular guards looked anything but. One was a tall man, and stood ramrod-straight, his chest thrown out. The other, shorter and stockier like Haukelid himself, kept turning his head to scan the darkness. Haukelid did not spare the energy to mentally curse the thoroughness of Nazi army discipline. Instead, he and Poulsson exchanged glances.

As quietly as possible, kill the guards on the bridge.

The orders from London had specified using a knife—but in this detail at least Haukelid was permitted to use his own judgment. Between the swirling wind, the thundering waterfall, and the roaring turbines, a pair of swift shots would never be heard. Knife work could too easily go awry, could too easily attract attention. A shot would only attract attention if it missed.

And there was simply no chance he or Poulsson would miss.

Haukelid had spent his entire childhood hunting in the woods. Poulsson similarly had been shooting grouse since the age of eleven. During the long winter months when Grouse starved on the Vidda waiting first for Freshman and then for Gunnerside, he had hunted reindeer to augment their meager rations. And before Grouse had left for Norway, he and Haukelid had hunted stag in the Highlands during breaks from their training—an illegal practice, but another rule made to be broken.

Now, moving almost in unison, they unslung their rifles, knelt, and took aim.

The guards dropped almost simultaneously, the sharp shots swallowed by the noise of the turbines, and Haukelid was instantly up and running.

The third guard was in the little house on the Vermok side of the bridge. In the fitful moonlight, he would not expect to be able to see his fellows, and he would not be able to see their absence. Haukelid wrestled the hood off the stockier guard and tied it to his own head. He didn't have to fool the third guard for long—only present a silhouette that would not cause the instantaneous sounding of the alarm. How fortunate he was built more or less along the same lines as the man he had killed. Poulsson might have impersonated the taller, thinner one, but Haukelid was determined to take this risk himself.

Poulsson donned the second hood and rose to his feet, taking up the taller guard's position, maintaining the illusion as long as possible. Just in case.

Haukelid acknowledged his nod, then started across the suspension bridge.

What we do in the next hour will be a chapter in history for a hundred years to come.

It was the longest seventy-five feet of his life.

As a child, the only relief from the smothering constraints of school and family life had been the weekends and holidays he had spent hunting and fishing with his grandfather in the mountains. There had been trolls in the mountains then—or at least, his young mind, full of his grandfather's stories, had seen their outline in every high rock formation and glimpsed their eyes glinting in every dark woodland dell. Long after he was too old to even half-believe in fairytales, trolls had formed part of his mental landscape. His eye still traced their outlines in mountain crags.

More recently, they had come to seem like a different sort of metaphor. Icy mountain crags, crouching boulders, seemingly quiescent—until magic awoke them and they exploded alive from the earth. If Haukelid lived through this night, he was not to return with the others. He had been given permission to stay in Norway and organize those long-promised resistance cells. The Nazis would never be able to hold what they had taken, once the sleeping earth awoke.

And if he did not live through the night—well, he was still striking a blow for Norway, following in the footsteps of the heroes of the old tales. Here was a mountain fortress to be entered, the bridge over the moat to be crossed, the quest on which the fate of the world hinged, a trick to get past the first obstacle, even a magic spell of sorts to get past the second. His German was fluent and without accent, and he had been provided with the password call-and-responses in use among the bridge guards. Whichever one they were using tonight, he would able to answer it and gain a few more seconds, a few steps closer, before arousing their suspicion. And his father had wanted him to work in a *bank*. Wouldn't that have been ridiculous?

His entire life had been leading to this one night. He just hadn't know that for most of it.

He was never to know what gave him away. Perhaps his gait was too different from that of the guard he impersonated, identical silhouette notwithstanding. All he knew was the guard on the Vermok side of the bridge emerged from his guardhouse immediately after Haukelid entered his field of vision. The guard called out, "*Zweihänder?*"

Which was not one of the passwords with which Haukelid had been provided.

There was no time to curse or hesitate or bluster. Haukelid was already charging in at a dead run, knife in his hand.

He was under the Nazi's guard before the man could aim his machine gun, stabbing upward with the knife. Haukelid had been taught all the ways to kill a man at close quarters—and his instructors in Scotland had called him fearless—but this Nazi had apparently been taught them too, and the ways to defend against them.

Knife work could so easily go awry, could so easily attract attention.

The guard was shouting as he fought, straining to be heard over the turbines and the waterfall. Haukelid had to kill him before he could reach the alarm.

He knew Poulsson would have seen his sprint, knew without hearing that Poulsson was pounding up the suspension bridge after him. The guard threw Haukelid off long enough to aim and fire, and Haukelid heard the scream as Poulsson fell in a shower of bullets two thirds of the way across the bridge. Haukelid lunged upward again, forcing the muzzle upward, slamming the Nazi against the side of the guardhouse. He jabbed upward with the knife again, and this time managed to hit a vulnerable spot—but as the guard collapsed, he reached out one desperate hand. In a movement Haukelid would have considered heroic if they'd been fighting on the same side, the guard brought his bloodied hand down on the alarm button as he fell.

The rest of the cover party had pounded across the bridge by this point, the demolition team right behind them. The alarm brayed through the night air, easily drowning out turbines and waterfall. Lights went on in the Nazi barracks.

The last thing Haukelid had wanted was to attempt the sabotage in the middle of a firefight.

"Go!" he snarled to Rønneberg, unslinging his rifle and herding the demolition team toward the plant. "Run!" He and the rest of the cover party were no longer leading, but now protectively surrounding, the demolitionists. One of them at least had to get inside.

The sudden floodlights blinded them all. "*Keep moving*," Haukelid ordered. The Gunnerside saboteurs had all boasted they could do their job blindfolded, and it seemed it was time to make good on the bluff.

Through the klaxon came the snarling and barking of dogs, the shouting of men, and the stutter of machine-gun fire.

Haukelid fell in a spray of heat and ice, the world tilting crazily around him.

He found his cheek on the frozen ground, his vision blurring but no longer night-blind. He could see the booted feet of a Nazi guard pounding toward him. He could see Rønneberg's fallen body, its chest flayed open and its eyes staring sightlessly upward.

None of them had expected to get out of Vermok. Haukelid had thought himself privately pessimistic about their chances of getting in—but he knew now that he had still retained hope. He knew he had been cherishing it, because now he felt it die. They had failed. The winter fortress could not be taken. Not by Freshman and not by Gunnerside.

The thought of Freshman reminded Haukelid of what he must do next. His fingers felt as though they belonged to someone else. He felt as though he reached into a separate universe entirely to fumble with the layers of cloth that covered the suicide capsule in his thigh pocket. They must not be taken alive.

He could hardly feel his hands. His fingers were utterly incapable of the dexterity required to tease the cloth apart. But in truth there was no need. His blood hissed and steamed, hot in the frozen air, spurting with each pump of his heart. Even without the suicide capsule, he would not live long enough for the sprinting Nazi guard to reach him.

He had two or three heartbeats left. That was long enough to think of his family. His body would be identified, and the reprisals would be terrible. The fate he had cheated would be visited upon them.

Three heartbeats was long enough to imagine his wife and mother dying in the concentration camp at Grini.

Long enough to imagine a world where the Third Reich had a weapon that could annihilate cities in one stroke, a world where Oslo and Paris and London and New York were smoking craters.

Long enough to imagine a time where there was no one left to stand against the Nazis, and their horrific empire presided over the entire globe.

Chapter 12

Maxwell hit the ground shoulder-first and turned it instantly into roll. He'd learned how to fall long ago. The air was sharp and cold, gritty with dust and mountain-thin, but at least Schwieger's grip was gone from his throat, and his frantic convulsive inhalation brought air as well as dust into his lungs. He gasped and choked, desperate to cough, desperate to take a moment just to breathe.

He didn't dare take even that moment. He struggled upright somehow. Schwieger was still on the ground, seemingly stunned by their impact with the soil of whatever new time and place this was. Maxwell kicked him once, savagely, to keep him down, then snatched his own timepiece from his waistcoat pocket. He didn't attempt to wrest Schwieger's away from him—let Schwieger keep it, he could do nothing immediate with it in any case, and Maxwell did not have time to waste on another physical contest. He dared not delay an instant in returning. He had to get back to September 2, 1885, to his mother and father and a situation with Katarina that was clearly painted in more shades of gray than any of them had realized—

He spun the dials, pressed the side button twice and the top once, and nothing happened.

No. No no no no no—

The fourth face awoke, brightly flashing as it cycled through its usual roster of images. On the other side of the—where were they? Maxwell looked about himself for the first time.

He stood in a ruin of some sort, with sand and gravel underfoot and the fallen walls of a long-crumbled building strewn about like boulders. On the other side of the ruin, Schwieger lay face down in the dirt, but he was stirring. Maxwell darted glances between his timepiece and his foe, until finally the fourth face showed him the quiet, construct-free street of 1885. As Schwieger groggily lifted his head, Maxwell depressed the side button once and the top twice—

And again, nothing happened.

"You son of a bitch," he said, breathless with the horror of it, as the Prussian rolled up onto one knee. "It's a junction. It's a junction, I've had my one chance, I can't get back. *I can't get back.* They're trapped there with a broken timepiece, *and I can't get back to them,* you son of a *bitch.*"

Schwieger glared as he staggered to his feet. "Serves them right. The time-pieces aren't toys for children to play with."

The exaggerated Prussian inflection was gone from his voice. His English was almost accentless. Even that had been a disguise. Maxwell's entire body tingled with the impulse to cross in a single bound the distance between himself and this imposter, but he overcame it by clenching his hands hard. "And what the devil gives you the right to say so?"

"Work it out for yourself," Schwieger snapped.

The realization landed on Maxwell like a boulder dropped from above. "You know where the watches come from."

Schwieger spread his hands in angry acknowledgment.

"Are you *from* where they come from? That time, that place—that future? Then Katarina wasn't the thief after all. It was you who stole Elizabeth's time-piece and the Frankenstein papers—"

"No," Schwieger said, "Katarina did steal Elizabeth's timepiece. Though I would have taken it if I could; I have standing orders to gather up any that have been left lying about. To prevent locals such as yourselves from wreaking the kind of havoc you have wreaked."

So Katarina was still a thief. She had still betrayed them— Maxwell wrenched his attention back to the moment. "Why the Frankenstein papers, then?"

Schwieger's mouth twisted. "A last-ditch effort. What is sometimes called, in an era after yours and mine, a Hail Mary pass. The Frankenstein monsters are the type of weapon that provides an incremental rather than an exponential advantage. Sometimes an incremental advantage is what you want. They'd be enough to win a border conflict in 1914, a short victorious war. Enough to stop the first tilting domino, so the world does not turn into—" He gestured. "—this."

Maxwell looked around again. Inside their ruin, the ground was gravel; on the other side of the almost-non-existent walls, it was rubble. The rubble stretched to the limit of his vision in every direction, except to the west, where a single building rose to the height of about half a story. Maxwell was reminded of Shelley's poem: *vast and trunkless legs, lone and level sands*. "Where are we?"

"The same latitude and longitude we left." Schwieger made a sound that was not a laugh. "This is our future, Maxwell."

"This is *London?* Is this where you're from?"

"No," Schwieger said. "But the timepiece I'm carrying belonged to Rosamund before it belonged to me. And Rosamund...always has a shortcut to London. This London. AfterLondon, she calls it. She will not let herself ever forget."

"Who's Rosamund?"

Schwieger did not answer.

But it didn't take much to put the pieces together. "She is another time traveler?" Maxwell seized on the new possibility. "She always *has,* not always *had,* and so she is therefore still alive?" If so, there was a way to solve at least one part of this mess. "Take me to her. She could go to 1885 and get Elizabeth and William safely back to—"

Schwieger stared at him in shocked disgust. "Is that *really* the only problem that concerns you?"

"No," Maxwell retorted, "not the only one. I'm quite concerned over Waterloo, Napoleon's empire, the 1910 I originally went back in time to stop, and whatever the hell this disaster is, but the woman you had the audacity to lay hands on is my mother, and though we've had our differences, she and my father both deserve better than to die trapped in an occupied London that's not even their time period. That is, therefore, the *first* of the problems that concerns me. Take me to Rosamund."

"Go to hell." Schwieger turned away.

Again Maxwell thought of crossing the alleyway in a bound and seizing Schwieger's collar, and again he converted the impulse into clenching and unclenching his fist. "No," he said after a moment. "I believe instead I'll go to Vienna."

Schwieger stopped. "What?"

Maxwell waited, balancing his weight and with every nerve tensed, until Schwieger turned around. Then he ostentatiously let Schwieger see him setting the dials. "Trevelyan said I saved his life from a fire in the Viennese *miethaus* district on the second of April, 1882. That seems like an excellent opportunity to warn him and by extension Seward about you and your nefarious plans." He held his thumb visibly above the side button. "You can't very well strand my parents if you've already been unmasked as a—"

"Don't! Wait!" Schwieger seemed honestly taken aback. "You can't do that."

"The hell I can't. It seems to be the one thing I absolutely can do. Trevelyan saw me in Vienna; I haven't been there yet; I can use that encounter for anything I—"

Schwieger was shaking his head. "Do that and you'll kill your parents for sure. Not to mention, I have spent years, *years* trying to change this history. You cannot condemn the world to this future!" He gestured to the alleyway and the city beyond.

"You think this is worse than Napoleon conquering the world?" It *obviously* was, but there was no need to let Schwieger know he thought so.

"You have no idea how much worse," Schwieger said, almost pleading now. "It could have been a small border war in an era of small border wars, but in 1914 this conflict engulfs the world in blood. Then a vanquished Germany rises from the ashes, not as a phoenix but as a vampire, and begins its conquest all over again. From the German vampire comes a weapon that can obliterate entire cities, we wipe out entire races of people, and this barren wasteland is our legacy."

"And you think *reintroducing Frankenstein's monsters* will nip such a thing in the bud?"

"I think it's worth trying! I think it's something we haven't tried yet. Stach has tried almost everything else."

A last-ditch effort. Maxwell knew something about last-ditch efforts. What Schwieger didn't realize was that Maxwell was enacting one right now.

"You cannot warn Trevelyan in Vienna," Schwieger said.

Maxwell smiled at him. "Oh yes, I can." He depressed the button.

Schwieger paled. "No."

Maxwell said quietly, "I am rescuing my parents from Napoleon's 1885 one way or the other. Either I go warn Trevelyan about you now, or together we save his life as he told us he remembered it and you then take me to see this Rosamund so *she* can rescue them."

Schwieger hesitated. Maxwell pressed the side button a second time.

Schwieger still said nothing, and Maxwell felt a surge of impatience. "As you like," he said, and jammed the top button down. As the world shimmered out of existence, he felt the now-familiar sensation of a hand closing over his sleeve.

❧

He was wrenching away before the world was solid around him, bracing himself for Schwieger's attack. But this time Schwieger did not try violence. The young Prussian stood instead with his hands spread, blocking Maxwell's path. Maxwell was, for once in his life, attempting neither to bluff nor to manipulate. His threat was absolutely sincere, and Schwieger could see that.

"Wait," Schwieger was saying, "wait, listen to me, *listen* to me."

The morning was golden all around them, the air rich and heavy and damp. They were enclosed by hedges, not rubble and crumbled walls. It would have been an overwhelming physical relief, had Maxwell's entire being not been focused on his adversary.

"While I was working with Frederick Kent's organization," Schwieger said, "I saved his life twice and Trevelyan's once. And Katarina and I saved each other more times than I can count." He looked Maxwell straight in the eye. "Make Trevelyan distrust me and I won't be there to do any of that. You could arrive in 1885 with your parents and find no one to offer you sanctuary. Right now they are stranded without a timepiece in reasonable comfort and reasonable safety under Kent's roof. They could be stranded without a timepiece in an Imperial prison."

Maxwell watched him narrowly. He did not think Schwieger was bluffing either.

"And that's if you're lucky," Schwieger went on. "They're there without a timepiece. If you change the timeline around them, they change with it...and they're not supposed to be there at all. They're time travelers, in a time and place where they do not belong, with nothing to keep them anchored once the timeline changes around them. They *might* survive it, but that's not where a gambler places his money. It's more likely they'll cease to exist right then. I've seen it happen."

Maxwell met his eyes. "A possibility that carries no weight with you. You already declared yourself unconcerned for their welfare. Therefore, you have reasons of your own for wanting Trevelyan unwarned."

There was a long pause.

"Fine," Schwieger said then. "Fine. We'll rescue Trevelyan and Zimmermann. You will say *nothing* about me. And then I'll take you to Rosamund, and you can negotiate with her the rescue of your troublesome parents."

"*Thank* you," Maxwell said. He gave it a breath. "This is an alliance out of necessity only. It does not mean I trust you."

"Then we agree about something after all." Schwieger looked about, seeming to notice the hedges for the first time. "Is today the day of the fire? And where the hell are we? This isn't the *mietshaus* district."

"Of course it's not. Did you think Trevelyan had used latitude and longitude to describe the location of his alleyway fire? We're in the Belvedere Gardens. I took the chance Napoleon hadn't destroyed the entire palace out of spite in vengeance for the Congress of Vienna—which it seems he did not. And no, the fire was two days ago. I thought there would be information in the papers by now. We'll take our time and do this the right way round. I might have finally learned something from my father's methodical nature after all."

Schwieger looked to his left and then to his right, and snorted derision. "You realize you've transported us into the middle of a hedge maze? I don't think you should be bragging about your skill at planning campaigns."

"Do you mean to imply a little hedge maze is enough to baffle you?" Maxwell inquired, and led the way, with a confidence he did not feel, to the left.

⁓

First there was the tedious process of working their way out of the maze. At least they encountered no armed resistance, Napoleon having apparently not appropriated the palace as an Imperial residence, which was the other risk Maxwell had known he was taking. The Belvedere had been a museum of art and antiquities back during young Maxwell Carrington's Grand Tour—a *very* long time ago, by any measurement of time—and it seemed to be one still. Well-dressed couples strolled its Versailles-style gardens and laughed their way through the hedge maze. They were all speaking French.

Then there was the tedious walk back to the city center, the tedious business of exchanging gold for coin (Schwieger, interestingly enough, traveled with gold sewn into his clothing, just as Maxwell once had) and the tedious business of purchasing a gentleman's outfit for Schwieger. If Maxwell had thought for an instant Schwieger could be trusted out of his sight, he would have gladly abandoned him and pursued his researches unencumbered—but Schwieger, though he could not use his pocket watch for twenty-four hours, might still create a variety of other complications. Fortunately, Schwieger clearly didn't trust Maxwell out of his sight either, so they spent the day locked grudgingly into each other's orbit.

Finally, the afternoon well-advanced, they finally arrived at the Hof-Bib-liothek. There might, under other circumstances, have been something mildly amusing about the name. It had been the "Imperial Library" for some centu-ries before Maxwell's 1838 visit; it was the "Imperial Library" still. The Empire had changed underneath it, from Hapsburg to Napoleonic, but the library still stood. Surely a metaphor for time travel lurked somewhere in that observation.

The library did, as hoped, have the daily papers. Actually, it had the daily paper, singular. Named *La Terre*—"The Earth"—it was the sole paper per-mitted in the Empire, and its masthead claimed itself "proud to publish the Decrees of the Emperor since 1816." This was not encouraging, but further in-vestigation showed it to be the Viennese-specific edition of *La Terre*: publishing the Emperor's decrees and news of the Empire on its front pages, but containing records of local occurrences toward the back. Hopefully they would be *factual* records of local occurrences.

Buried deep in the fine print, Maxwell found the account of the unim-portant (but rather odd) fire that had occurred in the *meitshaus* district shortly after seven o'clock in the evening two days before. The dead were listed as two workers from the Arceneau-fabrik and two unknown persons. One of the workers was named Zimmermann, so although the other name was unfamiliar, it seemed worth the risk to assume it was Trevelyan's alias. The article reported the fire to have proceeded from an apparent altercation between the four men, and to have been caused by the application of a match to a quantity of spilled lamp-oil, resulting in the igniting of all the debris in the alleyway. Fortunately, the brick walls of the buildings on either side were impervious to the flame; fortunately also, one of the two buildings was uninhabited.

As a last step, Maxwell and Schwieger went to survey the scene itself. The bodies had been cleared away, but the rest of the debris remained, as did a heavy wet odor of ash and oil. The debris had been sufficiently disordered in the re-moval of the bodies that it no longer told much of a tale—except for the bizarre presence of the smashed kerosene lamp. From the incongruous lamp had spilled the oil that had been ignited by the man with the match.

What the devil had a kerosene lamp been doing there in the first place?

Maxwell stared at it and slowly the realization came to him.

∽

After that, there was the traveling backward three days. The purchase of the oil lamp and its oil. The placement of same.

And then there was nothing but the waiting, sitting side by side on the floor of the empty house. Neither of them dared trust the other enough to sleep.

"A weapon that levels cities," Maxwell said into the silence. "A world empire worse than Napoleon's."

Schwieger's face went expressionless. "So much worse."

"So tell me. After all—" It was not that amusing a jest, but he made it anyway. "We have plenty of time."

Schwieger was silent for a long while. At last he said, "What do you suppose is worse than failing to save your parents from a monster?"

After a moment in which it became clear that he was actually waiting for a reply, Maxwell uttered the line apparently assigned to him. "I don't know."

"Watching as they become monsters," Schwieger said. "The entire Fatherland…" He sighed and started over. "I was born in 1908, six years before the conflict I will always think of as the Great War, though it later became known as 'the first World War' when a greater supplanted it. *My* Prussia was enslaved by France only until 1813, not all the way through the nineteenth century. The intrepid Family Carrington—" He inclined his head ironically in Maxwell's direction. "—changed that history under my feet while I was hopping through time chasing after the Frankenstein papers. When first I landed in the 1885 in which you found me, when first I understood the change, I— For a little while, I hoped for a silver lining. Perhaps with a different history behind it, the Germany in which I was born would never come to be…" He sighed. "But you saw AfterLondon. It exists still. As in my timeline, Germany starts its militarization throwing off France's yoke—and never stops. We never stop."

"How are you still here if you were born after Waterloo?" Maxwell asked. "Why didn't you change into a new version of yourself, like Seward and Katarina? Is it because you were in a time not your own?"

Schwieger looked up, surprised. "No, it is because I had the protection of this." He indicated his pocket watch. "Those who are in contact with a timepiece at the moment a timeline changes endure the change unaffected. Those who are not, change with it and never know."

Maxwell nodded, storing the information away.

"Sometimes changing with the timeline means they cease to exist," Schwieger said. "I have seen it happen, and it is a truly…disconcerting event to witness. Painless, one assumes, but still." He added after a moment, "Not that it is pleasant to survive the collapse of one's timeline either. I had the experience once. One of Stach's experiments altered time sufficiently that I was among those not born. Rosamund made him correct it, but the intervening time was—" He shook his head. "Very strange."

"Did it feel like being a ghost?" Maxwell asked. "Looking in from the outside?"

"As though sounds were muffled and my hands were gloved," Schwieger agreed. "As though the air was too thin to breathe. So that's where you are, then?"

"Yes. Since I lifted my lantern to see my mother's face in the first 1885."

"Congratulations," Schwieger said. "You've joined the ranks of the unmoored time travelers. I'm told the worst of the side effects fade. With..." He almost smiled, but without much humor. "With time."

"Unmoored." Maxwell considered it and almost laughed. "Well, that's appropriate. For me. Never mind," he added to Schwieger's inquiring look. "Private jest."

"Rosamund says the effects fade," Schwieger repeated. "Or, of course, if your timeline is restored, then—"

"No." Maxwell could still see his hand lifting the lantern past kid boots and ruffled Regency frock to the face that might have been his locket miniature come to life. "I don't want it restored. In that timeline, the two of them died in the court of Henry VIII when I was an infant; I've no fondness for that timeline. It no longer has anything to do with changing my childhood, it's only that I... don't want that to happen to them."

"Nothing will ever change your childhood," Schwieger agreed. "Restore your past or reinvent it, you are the artifact of it. The 'revenant,' Rosamund says."

Maxwell sighed. *Rosamund says* had become a wearisome phrase over the past two days. He himself might have spent a decade recollecting at every turn Katarina's principles of engagement, but at least he had never done so out loud. "Tell me about Rosamund," he said now. "Or is there some other manner in which I ought to refer to her? What is the rest of her name?"

"Rosamund Holborn," Schwieger said, "and when you meet her, 'Miss Holborn' would be most appropriate. She will understand that to be courtesy from a man of your era. She understood it to be courtesy from a man of mine. I should say," he added after a moment, "from a boy. I was so young."

Maxwell bit his tongue on *How old are you?* Schwieger still looked like a boy to him, but it was not the most pressing piece of information to gather at this time.

"Rosamund is the last of the original travelers," Schwieger said. "From far in the future. I don't know how old she is. She looks younger than you—" He eyed Maxwell critically. "Kent's age, maybe, or Trevelyan's? But when one adds together all of her stories, it is clear she has lived many years more than that. She tells me the medicine was better in the time she came from, as the medicine of 1939 was better than that of the medieval era."

Maxwell focused on the most unexpected part of that paragraph. *"Original travelers?"*

"There were twelve," Schwieger said, settling down as though to tell a folktale over a campfire, or perhaps in preparation for reading a page of Scripture. "Each carried a timepiece. They came as explorers, they plunged into the past as giddy children plunge into play, they romped about and touched what they shouldn't have and tried to change those parts of history they disapproved of— and they destroyed their way home. Because of what they did, because of all the things they did, their timeline collapsed.

"At first they didn't know the cause of the feelings of faintness and illness that plagued them. The timepiece protects the traveler and what the traveler carries, and some similar protection guards the place they call their 'observation post,' their 'headquarters.' When they realized, they spent many years in attempts to restore the future from which they had come. They discovered…" Schwieger smiled a little. "What you and I have also discovered. Romping about like an idiot with a cannon, it is easy to *change* the past, and thereby the future. *Crafting* the future you desire is a far different proposition. Far more difficult.

"And so the Twelve came eventually to realize they could not return home. Then a schism developed between them—the Twelve became the Five and the Seven. The Seven went out into the world, into all the worlds open to them, all the times and all the places, each in search of a time and place in which a new home could be made. A different time and place for each, and there they lived out their lives. Rosamund does not know where any of the Seven finally settled. She says once she might have tracked them by the ripples they made in the time flowing past them, but they had all determined to set their powers aside and live ordinary lives, and their small ripples were lost in the cataclysms of the Five. The Seven are all dead now, of natural causes or accidents or in the cataclysms."

"Yes, but—wait." Forgetting his resolution not to interrupt Schwieger, Maxwell held up a hand. "They're not truly dead, surely? Not in all times and all places. A given time traveler might be dead on the twentieth of April in the court of Henry VIII, but she is alive on the nineteenth of April—why could she not be retrieved?"

Schwieger looked at him. "How easy did you find it?"

Maxwell had no answer for that.

"The moments of their deaths are all lost behind layers of timeline collapse," Schwieger said. "Like layers of rockslide. None of them can be rescued—but their timepieces, built to survive the collapse of a timeline, still linger in garrets and graves and bank deposit boxes, occasionally falling into the hands of locals such as you and your parents."

Maxwell took a moment to digest this. "And the Five?"

"The Five considered the Seven selfish and foolish. Left alone, the Five set out to build a paradise. If they could not rebuild the future they had come from, they would build a better one, a heaven on earth. And so they proved over and again that craftwork cannot be successfully executed when one's only tool is a cannon. The future they finally created…is the nightmare you saw. My country rises like a vampire from the ashes of the Great War, crafts a weapon that annihilates cities at a stroke, then, unopposed, systematically murders all who—" Schwieger swallowed hard, as though on bile. "—are considered to represent a threat to it. All considered…lesser."

Maxwell could tell there was more unsaid than said in those carefully chosen words. Schwieger was talking around a concept so horrific he could not bring himself to more plainly speak about it. Maxwell did not wish to press him at the present moment. He feared that any further interruption would silence Schwieger's story permanently.

"They are still trying to undo the harm they wrought," Schwieger said. "Four of them have died trying; Rosamund is the last of the Five. But she has recruited successors. She has plucked local men and women from various timelines and trained them to carry on the work. I am one such; the others are Wadi, Sui, and Stanislaus—'Stach.' If Rosamund dies before the work is completed, we will complete it for her. We'll manage it someday. And if not, then *our* successors will." Schwieger's smile was grim. "We have all the time in the world, after all."

Somewhere in the blue-gray night outside, a church bell began to toll. The quarter-chime, the half-chime, the three-quarter chime, and finally the strokes that told the hours. Seven deep, sonorous peals. The church happened to be called St. Clemens, Maxwell had discovered during their researches the previous day. *Oranges and lemons.*

Schwieger got to his feet, to take himself off to where the soon-to-be-arriving Gavin Trevelyan could not glimpse him. Before he left, he fixed Maxwell with a glare. "I'll know if anything you do unmoors me. Say one word that undoes my past and I'll see to it you never see Rosamund. Your parents will rot in Napoleon's 1885."

Maxwell was hardly discomfited by the threat, having expected no less. "You may trust me," he said with icy courtesy, "to keep my word as I have given it."

Schwieger snorted with truly offensive disbelief and left for his hiding place.

❧

nce he was gone, Maxwell cracked the heavy metal door open just enough to be able to see into the alleyway.

The night outside was layers of blue and gray. Not true blackness; not yet. The brick wall on the other side of the alleyway was lost in shadow, but the monochrome outlines of the piled barrels and boxes were still visible. Atop one crate perched the incongruous oil lamp. Maxwell worried it was too obvious, but there was nothing to be done about that now.

He tilted his head the tiniest fraction, reluctant to open the door any further or risk any noise. It was easier to see silhouettes against the light that filtered in from the mouth of the alleyway. He could just make out the shadow that lurked there in wait.

Trevelyan's phrasing had been clear: *You rescued me and my friend Zimmermann from a fire.* Not from an ambush, not from a street fight, not from a beating, from a *fire.* Maxwell could not act until the fire had started, no matter how much he might wish to save this ghost-of-his-friend from what was about to happen.

Three different figures passed by the alleyway mouth while Maxwell waited, and each time Maxwell saw the shadowy ambusher tense. Each time, Maxwell tensed as well, but each time he knew even as he did so than none of these were Trevelyan. The first man was going in the wrong direction. The second was too short. The third strolled as though he were a country gentleman taking the air on a fine afternoon, not a factor worker late for his shift.

When Trevelyan appeared—walking briskly—Maxwell was sure of him. So too, apparently, was the waiting shadow. It leaped, flinging a cloak or blanket over its target's head as it moved. Another figure appeared from behind Trevelyan, and struck the inventor smartly in the back of the skull.

A fire. Not an ambush, not a beating. Maxwell dared not interfere until there was a fire.

The two dragged Trevelyan into the alley, forced the semi-conscious man to his knees, and bound his hands behind him. Maxwell could not help but wince at the roughness that wrenched Trevelyan's arms nearly out of their sockets. The larger of the two stood with his hands on Trevelyan's shoulders—whether holding him steady or keeping him down it was hard to say. The other stood where Trevelyan's eyes would light upon him once those eyes were open, and drew something from his pocket. For a moment Maxwell thought it was a knife, and almost abandoned his resolution to wait until the fire—

But no. It was a box of matches. The man struck one, and a sharp pinprick of light illuminated the darkness. Maxwell could see the lower half of a pale face and a black beard, and the upper half of a shabby patched shirt.

At least his adversaries were ruining their night vision with the light.

"Trevelyan," the man with the match said, in quiet satisfaction.

Trevelyan's head came up slowly, and he stared for some uncomprehending moments at the face of the man with the match.

"Miss me?" the man inquired. It was hard to tell from so few words, but Maxwell thought he might be hearing a Russian accent.

"I…thought you were dead," Trevelyan managed.

"You hoped," snarled the man whose heavy hands kept Trevelyan on his knees. Definitely a Russian accent. "You hoped, is it not so?"

"No," Trevelyan gasped.

"No," agreed the man with the match, in a pleasant tone that raised the hair on Maxwell's arms. A dangerous man, this. The match spluttered between his fingertips, sparking against his skin but drawing no reaction—another useful and unwelcome piece of information. "You did not hope, but you thought. You thought we could not endure the punishments awaiting those who failed to escape Cayenne. An understandable mistake, old friend. Most men would have died from what they did to us after you and Cieśla abandoned us and escaped alone." With no further warning than that, he plunged toward Trevelyan and fastened his hands around the inventor's throat.

Trevelyan thrashed frantically in the struggle for air, but the bigger man held him down easily. The man with the beard did not loosen his grip from

Trevelyan's throat. "It was anticipating this moment that kept me alive," he purred.

Trevelyan thrashed again—and again—and more feebly—and Maxwell had almost decided to abandon the plan and rush to his defense—when a shout came from the alleyway mouth. The strangler jerked toward it, surprised.

At the alleyway mouth, the shadows seemed to spontaneously coalesce into human form, and a tall thin figure sprinted toward the confrontation. It roared a distraction, and it swung a length of pipe into the Russian's face.

This could only be Zimmermann, come to Trevelyan's rescue.

His howling headlong rush gave Trevelyan a moment in which to act. Gasping for air, the inventor pushed back against the hold on his shoulders, and the bigger of his abductors rocked back for an instant off-balance. Trevelyan followed the momentum, staggering to his feet.

His hands were useless, but he kicked at the crate upon which Maxwell had placed the oil lamp, and the lamp sailed from its precarious position and crashed into the cobblestones, splashing kerosene in every direction. Trevelyan ran a few steps, then slipped and staggered. The big Russian grabbed hold of him again, and they folded against the wall no further than an arm's-length from Maxwell's door. The Russian got back up, but Trevelyan did not.

Maxwell dug his fingers into the brick wall and forced himself to hold still.

Trevelyan was down. Zimmermann was likewise faring badly against his opponent, who was shouting accusations and abuse—mostly in Russian, but the names "Cayenne," "Trevelyan", and "Cieśla" were plainly audible. Zimmermann landed one lucky blow with his pipe, catching the strangler in the gut and dropping him momentarily to hands and knees in the puddle of lamp oil. Both the Russians were splashed with it now, and they stood between Trevelyan and safety.

Zimmermann stumbled a pace toward the mouth of the alley, snatching toward his shirt pocket. He hesitated one instant.

He had a brain like Trevelyan's, Maxwell could see in that moment. Ice-cold, precisely calculating, focused upon the larger picture. Zimmermann took one deep breath and struck the match—

—Maxwell was already moving, banging open the door and grabbing hold of the limp Trevelyan—

—Zimmermann threw the match and ran.

Maxwell slammed the door closed and bolted it as the spilled lamp-oil went up in a rush of orange flame.

S chwieger was waiting to direct Zimmermann toward the front entrance of the abandoned building, but there was no need. Zimmermann had seen enough of the unexpected rescue to find his own way in. He burst through the front door and then down the cellar stairs while Maxwell was still waiting for Trevelyan to open his eyes.

Maxwell rose from Trevelyan's unconscious form, spreading his hands to show he held no weapon.

Zimmermann barked a question at him in German, then switched impatiently to French. *"Qui êtes-vous?"*

"A friend," Maxwell answered in English. *Keep them off balance.*

Zimmermann hesitated. "So it appears," he said in awkward English. "But appearances deceive, no?"

"Indeed they do," Maxwell agreed. "But I truly am Gavin Trevelyan's friend."

Zimmermann watched him narrowly. "You are friend to Gavin Trevelyan by that name?" He jerked his chin toward the alleyway. "And those others?"

"Those others are the enemies of my friend Gavin Trevelyan. I am not here to rescue them. Only the two of you."

Zimmermann slowly circled Trevelyan's body, and Maxwell let him come near, holding himself ready but not making an aggressive first move. He was fairly certain he could take the emaciated old man in a physical contest, but Zimmermann had proven himself both ruthless and inventive, and Maxwell would therefore rather not test the assertion.

"Shall we sit?" Maxwell offered eventually, and after a long pause, Zimmermann nodded.

There was no furniture in the dank little cellar with its low, wood-timbered ceiling. Maxwell sat cross-legged on the floor, his back toward a wall, letting Zimmermann take a position between him and Trevelyan's body. *Grant concessions that do no matter, allow them to feel they have the upper hand.*

"We must leave Vienna now," Zimmermann muttered after a while. "We must find a new place to go."

"Have you thought about Wales?" Maxwell offered.

"Is it there you know him from?" Zimmermann asked. "The Welsh Rising?"

"No." Maxwell had entered this determined to tell the truth, or at least most of it. As unfamiliar as the practice was, it seemed the only way to ensure this encounter played out correctly. "But I do know him. And I know—" *Half-statements are more valuable than whole statements. Pique their interest.* "I know that he will be in Wales in 1883 and London in 1885."

He had Zimmermann's attention now. "How?"

"The same way I knew how to find you today." Maxwell detached the timepiece from his waistcoat, wondering if any of his various attempts to change the past would have succeeded if he had ever once, in all those convoluted conspiracies, simply demonstrated this truth. He let the pocket watch fall open in his hand and held it out for Zimmermann's inspection. Zimmermann went still.

"This allows me to travel through time," Maxwell said, and it was the oddest relief he could ever have imagined, to just say the words.

On Zimmermann's far side, Trevelyan groaned and stirred. Zimmermann tore his attention from the pocket watch with some difficulty. "I think he wakes." He bent over his colleague. "Gavin?" The name sounded strange on his tongue.

Trevelyan reacted with reassuring bad temper. "Don't be calling me that."

"Less damaged than I feared," Zimmermann said dryly, which was more or less exactly what Maxwell had been thinking, and put a hand out to help Trevelyan sit up. Trevelyan paled and blinked in the manner common to those with head injuries.

"Am I dreaming this?" he asked Zimmermann.

"If you are, I am as well," Zimmermann said, but then answered the question. "No. This man who can travel through time landed in an alleyway in Vienna to save two *fabrik*-workers from their past." He fixed unsettling blue-gray eyes on Maxwell. "Why?"

"Truthfully?" Maxwell found he needed to take a deep breath. Yes, truthfully. Truth was the only path that would get him through this. "Because I need your help. I will need your help." Had he ever said that before? "I need you to choose to help me."

"Help you do what?" Zimmermann demanded. "You have *that*." His arms were still occupied in holding Trevelyan upright, but he indicated the pocket watch with his chin. "What need can you have of other aid?"

Maxwell had to smile. "You would be surprised."

"Help you do what?" Trevelyan managed, addressing Maxwell for the first time.

"I have been trying to save my mother's life for many years now," Maxwell said, and it was both a wonder and a terror to actually say it. "In 1885, I will be traveling in time with her and with my father—but it will be, for them, before their marriage and my birth. They will not know who I am. The three of us will show up at your door, two steps from arrest and in need of a safe place to stay. You'll be in a position to provide me one. I ask firstly that you do so, and secondly that you not tell either of them about our relationship."

Trevelyan blinked at him. "Done. And done. Simple enough."

Would it truly be that easy? "Then I thank you," Maxwell said. "And now I must go, and so must you. Be well away from here before the Imperials come to put out the fire and recover the bodies of your attackers."

"Wait," Zimmermann said as Maxwell rose to his feet. "What else can you tell us of the days that lie ahead?"

The Rising fails, Maxwell thought. *You die under fire. Emil Schwieger is a time traveler. In the future London is a lifeless crater.*

But no. A bargain was a bargain. A gentleman did not betray his given word, and besides, Maxwell had absolutely no doubt that Schwieger would make good his threat. Schwieger represented Maxwell's only path to Rosamund Holborn, and Rosamund represented the only chance of William and Elizabeth's rescue. Therefore—

"What else can you tell us?" Zimmermann persisted, one hand leaving Trevelyan's back to grasp Maxwell's arm.

But Maxwell shrugged aside the hand and rose to his feet. "Nothing. I'm sorry."

Schwieger was waiting for Maxwell on the top floor of the building—a good thing, too, for if he had abandoned Maxwell here, with no way to Rosamund, Maxwell would have turned straight about and told the two revolutionaries all about the young Prussian's future treachery. At least the threat cut both ways.

Schwieger did not ask how it had gone, but he did keep flexing his hands and looking down at his moving fingers, as though to ensure there was no feeling of fading. Past him, a dingy cracked-pane window showed the fire still merrily burning in the alleyway below.

"I kept my side of the bargain," Maxwell greeted him.

"You did." Schwieger left off examining his hands and drew out his time-piece. He opened it, careful to tilt the face from Maxwell's line of sight. He indicated that Maxwell should come and join him, and Maxwell crossed the room unwillingly, pace by pace. He found the idea of physical contact with Schwieger to be deeply distasteful, but there was no help for it, so he reached out to lay fingertips Schwieger's shoulder from the furthest possible distance.

Again Schwieger tilted the watch away from his line of vision before pressing the buttons. "So I'll keep mine. I'll take you to Rosamund." He pressed the first button. "Let's go home."

Chapter 13

When the rainbow-shot dark and faint ringing vibrations of time travel passed away, Maxwell found himself in the largest room he had ever seen—an empty, echoing cavern, frigid as a winter ice storm but utterly still, with walls that stretched upwards until they vanished into dimness. On three sides, the room likewise stretched empty until it disappeared into shadow; but directly before Maxwell was a wall that put him in mind of Byzantine mosaic, except for one section of it, which seemed to be made of flickering flames. There was no hearth, nor sight of anything that could burn—the flames shimmered in midair, starting nowhere and ending nowhere, disappearing into the shadows at Maxwell's feet and the shadows above his head. But the flames gave off no heat, and Schwieger strode through them without hesitation—so very likely they were not fire at all.

"Rosamund?" Schwieger called. His voice echoed off impossibly high walls. "Sui?"

Maxwell touched the tip of his finger curiously to one of the crystals. It was so utterly cold that his skin burned as though from fire, and he snatched his hand away. He eyed the flames for a moment, but when he stepped through them, they neither scorched nor did anything else untoward, nothing more than whisper like a breeze over his skin. He was so cold that he was hard-pressed to keep from shaking. This was undoubtedly the strangest place he had ever been.

It was also empty. Maxwell was abruptly certain of that. This silent chill spoke of abandonment.

The room he had stepped into was smaller than the first—still large, but he could at least see where it began and ended. It was also somewhat better lit, the illumination coming from pale gold tubes that ran along the ceiling and floor. There was a large chair in the center of the room, made not of wood or cloth, but of some slick material Maxwell had never before encountered. Its base ended not in feet but in a solid cylinder attached to the floor. There were several smaller chairs with desks in front of them, likewise attached to the floor. Each desk had a screen that reminded him of the fourth screen of his timepiece; each screen was dark. Maxwell had just enough light to see his own breath puff in the dry air.

Schwieger was disappearing through a second doorway made of the same flickering not-fire as the first. Maxwell followed him into a corridor where the walls and floor were crystal, where light came from more pale gold tubes, and where there was no trace that anything was living or ever had.

Schwieger strode rapidly through the echoing halls, calling, until Maxwell, exasperated with this performance, grabbed his arm to turn him around. "You can stop your pretense. There was never anyone here. You've tricked me, and I swear I'll—"

"I haven't!" The panic on the younger man's face certainly seemed real enough, and Maxwell was forcibly reminded just how young he was. "Rosamund never goes on excursions any longer, she watches everything from here! If she were to leave, Wadi would take over, or Sui would! There's always someone here!"

"There isn't," Maxwell stated the obvious with a calmness he did not feel, "anyone here now."

∞

I f one thought of it as a faerie hill, it was easier to comprehend. For that matter, those folktales of faerie hills might well have been rooted in visits to this very place. Time travelers from the future would fit most descriptions given of the Fair Folk: taller, immensely long-lived in comparison with for instance a peasant from the Dark Ages, masters of magic and able to tell the future. Moreover, this place, for which Schwieger had no name except "headquarters," had been in existence for…for all of human existence, if one cared to look at it that way.

Maxwell sat in one of the strangely-covered chairs in the room Schwieger called the "library," wrapped in a blanket and sipping a hot drink while the "environmental controls" gradually restored a comfortable level of heat and light. Schwieger was off prowling the place in search of a clue, any clue, as to the whereabouts of his comrades. All he could say for certain was that the meddling of the Carrington family in the events of the nineteenth and early twentieth centuries had not caused the erasure from existence of the headquarters' inhabitants. As unmoored time travelers, they were impervious to any additional changes to their pasts.

The strangely-named "library" had no books. Instead, the walls were made up of what seemed to be windows looking onto a moonless night. They were not *actual* windows as Maxwell understood the concept: not portals to a true outer world, but rather pictorial representations of answers to questions. Moving pictures, like the timepieces. "Screens," Schwieger called them. The library would use its "screens" to show Maxwell the answers to questions he asked—or so Schwieger said, at least, though the Prussian had declined to explain how. "Think of it as a jinn," Schwieger had said impatiently. "Now just sit here and let it entertain you and don't *touch* anything—" and he was gone in his search for clues.

Now Maxwell set his tea aside, cleared his throat, and gave it a try.

"Scheherazade?" The inhabitants of this place had so named the library. As a joke, Schwieger said.

A disembodied voice answered with a cool, "Yes?"

Tell me a story, Maxwell thought. He understood the joke well enough. But would that be too broad a request? He tried instead, "Tell me about the people who have lived here."

"Original roster," the cool voice replied, and the windows around Maxwell flickered simultaneously with colored light. He had time to think, *Prism?* before each resolved into a portrait. The colored-light border remained around each, flickering as the images of the timepiece flickered, momentarily brighter around each portrait as Scheherazade spoke the name of, presumably, the person whose portrait it was. They were an astonishing collection, representatives from every race that walked the earth and some Maxwell did not recorgnize, men and women and a few whose gender he could not identify.

"Shaimaa Akbari," Scheherazade said. "Born 5th T.S., Relative Day 402, Monaco-London Sphere, collapsed timeline. Status: departed, presumed deceased. Timepiece: missing.

"Renee Akintola, born 5th T.S. Relative Day 8, Nairobi-Istanbul Sphere, collapsed timeline. Status: departed, presumed deceased. Timepiece: missing.

"Wei Dahan, born 5th T.S. Relative Day 8009, Sao Paolo-New York Sphere, collapsed timeline. Status: confirmed deceased J2000 Day 302, United Federation of the Americas, collapsed timeline. Timepiece: recovered."

Confirmed deceased, Maxwell thought. *Not departed and presumed deceased. So those who live here know what happened to her. She is therefore one of the Five rather than one of the Seven?*

"Santiago Grigoriyan, born 5th T.S. Relative Day -16, Auckland-Ulaanbataar Sphere, collapsed timeline. Status: departed, presumed deceased. Timepiece: missing.

"Rosamund Holborn." Maxwell looked up at the familiar name. Green light outlined the portrait of a woman of perhaps thirty years, with warm red-brown skin, high sculpted cheekbones, no hair at all, and amber-colored eyes steadily regarding the viewer. "Born: 5th T.S., Relative Day 120, Monaco-London Sphere, collapsed timeline. Status: missing. Timepiece: missing."

Well, that was singularly uninformative. Maxwell and Schwieger already knew Rosamund and her timepiece to be mysteriously missing. Maxwell resisted the urge to sarcastically thank the disembodied voice.

"Mohamed Jones," the voice went on. "Born 5th T.S., Relative Day 8009, Sao Paolo-New York Sphere, collapsed timeline. Status: departed, confirmed deceased 12024 HE, United States of America, collapsed timeline. Timepiece: recovered.

"Lucia Kari. Born 5th T.S., Relative Day -95, Sao Paolo-New York Sphere, collapsed timeline. Status: confirmed deceased 1656 AM, Nakhchyvan, collapsed timeline. Timepiece: recovered.

"Li Lopez. Born 5th T.S., Relative Day 8, Sao Paolo-New York Sphere. Status: departed, presumed deceased. Timepiece: missing.

"Anya Maxwell. Born—"

"*Wait.*" The sound of his own name sent a jolt down Maxwell's spine, like lightning sizzling down the rod to charge Trevelyan's lost rail-gun. In the next instant, rational thought raised an impatient voice to make itself heard over the pounding of his heart, pointing out that he was a fool and that it had to be a coincidence. Many people had the surname *Maxwell.* There was nothing here of value to him. He should continue through the catalogue.

But by then, Scheherazade had already stopped her recital.

Maxwell, blinking eyes dry with sleeplessness, suddenly no long feeling his exhaustion, leaned forward to examine the portrait outlined in green. The woman depicted there was perhaps twenty, and looked out at the world with an insolent grin. Her skin was alabaster, her hair fell in black ringlets over her shoulders, her eyes were piercing green.

A coincidence, the voice in his head repeated impatiently. But this time his pounding heart would not be overruled. "Scheherazade?"

"Yes?"

"Er—" He wasn't entirely certain how to make his wishes known, but the voice stepped in smoothly as he hesitated.

"Shall I continue?" it suggested.

"Er," Maxwell said again. But it was actually the simplest path to the information he sought. "Yes. Er, if you please."

"Anya Maxwell," Scheherazade resumed. "Born: 5th T.S., Relative Day -13, Auckland-Ulaanbataar Sphere. Status: departed, confirmed deceased 1536 CE, Kingdom of England, collapsed timeline. Timepiece: missing."

Fifteen-thirty-six. Kingdom of England. The court of Henry VIII.

It could not possibly be healthy for Maxwell's heart to hammer so hard when he was sitting still.

Maxwell licked his lips. "Did she— Where did she travel before that?"

"Upon departure from headquarters," Scheherazade said, "Anya Maxwell's stated destination was 1814 CE, Kingdom of Great Britain—"

"Stop."

Maxwell leaned his elbows on the polished desk and rested his forehead in his hands, muscles sagging and shivering as though his pounding heart had represented a literal physical sprint and as though he had now reached his goal.

He could see it, he could see how it could have happened. How it must have happened. The girls would have met at an Assembly, or perhaps Anya Maxwell would have set herself up as a war widow or an adventuress. Elizabeth Barton liked the company of adventuresses, after all. She would have liked the wicked twinkle in Anya's green eyes.

He wondered how many adventures the two of them had enjoyed, back in that collapsed timeline, and how many had involved time travel. Some had probably been of the more mundane variety that two strong-willed women could manage even through the smothering protections of the Regency. They had very likely donned trousers and explored the dark recesses of London in male disguise. He could see them doing it.

Perhaps it had been not the *two* of them who had enjoyed adventure together, but the *three* of them. William Carrington would, after all, have been required to legally give his consent to his son's second name, back in this vanished idyllic green haven timeline. He too must have had some fondness for his wife's friend.

Maxwell snorted. Of *course* he had. William might seem the more conventional of the pair, but that was only by degrees and only by comparison. William by any other standard, compared to almost anyone other than his wife, was unconventional in the extreme. William too had a proven fondness for adventuresses.

Anya Maxwell had lived for a time in 1814. Elizabeth and William had given her name to their child, and she had given them a pocket watch, perhaps as a wedding present. Which meant she must have been carrying two timepieces, since one had carried her to Tudor times and another had carried Elizabeth and William after her. Maxwell was absolutely, definitively certain, as he had been certain of nothing else in his life, that Anya had been "the fool in need of saving" that Elizabeth and William had chased after on that last fatal journey.

He looked around the silent echoing room. In this "library," no doubt, lay the evidence that would prove the theory.

But that could wait. He would have time for it later. For now, Maxwell straightened and rubbed his hands over his face. For now, it was more important to discover what had happened to Rosamund Holborn.

"Scheherazade? Continue...ah..."

Again the voice came patiently to his aid. "Continue Anya Maxwell's record, or continue original roster?"

"Continue the original roster."

The final three names Scheherazade gave him ("Nikau Patel, confirmed deceased, collapsed timeline," "Malik Pichler, confirmed deceased, collapsed timeline" and "Mareva Zhao, departed and presumed deceased, timepiece missing") gave Maxwell no new information. He sat for a moment trying to formulate his next question.

He finally settled on, "Who lives here now?"

"Current roster in order of seniority," the cool voice replied, and the windows went dark momentarily, before flickering back to life. Only one face was the same.

"Rosamund Holborn." The intensity of her gaze, inanimate though it was, made Maxwell shift uncomfortably. "Born: 5th T.S., Relative Day 120, Monaco-London Sphere, collapsed timeline. Status: missing."

Yes, Maxwell restrained himself from answering, *I already know that.*

"Wadi Bardo." This was young man, surely no older than William, strongly-built, with a blunt-featured face and obsidian skin. "Born: 41st of Balnba, Gulumoerrgin Federation, collapsed timeline. Status: missing."

"Sui al-Farsi." A young woman perhaps Elizabeth's age, dark eyes, golden skin, hair hidden under a scarf. "Born: 1638 AH, United Federation of North America, collapsed timeline. Status: missing."

"Enoch ben Jared." A man of late middle age—a lined, craggy face, dark eyes like Sui's, hair as white as Maxwell's. "Born: 622 AM, Nakhchyvan, collapsed timeline. Status: confirmed deceased 1656 AM, Nakhchyvan, collapsed timeline."

"Stanislaus 'Stach' Lis." A man of perhaps Trevelyan's age, a hard-used thirty-five, short and wiry, white-blond hair and narrowed ice-blue eyes. "Born: 1960 CE, Aryan Empire, viable timeline. Status: traveling, last known location Europe, 1943 CE, viable timeline."

"Emil Sch—"

"Wait," Maxwell said again. The voice paused obediently. "What did you just say? *What* is the status of Stanislaus Lis?"

"Traveling. Last know location Europe, 1943 CE, viable timeline."

"What in flaming hell is he doing in 1943 Europe?"

"Extrapolation possible from log entries of Stanislaus Lis and Rosamund Holborn," Scheherazade said pleasantly. "Please state preference: raw data or synthesized summary extrapolation."

Maxwell hesitated. "Tell me his story."

"Synthesizing," Scheherazade said. "Ready."

"Er," Maxwell said. "Proceed?"

Scheherazade made a sound like a woman clearing her throat. Maxwell leaned back gingerly into the cushions of the chair to listen to the tale.

Chapter 14

Stanislaus Lis could feel the repetitive thud of the turbine as a dull throb in his breastbone. At first it had been hard to pick out the sound over the swirl of the wind and the roar of the waterfall, but now it filled the air, overwhelming, inescapable, signaling the journey's end.

This *would* be the journey's end. It had to be.

He'd said that to himself before, of course. Every time. Every attempt had been conceived as the last one, the successful one, the journey's end. By *definition*—it was not as though any time traveler would don an SS uniform and a persona and stalk the Fuhrer's afternoon walk from Obersalzberg with an endgame plan of "get arrested and escape only by the skin of the teeth and the grace of a timepiece." No one went into these things *intending* to fail.

The timeline locals hadn't intended to fail either, of course. The brave men of Operation Freshman had not intended to deliver themselves and their plot straight into the arms of the Gestapo. Tomorrow night, the equally brave men of Operation Gunnerside would arrive at Vermok equally determined not to fail—but once they set foot on that well-guarded suspension bridge, they and their plan would be doomed. And no subsequent attempt would get even as close as they did, and this very power plant would provide the heavy water for the nuclear bomb that would allow the Nazi Empire to destroy its enemies. Unopposed, the Empire would then spread like a poisonous mold over the entire planet. Tomorrow night marked the beginning of the end of the free world.

Stach studied the suspension bridge—a surprisingly delicate-looking structure at this distance, black against the green of his night-vision goggles. It had been utterly insane for Gunnerside to attempt that means of entrance. It hadn't been entirely their fault, of course. And it wasn't even really fair to blame those who had given the orders. It was understandable that those who plotted the sabotage in London had preferred the risk of the bridge to the risk of the gorge. After all, even the Norwegian locals had believed the gorge could not be climbed.

The problem was—and this was the stupidest, most heartbreaking part of the whole business—the gorge *could* be climbed. It had been proven climbable by curious students of history in the decades since Vermok ceased being an active military installation and became a museum to the might of the Reich. Such experiments were still called Monday-morning-quarterbacking in the era of Stach's childhood—not that *futbol amerykanski* was ever played any longer, but the idiom had outlived its sports-game origin and its later adoption by Allied military training manuals to become a nearly universal term.

Except it wasn't Monday-morning-quarterbacking if one had a time machine.

The gorge could be climbed. Stach would climb it. The quarterbacking was his to do, in real time. And then that would be the end of it. Surely *this* would be the tactic that worked, the success that would redeem the other failures.

So many failures.

The first time, he'd trusted the tactical skill of the time traveler who had recruited him. Stach and assorted others born in the rubble of various Nazi-annihilated cities had crouched in wait at the treacherous tight curve of the road near Strausland, prepared to overwhelm Hitler's car by sheer force of numbers and execute its occupants. As he looked back on the strategy now, from the remove of several years' experience, Stach still considered it to be solid—but even so, the plan had failed that night. The assassins' initial shots had not succeeded in blowing out the Fuhrer's tires, and the driver had managed to take the tight turn at an impressive skidding speed, against all odds getting Hitler away to safety.

The next two times Stach had worked alone, playing a long con, trusting his sniper's skill and his ability to act a part. But at Wolf's Lair in 1943 he missed his shot, and at Obersalzberg in 1937 he was—against all odds, again—spotted and arrested before he could make the attempt.

The problem was *timing*, he'd decided then. Trying to assassinate a political leader would always be a difficult proposition, as political leaders were always surrounded by guards and safety protocols. But Stach had a *time machine*. He could go back earlier, to a time before bodyguards and fame or infamy, before Hitler had risen to a prominence sufficient to call for assassination. That first plan, the ambush back in 1932—that had been the right timeframe.

And so Stach Lis had traveled to 1932 to fire a sniper's shot into a train carriage bound for Weimar. He had traveled to 1923 and taken the far greater risk of firing from a crowd in Leipzig, then tried the tactic again in Thuringia earlier the same year. In 1932, he attempted a more elaborate poisoning plot in Berlin, which succeeded in sickening everyone at Hitler's table except the man himself.

And finally, Stach had gone back to 1921, to a beer hall in Munich where the relatively unknown new chairman of the NSDAP was exciting half the crowd and angering the other half with one of his trademark vitriolic speeches. Riots during such speeches were not only commonplace, but considered half the fun, audience members spending the early evening consuming as much beer as possible so they might have as many steins as possible to use as weapons in the later evening. And in fact, the history books happened to mention one such riot occurring during this very speech.

There could not have been a more perfect opportunity.

And yet he had failed again.

Now, outside Vermok, Stach ground his teeth in the cold Norwegian air. Even yet he could not think of that night without frustration. He had been *so close* to victory, the crowd of three hundred rioting men providing better cover than he had even hoped for. Despite the beer steins and chairs flying through the hall, Stach's first two bullets had hit the podium, and with the range established, he knew his third would have hit the speaker—

—had it not been for Emil Goddamned Schwieger, thirteen years old and a nascent Nazi already. A kid like Emil should never have been in such a gathering in the first place, but had intrepidly disobeyed his parents and snuck out of his bedroom to follow an older cousin. Emil had seen the first two shots, had seen Stach carefully setting up the third, had considered it unsportsmanlike, and had careened into Stach like a missile, knocking into him hard enough to spoil his aim and ruin his chance. Stach couldn't help still resenting that moment—even though the kid had developed into a decent enough human being after Rosamund took him in hand and painstakingly undid the harm of his earliest education. Emil, now enlightened enough to be horrified at what his country turned into in the years after an enraged Stach yanked him out of his proper time, was now at least spending his young adulthood trying to atone for the acts of his childhood and his Fatherland.

Stach Lis had wanted to kill Hitler since his own childhood in the bombed-out radioactive ruins of Warsaw. Back then, he'd thought all he lacked was opportunity. But then he'd acquired a timepiece and all the opportunity he could want, and it hadn't helped. Despite dozens of efforts, he had been unable to bridge the gap from possibility to reality.

Every time he returned to headquarters to check the history books, he found another "failed assassination attempt" added to the list of thirty or forty under Adolf Hitler's name. About half of those attempts had been made by brave people local to the timeline and identified as such, and good for them; but at least as many were listed as "by unknown assailants." *Shooting in Munich by an unknown person. Shooting in Thurigia by an unknown person. Shooting in Leipzig by an unknown person. Attempted poisoning by an unknown person. Shooting by an unknown man in an SS uniform. Assassination attempt by an unknown Pole.* The history books didn't know it was the same unknown man, failing in his life's mission every time.

Watching Emil grow up under Rosamund's guidance, seeing him overcome his early brainwashing, Stach slowly began to consider the problem in a new way. Killing Hitler would have been viscerally satisfying, of course. But *Kill Hitler* had never been the end goal. *Stop Germany* was. And there were other ways to slay the evil double-headed eagle than to slice off its head.

Emil, a fan of first causes and one for whom the Great War was personal history, wanted to reduce Alsace and Lorraine to a border squabble, quickly resolved. He'd had become convinced that supplying Germany with superior firepower back then, giving them swift victory, would paradoxically make it unnecessary for the Fatherland to rise like a vampire from the humiliating ashes of World War I and enslave the world. Emil's tactics in pursuit of this strategy had grown increasingly hare-brained as the years went by—resurrecting the

Frankenstein monsters was surely more than half-mad—but Stach supposed they were all a little mad by now, living the way they did. His own sanity wasn't likely to stand up to close scrutiny.

Rosamund had certainly thought he had snapped. When, during an absence from headquarters of the others, Stach had informed her of his intention to undo Vermok, Rosamund had asked not *if* he had lost his mind, but *when*.

From Stach's point of view, the situation was straightforward. Stopping Nazi Germany from developing the nuclear bomb would surely save Warsaw (and the rest of the world) from being bombed with it. From Rosamund's point of view, the situation was equally simple. Assassinating Hitler was a job for one man with a rifle. Collecting the Frankenstein notes was a job for one man with a burning need for redemption. Bringing down Vermok was a job for a carefully-coordinated team; it was *not* a job for a single person working alone; *seriously, Stach, this is crazy, can't you see that? How long has it been since you've slept?*

Emil had been off on his quixotic Frankenstein quest, Sui and Wadi returning the accidentally-acquired Enoch to something approximately his own time. Stach and Rosamund had had the headquarters to themselves. Their final explosive conflict had been a long time brewing.

They spent days arguing in one empty room after another, shouting up and down the long echoing corridors. He had finally silenced her with the truth that always silenced her— *You have no right to tell me what I can't risk! This is all your fault!* He had made Scheherazade display images of all the bombed-out cities, dragged Rosamund into the control room and made her look at them. *All of this is your fault!*

There was no answer she could make to that accusation, no defense, no exculpation. In her momentary silence, he had stormed back to his quarters for his supplies and was gone before she could stop him. He'd known she would not chase after him. She would not leave headquarters unguarded.

∞

Now Vermok lay before him, shining in the moonlight, on the other side of a seventy-five-foot-long suspension bridge swaying over a six-hundred-foot drop, on the other side of a gorge thought to be too steep to climb.

Thought *incorrectly* to be too steep to climb.

Stach lowered himself into the gorge.

It was not unlike descending into hell—the frozen rather than the fiery kind. The branches and shrubs he clung to bent under his weight; his feet slipped on the slick, steep, snow-covered rocks, sending miniature avalanches ahead of him to trumpet his presence to anyone who might be looking. He thought of the eagle-eyed Nazi patrollers, imagined the sudden sear of the searchlight, and felt his stomach twist.

The bottom of the gorge was treacherous in its own right. An unexpected thaw was causing an early melt of the Mana River, and for a moment Stach could not see a way across. Finally his searching eyes found an ice bridge—already melting, already covered by three inches of water—and to his relief it supported his weight. It might not be there in an hour or so, but he would not need it for a return trip. The twenty-four-hour recharge time of the timepieces had led to a simple procedural rule of thumb. In situations where the ability to make a quick getaway was essential (which was every situation, more or less) one either waited in hiding for twenty-four hours before taking any action, to ensure one had a watch that would function as an escape route; or one took two watches, one for the journey in and one for the journey out. Stach had chosen the second protocol. Once the Vermok heavy water supplies and mechanisms were destroyed, he intended to blink out and instantly home.

He looked up. The mountainside soared above him, an almost sheer face disappearing into darkness. Six hundred feet above, Nazi boots thumped on the bridge he was avoiding; six hundred feet above, the railway offered another way into Vermok.

Six hundred vertical feet was more than enough opportunity for a climber to lose his footing and plunge to his death in the iced-over river below.

But spruce and pine grew out of crevices in the rock face, and where trees could grow, a man could climb. Stach set his hand in one crevice and his boot in another, and began.

To call the ascent a nightmare was to underrate nightmares. Mountaineering best practice instructed the climber to have supports for both hands and both feet before attempting to change position—but it seemed no one had informed the rock face of its duty to provide them. Stach found that he must count himself lucky to have one handhold and one foot support, and sometimes, more terrifyingly, he was forced to manage with only supports for his feet, sliding his hands up the slick slippery surface that might or might not actually have a higher handhold to offer him. Every time he stopped to breathe, he could hear the whisper of melting snow sliding down the cliff around him, until he began to hallucinate the certainty that the early melt was an ally of the Third Reich, that it took malicious delight in making every inch of the journey that much more treacherous.

Finally, every muscle trembling, Stanislaus Lis hauled himself onto solid ground. Beneath his shivering belly was the rock ledge on which the railway ran. Once more the sound of turbines filled the air. They had been running all through his laborious ascent, but he hadn't heard them.

Once he had his breath back, Stach got carefully to his feet. History had not recorded German mines around the train tracks, but unrecorded history had bitten him before. He put one foot carefully down, then another, slowly, cautiously, inching his way up the train tracks until he chanced to see a trail made in the snow earlier that day. By a plant worker, presumably, so at least he could be sure that path was mine-free.

After that he made progress more quickly, coming at last to a small transformer station about five hundred yards from Vermok. Here he paused a moment, to rest and reconnoiter.

The air was filled with the sound of the turbines. His own heart seemed to beat in time with the pulsing roar. Down below and to the right, he could see the fatal suspension bridge and the silhouettes of the soldiers guarding it. Straight in front of him was the railway gate. Stach checked his chrono; it was a quarter to twelve.

At midnight came the changing of the guard. Stach watched it happen, noting with unhappiness the crisp alertness of the new guards, despite the hour and the cold. Even the relieved guards, retiring to their barracks after a long shift in the cold, walked with brisk steps and looked warily from side to side. They knew the importance of what they guarded, damn them.

Stach intended to follow Rønneberg's plan of allowing a half hour or so to elapse before attempting the sabotage, to maximize the chances of cold, bored, complacent guards. Unfortunately, these particular guards looked unlikely to succumb to complacency. One was a tall man, and stood ramrod-straight, his chest thrown out. The other, shorter and stockier, kept turning his head to scan the darkness.

At half past twelve, Stach decided these men were simply not going to relax, and that he couldn't wait any longer.

The gate that led into Vermok's yard was intended to be easily opened for the convenience of the train, so only a padlock blocked the way. The chain was trivially easy to cut, even with the tools of the time, as long as one had the upper body strength required. For a moment, Stach feared he did not, but then the chain gave. The gate swung open, and Stanislaus Lis crept into Vermok.

He paused to look all around, to strain his ears for sounds above the roaring of the turbines and the roaring of the water. He knew there was at least one sentry patrolling the penstocks nine hundred feet above. He was very aware of those very alert guards on the suspension bridge.

The hydrogen plant and the power station loomed before him, eight stories high, two enormous buildings with the German guard barracks nestled between them. Stach ran lightly across the yard and tried the basement door of the hydrogen plant.

It was locked.

He had brought along explosives sufficient to blow it off its hinges, but now, at the moment of truth, he hesitated. The guard barracks were *right there*. He did not dare an explosion that might rouse them, might position them to stop the explosion he was *actually* here to execute.

He ran around the building in search of another way in, in search of any other information at all. The plant's windows had all been painted black, but here and there a chink of light showed through. Stach peered through one, and luck was on his side for once, because right there was exactly the room he wanted. Six feet below sat two sets of heavy water cells. In the middle of the room, a man in overalls hunched over a desk, writing something in a book.

Overalls. Not a uniform. So this man was a Norwegian worker rather than a Nazi guard. There were risks to breaking the window, of course—the sound, the light that would suddenly pour across the dark yard, the chance of alarming the workman—but standing here with his back to the German barracks was a risk too.

Stach wagered it all on one throw of the dice. And broke the window.

The Norwegian jumped like a scalded cat. Stach swung himself into the room, heedless of the broken glass, starting to utter reassurances, but the Norwegian bolted before Stach's feet landed on the concrete floor.

Dammit.

Between the light pouring from the broken window and the alarm the Norwegian was no doubt about to raise, Stach had just put himself under a hellacious deadline.

But he had drilled for months until he could do this routine in his sleep. When all of time and space was open to you, it was not so very difficult to get in the practice you needed, away from your colleagues' notice.

Stach pulled the explosives from his pack. He would have preferred to use something more sophisticated and reliable than old-fashioned nitrocellulose, but he was not about to deliver future bomb tech into the hands of whatever Nazis picked up the pieces of Vermok's destruction, so he'd had to make do with period-appropriate materials. The resulting charges reminded him of sausages, and made him wish for a nearby comrade-in-arms who might appreciate the cheap jokes running nervously through his brain.

The eighteen heavy water cells seemed to stare at him as fitted the explosives around him. There were impressive to look at—stainless steel cylinders four feet high, decked out with a bewildering array of pipes, tubes, cabling, and seals. Behind these seals lay the damnation of mankind. There was a Biblical joke to be made somewhere in there, about breaking the seals to cause the Apocalypse.

Or prevent it, in this case.

There was shouting outside, barked clipped orders, heavy boots on the stairs. *Nazi guards. Shit.* Had they been alerted by the watchman? By the light shining through the broken pane? By an inopportune glance out the window from a man playing cards in the barracks? Did it matter?

Following Gunnerside's plan of record, Stach tied the eighteen fuses in pairs. (The shouts and feet outside were growing closer.) Gunnerside's plan called for detonators to be trimmed to the two-minute length, giving the saboteurs enough of a margin to flee. (He heard dogs barking.) Stach didn't think he had two minutes to play with. (Fists were pounding at the door.) He trimmed one detonator to the thirty-second length, lit the fuse, and backed away from it.

He had brought period-appropriate British paraphernalia to leave behind. Like the men of Gunnerside, he wanted to provide an external enemy for the Gestapo to blame, to shield the locals as much as possible from their retribution.

Now, even though he was down to maybe twenty seconds of fuse, he rummaged for the British parachute insignias at the bottom of his pack.

Once the badges were scattered artistically over the floor, it was time to go. He had the timepiece ready in his hand, had his finger poised to enter the coordinates of space and time that were never *ever*, even by the most reckless of rogues, saved as a shortcut among the fourth face's images. The spitting fuse had maybe ten or fifteen seconds left. The Nazis were breaking down the door. He really needed to leave.

But the Nazis were *breaking down the door,* and there were still ten seconds left on his charges. Enemy soldiers working quickly might still be able to stamp the charges out. And Stach couldn't let that happen—he had come too far, risked too much, lost too much.

He raced back, flicking open his lighter. With one quick movement he would be able touch the flame to the bottom of the fuse, detonating it in a complete and spectacular explosion at the same instant he pressed the top button of the timepiece with his other hand.

But he had crossed no more than half the short distance when the door behind him flew open and a burning hot pain embedded itself in his back.

He fell, the lighter tumbling uselessly from his hand. Jackbooted thugs ran past him and stomped out his fuses.

❦

They hurt him badly, but they did not kill him—because that was what Nazis did, he'd known that going in, that was what they'd done to Freshman, that was the hell of it, the way they didn't let you die.

Stach lay helpless, blood oozing and vision clouding, unbearably cold. From where he lay, he had a perfect view of the castrated fuses, rendered harmless mere seconds before they could fulfill their purpose.

A man in Nazi uniform bent over Stach and plucked the timepiece from his limp outstretched hand. It glittered through the air as the Nazi straightened. Its traitorous fourth face flickered to life, displaying all of its secrets in lazy elegant striptease.

"What's this?" the man said, and Stach had time to know the depths of the disaster he had caused before unconsciousness claimed him.

Chapter 15

Schwieger entered the library as Scheherazade's voice was fading. Maxwell turned to look at him. "It seems the whereabouts of one of your comrades is known." He stumbled over the pronunciation of the Polish name. "Stanislaus Lis?"

Relief washed over Schwieger's face, succeeded immediately by wariness. "What's Stach done? Where is he?"

"If your jinn is to be believed, a place called Vermok," Maxwell began.

"*Vermok?*" Schwieger echoed in disbelief.

"Voiceprint recognized," Scheherazade said over their heads. "Password recognized."

"Password—?" Schwieger turned bewildered eyes to the blank screens.

"A communication was left for you by Rosamund Holborn," Scheherazade said, "encoded to your voiceprint and the password 'Vermok.' Do you wish to play it?"

"*Jawohl,*" Schwieger snapped, as though out of patience with the voice, and the largest of the blank screens lit up, displaying a portrait of the beautiful dark-skinned woman with the unsettling gaze.

Not a portrait, Maxwell corrected himself in the next instant, for it moved as the images on the timepiece did. It did more than move—it *spoke*.

She spoke. It was indeed like watching her through a window. Perhaps the "screen" should be thought of as a window of sorts, a window into another time, when this woman Rosamund had sat at this desk and spoken these words? Very likely that was how it worked.

Rosamund was older than in the still portrait Scheherazade had displayed earlier, and her face was drawn with fatigue. Schwieger sat down slowly in the chair beside Maxwell, his eyes fixed upon her, looking aghast. He stretched out fingertips toward the image, then stopped himself.

"Emil," Rosamund's image began. "I hope you never see this."

She broke off and rubbed her face with her hands. Her fingers were long and elegant, but the nails were bitten raggedly to the quick. "That's a seriously stupid thing to say. I don't know where the impulse comes from, to start this sort of message that way. Everybody does it. It's some sort of weird compulsion. By definition, if you're listening to me say this, the worst has come to pass, and it doesn't matter what I hoped."

She looked back up at the screen. Her eyes were bloodshot with exhaustion. "All right. If you are seeing this, you returned from your jaunt to recover the Frankenstein papers and found headquarters deserted. You investigated sufficiently to discover that Stach went to Vermok, and to guess that's how I password-protected this message—"

"Er," Maxwell spoke over her.

"Scheherazade, pause message," Schwieger ordered. He looked at Maxwell. "What?"

"She told me about your companion's journey to Vermok. I am sure she could repeat the tale, if it's necessary to understand Miss Holborn's communication—"

"No." Schwieger shook his head. "I know what Vermok is. I can guess what Stach went to do. I'll get the details later. Scheherazade, resume."

"—so you have some idea how bad this is," Rosamund continued. She shook her head and looked away. "What's the only thing worse than Nazis with the A-bomb? Nazis with time travel." She looked back into the screen, her eyes dry and bleak. "The A-bomb thing was my fault, as Stach never stops reminding me. I'd say he's finally managed to top me, except it's *all* my fault really. One-twelfth my fault. If it weren't for us, there would be no Stach. In my timeline, World War II was responsible for horrific loss of life—and we made it *worse.* Because of us, because our interference, the Nazis developed atomic weapons first and won the war, and turned the world into—"

She didn't finish. She didn't have to. Maxwell's brief glimpse of AfterLondon was still with him. And Rosamund kept a shortcut to it on her timepiece, so that she could never for one instant forget.

"And Stach was born into this world, in the smoking radioactive crater of Poland. And because of that, he took this desperate act. And he must have been captured, he and his pocket watch must have been captured, because now suddenly the Nazi regime has *time travel,* and we thought it was bad before, but we had no idea how bad it could get.

"I started noticing changes almost at once. Little things, trembles in the threads. The Nazis haven't figured out how to make big changes yet. But they will. They'll be able to recreate the world from the ground up, from pre-history, from—" She turned all at once back to face them. Her eyes seemed to reflect the burnt-out abandoned shell of a city Maxwell had seen a few days before. "I come from the time after the seas rose," she said. "But I went to visit the time when they were rising, before the dykes were built. Since the Seven left us, my life has felt like that—standing on top of the tower with water rising all around me, waves crashing high against the fortress walls. You can't argue with the ocean, but you can build the walls higher and stronger a bit at a time.

"This is—so much worse, *so* much worse than waves crashing against the tower. It's the tower crumbling from its lowest brick. It's looking down to see that the foundation isn't there any more, watching it cease to exist stone by stone. Not destroyed. Never there in the first place."

The room was absolutely silent. Neither the two men in the library nor the woman on the other side of the time window said anything.

Then Rosamund took a deep breath and spoke in a deliberately businesslike tone. "Sui and Wadi and I have made several attempts to stop Stach. It's just me left now. I'm off to try again. If you're listening to this…I hope you never listen to this. I want to tell you it will be fine. I'll grab Stach by the scruff of his tortured reckless neck and drag him back here and it will all undo itself and all will be well, and by the time you're back with Frankenstein monsters, we'll be here waiting for you… But if you're listening to this, it didn't happen that way. If you're listening to this, I'm not coming home, and what happens next is all up to you. The trust passes to you, like I always intended it to…just not like this…we are so far past your Frankenstein monsters."

She shook her head. Her distant eyes seemed to evaluate future possibilities. "I suppose it is some cold comfort to think that you have advantages I do not. *You'll* be fine in any world they choose to create. Even without a timepiece, you wouldn't be overwritten. You can walk among them…Maybe you can survive long enough to take an effective action. You have the privilege of a little longer to act." She hesitated, then added, "But don't wait. They're taking apart the foundation, stone by stone, right now, while you're listening to this."

The screen went black.

Without its light, the library seemed very dark indeed. Schwieger got up, paced a step, stumbled, regained his balance.

"She's gone, then," he said at last. "They all must be. If an unmoored time traveler is killed, that's—that's it. No subsequent change can write them back in. They're all gone, they're forever gone, and your parents are—are forever trapped, because neither of us can get back to Napoleon's 1885."

"Never mind about my parents," Maxwell heard himself say, and to his surprise, found that he meant it. "We have bigger problems."

Schwieger paced to the other end of the room, into the darkest of the shadows. He turned and came back, walking like a man stunned. He stopped with his back to one wall, and all at once seemed to lose the ability to remain upright. He slid slowly to a crouch, and then the floor. "What does she think I can do?" he whispered. "What can I possibly do?"

"Stop Lis," Maxwell said.

Schwieger looked up. "How? When?"

"I imagine she meant stop him that night, that place. Vermok."

"I can't go to Vermok." Schwieger shook his head. "The years of the war are closed to me. I— Apparently it is ordained I go back and live straight in a line again. I can't go to 1943 because I am already there. The timepiece won't take me." He looked up at Maxwell, trying to assess whether Maxwell understood him. "One can't cross one's own timeline."

There was a long pause. The shouts of Waterloo echoed in Maxwell's brain.

"As it happens," he said at last, slowly, "one can. It costs the timepiece, but it can be done."

"How the hell do you know that? Who would risk—"

"My mother is an unconventional woman."

Something like wary hope crossed Schwieger's face. "Tell me."

"My timepiece was set to take me to Waterloo—had just started to take me there—and Elizabeth grabbed my sleeve. She forced it to take her and William along as well. So Elizabeth Barton and William Carrington spent June 18, 1815, both in a garden in Kent and on the field of Waterloo. It can be done. It costs the watch, but…but that's all right. We have two." Maxwell looked about himself. "At least two. More, if those recovered timepieces Scheherazade mentioned are stored here." He took a breath. "So that part is all right. You can get to Vermok if I take you there."

The silence this time was even longer.

"Why would you do this for me?" Schwieger asked at last, in barely more than a whisper.

"I'm not doing it for you," Maxwell said. *I can't save Elizabeth Barton, William Carrington, or Katarina Rasmirovna.* "I thought the Spider's 1910 was the worst future imaginable, and it would appear I…was very wrong." *I can't save them, but the world still needs saving.* "The world your Miss Holborn describes, the AfterLondon I saw…" He shook his head. There truly were not adequate words. "And the idea of those people having the ability to author history however they choose? That's unthinkable." *I have to save something, somehow. I have to make this all worth something.* "This evil empire of yours can't be allowed time travel. I'll help you stop it. It won't save Rosamund or Lis, but—"

"It will save history," Schwieger said, getting unsteadily to his feet. "This is bigger than both our families."

Chapter 16

Stanislaus Lis could feel the repetitive thud of the turbine as a dull throb in his breastbone. At first it had been hard to pick out the sound over the swirl of the wind and the roar of the waterfall, but now it filled the air, overwhelming, inescapable, signaling the journey's end.

This *would* be the journey's end. It had to be. This would be the success to redeem all his failures.

Every muscle trembled as he hauled himself out of the gorge and onto solid ground. He had been right. Where trees could grow, a man could climb. Beneath his shivering belly was the rock ledge on which the railway ran straight into Vermok's yard. He had to take a moment to breathe.

Once he had his breath back, Stach got carefully to his feet. History had not recorded German mines around the train tracks, but unrecorded history had bitten him before. He put one foot carefully down, then another, slowly, cautiously, inching his way up the train tracks until he chanced to see a trail made in the snow earlier that day. By a plant worker, presumably; and it at least would not be mined. After that he made progress more quickly, coming at last to a small transformer station about five hundred yards from Vermok. Here he paused a moment, to rest and reconnoiter.

His heart seemed to beat in time with the pulsing roar of the turbines. Down below and to the right, he could see the fatal suspension bridge and the silhouettes of the soldiers guarding it. Straight in front of him was the railway gate. Stach checked his chrono; it was a quarter to twelve.

At midnight came the changing of the guard. Stach watched it happen, noting with unhappiness the crisp alertness of the new guards, despite the hour and the cold. Even the relieved guards, retiring to their barracks after a long shift in the cold, walked with brisk steps and looked warily from side to side. They knew the importance of what they guarded, damn them.

Stach intended to follow Rønneberg's plan of allowing a half hour or so to elapse before attempting the sabotage, to maximize the chances of cold, bored, complacent guards. Unfortunately, these particular guards looked unlikely to succumb to complacency. One was a tall man, and stood ramrod-straight, his chest thrown out. The other, shorter and stockier, kept turning his head to scan the darkness.

At half past twelve, Stach decided these men were simply not going to relax, and that he couldn't wait any longer.

The gate that led into Vermok's yard was intended to be easily opened for the convenience of the train, so only a padlock blocked the way. The chain was trivially easy to cut, even with the tools of the time, as long as one had the upper body strength required. For a moment, Stach feared he did not, but then the chain gave. The gate swung open, and Stanislaus Lis crept into Vermok.

He paused to look all around, to strain his ears for sounds above the roaring of the turbines and the roaring of the water. He knew there was at least one sentry patrolling the penstocks nine hundred feet above. He was very aware of those very alert guards on the suspension bridge.

The hydrogen plant and the power station loomed before him, eight stories high, two enormous buildings with the German guard barracks nestled between them. Stach ran lightly across the yard and tried the basement door of the hydrogen plant.

It yielded to his hand.

He had brought along explosives sufficient to blow it off its hinges, but was relieved that he did not now have to use them, as the guard barracks were *right there*. He would have broken one of the black-paint-covered windows if he'd had to, but that too would have carried a risk; one of those frighteningly well-trained guards might have noticed the light. His chances of success had just noticeably improved.

The door led into a stairwell, and at the bottom was exactly the room Stach sought. Two sets of heavy water cells met his eyes. In the middle of the room, a man in overalls hunched over a desk, writing something in a book.

Stach drew his pistol and crossed the room in a bound. The man in overalls leapt around to face him, but Stach already had the pistol clapped to his head. "Put your hands up," he said in Norwegian, and the man obeyed instantly. "Good," Stach told him. "What's your name?"

"Gustav Johansen," the man stammered.

Stach relaxed minutely. That was the name of the Norwegian night guard, recorded by history to have been loyal to his country and no friend to the Nazis. "Nothing will happen to you if you do as you're told," Stach told him. He motioned with the gun. "Go lock the door."

Johansen slowly crossed the room and did so. "You're not Norwegian," he ventured.

Polish, Stach wanted to say. "British," he said instead. Stick to the plan.

Keeping his pistol pointed at Johansen, he swung his rucksack to the floor. "Open it," he told the Norwegian.

Trembling a little, Johansen unpacked the explosives and fuses. Stach had drilled for months until he could do this routine in his sleep. When all of time and space was open to you, it was not so very difficult to get in the practice you needed, away from your colleagues' discerning eyes. Instructing someone else in their assembly was only a little harder. It would have been quicker to do it himself, of course, but he could not take the risk of leaving Johansen uncovered.

The charges reminded him of sausages, but he restrained the half-hysterical impulse to indulge in low humor. They were made of nitrocellulose, a malleable plastic explosive. Stach might have gotten a more sophisticated explosive from any future point, but he had no wish to deliver futuristic explosives into the hands of the Nazis. These detonator fuses could be trimmed to allow for different burning times. A full-length fuse took two minutes, time enough for a saboteur—and his unwilling accomplice—to flee.

The eighteen heavy water cells seemed to stare at him as Johansen fitted the explosives around them. There were impressive to look at—stainless steel cylinders four feet high, decked out with a bewildering array of pipes, tubes, cabling, and seals. Behind these seals lay the damnation of mankind. There was a Biblical joke to be made somewhere in there, about breaking the seals to cause the Apocalypse.

Or preventing it, in this case.

Once Johansen grasped what he was being ordered to do, he worked faster. Yes, he was indeed a loyal Norwegian. At Stach's order, he scattered some paraphernalia Stach had brought along, designed to reinforce the cover story of a British sabotage team, to protect the locals from reprisals. "You'll tell them two British soldiers were here," Stach instructed him. "One held you at gunpoint while the other did this. No one will blame you."

Johansen nodded. Stach instructed him to unlock the door, and he did so. "I'll light the fuses," Stach said, keeping the gun trained on Johansen as he drew his lighter out with his other hand, "and then you'll have just enough time to run."

But as he bent over the fuses, Johansen balked for the first time. "Wait! Sir! My eyeglasses!"

"Your *what*?" Stach stared at him. It might have been considered a moment of comedic relief, except this situation was too dire for comedy.

"My eyeglasses," Johansen pleaded. "I need them for my job. They're impossible to replace these days!"

Stach remembered reading something along those lines, in some history book or another: the Nazis had seized all optical goods and equipment in Norway. "I'm sorry," he said. "We can't wait." He flicked open the lighter.

And to his horror, heard footsteps on the stairs.

Nazi guards.

Stach touched the flame to the thirty-second fuse and whirled for the door, leveling his pistol as he moved.

The German guard was already framed in the doorway, his pale blue eyes wide, his own gun raised. Stach fired; the German fired; Johansen fell. The German got off another shot before he, too, collapsed, and then there was an absolute stampede of feet on the stairs.

The thirty-second fuse had not properly lit. Cursing, Stach lit the nine two-minute fuses as fast as he could. Outside the room, there were shouts. Gunfire. A clipped German voice was cutting through the racket, cursing, demanding to know how the *hell* these saboteurs had gotten in. The suspension bridge was guarded, after all; the penstocks were mined; guards patrolled the grounds; up until this moment there had been not a single shot—

For the second time, Stach tried to light the thirty-second fuse.

He knew he needed to leave. He had the timepiece ready in his hand, had his finger poised to enter the coordinates of space and time that were never *ever,* even by the most reckless of rogues, saved as a shortcut among the fourth face's images. The Nazis were at the door and he was out of time.

But the Nazis were *at the door,* and the thirty-second fuse would not light. Enemy soldiers working quickly would certainly be able to stamp out the other ones. And Stach couldn't let that happen—he had come too far, risked too much, lost too much.

He flicked open his lighter to try again. With one quick movement he would be able touch the flame to the bottom of the fuse, detonating it in a complete and spectacular explosion at the same instant he pressed the top button of the timepiece with his other hand. It didn't matter where he went, after all. He could set the headquarters coordinates from a safer vantage point.

He bent to the fuses.

A burning hot pain embedded itself in his back.

In the scrum that followed, Stach could have sworn he saw Emil Schwieger, wearing a Nazi uniform that fit him like a glove, in desperate hand-to-hand combat with the other Nazi guards.

A hallucination, of course.

The hallucination shot two or three of the jackbooted thugs pouring into the room, but that still left plenty of steel-toed boots to stomp out Stach's fuses. And plenty more to wreak vengeance upon Stach himself, already rendered helpless by the bullet in his spine. They would not kill him, of course—because that was the way of it, he'd known that going in, that was what they'd done to Freshman, that was the hell of it, they didn't let you die. He lay helpless, blood oozing and vision clouding, and he was aware of an unbearable cold—

A man in Nazi uniform bent over Stach and plucked the timepiece from his limp outstretched hand. It glittered through the air as the Nazi straightened. It flickered to life, its traitorous fourth face displaying all of its secrets in lazy elegant striptease.

"What's this?" the man said.

The hallucination of Emil Schwieger hurtled across the room and flung himself upon the guard holding the timepiece. He was aided in his struggle by a white-haired man who might also be a hallucination. Both were hampered by two or three other Nazis who were clearly trying to take all three prisoners alive. The white-haired man struggled to pry the guard's fingers off Stach's timepiece—and almost managed it before he was torn away. Emil had taken out his own pocket watch in what looked like a bid for escape, but it was knocked from his hand.

The knot of humanity struggled on the floor a few feet away, thumbs smashing the buttons of the contested timepiece in no pattern Stach could see. He couldn't help counting side button presses and top button presses.

The older man threw off the two Nazis who were trying to hold him and plunged back into the struggle to aid Emil, and Stach knew what was going to happen a second before it did. Someone's thumb hit the final button, and the trio—Emil, the Nazi guard, and the white-haired man—vanished in a momentary brightening, then dimming, of the ambient light, as though the universe had folded itself around them.

Emil's timepiece fell to the floor where they had been.

A steel-toed boot was swinging toward his face. But Stach still had time to know the depths of the disaster he had caused before unconsciousness claimed him.

Part Three:
Uncharted

What's past is prologue.
— Shakespeare, *The Tempest*

Chapter 17

Madame Katarina Rasmirovna—sometime *prima donna* of Milan's Teatro alla Scala, toast of all Europe for her breathtaking performances of Cinderella and of Carmen, newly returned to London for a brief engagement—leaned against the door of the luxurious hotel suite that was serving as her home this fortnight and closed her eyes.

This is ridiculous. I should be happy.

She was not *unhappy,* to be sure. There was nothing to be unhappy about. Tonight she had sung before the packed Royal Opera house with the famous Italian emerald known as the "Cat's Eye" glittering at her breast. She had received a standing ovation and armloads of roses afterward. There was an undeniable thrill in this triumphant return to the city she had left what felt like a lifetime ago, and she greatly enjoyed the attention, the luxury, and the wilderness of appreciative bouquets that crowded her hotel sitting room. She did not exactly approve of the large pink and yellow flowers embellishing the carpet of said sitting room, but she did like the feel of them under her bare feet, and she enjoyed the naughtiness of walking about with shoes cast off now there was no one to see her. She was looking forward to collapsing into the decadent feather mattress of the four-poster bed in the other room, and to a cup of good strong English tea in the morning.

There was nothing to be unhappy about.

Perhaps it was only that unhappiness was familiar?—or, no, not unhappiness, she corrected herself again—but dissatisfaction, the frame of mind that made the best of today but derived its true pleasure from a contemplation of tomorrow, next year, a distant horizon. As the probably-illegitimate daughter of a probably-not-noble foreigner and a retired opera singer, she had spent her childhood feeling like an outsider in the little Devonshire village in which her mother had raised her. Happiness back in those days had been found in thoughts of escape, in plans of what she would do someday. Her girlhood in London after her mother's death had been a hardscrabble struggle, music halls and male impersonation acts, pennies pinched for voice instruction and elocution lessons, tiny respectable parts obtained under a different name than the music hall girl's, fighting to ascend one rung of the ladder after another. Not precisely unhappy, actively satisfying in many ways, but still fueled by the distant horizon. *When I escape, when I succeed, when I am known, when I am prima donna, when—*

When I am rich, say the bells of Shoreditch.

Now she sang to sold-out opera houses, received bouquets from foreign suitors, had money enough to enjoy herself (and plenty left over to properly invest; she still took the long view), and even Mr. Colin Ramsey when she needed a brief escape from it all. Watching the scenes of her life from the outside, Katarina knew that these were the circumstances in which she had expected to find that elusive sense of completion. Not someday, but now. This. Happy, forever after.

What did one do after one got what one wanted?

Katarina pushed off the door, angry with herself for even posing the question, even thinking the question. She knew quite well it was a question most people did not have the opportunity to contemplate.

She bolted the door behind her, turned down the gas, and walked across the colorful floral carpet to check the fastenings of the window. A misty drizzle fogged the panes, but in the morning, she would be able to see Hyde Park. She had a first-floor suite looking out onto *Hyde Park*.

It would be better in the morning. It was always better in the morning. She would sip strong English tea and read English newspapers, looking out over Hyde Park. Later she would make her way to the Opera House to prepare for the evening performance. Perhaps on Sunday, when she had no engagements, she would go for a drive. She would be one of those ladies who drove out in a fine carriage on a Sunday afternoon.

Katarina entered the bedroom, closed the door behind her, and sat down to brush and braid her thick hair. It was coal-black still, no white strands visible yet. She told the story to herself, seeking the self-satisfied thrill in it: Young enough that her hair was still black, she had achieved a gilt-edged mirror, a silver-backed hairbrush, a four-poster bed, and gentlemen who sent bouquets and cards instead of shouting raucous suggestions from the shadows beyond the stage door. This was altogether a pleasant change from the last time she had worked in London.

Although…Absurd as it was, she could not help the thought. Her old life, for all its dangers, uncertainty, and poverty, had had its moments. She did not exactly miss walking home from a third-rate music hall with every nerve on alert—and to the extent she did miss it, she had Colin Ramsey, who might safely prowl the streets once inhabited by Katherine the music-hall girl—but there had been something real and vital about that life, the daily struggle and the promise of the horizon, the certainty that tomorrow was bound to be better than today.

What did one do after one got what one wanted?

It seemed she could not smother the question into silence. Well, it was a fair enough question, was it not? There was always "next" and "after" to be considered. One could not stay a diva forever; eventually one's voice roughened and one's physical beauty faded. A voice like hers might eke out a living a little longer playing mothers and witches, but there was an apex, a tide that eventually turned. One could not be an opera singer forever, so what next?

What did one do after one got what one wanted? One got married, she supposed. One selected from among the foreign gentlemen angling for one's hand, or, if one wanted a life of more security and more stability, one might choose an Englishman, a barrister or something of the sort. One might even have children and live in an obscure country village, as one's mother had.

But one could as easily establish oneself in Vienna or Milan, hold salons and teach youngsters, establish scholarships perhaps, be venerated as a Grande Dame of the opera. That thought was somewhat more appealing. Or perhaps one took the money and vanished—perhaps Mr. Colin Ramsey became one's primary habitation and one went and explored the world. There was a great deal of world to explore, and much more freedom to be found if one explored it in a male persona. Perhaps exploration was the solution that would slake this nagging thirst. Though the male persona would make it difficult to engage in certain social activities Katarina quite enjoyed...

From the outer room, something hit the floor with a heavy thump.

And instantly she was back in this world, here and now, distracted by no daydream of the future.

And on her feet without conscious thought. There were instincts that soaked into the skin, reflexes that no subsequently-acquired safety could smother. She was careful to make no sound as she stole across the mercifully thick carpet to fetch the little pearl-handled revolver she kept under her pillow. Its presence might have shocked those who did not know her antecedents; it actually had shocked one or two lovers, but she had been able to brush off their exclamations of concern. She traveled with her jewels, after all—jewels that included a famous and priceless emerald given to her by a famous and wealthy Italian count. She preferred to know she could protect herself and her property if necessary.

From intruders in a hotel, for instance.

She reached the sitting-room door and paused there to listen. Were there in fact intruders, plural?

Yes. She could hear at least two out there, engaged in some sort of struggle, quite possibly distracted. Her eye to the keyhole saw nothing, not one speck of light, so their eyes would have adapted to dimness. Katarina therefore seized the moment and turned the bedroom gas lamp as high as it would go. Thinking *All the better to blind you with my dear,* she jerked open the door.

There were three of them—a slim blond youth, another fair-haired man who was some years older and wore a military uniform, and an older man with white hair. It seemed to be two on one, the eldest and youngest of the trio attempting to subdue the soldier. Which pleased her, as far as it went, dissension in the ranks of one's enemies being a desirable situation. Sometimes if one stayed quiet in the shadows, said enemies spent their energy in reducing their numbers—

The white-haired man flinched back from the sudden light, and the soldier succeeded in landing a solid blow to his jaw. He followed it up with a kick that doubled the older man over. The solider shoved his opponent to the ground hard enough that the door shuddered despite its fastened bolts when the white-haired man landed against it—and then swung for the window, light glistening on strange military insignia the like of which Katarina had never seen. There was an oversized pocket watch clenched in his hand.

The youngest man flung himself upon the soldier with a tiger's fury, succeeding for an instant in pulling the soldier's hand from where it was fumbling at the window latch—

—but the soldier at once jerked him off balance. The soldier's hand dipped into his pocket, then his arm flashed—

—and the blond youth collapsed with a sound more like a cough than a cry.

The white-haired man was on his feet now, but still doubled-over, too slow and too late. The soldier yanked the window open and leaped through it, crashing into the shrubbery below. He apparently regained his feet at once, for Katarina heard his running steps on the pavement while the white-haired man was still lurching across the room.

The white-haired man gave one single despairing look out the window—turned a horrified gaze upon his young companion, bleeding from what looked like a knife wound to the side—and for the first time looked to where the occupant of the suite stood watching.

And froze as though turned to stone. *"Katarina?"*

She ought to have definitely had the upper hand, with both the intruders injured and her revolver already cocked and aimed—but her name, *that* name, said in a British accent and with that note of astonishment, took the wind from her sails and the breath momentarily from her lungs. She could have shot, but she lost an instant to staring.

After a moment she riposted with, "Have we *met?*"

Impossibly, something in his face seemed to soften at that. He was younger than she had first thought, a man still in the prime of life despite the premature gray of his hair. "No," he said, as though the realization were a discovery of some treasure. "No, I suppose we haven't."

"Then that's 'Madame Rasmirovna.'" Which was an absurd thing to insist upon, but she had to keep the upper hand. This was her stage to control.

The expression on his face was amused, even affectionate. Certainly it was more familiar than respectful. His lips parted to say something in response—

The boy at their feet moaned, and the older man's brown eyes dropped back to his fallen comrade. "Emil," he said, momentary warmth vanishing from his face, and he made as though to move to the younger man's side.

"Stay where you are," Katarina ordered.

The white-haired man looked back at her in surprise and alarm. "You have to let me help him."

"I don't have to do anything." Though perhaps she ought to let him burden his hands with the injured man. If he were crouched by his friend, he would be less able to pose a threat in the endless seconds it would take her cross the room, unbolt the door, call for hotel security—

"Please," the white-haired man said, spreading his hands as though in supplication. "Let me help him. Then let me go; I have to follow that man. I have to stop him. He stole something—something indescribably precious, and we have only twenty-four hours to retrieve it before he uses it to do harm—"

"He acted as though you intended to do *him* harm," Katarina countered, but she was only half aware of what she was saying. Something was wrong. Some instinct prompted her to keep this man here and keep him talking, instead of calling the authorities like a sensible person, because she had seen something wrong.

"I intended to stop him, that's all." The white-haired man's face twisted. "I failed. It seems I do nothing but fail, I make it all worse with every step, but I was only trying to prevent him escaping."

It was true enough, the soldier *had* been intent on escape. Katarina replayed the sequence in her head, recalling each movement as though it were a stage direction. The soldier had used violence to facilitate his escape. He had thrown the older man into the door so hard it had rattled despite its bolts, then stabbed the younger man when the latter tried to prevent his unfastening of the window latch—

"The window was fastened," Katarina said. That was what had caught her attention. "The window was fastened and the door is still bolted. Neither lock has been forced." And the furniture in this sitting room was the elegant modern sort, with slender carved legs that provided no concealment. "How did you get in here?"

The white-haired man hesitated. "It's a long story."

Katarina raised her eyebrows. "Then I suggest you talk rapidly."

Her opponent looked down at his friend, then back up to her. "Please let me help him."

It was a reasonable enough request. Truthfully, even without the plea, Katarina would have found it unacceptable—both ethically abhorrent and legally unpleasant—to let the blond man bleed to death while his companion told their tale. Without taking her eyes from the white-haired man's face, or her finger from the trigger, Katarina reached into the bedroom behind her, pulled a towel from her dressing table, and tossed it. It fell at the older man's feet.

He dropped down at once, catching up the towel and pressing it to his companion's side as he checked for the pulse and for other injuries. The younger man—Emil, was it?—moaned again, but his eyes stayed closed.

"Start talking," Katarina instructed. She had learned that tone of voice years ago.

The white-haired man sighed. "My friend's name is Emil Schwieger," he said. "He was born in the year of our Lord nineteen hundred and eight." He did not pause to allow a response before continuing. "My name is Maxwell. I was born in 1818, and ninety-two years after that, I had the honor of getting to know you quite well. Are you..." He looked about himself. "Are you actually an opera singer, this time? It was what you wanted to be, the other times."

There was so much strangeness packed into one paragraph that Katarina hardly knew what to question first.

Maxwell answered his own question. "Hotel room. Flowers. It would seem though you are. Are you among a small elite, then? Or is this London free from Wellington monsters, constructs, and Napoleon alike?"

"What?"

"Oh," Maxwell said, as though overcome by it. "Oh, that's…that's good. That's…something good. But how—?"

"Are you *mad*?" Katarina managed at last.

Maxwell shook his head. "Let me show you something." He carefully unhooked the pocket watch stretched across his waistcoat—overly large, a twin to the one the soldier had carried away—and tossed it so that it landed at her feet.

Still with her eyes on him, Katarina picked it up. It fell open in her hand, revealing an intricacy of clockwork, wheels within wheels, not one large face but four small ones nested together, each with a crack running across its center.

If it was a ploy to distract her attention, it was a good one, but Katarina wrenched her eyes away from it and back to Maxwell. "The soldier. He took one of these when he escaped."

"He took the one still in working order," Maxwell said. "He'll use it to get back to 1943. There's a terrible war being waged, and that man is a soldier for the army that will *begin* by wiping London from the map, and that's the least of their evil. I only have twenty-four hours before he can—"

The man on the floor caught his breath in a gasp. "…happened."

Maxwell turned to him at once.

"It happened," Emil said, eyes glassy. "We didn't stop it. We can't go back."

"It happened," Maxwell agreed heavily. "We didn't stop it and we can't go back. But Emil, it's worse than that."

"I…know," Emil said. "I…saw. Window." His eyes wandered away from Maxwell's face—and widened. "Katarina?" he managed in a gasp.

"You have the advantage of me," Katarina said, infusing as much irony as possible into her voice. "Emil, I believe?"

"She doesn't know us," Maxwell told the younger man. "We've just appeared in her sitting room, and she doesn't know anything about any of this. She has no reason to trust us."

"Give her…as much reason…as she needs," Emil said, his eyelids sliding closed again. "She's the best ally…we could…hope for."

"Strongest piece on the board," Maxwell agreed.

Katarina raised her eyebrows at him. She knew she was indeed far more powerful than any admirer of Madame Rasmirovna or acquaintance of Colin Ramsey could know, but how could this stranger sound so certain of it? How much *did* he know about her?

Maxwell looked up at her, still holding the folded cloth pressed to Emil's side. There were lines of strain around his eyes, but they met hers straightly, without any apparent intent to deceive. She was good at spotting deception, after so many years using it as a tool herself. "What if I told you," he began carefully, "there was another life you could have had, one that you simply don't remember?"

"Under other circumstances," Katarina said, still with as much irony as she could manage, "I would call you mad. Under these—" She indicated the watch, the latched window, and the bolted door, and lifted her shoulders in a shrug. "—I might be willing to listen."

"What if I told you that the world is literally in danger and you are the person who can save it?"

"I thought that role was yours. Didn't you say you needed to pursue that man?"

Maxwell cast a disgusted look at the window. "I lost my moment. I wasn't in time to see which way he fled, and once he got out of earshot, any chance I had was gone. I don't know this city, you see. I once knew a city *like* this, but that's not the same thing. I don't know where he'd go, I don't know who might hide him, I don't know who could be persuaded to provide aid in hunting him down—and twenty-four hours isn't time enough to learn." Again the brown eyes met hers. "This fight has to be yours."

She could have screamed for help. Someone would have come to her aid.

She could have shot. No one would have faulted her for shooting intruders.

She could have decided he was a madman babbling nonsense. There was enough evidence to support that conclusion.

Instead she lowered the revolver and said, "Tell me why I should. Why must that man be stopped?"

Maxwell kept the cloth pressed tight to Emil's side. "Imagine," he said, "a German Empire led by madmen, running rampant over Europe. Imagine Vienna and Milan and Paris ravaged, imagine forty million people dying in the Empire's first attempt to control the globe and eighty million dying in its second—and now imagine they have achieved a weapon that can rain fire from the sky and obliterate cities whole." He swallowed. "I saw London after such an attack. It was...it was a smoking hole in the earth. One of Dante's levels of hell." She could see that hell reflected in his eyes. "And *now* imagine these men have the ability to travel through time. The man who stole that watch is one of their foot soldiers. The watch has spent its power, and he will not be able to use it until twenty-four hours have passed. But then he will bring it home to his masters, and they will fall eagerly upon the chance to remake the world in their own image. They will rain destruction upon the past and the future, slaughter three-quarters of the inhabitants of the globe at least, and rewrite history so that *nothing* of value survives, no achievement of art or medicine or philosophy or invention not produced by German hands." He met her eyes. "No coffee houses in Vienna, where the great men of the day debate their ideas; many of those ideas will be considered heretical, and some of those men were Jews. No pyramids in Egypt or South America, monuments to bygone magnificence; no Egyptian or Mayan empires will be permitted to form and build them. No operas written by Italians, a degenerate mongrel race. No medicine pioneered by Arabs, who are even worse offenders. No centers of trade or learning in Timbuktu or Magadha or Baghdad—" He took a ragged breath. Katarina could tell this was no rehearsed speech. "I saw the records of what they did, living forward. I'm not sure the human race survives at all, if they have the ability to change everything from the dawn of time."

There was a silence. Katarina half-wondered if that was his heart she heard pounding, or only her own. "You're telling the truth," she said after a long pause. She had heard other people speak of moments when they felt their lives dissolve and reform—moments mostly surrounding the births of children or the deaths of loved ones. She had never experienced the sensation herself, but it was impossible to mistake for anything else.

"For once in my life," he said, "yes, I am. Nothing more and nothing less."

"I'll help," she said. Some enormous cosmic tuning fork vibrated with the words.

Maxwell sagged in relief—then caught the expression on her face and looked at her curiously.

"Nothing." Katarina shook her head. "It's nothing." His curiosity did not abate. "It's only—" She let out half a laugh. "I have the oddest feeling that all my life up to now has been the Overture."

Maxwell smiled a little despite the desperate gravity in his eyes. "Madame Rasmirovna, you have no idea."

"But there's one thing that must be settled between us before we go any further. You said this was my fight?"

"It's your city," Maxwell said, "so it has to be your fight. I'll aid in every way I can, but I don't know the terrain or the players."

"Then you are saying you are willing to follow my lead." If such an arrangement were to be unpalatable to him, as it would be to some men, it was better she discover that fact at once.

Maxwell almost laughed. "I've been following it for well over a decade already." He sobered. "What shall we do?"

Katarina thought hard. "Your friend needs a doctor. And then we need a net, a *much* larger net than we can spread alone." Two sources of said net suggested themselves. Which one? Well, the official first, and then she could consider the pros and cons of using the other. "Very well, I know what we must do to acquire one. Herr Schwieger—" The young man dragged his eyes open at the sound of his name. "You've just become Mr. Colin Ramsey for the duration, can you remember that? Mr. Ramsey has a suite of rooms next door, and he and I have an…understanding. You're enough of a height, and though he's dark rather than fair, hardly anyone has gotten a close enough look at him to have noticed one way or the other. You were coming home late with your latchkey, Mr. Ramsey, when you saw a man sneaking in through the back door. You challenged him and he stabbed you, then stole your pocket watch before he departed. Mr. Maxwell, passing by soon after, saw you bleeding to death in the shadows and ran to your aid. He will bring you to your room and call for the hotel to send for a doctor. It's…a bit unlikely, and a bit scanty as to details, but it can be done if you brazen your way through it. Do you understand?"

Emil nodded weakly.

"Yes," Maxwell said, "I understand, I can help him do that, but wait. What will you be doing while we enact that melodrama?"

"Discovering the same man in my room, stealing my jewels and escaping by that window there." Katarina indicated it with her head, smiling. "The police cast the second most efficient net of anyone I know. To make such a story stand up to scrutiny, however, I'll need to force the lock to my room—so let's get Mr. Ramsey here settled next door and then you can keep watch while I do that."

She wasn't sure what she expected. Objections? Demands for details? At least an inquiry as to whether the real "Mr. Ramsey" was expected back to-night? An open-mouthed stare and questions as to her own sanity?

But Maxwell only said, "Where are we going? If it's truly next door, I can carry Emil that far."

She took them to "Colin Ramsey's" apartment. It was a suite like her own, but smaller, and decorated with the stern polished-wood elegance that befit-ted a man rather than the pink-and-yellow opulence considered appropriate for housing a *prima donna*. Katarina gestured for Maxwell, carrying Emil, to precede her inside, then shut the door behind the three of them before reach-ing for the gas lamp and turning up the flame. The sitting room was almost aggressively devoid of personal belongings or clues to the occupant's tastes and character—only some cigarettes on one end table and a walking stick leaning up against the desk.

The bedroom was little better. Mr. Ramsey appeared to have traveled to En-gland with nothing beyond some linen in the chest of drawers, a shaving kit set neatly atop it, three suits of differing levels of formality hung in the wardrobe, one high silk hat, one bowler, one flat cap, and two pairs of boots. There was not even a book on the bedside table. Fortunate in a way; this iteration of Mr. Ramsey could conform to whatever tastes and character Emil Schwieger found it easiest to portray. The bedsheets were tightly tucked in and the pillows un-disturbed, indicating that Mr. Ramsey had not been in his room this evening.

The sitting room door swung shut behind them, plunging the room into darkness, but Katarina again found the gas lamp by touch and turned it up. "You seem to know the room well," was Maxwell's only comment, delivered in a tone of amusement rather than censure. Katarina almost paused to question him, but they didn't have time. Maxwell got Emil settled in the bed, towel pressed hard to his side, and Katarina kept well away while he did so, for blood on her gown would give the lie to the story she was about to spin.

Then Maxwell returned with her to the corridor and, without being asked, positioned himself to keep watch while she fetched the lock picks from her bed-room—he didn't question those, either—and swiftly forced the lock of her own chamber's door. She wiped her fingerprints off them and tossed them into the room, in line with the window, where a fleeing man might have let them fall.

Then, as Maxwell set up a clamor, calling for help for his injured friend from the hotel staff, Katarina opened her sitting room safe, grabbed a handful of jewelry from the jewel-box in the bedroom, strewed the contents artistically between safe and window, set the Milan Cat's Eye and a green glass vase of flowers on the hearth, and used a poker to smash both together. She replaced the poker in the rack, shoved the shutter wide, backed toward her bedroom door, took one deep breath, and put all her operatic training into a scream.

Chapter 18

The headlines in the early edition of *The Times* were everything she could desire. PRIMA DONNA'S HOTEL ROOM BURGLED; FAMOUS EMERALD MISSING. Katarina's detailed description of the man and a lengthy story about the Cat's Eye were included—above the fold, no less. Everyone in London, on both sides of the river, would be looking for the soldier. She refrained from smiling too broadly, lest it strike a discordant note in the mind of the private inquiry agent who was currently watching her from the other side of the tea-table.

The Scotland Yard Inspector had asked her permission to send for this friend of his, one Mr. Hewitt, whose unconventional methods sometimes garnered more rapid results than the police could manage working alone. The role Katarina had assumed required her to assent at once—was not the discovery of her priceless emerald a matter of the first importance?—and she had initially been glad to do so, for truly, the more eyes looking for the soldier, the better. Even when the pleasant private detective made it clear that he expected the famous *prima donna* to pay him for his efforts, she had felt no regret at involving him. But now that she sat with Mr. Hewitt in the outer room of the new suite to which the hotel had moved her, Katarina felt a *frisson* of concern. This was not a stupid man. The eyes in that bland, pleasant face were sharp and watchful. She would have to tread carefully.

At least she had provided herself with a simple, believable story, well-supported by physical clues.

"You were asleep when the incident occurred?" Mr. Hewitt peered down at the notes with which Inspector Plummer had provided him.

"I had retired to my bedchamber," Katarina corrected, "but I was not yet abed." This was easily the tenth time she had repeated her night's adventures. Each of the interviewers had relayed some detail incorrectly as he made his report up the chain of command, requiring Katarina to set matters straight over and over again. They were a disorganized lot.

Or else it was a deliberate tactic to probe her story. The possibility did not worry her overmuch—this wasn't her first time rapidly learning a part, nor for that matter her first police interview, though admittedly her first in this persona. But it was yet another a reminder not to underestimate any of these men.

"And what prompted you to return to the sitting room?" Mr. Hewitt asked.

"I heard the sound of smashing glass."

"The vase." Mr. Hewitt nodded.

"At the time, I thought it was the window, but yes, it must have been the vase."

"And you went to investigate yourself?" Mr. Hewitt put a great deal of middle-class sensibility into the question.

"Of course," Katarina replied, countering with Continental worldliness. "What were my other options? I hardly had someone to send in my stead, and the bedchamber has no other exit I could have used to retreat."

"You might have called for help," the detective pointed out.

"I did that simultaneously."

"You did, yes." Mr. Hewitt peered at the notes again. "You entered the sitting room and saw—?"

"The safe was open, and a man unknown to me was three-quarters of the way to the window. I screamed for help, which startled him, and he dropped some of my jewels, but made his escape with the rest before hotel security arrived."

Mr. Hewitt once more examined the notes. "You provided a most detailed description of him. Most useful, and most impressive. Surely he would have had his back to you in his flight to the window, and the room was in darkness?"

"The light from my bedchamber was quite bright," Katarina replied, "and the man turned when I called for help. I saw his face quite distinctly. I am certain of my description."

"Hm. Tell me about this emerald, Madame Rasmirovna."

She played up the romance of the story as much as possible—the Italian count who had sought her hand, bestowing the famous jewel as his parting gift when she refused him. The emerald known as the Milan Cat's Eye had possessed a history of checkered romance and tragedy before it ever came into her possession, and it had become an iconic trademark of the renowned diva during her European tour.

"Who knew you had this emerald in your possession?"

"Literally everyone who reads the society papers, I'm afraid."

"I am surprised a jewel of such value is not kept in a bank."

"It's rather hard to wear onstage when it is in a bank," Katarina said, irritated. "I had thought a safe in a first-class hotel would have been good enough."

"Indeed, I would have thought so as well. Erroneously, so it would seem. That has some interesting implications." Mr. Hewitt frowned into the middle distance.

"You can find it, though, can't you?" Katarina opened her eyes a little, let a little emotion 'crack' her elegant façade. "Quite apart from the monetary value, which is considerable, the stone has great sentimental value for me. I would be....deeply distressed at its loss."

"Of course," Mr. Hewitt soothed. "Was anything else taken?"

"Two pieces," Katarina improvised. "A pair of pearl earrings, and a garnet broach that belonged to my mother—garnets set in a circle around a lock of *her* mother's hair. I kept it for sentiment, but I will be honest with you, Mr.

Hewitt, I never liked it. And as for the earrings, well, they I can replace! But the emerald is quite irreplaceable. As is, I believe, the pocket watch belonging to the poor young man who was stabbed. I understand it too carries great sentimental value."

"Well, I will certainly do all I can to recover your emerald." Mr. Hewitt rose. "Oh, one last thing, Madame—you have a jewel-box in your bedchamber, do you not? I observed it during my initial investigation."

She took care not to react. "I do. What of it?"

"Why do you keep some jewels in the box and others in the hotel's safe? Why not keep them all in the safe?"

Katarina shrugged. "No reason. The safe is not large enough to accommodate my jewel-box itself—" *Please let that be true.* "—or, at least, the safes of most hotel rooms have not been large enough; I cannot remember if I performed the experiment here. In any case, I have become accustomed to the jewel-box not fitting within the safe, and one hates to tumble jewelry together with nothing to protect it, for that is how pieces are scratched. I therefore remove only the pieces of greatest value to the safes provided by the hotels I stay in, and keep the rest in the box." She raised troubled eyes to his. "It's quite distressing to think my emerald would have been safe if only I had kept it in the bedroom with me."

Mr. Hewitt shook his head. "Or I might now be investigating your assault or your death, Madame. I would far rather be chasing a thief than a murderer. The world—" He suddenly flushed a little, to Katarina's surprise. "The world would be a poorer place without your music in it."

"That is so kind of you to say." Those words came easily; she did not need to feign pleasure at the clumsy compliment.

"And I pledge to do all I can to restore your emerald to you."

Katarina thanked him prettily, with a gratitude she also did not have to feign. It appeared Mr. Hewitt accepted her story, as had his colleagues in the police force. A great relief, and one hurdle cleared. When Hewitt had bowed himself out, Katarina left her new sitting room—which notably did *not* overlook Hyde Park, but rather an inner courtyard—and tapped on the door of Mr. Colin Ramsey's more modest apartment on the other side of the corridor. Emil's weakened voice called for her to enter.

It was the world's strangest sensation to enter those rooms and find them occupied, as though the character of Colin Ramsey had escaped the boundaries of her imagination and now enjoyed independent locomotion. The sitting room now showed signs of occupation: Maxwell's coat flung across the back of the sofa, the remnants of a hastily-eaten meal on the table, the doctor's business card propped against the cigarette case. Someone had knocked one of the armchairs out of alignment in a hasty entrance or exit and had not returned it to its proper place.

The bedchamber was likewise transformed, surfaces cluttered now with medicine bottles, bandages, mugs of tea, and the other impedimenta necessary for nursing. Herr Schwieger lay in the bed, propped upright by pillows, looking pale and drawn indeed—so perhaps it would be inaccurate to call Mr. Colin Ramsey capable of independent *locomotion* precisely. Katarina smiled at the jest inwardly, but did not make it aloud. It would require too much explanation, for one thing; and for another, no humor was wanted here. The doctor had pronounced Emil Schwieger in no danger, barring infection, yet Maxwell, sitting beside him, was concealing his agitation as poorly as though he watched by a deathbed. The night spent in silent waiting had apparently not suited his active nature.

"Seventeen hours," Maxwell greeted her. "We only have until midnight. The instant that watch comes alive in his hand, he'll be gone. Do you think your police will find him before then?"

"Good morning, Mr. Maxwell," Katarina answered evenly. "Of course you are most welcome to the extraordinary efforts I have made on your behalf, and your thanks are quite unnecessary." Maxwell had the grace to look embarrassed, but only briefly. "The police are chasing a famous emerald," Katarina went on, "so I think the odds quite good. Moreover, there is another net I can deploy." She looked over to the man on the bed. "How are you feeling, Mr. Ramsey?"

"Better, thanks to you," Emil rasped. "But we must take council on this matter, now and not later."

"I think you're meant to be resting," Katarina reminded him gently. "Surely it can—"

"I don't have time. We don't have time." Emil struggled to sit up straighter, and after a moment Maxwell seemed to realize what was needed, and moved to adjust the pillows for him. "Even if you find the one afloat in 1895, they still have the one we left in 1943."

"The one left in—" Very well, then. This was a more complex situation than she had been led to believe, and that was saying something. Katarina looked about, decided on the other armchair, spread her skirts and seated herself in it, folded her hands on her lap, and only then turned her attention to Maxwell. "You did not," she said with a touch of frost, "mention this last night."

"I didn't have time to go into those details with Emil bleeding to death on your carpet," Maxwell defended himself.

"True enough," Katarina said, "but if your evil empire already has one or more of these pocket watches, what good are our efforts here? They're already—"

"—rewriting history as fast as they can. Yes. Yes, they are." Emil pushed himself upright despite his weakness, fastening feverish and urgent eyes upon her face. "You're in danger, Katarina. Madame Rasmirovna."

"*I* am in danger?" Katarina repeated. "I personally?"

"Your father was Romani, was he not?"

Katarina took a moment to exhale. If these men were to be believed, they had more pressing concerns than selling secrets to the society papers. She ought not to interpret Emil's statement as a threat of blackmail. She kept her tone pleasant. "Wherever did you come by that extraordinary piece of incorrect information?"

"He was a gypsy in the last two timelines," Maxwell said quietly. "Or at least you had reason to believe he was. Your mother always said he was a Russian nobleman, and even after you were old enough to question, you never asked her outright, because she would have answered honestly. And in lieu of the honest answer, there was still the chance that he had been a nobleman. That he had married her. That he loved her. That your mother had not sacrificed her career for a tumble with a gypsy stagehand."

Extraordinary. Beyond extraordinary. A figure her imagination had created lay injured in her bed, and another spoke words she had only ever said in the privacy of her own mind, in exactly the cadence she was accustomed to saying them. If she had needed any further proof that they knew her, that they had once known her very well indeed, here it was.

Maxwell's serious brown eyes met her own. "I don't imagine your childhood was as hard in this timeline as in the others, but I do not imagine it was easy, either."

"No," Katarina said after a moment. "It was not." She eyed Emil. "Those of gypsy blood do not fare well under your evil empire, is that it?"

Emil shuddered. "No. They— We— I was a child, you know. I didn't know any better, and I didn't actually, myself— But we, Germany, the Third Reich, we exterminated the Jewish and the Romani races. They—we—started the extermination during the war and then they—we—completed it after their—after our victory." He leaned forward again, weakness overcome by urgency. "Nazis with a timepiece will have no need for such conspiracies. They can wipe out the populations of, of those they call *untermenschen,* at the, at the source. At the dawn of history."

Untermenschen. Not a word one usually encountered in operas, but Katarina had learned enough German playing her offstage part as a fine lady to enable her to decipher it. *Less-than-human.*

There were so many appalling parts to Emil's statement that she scarcely knew which to address first.

"They can destroy whole races at the dawn of history," she said at last, slowly. "They *will* destroy whole races at the dawn of history. But—it happens then and now at the same instant, does it not? Their action and the downstream consequence. They have, right now, since the moment you left, a timepiece that will allow them to go to the earliest days of human history. Therefore, they have had the power to destroy whom they will since the earliest days of human history. I am living in a world where they have always had this power, am I not? How am I still standing here?"

Emil shook his head. "You are not yet living in a world where they have always had that power. They have the pocket watch, but it appears they have not yet determined how to use it."

Maxwell murmured, "The past can be very resistant to change."

"So it is still 'they will,'" Emil continued. "When they learn what they need to know, it becomes 'they always have'—it all changes at once, backwards and forwards, and those who live in the timeline change with it."

Katarina took her time to think that over. "I won't notice the change. But you will."

Maxwell nodded. "Our fear," he said, "is that we will watch you disappear." He held out to her the pocket watch with the smashed, impossible faces.

Katarina looked at it. "This is a talisman protecting against such a fate?"

"If it were working, it would be," Emil said. "As it is, we cannot be certain, but it is better than you having no recourse at all."

"A gentleman's pocket watch will be difficult to conceal among a lady's clothing," Katarina said, but she put out her hand for it.

"You should know what you are choosing," Maxwell said, suddenly and all in one mouthful, as though uttering a foreign phrase.

Katarina raised her eyebrows at him and deliberately lowered her reaching hand. *You're damned right I should* rose to her lips, but she took a moment to rephrase it. "Indeed, Mr. Maxwell, that would be preferable."

"It is…it is unpleasant, becoming unmoored," Maxwell said. "Like trying to breathe thin air on a mountain peak. One sees other possibilities, flickering at the corner of the eye. One grows accustomed to it after a time, but—but I'm not certain I would have chosen this unmoored life if anyone had offered *me* the choice."

"If I survive the destruction of my father's people while wearing this time-piece of yours, I will see both worlds? The ones where the Roma people never existed and the one where they do?"

"Yes," Maxwell said. He was still holding out the timepiece.

This time Katarina took it. "But if I don't wear it, I'll die with my timeline," she said, and that seemed like the end of the discussion to her.

But Maxwell was not yet finished. "If you don't wear it, you'll *vanish* with your timeline," he corrected, "and you may reappear, if and when we are successful in stopping this atrocity." From the bed, Emil gave a dismal snort. Maxwell ignored him. "But if you take it and adventure with us, and through evil chance you die outside your timeline, unmoored—that's the end. You won't reappear." He cleared his throat. "You need to know what you are risking."

"Death, without possibility of resurrection?" Katarina had to smile. "How is that different in from every other time I've risked death?"

Maxwell smiled too, reluctantly. "I suppose, when you put it that way, the warning is foolish," he admitted. "But my mother would have wanted me to ensure you understood."

"I understand," Katarina said. She closed her hand decisively around the watch and held it up for the two of them to see. She thought they both relaxed a little.

"Seventeen hours," Katarina said then, and both of their expressions sharpened as they refocused on the larger picture.

"Seventeen hours," Maxwell agreed, looking tense again.

"I believe it is time for phase two."

Maxwell nodded. "And what is phase two?"

Katarina smiled. "I said the police spread the *second* most efficient net of anyone I know. The time has come for me to renew some old acquaintances."

Chapter 19

"When I said I would give you all the aid I could," Maxwell said, trying to keep a rein on his temper, "it was with the assumption that you would, on occasion at least, accept the aid."

Twelve hours ago, his first sight of Katarina had brought a wave of joy and relief so profound his knees had gone weak. Those feelings had not faded exactly, but they were currently being dampened by a rising annoyance. Enlisting the great Katarina Rasmirovna in his battle had not, as it briefly seemed it would, solved all his problems. It was not unlike his first attempt to work with his parents—they too had been different from the images in his head, strange beings with minds of their own and opinions that conflicted with his.

Maxwell was keeping himself from hysteria only by the very narrowest of margins. The Nazis of 1943 were still in possession of time travel. The Nazi who had accidentally brought them all to 1895 was still in possession of the working timepiece. Maxwell's timepiece had been broken during the journey to Vermok, Schwieger's accidentally abandoned there. And somehow, in the midst of all of this, the past had been rewritten to eliminate a Napoleonic Empire that had once stretched to 1885 and to London—and what did that mean for the Elizabeth Barton and William Carrington who had been stranded in it? Maxwell wrenched his attention away from that question. He *did not have time* to think about it now. He had bigger problems to solve.

"You can't help me," Katarina said. "Besides, someone needs to stay with young Mr. Ramsey here, and you ought to take the opportunity to sleep while you can."

"I couldn't sleep if I wanted to," Maxwell snapped back, "and I believe I can be of more help than you realize."

They stood glaring at each other from opposite ends of Colin Ramsey's sitting room. Behind the closed door of the bedchamber, Schwieger lay in an uneasy, feverish doze. Katarina was now arrayed in an outfit that made clear that she was headed to the East End to renew those acquaintances of which she had spoken—a gown that had started as a respectable dark red walking suit, but had been magicked into something cheap-looking and showy by the addition of carelessly-hand-sewn silvery lace, ruthlessly harvested from an evening dress. A frowsy hat with stringy feathers and gloves with obvious patches completed the image. Nothing could be further from the elegant Madame Rasmirovna, but this was exactly how Katherine the music hall girl would look after an interval of twelve years. Maxwell got the impression that Katarina had quite enjoyed mutilating two gowns, a pair of gloves, and a hat to create this costume.

He was almost certain he knew where she was going, but she refused to share with him so much as the outline of her plans.

"I've done this before," she said, "I know what I'm doing, you do not look the part, and you will be under my feet. As you yourself pointed out *when you promised to follow my lead,* I know this city and you do not."

"I also have done this before," Maxwell said, "I can costume for the part, and if you're headed for the East End you'll want someone watching your back—"

"—you know nothing of the political situation in the East End, and I do not have time to school you in all the ancient history I intend to leverage—"

"There are a few things I do know," Maxwell said, exasperated. "I know that gambles of this kind proceed more smoothly when one carries an ace up one's sleeve. I know that negotiations with Arcturus Bastion require something of value to trade. And I know that Adolphus Bastion intends to make a play for his father's throne later this year."

Katarina stared at him.

"Tell me you don't know who Arcturus is, tell me his son is already in command, tell me the father treats the son with loving respect and a revolution is therefore unthinkable, and I'll agree I know too little of this version of London. But otherwise, *let me help.* I have pieces of this puzzle that you do not, and the stakes are too high for you to plan your strategy with anything less than full information. Let my fractured life be of some use to you."

There was a long pause. Then Katarina gathered the folds of her silver-trimmed skirt and seated herself in one of the armchairs.

"Adolphus is staging a revolution?" she said.

Maxwell sighed and took the chair opposite. "Now that I have your attention, it would be more accurate to say that Adolphus is *probably* staging a revolution. In the timeline I knew, he did so during a time of upheaval in 1895. An acute judge of character I had the honor to know—" He inclined his head to her. "—believed Adolphus would have struck that year even without the chaos. But in that case he would probably have failed, and it would have been better so. The London Underworld would have done better if Arcturus had remained in charge of it."

Katarina considered. "You think my judgment as an old woman is enough to drive a strategy now?"

"I've taken more drastic steps on a lighter word of yours."

"Hm." She turned it over in her mind for a moment. At last she said, "Yes, I could envision Lord Arcturus appreciating such a warning, particularly if it came in time for him to diffuse the situation quietly. In exchange, he might indeed be willing to turn over any thief and pocket watch that happened to fall into his possession. Very well, then, you may come." She smiled at him suddenly—and for the first time since he landed in 1895, genuinely. He had once known her well enough to tell her diplomatic smiles from her real ones. "Mr.

Maxwell, I should be very pleased if you would escort me to the Zoo. There we will find one Mr. Bill Ellis, who can pass the word to Lord Arcturus that I wish to—" She caught sight of his expression. "What now?"

"That's not the best idea," Maxwell said. "Ellis is helping orchestrate Adolphus' insurrection—or, at least, he orchestrated it in the world I knew. This right here is what I mean when I say we should pool information before deciding on a strategy."

"My sainted great aunt, can nothing be simple?" Katarina sighed, but changed direction gamely enough. "Very well, we'll stay here long enough for you to tell me everything else you know. But once we're in Bastion's stronghold, I do the talking."

"Of course. Will we need to find a different go-between?"

"It's not necessary. An intermediary would have been useful, as Bastion and I did not part on good terms, but I don't need a guide. I know where Lord Arcturus holds court."

"Still in the sewer?"

"Yes, indeed."

∽

rcturus Bastion's sewer continued to be one of the constants of the universe. The ceiling dripped as it always had. The throne loomed as it always had. The white-haired cadaver atop the high seat had changed hardly at all in the ten years that had passed since 1885 and Maxwell's last encounter with him, in a now-forever-lost timeline. The middle-aged Adolphus still smiled and leered as he conducted Katarina and Maxwell into his father's presence.

"You're not needed," Lord Arcturus said to his son, without actually looking at him. "Go."

Adolphus' lips tightened as he backed away. His heavy, deliberate footfalls receded, and somewhere in the darkness, a door ground shut.

The hall was so silent that each plop of dripping water echoed and re-echoed. Katarina stood quietly, without shifting her weight, but Maxwell was close enough to see the pulse jumping in her throat.

Finally the man on the throne leaned forward. In the dim light he seemed to be composed of suggestions only—glistening sharp cheekbones, wisps of hair, skeletal fingers gripping the chair arms—a charcoal sketch rather than a portrait. "My *dear* Miss Katherine. I always did admire your pluck, but even so, I must say it is a surprise to see you again."

"I'm here to pay my debts," Katarina said sweetly, in her Cockney music-hall-girl voice. Maxwell was impressed by how she had roughened it, implying a reasonable aging effect. It made him think of the Widow Ramsey, which was an association somewhere between comforting and unsettling. "And to apologize I left so sudden twelve years ago."

Arcturus leaned back in his throne. "And what else? You would not bother to come here and pay debts unless you wanted something. You never lacked for audacity."

"I also wish to share a piece of news that's to do with you," Katarina continued as though he had not spoken. She looked him straight in the eye. "It wasn't you who masterminded the burglary of that opera singer's jewels yesterday, was it?"

Arcturus steepled his fingers. "It was not."

"Then there's someone plying the trade in your territory without your leave, isn't there? And surely that's of interest to you."

Arcturus inclined his head grudgingly.

"I can put a name to the rogue burglar," Katarina said. "He's a German, newly come to London. It happens I know him. My friend and I—" She gestured to Maxwell. "We've been working with him in the south of France. But he betrayed our trust, and fled here with so much of our joint spoils it took us quite a time to follow. That burglary of the opera singer's emerald, it's his work through and through." Katarina drew from her reticule the front page of the morning's *Times,* raggedly cut from the rest of the paper. "Even if I weren't sure, this description here clinches it. Just under six feet tall, broad shoulders, clean-shaven, straw-colored hair worn close-cropped, heard to speak German by the man he stabbed—that couldn't be anyone but our old friend Fritz Mueller. And I thought my former employer—" Katarina raised innocent eyes to Bastion's face. "—would want all possible detail about the rogue who has the gall to operate without your leave."

Arcturus watched her.

"I hope you punish him," Katarina said. "Then I'll be well-satisfied for what he did to us."

"He took spoils rightfully yours and fled the country?" Arcturus repeated in a tone of consideration. "And that's an act you believe merits punishment? How interesting. I share the opinion."

It seemed to take some effort for Katarina to maintain her composure—which told Maxwell it was all part of the performance, for any real effort would have been better masked. "In this bag here, I have what I owe you," she said. "Plus twelve years of interest. And if you should discover Mueller and this enormous emerald he has stolen so publicly, why, the emerald would be yours too, of course. But maybe in that case you'd see your way clear to return to my friend and me the jewels we acquired with Mueller in the south of France? Or, if not, at the very least there's a pocket watch—my friend's personal possession. Muller took it only for the insult."

Katarina waited, poised gracefully before the throne.

After a moment, Arcturus crooked a finger at her. She came up the steps to set the reticule full of money into his hands. "You'll want to count it yourself," she said, "to be sure it's adequate."

Maxwell watched as Arcturus turned over banknotes and coin, and marked the moment when he came upon the note. In Katarina's handwriting, it laid out the specifics of Adolphus' imminent rebellion as Maxwell recalled them. Not so much of a reaction as a careful absence of one crossed Arcturus' face.

"The emerald is yours," Katarina said softly. "All I want are the lesser jewels and my friend's pocket watch. Surely the payment is sufficient for that?"

A long silence went by before Arcturus raised his eyes from the paper. "You're lying," he said, but it sounded like a desperate denial instead of a calm statement of fact.

"I am not."

"Why would you bring me a warning? You? After the disgraceful way you left my service?"

"Because the East End is better off under you than under him."

Arcturus snorted—not because he disagreed, Maxwell thought, but because he was disgusted by the truth of it.

After another moment, Arcturus turned his attention to Maxwell. "This information comes from you."

Maxwell straightened his shoulders. "Yes."

"You didn't bring it here out of the goodness of your heart. What game are you playing?"

"I've a score to settle with Mueller," Maxwell said. "I want to see him punished for what he's done, whether or not my hand strikes the blow. And I want my father's watch back."

Arcturus watched him closely. "There's more to it than that."

Maxwell met his eyes. "There is. But that's the part that concerns you." Nothing more or less than the truth.

After a moment, Arcturus nodded acceptance, and Maxwell found himself unable to breathe. Who knew the truth could be so powerful a weapon?

"Where did you get your information?" the old man demanded.

Maxwell pulled air back into his lungs. "I can't tell you that."

"Then I can't accept it as truth." Arcturus turned his attention to Katarina. "Here are my terms: In exchange for your payment of your monetary debt to me, you and your friend walk free tonight. Because I will not tolerate a rogue drawing attention to the Underworld with spectacular thefts of emeralds, I will find Mueller and deal with him. As to whether I will bestow upon you any portion of what the German may have taken from you—well. For that, my price is proof of this accusation." He indicated the folded note with disgust.

Katarina stared at him. "How am I to get proof?"

"That is your affair."

"It's not as though these people leave elaborate written plans lying about!" Katarina protested. "What would be proof enough for you? Coded letters? Photographs? A gramophone recording of a plotting session?"

"Any of those will do," Arcturus said with a humorless grin, and lifted a white hand to ring a little bell that would summon his grandson to show his guests out.

❦

They stepped out onto a cobblestone alleyway, into a rush of surprisingly cool night air. *The storm will be here soon,* Maxwell thought before he remembered he didn't need to watch for one any longer. That plot was ten years ago, two timelines ago, more than a week ago.

At his side, Katarina muttered an exasperated, "Photographs!" But then she lifted her face to the rushing wind, letting it blow her stringy feathers back from her face and taking a deep breath as though celebrating an escape. Possibly from Bastion's dungeon, possibly from something more profound. The wind turned the stinking air of the stews into something almost palatable—though now Maxwell came to notice it, the smell was not as nauseating as it had been the last several times he had walked these streets.

"That didn't go so badly," Katarina said, still speaking in a Cockney rhythm, though in an accent closer to her own. "Where on earth we're to get proof, I don't know, but at least he'll have his people looking for the German the meanwhile."

"Did you think he wouldn't?" Maxwell asked. "It's in his own self-interest, after all."

Katarina lifted a shoulder. "It is, but he does have reason to be quite angry with me. I thought him too clever to cut off his nose to spite his face, but you never know. I'm glad he restrained himself to that bit about proof at the end."

"What *did* you do with the money? Or whatever it was you were supposed to bring to him twelve years ago and didn't?"

Katarina gave him a sidelong glance. "A train ticket to the Continent, decent clothing, and proper music lessons."

Maxwell raised his eyebrows. "It must have been quite a lucrative mission. Quite a 'haul,' I believe is the correct term?"

"Indeed it was." She slipped her arm through his, surprising him a little before he considered it would be an appropriate action for the roles they were playing. The better they played those roles, the safer they would be as they made their way out of the stews.

"Photographs may actually be possible," Katarina said suddenly, several streets later. She must have been thinking over the problem all this while.

Maxwell ran a mental eye over his recollection of the photography equipment available in 1895. "Were you intending to hide a box camera in your reticule?"

"An American company has just begun selling a smaller model," Katarina informed him, "but no, I was thinking of something more elegant. There's a Welsh inventor working in London—I can't remember his name offhand, but he's truly a marvel—"

It was like hearing the tumblers of a lock falling into place.

"Gavin Trevelyan," Maxwell said, without hesitation and not as a question.

"Yes, I think that was it. I remember reading last year he'd created a camera in the shape of a pocket watch for some wealthy captain of industry. It's actually designed for corporate espionage, though one imagines it would enable other sorts of espionage equally well. The original model was utterly secret, of course, but that was a few years ago, and as of last autumn, they'd become more widespread. They can be acquired at the better sort of jeweler, and I know of at least one in London who carries them. There's something poetic in using one not-a-pocket-watch to retrieve another."

"Even if we had this secret camera," Maxwell objected, "what do you mean to photograph? I suppose you might entice Ellis and Adolphus to a meeting, but a still photograph wouldn't prove what they were saying to each other."

"You say 'a still photograph' as though you are familiar with other options. I don't suppose the future has a gramophone recorder small enough to slip into a skirt pocket?"

"It does," Maxwell said. "I've seen them. And even if I had one here, I wouldn't be showing it Lord Bastion, so why are we discussing this? Getting back to the topic at hand, what were you intending to photograph?"

Katarina shrugged. "I haven't gotten quite that far yet. Perhaps there may prove to be correspondence...? It's too soon to tell; this has all the hallmarks of a long game rather than a short confidence trick. It will require some thought to best decide how to insinuate myself."

"We don't have that kind of time," Maxwell said, suddenly gripped by the grim terror of it.

She pressed his arm. "I know. But do you have a better idea?"

The manky-smelling breeze flowed down the alleyway. A street away, male voices raised in argument. Katarina's arm was warm against his own. It seemed like the sort of moment when the proper course of action would reveal itself, diamond-clear.

After several seconds of waiting for it, Maxwell said, "No."

"Then we keep on until a better idea emerges," Katarina said, "or until we get there the long hard way. In the meanwhile, it can only be helpful to have a pocket watch camera. I can send you to Abramson Jewelers tomorrow with sufficient funds. I'll instruct you on what to obtain. Obviously I can't go myself."

"Madame Rasmirovna shouldn't be involved in this end of the puzzle," Maxwell agreed, "and Katherine the music-hall girl would attract too much attention, but perhaps you might go as Colin Ramsey—or as another gentleman of his sort, if you didn't want to use the name? It would be better for you to handle this transaction. You know what you're looking for and have an idea how to negotiate for it. There's less chance of you attracting attention."

"No, it is quite impossible that I go to Abramson's. In any guise." Katarina spoke so definitively that Maxwell looked over at her in surprise. The light of the guttering streetlamps was too poor for him to discern any change in her color, but he thought her expression might be a little self-conscious. Even a little embarrassed. Embarrassment was not an emotion he associated with Katarina

Rasmirovna. She lifted her chin in defiance of it. "Jacob Abramson and I once knew each other quite well. The last time I lived in London."

Jacob. The same Jacob the other Katarina had mourned one Christmas Eve? Well, and why not? Even if they had not been in Seward's conspiracy together, they could still have met in some kinder 1882. "You must have been close friends, if he knew both Colin and Katherine."

"My dear Mr. Maxwell, he even knew Katarina." She glanced up at him, quirking a smile. "Ah, and I see you understand the significance of that. Not many would. Is there *anything* you don't know about me?"

"Oh, there's plenty," Maxwell said. "I've only ever known what you've chosen to share. What your counterparts chose to share, I mean." That did not seem to satisfy her, so he offered, "You always knew all about me, far too much for my comfort."

"You mean *they* did."

"Well, if it comes to it," Maxwell said, "I knew them and not you. The things I think I know about you could prove to be wrong. My assumptions could trip me at any point." The buildings of that clustered financial district known as "the City" had come into view, and the sight of them made him think of the Exchange—of trades, of gambles. And there was an idea. He smiled privately at the symmetry of it. "A very long time ago, before either of us could trust the other, I played a game of questions with you, trading an answer for an answer. Shall we try that now, rebalance the scales a bit? I'll even spot you two-to-one odds, to compensate for the knowledge I brought with me."

"Hm." Katarina flashed a real smile. "That could be interesting. Very well, I agree to your terms."

"You first."

Practical woman that she was, she used her first two questions to ask him further details regarding Ellis' relationship with Adolphus. Maxwell answered as best he could, pointing out that she needn't have wasted her turn on that. She only smiled in invitation.

He hesitated. "You never told me much about Jacob Abramson."

"Oh, there's...hardly anything to tell," Katarina said. She ducked her head and cleared her throat. "Truly. There was never any chance of a future, and I knew that at the time. He had a duty to his family, a certain way he was obliged to live his life, and I could be no part of that. Nor did I wish to stay in London." She shrugged a little. "He's married now, to the daughter of family friends. They have children. Jacob is a partner in his father's business. He got the happily-ever-after he wanted." After a moment she added, "And I got mine. A shame they weren't the same one, but not a tragedy. Calf love, you know." She eyed him. "At least, I assume you know. Let's make that my next question. Have you a calf love story?"

"No, as it happens," Maxwell said. "I was...much older."

"And why did it not end happily?"

He tried to make his voice even. "She was half my age and in love with someone else. And even if she hadn't been— I'm a time traveler. I didn't belong in her where and when. I had and I have responsibilities that mean I couldn't have stayed, no matter how much I may have been tempted." Because that *was* the truth, that had to be the truth. "As with you and Mr. Abramson, we never had any chance of a future."

Katarina nodded slowly, then looked at him in invitation. "I count that as two. Your turn."

They passed into the halo of a streetlamp, then out again into the shadows, while he considered.

"You needn't answer this one," he said at last, "but I can't help wondering."

"Ask."

"Are you performing when you're Katarina or are you performing when you're Colin?"

She raised her eyebrows. "I'm always performing to some extent."

"Well, of course. I mean to say, when you're alone, which one are you?"

For a moment, he feared she had retreated into offended silence, but then he realized she was giving the question serious consideration. "I...don't know," she said at last, slowly. "I'm just...me. I never thought about it. I'm me when I'm in trousers and the world meets me squarely, and I'm me when I wear a gown and men kiss my hands." She spread her free hand for effect. "Couldn't both be real?"

Maxwell considered the matter in turn. "Yes," he said. "But that means you're always fracturing yourself to meet the world."

Katarina shook her head. "Oh, it's not quite so painful as all that. It's more...inconvenient, the need to maintain so many different personae. I admit it might be rather nice if there were a few more people acquainted with both Colin and Katarina. It's a shame the constraints of my particular circumstances do not allow it."

They walked in silence for a few moments. The stench and sounds of the river were noticeable now. "Your turn," he reminded her.

"I think," Katarina said, "that this time I shall skip the practical and the personal in favor of the philosophical. There's a question I've been pondering lately, and I'd be interested to hear your perspective."

"Yes?"

"What does one do after one gets what one wants?"

Maxwell paused. "I wouldn't know."

They had reached the river, and it stretched before them with gaslight scudding across its oily surface. The buildings of Parliament shimmered golden-brown on the other side.

Big Ben made a sound like a man clearing his throat, gave voice to the opening bars of *Westminster Chimes*, then plunged into twelve deep, clanging strokes like a death knell.

Maxwell stood in the windy night with Katarina's arm through his, feeling ice cold all over. "Twenty-four hours," he said softly, once the twelfth stroke died away. "The timepiece is awake now. Anyone who finds it can use it—including that Nazi soldier, if it's still in his possession."

"I *know*," Katarina said. "But we can't change that. We can only keep trying. That, or surrender now."

"We keep trying," Maxwell agreed. He did, after all, know something about battles given up for lost that yet were won in the final moments. He could still hear Elizabeth declaiming passionately that even if one's cause was as good as lost, one did not pin the tricolor to the Tower with one's own hands.

Chapter 20

Maxwell walked through London streets at once familiar and unfamiliar. Around every corner he could see, for a moment of shimmering mirage, 1550 and 1910 and 1848 and two different 1885s, carelessly layered. He was becoming accustomed to that, and could maneuver around the sights he knew damned well were not really there, but they were still disconcerting. Schwieger had said the hallucinations inherent in being an unmoored time traveler faded. It seemed that this was not exactly true, and more accurate to say the unmoored time traveler got used to them.

Tucked safely inside his coat was a camera in the shape of a pocket watch—which turned out to have indeed been invented by one Gavin Trevelyan, because it seemed the universe had many constants, and all of them Maxwell's personal touchstones. It had been a straightforward matter to purchase it from Abramson and Son, which was a pleasant, well-kept establishment in a street of similarly pleasant establishments. Maxwell had been waited on by Katarina's Jacob—the "young Mr. Abramson," or rather the middle-aged one, easily distinguished from his white-bearded father. Jacob's dark hair and beard were only lightly touched by gray, and Maxwell estimated his age as a few years senior to Katarina—which meant, in this time and place, he was only a few years junior to Maxwell himself. Jacob's expression and manners were open and friendly, but the eyes behind the half-rimmed spectacles very shrewd indeed. No, Katarina could never have hoped to pass unnoticed here. Whereas Maxwell, just one more middle-class gentleman indistinguishable from the rest, completed his transaction in the most unremarkable and unmemorable manner.

Now he walked back to the hotel. He was thinking about the camera watch, the Bastion family drama, the lost timepiece, and the Nazi soldier, still unable to discern how to use the first two tools to solve the latter two problems. Katarina, no surprise, was envisioning a lengthy costumed infiltration of Adolphus Bastion's conspiracy, or at the very least a prolonged verbal fencing match with Bill Ellis that would end with him tricked into betraying his planned betrayal. Maxwell found it somewhat soothing that she still thought the same way she always had, but the tactics made him more uncomfortable the more deeply he considered them.

For a moment it was as though he could hear Elizabeth's voice in their final impassioned confrontation, blazing with fury as she condemned him for treating her as a pawn on a board. Trevelyan's camera watch weighed down his inner pockets, and he could almost feel the mud of a Pendoylan duck pond under his feet, a frightened Brenda Evans fighting him off, prison bars enclosing him while the monsters swept down from the mountains. He had been undone by the mistrust he had himself engendered, as he had engendered it in George Brown and the Duke of Wellington and—

It had never worked. Never *once*. Every time he tried to change the past through trickery, he failed. The only times he had even approached success was when he'd had no choice but to apprise Katarina Rasmirovna of the whole truth and she had chosen of her own free will to join him.

Suddenly he didn't think *she* was the common factor. Or at least, not the only one.

He had quickened his pace with every mental connection and now was almost running. Realizing he was attracting the attention of the sedate passers-by, he schooled himself back to a brisk walk. Even so he almost burst through the doors of the hotel, and disdained the lift to take the stairs two at a time to Madame Rasmirovna's floor. Fortunately she was alone, because he barely remembered to knock before barging into her sitting room. He found her standing before the glass, wearing a smart dark blue walking dress and adjusting a hat that was both more fashionable and more flattering than yesterday's stringy-feathered travesty.

"We're going about this wrong," he greeted her. "I've had an idea."

She raised eyebrow at him in the mirror, but her expression was amused rather than annoyed. "Good morning, Mr. Maxwell."

"Good morning, Madame Rasmirovna. I have the camera watch. But I don't think we need it after all."

Katarina turned to give him her full attention. "Continue."

"You were envisioning a long game," Maxwell said. "Which, I assume from context, refers in 1895 to something other than merely an approach to whist—"

Katarina laughed at that. "It does. The term did start life as a form of whist-playing, now I come to think of it, but these days is used more broadly. For diplomacy, confidence tricks, business ventures. Sometimes in the context of gambling on the Exchange."

"Right. But we don't have time for a long game. No, listen to me—" He raised a hand as she started to protest with the same arguments she had made the night before. "I'm not proposing surrender, and we'd go with the long infiltration approach if it were the only one available to us; but it's not. Look at this from another perspective. Let's talk about Bill Ellis."

A briefly unhappy expression flickered over Katarina's face. Was she really not guarding her reactions from him, or did he actually know her that well? "Yes," he said, answering the expression, "that's what I mean. In the first 1885 I shared with you, you and he were friends. Do you really intend to throw him to the tender mercies of Arcturus Bastion?"

Now a succession of unhappy expressions flitted over Katarina's face. "I'm not enamored of the idea," she admitted at length, "but I didn't make his choices for him. I truly would rather see the Underworld in Arcturus' competent hands rather than Adolphus' incompetent ones, and the need to find the enemy soldier and your pocket watch is bluntly worth the cost of one man's life."

"But photographs won't tell Arcturus what he wants to know," Maxwell said. "And we don't have the ability to make gramophone recordings. And Ellis *has* made his own choices and is in a position to make more of them, or he would be if he were given the opportunity to freely choose. He's a player, not a pawn on a board."

"You want me to convince Ellis to switch sides and betray Adolphus," Katarina said slowly. "Well. Well, that is indeed the shortest distance between two points."

"Then let me escort you to the Zoo." Maxwell took conscious note of her outfit for the first time. "Wait, where were you intending to go?"

"The Opera House—but never mind. We're short on time, as you so rightly say, and if we can convince Ellis this afternoon we'll want to take him Arcturus tonight, so I couldn't perform this evening in any case. I'll send word that I am still so overcome by the burglary that I require one more day's leisure to recover. Let me—" She unpinned her hat and began shaking down waves of glossy hair. "—attire myself to present a sufficiently distraught appearance to the hotel staff, so that they may take a convincing message for me, and then I'll change into yesterday's clothing and slip out the back. You do the same, and I'll meet you at the end of the street."

❧

Maxwell had never chanced to visit the London Zoo before. He had a dim recollection that the Zoological Society of London had opened its doors to the public (instead of restricting the viewing of its animals only to Society members) the year before he left London. At least fifteen years elapsed time, nearly fifty years chronological time, and it surely felt to him more like fifty than fifteen. The Maxwell Carrington he had been in 1847 had possessed no interest in animal husbandry or ornithology. He possessed none now.

He walked with Katarina Rasmirovna's arm tucked through his, her fingers unobtrusively guiding him with little squeezes and nudges, down streets that were cleaner than he had ever known London streets to be. The houses in this part of town were fine and large and well-kept, and his companion's cheap showy finery was attracting disapproving gazes from respectably-dressed gentlemen and gentlewomen passing by. Katarina responded to the stares with saucy little smiles, and most of the watchers hastily redirected their eyes.

The marble arch of the zoological gardens rose before them, and Katarina withdrew her arm. "As the marginally more respectable of the two of us, perhaps you would be so kind—?"

He bought the tickets, ostentatiously counting out the small change Katarina had remembered to provide them with. Then there was nothing for it but to promenade the walks of the London Zoo in the hope of encountering Bill Ellis.

No Wellington monster stared with dull eyes out of a tower on the other side of a moat. Maxwell had just cleared his throat to comment on this fact and ask some questions when Bill Ellis emerged from the lion house and went as white as though he had seen a ghost. *"Katherine?"* he croaked.

"More or less," Katarina told him with an impish little grin, in her roughened Cockney voice. She cocked her head at him. "Miss me?"

Maxwell had not known Ellis well in 1885, but they had encountered each other now and again in Katarina's company. Ellis had aged little in ten years—or more accurately, appeared to have enjoyed a lifetime of better health in this timeline, such that he wore his years more easily. After a moment's staring, his hand went up to pull his cap off his head. "Every day," he said—and then abruptly took a step back, as though he had not intended to admit so much. "Er. That's to say. It's been—ten years, hasn't it, or more? Katherine, where'd you *go?* Alice said you'd taken up with a foreign gentleman and gone abroad with him. Is this—?" Ellis' eyes went to Maxwell, but then frowned in confusion. It was obvious Maxwell was neither foreign nor, in the clothes Katarina had provided for the visit to Bastion's sewer, quite a gentleman.

"No," Katarina said. "My gentleman friend passed away, and I've had to return to my own life to support myself since. I met Maxwell in the course of those activities. Maxwell, this is Ellis; Ellis, Maxwell."

Maxwell inclined his head fractionally. Ellis did the same, but his attention stayed on Katarina. "Your old activities," he repeated slowly. "Surely you're not plying that trade here, without leave from…?" Now he looked at Maxwell, and changed whatever he had been about to say into a suggestive trailing off.

Katarina shook her head at once. "Of course not. We've been working in the south of France. We've just run into a bit of trouble. Double-crossed by someone we'd been working with, followed him to London. But that's not what I've come to tell you about…" She glanced at Maxwell, and he drifted away far enough to allow them the semblance of a private conversation.

He leaned with his elbows on a rail, half watching the bears in the pit below, half watching his memory of a disastrous mistake near a duck pond in Pendoylan. Would it all have gone differently if he had only thought to offer Brenda a free choice back then? Could it be possible that offering Ellis a free choice was all it would take to solve their problems now? Or could he be wrong—still, again—about how this all worked?

The conversation behind him occasionally rose high enough in volume to penetrate his thoughts. Katarina's earnest voice: *Arcturus means to crush the rebellion. I came to warn you that you've only just enough time to switch to the winning side.* That wasn't entirely true. Did it still count as offering a free choice? Ellis' voice, dismayed. Katarina again, intense: *It's too late for that. I told you, he already knows. You have just the one chance.* Ellis, in despair over what Adolphus and the rest of those loyal to Adolphus would do to him for his treachery. Katarina, darkly: *I don't think you need to worry about them.* And then more brightly, more soothingly, painting a picture of a grateful Arcturus allowing Ellis to leave the city, a nice cottage in a village somewhere, fresh air and new chances. Ellis grudgingly allowed that might be better for his family. *Family?* Katarina asked. From the rumble of his voice, Ellis spoke of them for some time. In the end, he convinced himself to come with Katarina and tell Arcturus everything.

Maxwell turned a bit, just as Katarina leaned over and gave Ellis a swift kiss on the cheek. "Tonight, then."

"Yes—"

"Ellis!" came a sharp call from further along the path. "What do you think you're doing with that—"

"—and now clear out before you get me the sack," Ellis finished, exasperated, pulling out a dirty handkerchief and making a show of wiping his face. He turned to face his oncoming angry superior, and Katarina caught hold of Maxwell's arm and drew him rapidly in the other direction. "Er, sorry sir, that's, she's an old friend. I didn't stop for but a minute's chat."

"Ellis," the supervisor's voice carried clearly, "that 'friend' of yours is quite obviously not a respectable woman—"

Katarina looked exhausted but exhilarated. "He'll do it," she confirmed in a whisper. "For his family as much as anything. Turns out he's married an old friend of mine from the Shoreditch, and cares for her daughter as if she were his own. He'll take banishment in a village for their sake, and I'll finance it if Arcturus won't. Bill's stepdaughter was quite a pet of mine, back before I left London."

Constants of the universe. "Let me guess," Maxwell said. "Annie and Margaret Drew."

Katarina nearly laughed. "Of course, you knew them."

"Twice."

"When Meg was a child, she wanted to be on the stage. Like me. What did she grow up to be?"

Maxwell smiled. "Exactly like you."

"Heavens. She'll hate a quiet country village, in that case."

"She might come back to London," Maxwell suggested. "On her own. Later."

"The Shoreditch Empire is the London Theater of Varieties now," Katarina said thoughtfully. "It's very nearly a respectable line of work. Perhaps I'll see to it she has funds enough, if she ever does want to try making her way in that world."

❧

That night the three of them went through the crowded alleyways to Bastion's sewer and Ellis stammered out his confession. Lord Arcturus received it without a change in his grim expression. The drips echoed in the silence that followed.

"There's your proof," Katarina said.

"Yes." Arcturus looked older and more tired than Maxwell had ever imagined he could look. "It's not what I wanted the truth to be...but it is the truth. Very well." He turned cold eyes to Ellis. "If you're gone by morning I will not pursue you, and I'll let my son and his supporters think you dead."

Ellis paled, but nodded. Katarina turned to him swiftly, murmuring, "Don't worry. I can help you get away." Then she looked back at Arcturus in calm expectation.

Arcturus rose from his throne and made his way down the steps. With a jerk of his chin he summoned Katarina and Maxwell to follow him.

They fell in behind, hardly knowing what to expect. "I've had my people searching for your German," Arcturus said. "Not because I expected you to bring me the proof I required, but because it was in my own interest to find him. No one plies unauthorized trade on my soil."

"And so?" Katarina inquired carefully. "You must be on his track by now, surely?"

"My dear Miss Katherine. Did you really think it would take me more than a night?" Arcturus stopped and pointed. "There."

They had reached the far wall of the sewer, where it branched into alcoves, some large enough for a man to crawl into and some only large enough for a rat, some leading to tunnels and others to dead ends. A man trying to escape Bastion's sewer in this fashion might make it out, or might wander until the press of the ceiling allowed no further movement and entombed him, gasping, where he struggled.

Arcturus stopped before an alcove where something lay in a heap, covered by a tarp. He gestured. Maxwell went to lift the shroud.

The naked body of the Nazi soldier lay on its side, stiff and hard. At this angle, the crusted bloodied blow to the back of the head was plainly visible.

"Is this your man?" Arcturus inquired from above.

"Yes," Maxwell said, though doubtless Bastion had been addressing Katarina. "That's Mueller. Did your people—?"

"No," Arcturus said. "We found him this way. Coshed on the back of the skull, neck broken for good measure, stripped of all valuables, body left naked in an alleyway." Maxwell looked up in time to catch the little smirk on the old man's face. "An ignominious end."

"He deserved an ignominious end," Maxwell said, flipping the tarp back over the contorted body and rising. "What of my father's watch?" He remembered the tale Katarina had spun. "And the emerald?"

Lord Arcturus shook his head. "We found him naked. No emerald, no pocket watch."

No.

It was like falling through a suddenly-opened trapdoor. Falling into ice water, with his stomach left somewhere high up above. They were back at the starting line, all their plans successful but the prize withheld, all the threads they might have followed snapped and useless. Unless— Maxwell looked swiftly at Katarina, hoping the old man was lying.

But Katarina's dark eyes flicked to meet his, and she nodded once. Bastion was telling the truth too.

Not the truth I wanted. "Sick" did not even begin to describe this feeling. It had never occurred to him that the two spread nets might find the Nazi but not the watch.

"He's been dead nearly two days, by the rigor," Arcturus said. "He must have been coshed almost as soon as he ran from the emerald burglary. I find it fascinating that so valuable a gem should not have surfaced, with the police and my people both searching for it."

"I should rather call it astonishing," Katarina said pleasantly. "Surely someone will lay hands on it before another day or so passes. I do hope it is one of your foot soldiers, as the emerald is of course yours by right." She paused. "Our arrangement still entitles me to the lesser gems and the pocket watch. I have honored my half of the bargain in full."

Abruptly Arcturus Bastion looked his age. "Yes," he said. "You have. Now go. I have a heavy duty before me."

As Maxwell and Katarina left, herding the frightened Ellis between them, Arcturus remounted the steps to the throne, seated himself there, and reached for the little bell.

Chapter 21

Schwieger turned the color of new milk when they told him.

That might, to be fair, have been partially the effect of the fever that still plagued his healing torso wound. Maxwell had seen such recoveries in sundry places and diverse times, and would not have considered interrupting the invalid's sleep for anything less catastrophic than the situation in which they found themselves. It would have been an early waking even for an uninjured man; the sun had yet to make meaningful headway in lightening the sky when he and Katarina returned to the hotel from seeing off the early morning train.

Bill Ellis was on that train, along with his wife and stepdaughter, the last of the banknotes Katarina had been keeping on hand, and a letter she had written to the now-ancient Sir Charles Buford, prettily requesting her old patron's aid for her friends. To call it an exhausting night would be speaking too mildly, but at least Ellis and his family were out of danger.

Immediate danger. Relatively speaking.

"The timepiece could be anywhere," Schwieger whispered. At times like this Maxwell was forcibly reminded how young he still was. "Anywhen. Whoever robbed the soldier could have taken it anywhere at all."

"Or it might well still be in the city, here and now," Katarina countered. "We should do all we can to determine which situation we're actually in." She took the chair opposite from the sofa upon which Schwieger had half-collapsed, and commenced a matter-of-fact logical attack upon the situation. "If the timepiece is still in the here-and-now, that argues for a different strategy than if it is not."

"What different strategy could we possibly pursue?" Emil said, despairing. "We can't travel anywhere in either case."

"Couldn't we send up a flare?" Katarina asked. "Or—or something similar? A message requesting reinforcements? Aren't there more time travelers than just the two of you?"

The old rage rose up in Maxwell's throat. "There used to be," he snarled in Emil's direction. "But who the hell knows where my parents are now. Or if they are."

Katarina ignored his tone. "If the timepiece is abroad in 1895, we need to find it," she repeated. "And if it's not, we need to know that. We need a...a tracker, something like a truffle hound or a magnet." She reached into her reticule and drew out Maxwell's dead timepiece, turning it thoughtfully so that the lamplight danced on the scratches. "Can one of these tell when another is close by? I imagine it's not easy, or it would have been the first thing you tried, but is it possible?"

"It is most likely possible to rig a *functional* one to detect another," Emil said, "but we never did. Rosamund always played guardian angel, watching us from headquarters."

"Well, we're on our own now," Maxwell said. He eyed the timepiece Katarina was toying with. "If only we knew more about how it worked... I can't believe your headquarters didn't have a technical expert."

"We *did*," Schwieger snapped. "More than one. Sui. Rosamund. Wadi. Just not me."

Maxwell turned away from him in angry disgust. For several minutes he stared out the window at the early morning sky. There was a streak of blue in it today, piercing the cloud like the beam of a construct's headlamp. Meg Drew—Meg Ellis—would grow up under a country village's blue sky, she and her mother and stepfather safe away from the Bastion family drama, because Maxwell had known how that drama would play out, because the universe seemed insistent upon retaining certain constants.

Universal constants from timeline to timeline. Maxwell's fractured life was finally giving him the information he needed to tell the truth in a way that mattered. "Right," he said. "Then we need to come up with our own technician. What was that phrase you used back in AfterLondon, Schwieger? A 'Hail Mary pass'?"

"Now *that* sounds blasphemous," Katarina murmured.

Maxwell turned to meet her quirked smile, finding his spirits buoyed at once and drastically. "It does, doesn't it? What we need is a genius inventor. And I know where to find one."

"Here and now?" Katarina asked, surprised.

"Here and now. That Gavin Trevelyan you mentioned, the famous Welshman? The one who created the camera watch? I made inquiries. He lives in Kensington."

"Why in the world would—" Katarina visibly stopped herself. The little smile flitted over her lips again. "I'm sure eventually I'll get used to this feeling of context changing under my feet. It's exciting, no doubt about that, and in time perhaps it will become less unsettling. I don't know much about this Trevelyan, Mr. Maxwell, but I do know he's a recluse. Why would he open his door to you, let alone help you?"

"That's a long story," Maxwell said, re-energized at the thought of this new possibility. "I can tell you on the way. Or if you prefer," he amended, "I can tell you when I return. You're overdue for some sleep."

"So are you," Katarina pointed out, rising. "I'll come with you if we can go and return before I'm due at rehearsal. I really can't keep claiming I'm too upset to perform and yet keep running about town, even in disguise; each day increases the risk someone will call upon me and discover I'm not here."

❧

"Are you certain you wish to do this?" Maxwell asked one final time, as he waited with Katarina for a cab. "Perhaps you ought to be resting, if you intend to perform tonight. I wouldn't want to see you imperil your career." He hesitated. "It's…something nice, in the middle of all this wretchedness, that you did finally get what you always wanted."

She gave him a rather odd look from under the frowsy feathered hat. "Rather frivolous, in the face of the wretchedness."

"But still. I always knew you fighting wars, and singing was what you intended to do when the war was won. It does seem a shame to drag you back onto the battlefield."

She smiled at that. "Oh, Mr. Maxwell. I haven't felt this alive in—five or six years at least. Here's a cab." She waited until he had handed her in, settled himself beside her, and informed the driver of the address, then continued, "Now, this man we're going to see?"

"Professor Gavin Trevelyan, late of Pendoylan, Wales," Maxwell said. "A famous inventor, as you already know. He lectures twice a month at the University of London and approximately once a week he is to be found in its laboratories. Otherwise, he works in the private laboratory he has fitted out in the house adjoining his, which is accessible through a courtyard and closed off to the outside. He does not welcome visitors of any pretensions during working hours, save an occasional tour of inspection by his patron, Lord Seward." Maxwell looked more carefully at Katarina's face as he spoke the name, but she showed no recognition. "Many students at the University have asked to be taken on even in menial roles for the opportunity to learn from him, and he has turned them all down in blistering terms. He is known for his scathing manner in the classroom."

"And this is a friend of yours?" Katarina murmured. "I believe I'd cross the street to avoid meeting him."

Maxwell wished for someone with whom to exchange amused glances. "His rudeness has its own—" He was *not* going to say 'charm.' He settled on, "One gets used to it," then went on, "He enjoys music, and is often to be found escorting his wife to musical performances, either as the guest of Lord Seward or in humbler seats he purchased himself. He was overheard to speak with pleased anticipation of attending the performance of a noted European *prima donna* recently arrived in London." He managed a seated half-bow.

"Indeed? How flattering. A shame I couldn't have done this under my own name, as he might have suddenly become at home to visitors if I called."

"He'll be at home to us," Maxwell said, more confidently than he felt.

"Do you intend to spin a tale to get us past the threshold?"

"No," Maxwell said, "Trevelyan isn't a pawn on a chessboard either. We won't gain his trust by lying to him."

"You mean to tell him the truth?" Katarina stared at him. "He'll never believe—"

"You're right," Maxwell said. "I mean to show him the truth."

"It's a convincing sight," Katarina admitted. "Very well, what else do I need to know of this long story you mentioned?"

Maxwell got through the basic outlines, keeping his focus on the high level of monsters and constructs and revolutionaries, omitting the details of complex and unhappy interpersonal relationships. He had barely concluded the account when the cab pulled up to the Trevelyans' front door.

He supposed there was this to say for it: he had left himself no time to worry.

He handed Katarina down from the cab, paid the driver, and offered her his arm as they made their way to the front door. They were an oddly-assorted pair, he dressed as gentleman and she as an actress of a dubious nature, but perhaps that was as well. Piquing one's quarry's interest could still be a legitimate tactic, even if one meant to tell the truth afterward.

The door was opened by a maidservant in a cap and ruffled apron, and just beyond her, Brenda Trevelyan herself was stripping off her gloves and unpinning a pretty flowered hat.

Maxwell took a deep breath. "Good afternoon, madam. I'm afraid I haven't a card on me, but my name is Maxwell. It is most urgent that I see Mr. Trevelyan."

The maid looked back at her mistress, and Brenda Trevelyan stepped forward. Her smile was pleasant, even apologetic, but her stance was unyielding. "I am so sorry," she said, "but my husband's scientific pursuits take up the vast majority of his time. He is unable to be at home to callers. It would be better that you state your business by letter."

Maxwell looked to Katarina, who removed the pocket watch from her reticule. It was not as impressive a sight as it would have been when working, but even broken, the strange inner gears held the attention. Katarina held it out to Brenda, and Maxwell saw Brenda's attention catch.

"Would you please just take him this?" Katarina asked.

For good measure, Maxwell fumbled for the newly-acquired camera watch and opened it for comparison. "Tell him that we think the man who created *this* would be very interested in the technological developments that created *that*."

Brenda reached out for the watch in Katarina's hand and started to smile. "What in the world—?"

Maxwell tried not to cringe as Katarina's hand fell away, leaving Brenda in possession of the timepiece. If he watched Katarina Rasmirovna vanish now, after so much— He wrenched his mind back to the job at hand. "If your husband is not interested in discussing this technological innovation, we will of course be needing it back."

Brenda regarded him with measuring eyes. Then she motioned to the maid to step back and for Maxwell and Katarina to step inside. "Wait here," she said.

She returned some five minutes later, without the watches and with a small smile. "Come this way."

Brenda led them down a corridor whose polished floorboards were covered with rugs too evenly-hooked to be anything but machine-made, and whose walls boasted pretty blue-flowered paper, assorted framed sketches, and gas lamps every few feet. To the right, an open door led to a charming and impeccably tidy sitting room, obviously meant to entertain visitors, but Brenda Trevelyan's bustled skirts swept past it, past the formal dining room on the corridor's other side, and on toward the back of the house, where a side door led out into a little courtyard. On the other side of the courtyard sat the building that housed Trevelyan's laboratory, guarded as if by a moat from the demands of the outside world, and Brenda opened the door and gestured them to precede her inside.

Yet another constant of the universe. No matter what timeline he was born into, Gavin Trevelyan contrived the finest laboratory his funds could command—and his funds in this time were apparently quite comfortable indeed. He must have hired builders to knock out every non-load-bearing wall that had once made the ground floor of this house the twin to the one in which his family resided. The result was an enormous open space even bigger than what Maxwell remembered from the 1885 warehouses. And it was *bright,* blindingly bright, brighter than a farmer's field under midday sun, despite the heavy oil-cloth that covered the windows on three sides. Trevelyan had rigged electric lights in this timeline, as he had in the one in which Maxwell had first made his acquaintance.

There was the blacksmith's forge, its coals cool and its bellows resting today. There was the spinning wheel and the loom. There was the litter of sketches and models and metal bits and tools—in no timeline, apparently, was Trevelyan a tidy man. So exact was the resemblance to the timelines he remembered that Maxwell had a sudden flash of superstitious dread, and found himself looking around for a construct—but there were none, of course. No need of them.

Could that be called a silver lining of this Nazi-polluted timeline? He didn't wish to give them credit for anything. Surely there was some way to keep this effect, to render monsters and constructs unnecessary, after otherwise resetting the timeline. Surely?

One problem at a time.

Near the door through which they had entered was placed a combination desk and worktable with a relatively clear surface. A chair was behind it, facing the door, but Gavin Trevelyan instead awaited them leaning against the front of the desk. He was wearing his usual laborer's shirt and trousers and his usual cynical half-smile, and he had the broken timepiece in his hand, the chain trailing through his fingers. In the five minutes he had been in possession of it, he had gotten the back casing off, and a small blinking blue object cast rhythmic light on his face. He looked up from examining this marvel as his guests entered.

"Maxwell, is it?" His voice came as something of a shock—a cool, correct London accent with nothing of Wales about it. The smile was subtly wrong as well—more genuine warm amusement than Maxwell remembered ever having seen on Trevelyan's face. "So that cub Carrington wasn't trying to just humbug his way in here after all? You got your stories crossed, I think; he said I'd met you at dinner party, which I have not. If he'd showed me this to begin with, he'd've gotten considerably further considerably fas—" Trevelyan straightened suddenly, dropping the pocket watch on the worktable behind him. "Good God, man, sit down before you fall down."

Trevelyan's face was out of focus, with swirling black at the edges, and his voice was almost lost through the roaring in Maxwell's ears. Two sets of hands pushed Maxwell into a chair, and Maxwell dropped his own head between his knees.

When his vision cleared, he was sitting on the straight-backed chair apparently snatched from behind the desk, bent over with a cool hand applying pressure to the back of his neck. He could see his own shoes, new brown leather boots bought with Katarina's money two days previously, and further off, a set of laborer's workboots that could only belong to Trevelyan's feet.

Voices came as though from a great distance.

"—brandy. At once." Brenda Trevelyan spoke firmly, obviously to a servant. "Then tell Cook we will want tea and sandwiches, but the brandy first."

"Yes'm, at once—" The maid's voice, followed by a patter of feet over cobblestones, receding, running for the house.

"Maxwell." The pressure on Maxwell's neck eased, and Katarina came into his field of vision, slipping around his side to kneel in front of him. It must have been her hand on his neck. Yes, it felt the same—pleasantly cool—when she pressed her fingers to his wrist. She smiled up at him, but it looked worried. "Are you back with us?"

"Yes," he said, straightening in the chair and freeing his hand to rub both of them hard over his face. "Yes, fine. Everything's fine. Oh, thank God, I thought they were dead."

"'They'?" Trevelyan's voice. Maxwell looked up. Trevelyan gave him a measuring look, appeared to decide his guest was well enough that he need not hover, and stepped back to lean against the desk again.

"Yes," Maxwell said, "'they.' At least— Did he have a girl with him? A minx barely out of the schoolroom, brown curls and blue eyes? For that matter, was he well? Were they well, I mean? Injured at all? How did they look?"

"Well enough," Trevelyan said, half-closing his eyes as though to visualize. "Tired-looking. Not injured—at least—there might have been something wrong with the right arm? But not obviously injured. Dressed in the most extraordinary suit of clothes, like something out of a costume box. I didn't see a girl—"

"I did," Brenda said. Maxwell craned around in the chair to see her standing by a bell-pull she had apparently used to summon the maid and send her running for brandy. She smiled at him and Trevelyan both. "There was a girl selling flowers who seemed to be watching Mr. Carrington rather intently. I think she did have brown curls."

"Thank God." Coming to a belated remembrance of appropriate manners, Maxwell struggled to his feet. "Madam, I am so sorry to have imposed upon your household. I—"

"Don't apologize," Brenda reassured him. "You look to have traveled long and far."

"You—" Hysterical laughter would *not* serve him well here. He swallowed it down. "You have no idea."

"I have some idea." Trevelyan picked up the pocket watch again, opening the catch and examining the faces inside. "I did try the buttons, but nothing happened. I assume there's a sequence?"

"There is," Katarina said. "But the device is broken."

Trevelyan glanced at her, possibly for the first time, and stopped short. He hesitated—opened his mouth—then apparently decided not to ask the question that had arrested his attention. He resumed his study of the watch. "I hoped the cracked faces indicated only cosmetic damage," he said. "That blue bit appears to be functional, but perhaps other parts of the internal workings are impaired." He turned the pocket watch over and let it fall open in his hand. "Longitude, latitude," he said. "Day, month, year. An outfit out of a costume box. If the device were working and I had pressed the correct sequence..." He looked up, unexpectedly piercing eyes fixed on Maxwell like a falcon striking. "Where would I have found myself?"

"Anywhere and anywhen you like," Maxwell said. "Future, or any part of the past where you haven't already been."

"Right, so this'll be taking longer than a quarter-hour." Trevelyan looked around. "I haven't chairs enough—I never want to be encouraging folk to overstay their welcome—but those boxes are sturdy and can serve as seats."

Maxwell started to follow, to help shift them, but the maid pattered back in with the brandy at that moment. "My husband can see to it," Brenda said gently at his elbow. "Sit and rest and sip this."

Maxwell took it from her and touched it to his lips out of politeness, but did not resume the chair. "No, there's no need, thank you. I'm recovered, truly." And there was too much in urgent need of his attention for him to risk succumbing to the lure of strong drink. He set the untasted brandy on Trevelyan's desk.

"Cook says tea and sandwiches will be ready directly, ma'am," the girl said to Brenda.

Brenda nodded dismissal to the maid. "Bring a tray when it is ready, Ellen, thank you."

Trevelyan had by that time arranged some boxes and the two chairs in a semi-circle of sorts, with a larger box in the middle to serve as a table. Brenda gave it a pained look, and Trevelyan made an offering movement with a paint-stained dropcloth. Brenda sighed and shook her head. She gestured Katarina toward one of the chairs and took the other herself.

"Right," Trevelyan said, leaning back against his desk. "We got a bit de-railed over the matter of introductions, didn't we?" The cool London accent had almost entirely seeped out of his speech by now, and the familiar rhythm of Wales had replaced it. "Mr. Maxwell, I believe?"

"Yes, sir." Maxwell took a step toward him and offered his hand. "Professor Trevelyan?"

"Indeed I am. You've made the acquaintance of my wife already."

"And may I present my companion—"

"Miss Ramsey," Katarina said, overlaying her words with the usual delicate hint of Cockney. Trevelyan looked at her again, and again seemed to stop himself from commenting.

"So then, Mr. Maxwell," he said. "I must be commending you for knowing the way to catch an engineer's attention. You've mine, sir, not a doubt of it. Why have you brought me this unbelievable invention?" His eyes glinted. "Were you thinking I could fix it for you?"

"Is it *possible* for you to fix it for us?" Maxwell stared at him. "We were hop-ing for a method by which we may locate its mate."

"So there's more than one?" He had never before seen Trevelyan smile so much at once. "Fascinating. Yes, with a bit of time to study the mechanism of the working one, no doubt I could effect a repair, assuming it doesn't have need of materials beyond my reach. And then we could discuss how it might be tracked. That would depend on how it works—the theory that underlies the internal mechanisms. Are you intending to tell me what the blue bit is?"

"If I could understand it myself," Maxwell said, "I'd try to share the infor-mation."

Trevelyan barked a laugh. "I take it you had no hand in the creation."

"Not a bit," Maxwell said. "Not even close. I can't even truly claim to be an expert user; though I've owned it for many years, it's still surprising me."

"Who did create it, then?"

"That's…a long story."

"In that case, may I suggest you begin at the—" The door creaked, heralding the arrival of the maids and the tea service, and Trevelyan closed the timepiece in his hand, hiding the blinking blue curiosity and continuing smoothly for the servants' benefit, "Of course I can mend your watch while we talk; an old friend like you, after all, glad to do you a favor." He waited until the tea was laid out and the maids had departed, and then an extra few seconds for good measure, before he opened his hand, set the timepiece on his desk, and went for his tools.

A piercing cry, gull-shrill, rose out in the courtyard, and Maxwell lurched upright, heart in his throat. Katarina had jumped to her feet as well, but Brenda only smiled as she went about the ritual of pouring the tea. "No, no, nothing to be alarmed about, it's only the children. My three youngest—they will be just awake from their afternoon nap, and out for playtime with their nurse. They do make an embarrassing lot of noise, don't they? But I assure you no one's being harmed."

Katarina subsided, looking embarrassed. Maxwell likewise relaxed, not feeling any embarrassment at all. Katarina glanced curiously toward the windows that overlooked the courtyard. "Does the noise not disturb you, Mr. Trevelyan?" she asked.

She had beaten Maxwell by a bare second to the question. Both the Gavin Trevelyans he had met had been quite rigid in their insistence of needing peace and quiet to work.

But this Gavin Trevelyan only cast Katarina a puzzled glance as he returned with his hands full of delicate instruments. "What, the lads? I suppose it does sound as though they're murdering each other, now you mention it."

Maxwell took the cup Brenda handed him and wandered over toward the window that faced the courtyard. These alone of all the windows on the ground floor were free of oil cloth, covered only by a curtain, and there was a hook to loop the curtain over. One could sit at that worktable, Maxwell thought, with that curtain pulled aside, and look up from one's work to see three little boys shrieking as they chased each other, their nurse in good-humored attendance. Brenda might be found playing out there with the children, or she might— Maxwell's eyes found a first story window just above the courtyard, in direct line with this one—she might sit just there, at that desk in that window nook, writing. Maxwell turned back to the room to find that Trevelyan was absorbed in examining the timepiece, but that the other two were watching him.

"Is he your nephew, this young Mr. Carrington you're so worried over?" Brenda asked gently.

"He's...family," Maxwell said, and took a swallow of tea so that he need not say more.

He almost choked; the cup tasted as though it were half sugar. Brenda smiled at him blandly, and Maxwell conceded he probably looked as though he were in need of the accepted treatment for shock. He took another swallow.

"So then," Trevelyan said without looking up, "I take it you're not meaning to leave me one of these?"

Maxwell felt all his muscles tense. He tried to speak calmly. "No, I can't do that."

"Then you've no payment but your tale, is that it?" Trevelyan glanced up just long enough to cast him a look Maxwell abruptly realized was amusement. "Well, let's have it. I've set out chairs and everything. Start talking."

Maxwell exhaled. "Very well."

He spoke of chess games across time, of the evil empire waiting in the wings, of the Seven and the Five and the last remaining member of the fraternity, Emil Schwieger. That story led naturally enough to a conclusion where Maxwell found one of the abandoned timepieces in a garret and joined Schwieger's quest. In the interests of keeping to the most direct path, he chose not to speak of monsters, constructs, the various versions of Katarina, or the Welsh student who had turned Britain into a funeral pyre for the woman he loved and died in an attempt to redeem his mistake.

Trevelyan had ceased his work somewhere around the middle of the story, and as it drew to a close he sat with his hands uncharacteristically still and his eyes on Maxwell's face. An enormous time seemed to have passed, though of course there were no sunbeams shifting on the floor to hint at it. The children were still playing their shrieking game outside.

Brenda shook herself as though coming out of a dream.

Her husband's unsettling gaze stayed on Maxwell. "That's not all of it," he said.

"No," Maxwell said, which was not the same thing as promising to tell the rest.

Trevelyan smiled in appreciation of the difference. "I'll help," he said. "Of course I will. Once I have this one working, it's a matter of determining what byproduct it gives off when it does work. Heat? Low-spectrum light? Noise pitched too low to hear? And the constructing of a dowsing rod proceeds from there. I'm working with a young Italian, name of Marconi—he may have some ideas. I expect you'll be wanting me to keep this matter to myself, though?"

"If you please," Maxwell said. "And thank you. And—when?"

Trevelyan shrugged helplessly. "There's no way to tell. As quick as I can. Give me an address where I can reach you and I'll inform you the same hour I have something for you to test."

"You'll need to keep the timepiece here," Maxwell realized.

"I can't very well fix it or build a dowsing rod for it if it's somewhere else." Ah, and there was the impatient, caustic Trevelyan he remembered. It was comforting, somehow. "You'll have to trust me with it for a time."

⁓

"It's sweet of you to worry over me," Katarina said as the cab took them back to her hotel. "But it's all right, truly."

Maxwell had been riding with his eyes fixed straight ahead, resolutely not thinking about the danger she was in. Now he turned to look at her in surprise. How had she read the thought?

"He can't mend it with it clutched in my fingers," Katarina said. "You don't know that it keeps me safe, you don't even know that I need to be kept safe, and even if we did know, my safety pales in comparison with the true task at hand."

Maxwell had to unclench his jaw before he could answer. "All true. I still don't like it."

"I could be wearing it and be run down by runaway carriage horses," she pointed out. "If I vanish, you'll just have to carry on the fight for me."

That felt like standing under a cold shower-bath. "No."

She raised sculpted eyebrows at him. "No?"

"I've done that. Twice. I don't care for the experience."

She was watching him too closely, and he was utterly failing to keep his inner anguish off his face. He was on the cusp of giving too much away. "It's foolish," he said, "but I can't help thinking you'd be safer if you didn't sing tonight."

"That is factually untrue."

"I know. It just…feels as though we're balanced on top of a precipice."

"Mr. Maxwell," Katarina said, "all life is lived balanced on the top of a precipice."

He snorted.

They both were silent for a time, and then he said, "There is nothing I can say to stop you taking this risk, is there?"

"Your inventor has to keep the timepiece to fix it," she said. "Without it on my person, I am not less safe in the Opera House than in the hotel." She smiled a little. "And to answer the question—no, Mr. Maxwell, there isn't."

"Suppose," he said, after another long pause, "suppose you just say 'Maxwell'? You did, in Trevelyan's laboratory."

"Did I? It must have slipped out because I was worried about you." Maxwell turned his head to catch her expression, but Katarina was searching through her reticule for something, her head bent and her face half-hidden. He couldn't be sure if he really saw a hint of a smile or if it was only his imagination. "Very well, I'll carry on with that if you like. And in that case I suppose you had better call me Katarina."

Chapter 22

They reached the hotel without an instant to spare. Katarina changed clothing and persona, rushed off to the theater, rehearsed, performed, collected accolades on her performance and sympathies on the burglary, and returned to the hotel.

She had slept not at all the night before, and very little the two nights before that. When she finally reached her bedchamber, she had no energy to spare for philosophical contemplations while brushing her hair. She did not even bother braiding it before collapsing into bed.

This left her with plenty of opportunity to think the following morning, as she went through the irritating lengthy process of brushing out the snarled birds-nest that had resulted from her laziness. At least the sleep had cleared her head, for she found her thoughts arriving at a useful conclusion. Once her hair was brushed—not bothering to pin it up, and donning only a tea-gown so that she need not waste time fussing with corsets—she crossed the hall and knocked on Colin Ramsey's sitting room door.

Maxwell answered it. "Um," he said, and fastened his gaze on her face. "Good morning."

"Good morning." She breezed in past him. Too late she realized his slight flush was due to her loose hair and all the myriad social signals it conveyed, and lifted her eyes to the ceiling in silent exasperation both with herself and with him. It was so much easier to avoid sending these unwanted messages when dressed as Colin Ramsey, and she could almost welcome the idea of a life spent just in that persona, where men would deal with her as herself and not through this layer of artifice. She headed for an armchair, taking firm possession of the room.

"Any news from Trevelyan?" Only then did she see the figure stretched out on the sofa. "Oh, good morning, Emil. How are you feeling?"

"Better," Emil said. His color was still poor and his voice weak, but she thought the fever might be abating. "No, nothing from Trevelyan."

"And nothing from the police or Hewitt either, I suppose, or you would have said?"

Maxwell took the chair opposite her. "Exactly."

"It occurred to me that we need not sit idle while waiting for Trevelyan's mechanical bloodhound," Katarina said. "A little simple logic tells us where best to search for the timepiece under the circumstances."

Schwieger looked bewildered. "How so? It could be anywhere—"

"No, it could not be." Maxwell said it at the same time as Katarina did, a tone of realization in his voice, and she glanced at him with a small smile. He apologized and waved for her to continue. "It could not be," she repeated, turning to Emil. "None of Bastion's people have it, though they brought him the body. Therefore, it was stripped by someone else, someone not of Bastion's company—"

Schwieger interrupted, "Or one of Bastion's people has it and is lying to—"

"No," Katarina cut him off sharply. It might be another advantage to dressing as Colin Ramsey, or at least to wearing her hair pinned up respectably; the less feminine her persona, the less often she was interrupted by the opposite sex. She took back the stage: "Don't tell me how the underbelly of my city works, young man. You've spent no time at all here. I tell you from my own personal experience, twelve years old though it may be, that it is mathematically possible, but unlikely in the extreme, that any of Bastion's people would risk his wrath over something so trivial. As the local expert to whom you should be deferring, I am telling you we may safely assume none of Bastion's people have it. Therefore, someone else stole the watch when they stripped the soldier. It's a very old trick down in Spitalfields, and a very different class of thief."

"I don't understand," Emil admitted unwillingly, after a moment.

"Some burglaries are carefully planned," Katarina said. "Orchestrated works of art, where every piece is in place the instant it is needed. Stealing plate, for instance." Maxwell nodded, a small smile on his lips, but did not speak. "It runs like a military operation. There are those who watch the house that will be targeted, and those who watch the policeman who walks the nearby beat. There are the burglars who do the actual stealing, climbing trellises and employing lock picks and the like. There is the cabman who drives the cab. The burglars enter the cab with their spoils and are driven to the home of the receiver, who is usually set up in some other profession—bootmaker, watchmaker, tailor—but whose real income comes from theft. The burglars usually inform them when they intend the robbery to occur and what they believe they will obtain, and so the receiver keeps a silver pot ready on a slow fire. The burglar and cabman unload their spoils, the cabman is paid a percentage of their worth, the cabman drives off, the receiver immediately commences melting down the silver plate, and within a quarter of an hour there is no longer any crest available by which it may be identified."

"But if they do that—" Emil sounded distressed. "The timepiece might well already be melted to component parts, and—"

"No. That's the point." Katarina could not keep the exasperation from her voice. "That is the kind of operation Bastion runs, and that is not at all what happened here. We're not dealing with a gang of semi-professionals, only with one desperate person. Only the most base kind of thief kills and strips a body in the night. We're not looking for a receiver or a fence, not one under Bastion's control and not one under the control of one of his competitors. We're looking for a *pawn shop*."

Emil relaxed, both enlightened and relieved.

"The trick, of course, will be discovering *which* pawn shop it went off to. There's no way to shortcut that process—we must just do it. I have a few hours before I am due at the theater, if Mister—if Maxwell would care to accompany me?"

Maxwell nodded at once.

"Then I shall change my clothing." She rose and headed for Schwieger's bedchamber, remembering only when her hand was on the doorknob to turn and add, "It would be better for Colin Ramsey to survey the pawn shops. I won't be a moment."

At least they didn't blink an eye at that.

She played it off with confidence while Schwieger was nearby to hear, to quash his superior attitude as it deserved to be quashed. Alone with Maxwell, she was more honest. "I must remind you my information is twelve years old. Once I knew which pawn shops had sworn fealty to Bastion and which operated independently, but..."

"Once I knew similar things," he said, "but my information is likewise ten years old and two steps sideways on the one side, and twenty-five years... young, is that the right word?...on the other." He seemed unconcerned. "We'll manage."

They did manage, all that morning and early afternoon, up and down the City Road, in and out the Eagle. They tried the depressing "dolly shops" of the East End, the severely respectable licensed pawnbrokers of Cheapside, and even the opulent shops of Houndsditch, Katarina carefully modulated Colin's accent and bearing to suit each, noting that Maxwell did the same.

In the dolly shops, they pretended to believe the fiction of having entered a second-hand clothing shop, examining the plentiful petticoats, gowns, shawls and bonnets hanging from the walls, turning their attention then to the articles of male clothing sitting about in heaps, and gradually drifting by degrees toward the back room, where stolen or illegally pawned merchandise might be traded. In the licensed pawnbrokers, Katarina was more open—or at least, stuck more closely to the story she had spun for Bastion. She showed the pawnbrokers the artist's sketch of the Nazi thief that had appeared in the paper, carefully described the outside of the stolen watch, and promised a reward far exceeding its value (and incidentally no involvement of the police) if the pawnbroker in question could produce it. In the wealthy Houndsditch shops, she must be more circumspect, avoiding any hint of an accusation that the proprietor could ever have knowingly accepted stolen goods.

The proprietors represented each and every one of London's myriad ethnic groups, but not quite indiscriminately. They tended to cluster together, so that one might walk past a whole row of Irish dolly shops or a whole street of Jewish pawnbrokers. Katarina avoided only the ones whose loyalty to Bastion she had reason to believe firm, scouring the others tirelessly, repeating the same story over and over again.

She was at the point of excusing herself to return to the hotel and thence to the theater, when Maxwell, walking beside her, suddenly stumbled.

It was an odd, lurching movement, not that of a man catching his foot on a raised cobblestone, but that of a man missing a step when descending a staircase. Katarina turned to steady him, the easy motion of a fellow gentleman, or perhaps the deference of a younger gentleman to an older one, the casual physical contact that she would not have been allowed had she been garbed as a woman. She said, "All right there?" in a perfunctory manner, but she was thinking about the ludicrous differences between her male and female personae, and she did not realize at first how pale his face had gone.

They were standing across the street from Abramson's Pawn Shop, the only one in the entire East End she dared not enter. She'd been more than half hoping it would not be necessary, that they would find Maxwell's watch before reaching Abramson's, or that the little pawnbroker establishment would prove to be boarded-up and abandoned. No such luck, unfortunately. The name was still bravely painted on the unmistakable three-ball sign, just as it had been when she frequented this area twelve years previously; and through the unshuttered window, she thought she actually glimpsed Jacob himself waiting courteously on a customer. Interacting with him was a risk she simply could not take.

She turned to Maxwell. "I'll need you to handle this. I…haven't had the opportunity to tell you before now, but I know the man who runs this shop. Once upon a time I knew him quite well, in fact—"

That was when she noticed the wideness of Maxwell's eyes.

"You have told me this," Maxwell said hoarsely. "You told me this three days ago, the night before you sent me to purchase a camera watch from him. Three days ago he was a jeweler, not a pawnbroker."

Katarina shook her head impatiently. "Of course I never told you that. He's always been a—"

"He has *not* always been a pawnbroker." Maxwell's expression was a bare degree away from frantic. "Two days ago he was a jeweler and two seconds ago this shop had a different name painted over the door and *didn't you feel that,* just now?"

Belatedly she connected this bizarre conversation with Maxwell's stumble. "So this is what it's like," she said slowly, "when one changes with the timeline."

"We should go back to Trevelyan's," Maxwell said, pulling himself straight. "You might not survive the next timeline change."

Katarina shook her head. "I'm due at the Opera House."

"For how much longer?" Maxwell snapped.

"Listen to me." Katarina spoke quietly, dropping rather than raising her voice. *"Right now* I am still due at the Opera House. *Right now* Jacob Abramson still knows me well enough to recognize me in this persona. *Right now* you must

refrain from behavior that will draw his eye to the window and cause him to consider us closely, because Jacob isn't a stupid man. I don't form attachments with stupid men."

She was not entirely certain why she had chosen to include the final line, but the length of the speech had given Maxwell an opportunity to slow his breathing and more firmly set his feet on the pavement. "Yes," he said, "of course."

"To the best of my recollection, we have not visited Jacob's shop in search of the timepiece."

"It wasn't Jacob's a moment ago," he said, "but we didn't visit it under its former name either." He took a deep breath. "I'll go." Another breath. "Wait here." She could tell it took him some effort to turn away. For his sake more than her own, she hoped nothing would alter the timeline and cause him to return to an empty street corner.

She watched from her lounging post as Maxwell went through the pantomime with Jacob—explanation, reassurance, picture of the thief, promises. She saw Jacob look carefully at the drawing, holding it close to eyes apparently more nearsighted than they had been twelve years ago, before he shook his head. Was there a wedding ring on his left hand? There must be, after all this time. She wouldn't wish it otherwise.

Maxwell left the shop with a reasonable imitation of unconcern. But he looked at once and anxiously at her street corner—and when he saw her still standing there, closed his eyes for a moment in what could only be thankfulness.

❧

She did not disappear while rehearsing, or while performing. If the world changed around her in that time, she was unaware of it. Maxwell was still awake when she tapped on his door upon her late-night return, naked relief upon his face at the sight of her.

Emil Schwieger had chosen to wait up for her as well, stretched out full length upon the sofa. He had been sound asleep during her brief stop that afternoon to change personae, but she could tell Maxwell had informed him of the timeline shift in her absence. He looked as pale and frantic as his older friend, and as relieved to see her alive and unchanged.

"Any news?" she greeted the two of them.

"None from Trevelyan," Schwieger said. "But Hewitt called while you were out this morning."

"Hewitt?" She had nearly forgotten him amidst the shifting priorities and spinning plates of the past few days. Careless of her; he was a player on the board and she dared not lose track of him.

"I managed to persuade him you had taken a calming draught and were asleep, and he must not disturb you."

"And he believed that?"

"He did not seem overly interested one way or the other," Emil admitted. "He said he could just as well talk with me. He asked me to go over my account again—"

Katarina frowned at that. "And I hope you managed all the details correctly?"

"I have *done this before*. He also wished to examine your original suite of rooms a second time, and the manager permitted it."

That was disconcerting. What could he be looking for there? "Did he say if he discovered something?"

Emil shook his head. "He did not return afterward. I heard him rustling about in there, not for very long, and then he departed. The manager locked the doors after him."

"And my picks have gone off with the rest of the evidence," Katarina sighed, "so I can't check for myself. Well, there's nothing to be done about that now." She looked over at Maxwell, wondering if his features were more angular than they had been at the beginning of this week, or if that were only her imagination. Certainly the bags under his eyes were more pronounced. "I don't suppose you've managed to sleep?"

"I can't." Nor had he seated himself. His fingers drummed on the table he stood beside.

"I sympathize." It was not entirely true. Katarina was exhausted to the bone, and fairly certain a single glass of wine would have been sufficient to send her into deep and dreamless slumber. But Maxwell's agitation troubled her, and she found herself quite automatically casting about for a means of relieving it. "I don't think I could, either. Suppose I assume Colin's persona again and we go walking?"

"The pawn shops are closed, surely?" he said.

Katarina shrugged. "We might find another lead."

"At least you two can pretend to be doing something," Emil muttered in obvious self-disgust.

The pair of them prowled the streets mostly in search of further changes to the timeline. Maxwell said the portion of the East End controlled by Arcturus Bastion was dirtier and less welcoming than it had been, but Katarina was inclined to attribute that to his nervousness. *She* saw no such changes.

Finally, physical fatigue drove them home, and Katarina collapsed into bed just as the sky was lightening.

Three hours later, a maid tapped at the door with the news that Mr. Hewitt had called upon her.

⁌⁍

Eight o'clock in the morning was an uncivilized hour to be expected to play hostess even when one hadn't been awake for most of three nights, and Katarina felt no compunction about letting Hewitt cool his heels in the lobby while she washed and dressed. She once again chose her emerald green tea-gown so that she would not have to fuss with corsets, but she took the time to brush out her braids, pin up her hair, and rub a touch of greasepaint into the circles under her eyes. She was absolutely not about to meet the man with her hair loose—she was not inviting him into her boudoir, and it was better for the both of them that he entertain no such false impression—and there was no reason to start any speculative train of thought as to what activities she might have substituted for sleep.

Satisfied that she presented a sufficiently businesslike appearance given the circumstances, she pulled the bell-rope. When the chambermaid appeared, she requested tea and toast, and when it had been brought, indicated that she was now at leisure to receive Mr. Hewitt.

When the maid showed him in, she was awaiting him from a seat behind the teapot, angled so her back was to the window, perfectly coiffed and perfectly composed. He was composed as well, so much so that despite the morning light falling on his pleasant face, she could not tell if he looked annoyed at the delay.

"Madame Rasmirovna."

"Mr. Hewitt. Please, come in and sit down. Would you like a cup of tea? How do you take it?" If he had apologized for the early hour, she would have apologized for keeping him waiting. Since he did not, she carried war into the enemy's camp the instant they were both provided with cups. "I imagine you must have urgent news for me, calling so early in the morning?"

"Not news as such," Mr. Hewitt said. He set down his untasted tea and leaned back in his chair. "Madame Rasmirovna, I should like to tell you a story."

She raised her eyebrows at him and lifted her teacup deliberately to her lips. "If you wish, Mr. Hewitt, of course."

"I'm not much of a storyteller myself. I leave that sort of thing to my friend Brett, but I think I could probably master the way of it with a little effort. They have a certain form, those things one sees in *The Strand.*"

She had no idea to what he was referring, but she nodded as though she did.

"Once upon a time," Mr. Hewitt began, "—because that's the way we always start these stories, isn't it?—once upon a time, there was an Italian count of old family and great wealth. He lacked only a countess to make his life complete, and thought he had found her in the person of brilliant and beautiful opera singer, a *prima donna* at La Scala. Alas for the count, the woman he loved declined his offer of marriage, valuing too highly her freedom and her career. When they parted, he gifted her with a jewel worth millions, a dazzling emerald called the Cat's Eye. The opera singer wore this gem to every performance thereafter, until the night it was stolen from her hotel safe."

Hewitt paused for Katarina's reaction. She could not imagine what he wanted her to say, and therefore could not choose whether to meet or disappoint his expectations. She raised her teacup to her lips again, instead.

"A private investigator was summoned to assist the official police," said Mr. Hewitt, "a man perhaps not so well-known as others of his trade, but just as skilled as his more famous brethren, and possessing a particular knowledge of jewel thefts. This private investigator examined the scene of the crime, questioned the victim and nearby witnesses, followed footprints, and tracked the thief from the West End to the East. Unfortunately, he arrived too late. He did not arrive to find a thief he could question, but only a dead, stripped body."

Katarina did react to that. "You've found him?"

"The night before last, on the banks of the Thames," Mr. Hewitt confirmed, "although evidence indicates he was not killed there." He resumed his storyteller's voice. "The private detective thought for a time that his case had come to a standstill. The thief was dead, the jewel gone, the trail cold. How am I doing so far?"

Katarina blinked before correctly interpreting the question. "I am not a regular reader of *The Strand,* so I cannot answer for you matching the style you spoke of, but you do well at spinning an engaging tale."

Mr. Hewitt bowed. "Where was I? Ah, yes. The private investigator thought he might track the jewel if not the thief. Often these matters are resolved by thorough and backbreaking work, rather than a flash of inspiration, and so it seemed likely to be this time. The investigator set about a search of every pawn shop in the area where the thief's body had been found. And then every pawn shop in a slightly larger radius. And then a slightly larger radius than that.

"He was interested to discover that a dark-haired man had been circulating some of the same pawn shops as himself, some two or three hours earlier. This young man was said to be searching not for an emerald, but for a pocket watch—one of the lesser items listed missing from the hotel robbery.

"Which set me thinking," Mr. Hewitt said, dropping from the third person to the first without seeming to notice he had done so. "I came back to examine your sitting room once more, and I found what I had missed at first: a blood smear on your carpet."

Katarina sat still, breathing as calmly as she could. The surge of nerves now was like the surge on stage, and she masked her agitation there well enough.

"It was a lesson to me," Mr. Hewitt said rather dreamily. "I believe after this I shall always investigate the scene first, before taking the statement of any witness. The stories we are told suggest to us what we should see. Your admirably well-told account did not include any mention of violence, and so I was not expecting a blood smear. Yet there it was, blood soaked into a carpet that, by the facts as you told them to me, Mr. Ramsey could never have been near."

Katarina did no more than twitch her brows upward. It was far better that he talk than that she hasten her reply.

"I reviewed the scene with new eyes," Mr. Hewitt went on, "looking dispassionately for all that was there. I noticed for the first time that the direct path from the safe to the window goes nowhere near the table upon which that smashed green vase stood. I always thought it somewhat odd that you would keep your jewels in an outer room instead of by your side. And I could find no one, *no one,* who witnessed any altercation between the thief and Mr. Ramsey or witnessed Mr. Maxwell providing him aid. What I *did* find, after an annoying number of telegrams, was a trail of one Colin Ramsey staying at precisely the same hotels you have frequented throughout your European tour."

Katarina continued to concentrate on breathing evenly. Hewitt had almost all of it, very nearly all the pieces. But she would not allow herself to react until she saw the shape in which he put them together. She doubted very much he would think of the actual explanation, after all, and surely she would be able to navigate her way through anything less dangerous.

Surely.

"Here's what I think happened," Mr. Hewitt said, leaning confidingly forward. "I think you were not alone when your hotel room was burgled. I think Mr. Ramsey, with whom you clearly have a…friendship of long standing, was with you in your bedchamber. I think when you both heard a sound in the outer room, he went to investigate. He surprised the burglar at your safe, and was stabbed for his trouble. The burglar ran off with a few jewels of middling value, and with your friend Mr. Ramsey's pocket watch. Mr. Ramsey did not want to admit where he had been, for the sake of your reputation, and so concocted the story of the outdoor stabbing before hobbling his way to the room booked under his name."

Katarina exhaled. All right, that was material enough to work with. She could do this. "You are correct," she said, and deliberately spoke the exact truth. "Mr. Ramsey and I do indeed have an association of long standing. Mr. Ramsey was indeed stabbed in this room, not outside. And Mr. Ramsey indeed did not wish to publicly explain his presence here."

"It was of great importance to Mr. Ramsey to retrieve his watch," Mr. Hewitt observed. "So much so that he rose from a sickbed to make the round of the pawn shops, after the thief was reported dead. That watch is of great value?"

Katarina said, "It is of great sentimental value," and that, too, was absolutely the truth.

"It must be, extraordinarily so, for Mr. Ramsey, not yet recovered from a stab wound, to have dragged himself injured on a long walk through the dubious part of a city he does not know."

Katarina did not reply to that. It was not a question.

"Unless, of course—" Mr. Hewitt spoke as though absently, looking pensively at something over her left shoulder. "Unless, of course, someone else did it in his name."

That was not a question either. So still she said nothing.

"Male costume would be nothing new to an actress," Mr. Hewitt mused, "and I have heard tell that a woman who achieved some fame twelve years ago as an impersonator is recently returned to town, and has been seen near her old haunts." Now he cocked his head at her, a question of body language rather than words.

Katarina gave him a slow and deliberate smile. "Well," she said, "you are correct there. Male costume would indeed be nothing new to an actress."

Mr. Hewitt now watched her as closely as she had been watching him.

"If an actress *had* assisted Mr. Ramsey," Katarina said, as speculatively as he had done, "I expect her goal would have been to recover the pocket watch. Sometimes such a trinket is more valuable than its price would suggest. Sometimes a watch is all a son knows of his father."

"An interesting thought," Mr. Hewitt said. "You may be right." He studied her. "There's one thing more that perplexes me," he said then. "A large emerald is an awkward thing to steal. It's eminently traceable. If a thief wished to attempt such a *coup*, one would expect to hear of jewel cutters lined up in advance, a dozen fences standing ready, a heist of mythic proportions. I have found no evidence of any such thing.

"Now, it is remotely possible we are instead dealing with a lucky thief who did not know the value of the green bauble in his hand, but in that case one would expect to find it pawned with the rest, and it has not passed through any pawn shop anywhere in London.

"Which brings us to a third possibility. Perhaps the thief did not know the value of his prize, but the man who killed the thief had a better eye than his victim. Perhaps this second man has hidden the stone away and seeks to find a gem cutter now. If this is the situation, perhaps the Cat's Eye will surface in time."

"I hope so," Katarina said.

"But perhaps the fourth explanation is the true one." Mr. Hewitt tapped his finger idly on his notebook, then turned the pages to the sketch he had made of her original chamber. "This story we have concocted together, of the actress and the injured man—it still does not account for the smashed vase." He indicated on the paper. "Here is the safe. There is the window. That table is nowhere near the direct path between the one and the other. How did the thief manage to knock it so violently over as he escaped?"

"Perhaps," Katarina said, "it was in the struggle with Mr. Ramsey."

"Perhaps, but the blood smear was here." Mr. Hewitt indicated the rug in the drawing. "Also nowhere near the table. It is, I suppose, still possible that they fought all over the room, first knocking over the vase here before Mr. Ramsey took the wound that caused him to collapse here." He looked speculatively at the drawing, then up at her. "It must have been a violent struggle indeed. The vase was smashed utterly to bits, not as though someone had knocked it from its pedestal but as though someone had used an implement. A poker, for instance. I found slivers of green glass actually ground into the carpet." He paused. "Such an interesting color, green."

Katarina met his eyes steadily.

"Was there ever a real emerald, Madame Rasmirovna?"

"Of course there was," Katarina said. She had known this might happen. It had been one of the contingencies she had set up that night with the poker. Now to tell the truth, or almost all of it, and thereby distract him from the pocket watch. It might mean the end of Katarina Rasmirovna's career, but perhaps that was just as well. What did one do, after one got what one wanted? One cashed in one's chips and moved on to the next adventure. "When the count presented me with the Cat's Eye, it was duly examined, authenticated, and insured."

"Ah," Mr. Hewitt said, and resumed his seat. He took up his teacup, watching her expectantly.

He had ceded the stage, so Katarina thought she might as well give him the performance he seemed to be expecting. She rose. "But a famous emerald is an awkward valuable, especially when one travels as I do. There is no point in owning such a thing if one does not wear it, but every time it leaves the safe it is at risk from every passer-by."

"So a glass copy becomes a reasonable alternative," Mr. Hewitt said. "Where is the real one? A bank in Milan?"

She probably ought to say yes, but— "Truthfully, I sold it years ago. I had it cut, and I sold each smaller gem separately." She raised her eyebrows at him. "I am a practical woman. I prefer to have my funds liquid."

Mr. Hewitt nodded. "I understand. Moreover, you stood to double those liquid funds once the theft was reported to the insurers."

"That *would* have been very clever of me," Katarina said sweetly. "But perhaps I only smashed the emerald to ensure the interest of the police, so that my friend's pocket watch was more likely to be recovered?"

Mr. Hewitt snorted. "Indeed, I suppose that also is possible. But it would be absurd." He regarded her. "I cannot permit insurance fraud to take place," he said.

Katarina nodded. "I shall take care that none does."

"To that end—" He reached into his waistcoat pocket and pulled out a sparkling green gem. "I thought this might be of use to you. It's not real, of course, but as a replica it is rather fine. We could say I found it through a disreputable East End connection, of which I have a few. And then, with it returned to you, the case would be closed, and no one would look further into smashed green glass or a smear of blood upon your carpet."

Katarina took it. "Mr. Hewitt," she said seriously, "that is indeed very kind."

"Honored to be of service, Madame. I should hate to see anything else happen. The world would be bereft without your singing."

She dipped him a curtsy. "May I offer you another cup of tea?" She did not miss that he stood to gain as well—solving a large jewel theft case of this kind would make his career. But he had gone to some length to shield her, and she considered the exchange equitable.

"Are you very fond of music, then?" she asked, pouring the second cup, and they chatted amiably enough for ten minutes more before he rose to take his leave.

In the midst of conventional goodbyes, he suddenly said, "I can't help wondering if there's a piece I missed."

Her heart slammed against her ribcage.

"It was likely only the spur of the moment," he said, "the smashed green glass, taking advantage of the theft—but it was a cool-headed thing to do while your lover lay bleeding. The entire room had the feel of a staged set. I wondered for a time if you could have employed the thief yourself, but Mr. Ramsey's stab wound seemed to negate that. Do you know, no one has come to identify the thief's body? I can't find a boarding house, a doss house, a charity or a gang sleeping rough in an alleyway that knows anything of the man. He might have appeared out of thin air."

Katarina breathed carefully and said, "I assure you I did not hire the man who stabbed Mr. Ramsey and stole valuables from my room."

Hewitt watched her steadily. "The impulse to commit insurance fraud in the face of a severe injury to someone close to you—that still implies premeditation, Madame."

"It is possible that I have, before now, contemplated staging just such a scene," Katarina admitted. "Other than the attack upon Mr. Ramsey, of course. It is possible I had thought out the blocking ahead of time."

"But why do it now?" He studied her. "What's about to happen, Madame Rasmirovna? Are you—going somewhere?"

She did not make the decision in that moment. Rather, she realized that she had already made it. Earlier in the conversation, when risking the truth; or perhaps earlier even than that. *What does one do? One cashes in one's chips and moves on to the next adventure.*

"It did occur to me," Katarina said carefully, "that a dramatic disappearance might prove a more satisfactory crowning end to a career than a slow slide into obscurity. Hypothetically. If one were writing the opera, you know."

"Are you writing an opera?" he asked.

"Well, there is that old story, of the woman who vanished after attending the Prince Regent's ball, the night news came of the victory at Waterloo—have you ever heard it? She left her clothing behind and disappeared from within a locked room. Her ghost is still supposed to haunt the place. It's the sort of story," Katarina said, smiling, "no one ever stops telling."

"I see," Mr. Hewitt said. "I do hope—well, I've managed to secure tickets for your final performance, and I do hope—"

"My dear sir, I would never, even hypothetically speaking, renege on a contract. I shall fulfill all the obligations of this, the last stop on my tour. And I shall do it wearing the emerald you have retrieved for me." She assessed him for a moment, then leaned in to touch her lips to his. "Thank you."

He flushed to the tips of his ears and bowed himself out.

Chapter 23

Katarina waited until she was certain Hewitt had completely departed before she flew across the hall. Almost before she finished knocking, Maxwell opened the door—in his shirt sleeves, with his collar undone, but with eyes too bright and alert to be those of a man just roused from sleep.

"You will not believe the conversation I just had," she greeted him.

He stepped aside to let her in, brandishing a telegram slip with his free hand. He looked as alive as she felt. "No matter what your news is, I think mine trumps it."

"Indeed? Who sent that?" Katarina squinted at it.

"Trevelyan."

Katarina stared a moment. "In that case, you're absolutely right. Does he have progress to report?"

"I think he has *success* to report." Maxwell's voice vibrated with suppressed energy. He stepped closer, angling the telegram so they both could read it—an interesting choice, she had time to consider later, rather than handing it to her and maintaining a respectable distance, but in the moment, it felt completely natural to be standing so close she could feel the warmth of his skin through the fabric of his shirt. "He writes circumspectly, but his request is too odd to be only an interim dispatch."

Katarina read over his arm. "He wants to come here?"

"I mean to tell him no, of course. We can't let him set foot in Madame Rasmirovna's hotel or he'll realize who you really are—he being not a stupid man, and all. But there must be somewhere else we can meet him, somewhere nearby, a tea room or a park, where you could attend the meeting in one of your other personae. I think it is a significant point that he wishes to meet so far from his home."

And indeed, it proved to be so. When Trevelyan entered the shabby little tea room several streets away, he was carrying a small paper-wrapped parcel in his hand.

He set it down with some ceremony, equidistantly between Maxwell and Katarina.

Both of them looked at it.

Trevelyan's eyes crinkled. But he only said, in an impatient manner and in his London accent, "One or the other of you had better open it. We haven't all the time in the world, have we?"

Katarina made a motion of deference to Maxwell, who seized the parcel and undid the wrapping. The paper fell away to reveal a delicately-shaped pendant-watch, suitable for a woman to wear about her neck. It did not tick and its tiny hands did not move.

"I thought, since we had something of a theme established, the dowsing rod ought to take the form of another timekeeping device," Trevelyan explained in a low voice. "I...was not entirely certain which of you was senior partner in this enterprise, but there did seem to be a compelling argument for crafting an object that could not possibly be confused with a man's pocket watch. And my wife did happen to mention Miss Ramsey was the one actually carrying the timepiece you brought me, so I took a guess."

"I find all parts of that argument entirely reasonable." Maxwell slid the timepiece pendant across the table to Katarina. "Are you telling me this dowsing rod of yours actually works?"

"I'm telling you you're participating in a field test," Trevelyan answered. "It certainly works to locate a functioning...er, device such as your pocket watch from a distance of one-quarter mile. Which is as far as I can walk from my house without attracting undesirable attention from the general public. This morning, we will attempt a more meaningful distance."

Katarina stared at him. "Our pocket watch is functional? You...cannot be serious."

"I believe I ought to be affronted," Trevelyan said. "Of course I'm serious. You do *know* whose assistance you sought, don't you? It's functional and the dowsing rod can find it—I'm just not certain from what distance. The one thing this doesn't do is tell time," he added, picking up the pendant. "It didn't seem a priority, though a later model ought to, for the camouflage. You hold it in your palm like so, Miss Ramsey—" He gestured, and Katarina obediently closed her hand over it. "It will vibrate when it is within range of the pocket watch. The stronger and closer together the vibrations, the closer it is to the target. We'll keep a close eye on it on the drive back to my house, and then we'll know its maximum range."

"That's wonderful." Maxwell started to push back his chair, then stopped himself. "I'm sorry, Mr. Trevelyan. I did invite you to breakfast—"

"No need." Trevelyan was pushing his chair back as well. "I want to see this task done. I'll eat afterward. Then I'll sleep." His mouth twitched. "I've already promised my wife. Let's call a four-wheeler and be off."

The pendant lay quiescent in Katarina's hand for most of the slow drive to Kensington. Its first vibrations were intermittent, and so subtle she might have been merely imagining them. The tickle did not become regular until the cab turned onto Trevelyan's street, and did not achieve a noticeable intensity until the three of them had descended and were actually making their way up the flower-lined walk. Trevelyan frowned a little, whipping out a notepad to jot a few scribbles as he walked. "This is a shorter useful range than I meant to give you. I ought to be able to improve that in the next model—"

"You mended a time machine you had never before encountered and devised a method for tracking it in *forty-eight hours,*" Maxwell said. "I do not think you owe us an apology for any infelicities in the design."

Trevelyan smiled a little at that. He produced a latchkey to open his front door, waved aside the maidservant with the ruffled apron who hesitated in the hall, and led his guests with a brisk stride through his house and out the back door.

The space between the house and the laboratory had been turned into a playground by an astonishing number of children. Katarina was by this point too distracted by the pendant, now buzzing like a honeybee against her gloved palm, to properly stop and count them, but there were certainly a greater number than the three little boys who had been playing with their nurse upon the occasion of her last visit here. For that matter, there appeared to be more than one nurse in attendance. Brenda Trevelyan was in the middle of the tumult, and looked up with a cheerful greeting that was completely drowned out by the children's cries of "Da!"

Trevelyan skirted his way through the chaos without slowing, answering the children pleasantly enough but with reminders that he was working, and was this the polite way one greeted one's father's guests? No, it was not, and he would see them all in the evening. The nurses took on the task of restoring order, and Brenda joined the adults in continuing on to the laboratory. She closed the door between them and the children, which Katarina found to be a relief of sorts, even though the open window meant the noise did not noticeably decrease.

Maxwell's impossible pocket watch sat gleaming and ready atop Trevelyan's worktable, and the pendant's vibrations had achieved a positive frenzy that made the tender flesh of Katarina's palm itch even through her glove. She held the quivering thing toward Trevelyan. "How do I stop it, now that it's fulfilled its task?"

"Touch it to the timepiece." Trevelyan picked it up from the table so she could do just that, and the frantic buzzing ceased. "It won't be searching for this one now, not until it's taken far enough away again."

"Brilliant," Maxwell murmured, as though in awe. "And the timepiece—"

"See for yourself." Trevelyan flipped it open.

Katarina felt her mouth fall open at the sight of the moving images on the fourth face. Maxwell's and Emil's descriptions were nothing compared to actually seeing it alive and functional. "Dear...heavens."

"That was more or less my response as well," Mrs. Trevelyan agreed from behind her. "I take it all is satisfactorily completed?"

"And then some." Maxwell seemed to have shed twenty years in a moment. "Mr. Trevelyan, I cannot ever thank you enough. You've succeeded beyond my wildest hopes, and even if the second timepiece has been taken beyond our reach, we now have a means of travel, which means more than I can say. You've accomplished what I thought no one here and now ever could."

"Ah, there's no need for all that," Trevelyan brushed off the praise. "Mending the watch turned out to be not at all difficult. No, truly. It was the clockwork surrounding that flashing blue item that had broken, not the item itself, and clockwork I can fix. The blue bit proved to be in working order, which was fortunate, as I've no idea what it is or what it does. I've never seen anything even remotely akin to it, and nor has Marconi—"

Maxwell looked up.

"I know," Trevelyan said, "you wanted me to keep this to myself, and I mostly did, but I needed his help, and time is of the essence in defeating your evil empire, is it not? You can trust my judgment—"

"I do," Maxwell said at once, unhesitatingly.

Trevelyan's face softened a fraction. "Yes," he said, "for some reason you already do. I've been thinking about that, these past few days. You admitted you left out some important parts of your story, and I believe I am beginning to see the shape of the missing pieces."

Maxwell started to say something, then stopped. The laboratory was silent, except for the ticking of the pocket watch in Trevelyan's hand.

"You came *here*," Trevelyan said. "Not to the University, not to the Royal Society. You came to me personally. My skill is known to be considerable, yes, but skill and trustworthiness are different things, and yet you trusted me, without question, with *this*. I can only assume you knew me, in one of those other worlds?"

Maxwell bent his head in assent. "I knew you very well. We fought side by side. It was an honor."

Silence again, broken only by the ticking and the flashing lights from the fourth face.

"It was a terrible world, though," Maxwell said. "I'm not sorry it's gone. Even if we have a much harder task now, even if the future is darker, I'm glad to find that world unmade. I had thought it a side effect, a silver lining of all this horror...but I am beginning to wonder if we might not credit it to my parents, and thereby, in an odd way, to me, and to a version of you, and to a version of Miss Ramsey here. I think the three of us can claim some credit for unmaking that world as we once vowed we would, and I'm glad not to find myself there again."

"What a very Celtic tale I'm in," Trevelyan said. "Or not inside, but at the fringes of. A few lines in one of the middle verses, the smith who shoes a horse while the weary travelers warm themselves by the fire. A bit part in a grand saga."

"You could have more than a bit part," Maxwell said at once. "If you wanted to join this fight, I would like nothing better than to work with you again. I can promise you without exaggeration the adventure of a lifetime."

Trevelyan hesitated. His eyes went from Maxwell, to Katarina…and then past them to the courtyard, where the children's shouts echoed off the walls… to the desk behind the fluttering yellow curtain, where his wife wrote her articles urging social reform…and finally around his workroom, coming at last to rest on Brenda's face.

Trevelyan looked back to meet Maxwell's eye. "For what imaginable reason," he said, "would I want to do that?"

"You're a wise man," Maxwell said after a moment.

"Such a tone of surprise?" Trevelyan mocked him gently. "I thought you said you knew me."

"I knew a brilliant man. Wisdom is different. It takes a wise man to realize when he is happy."

Katarina moved a little, restlessly, and Trevelyan's sharp eyes went to her. She lifted her shoulders in a shrug at the question she saw on his face. "Forgive me, but I can't help wondering—are you certain you won't be bored?"

Trevelyan laughed. "Quite certain. I am handsomely paid to invent what I wish, and I have six children underfoot. Nine when the eldest three are home from school and University. When exactly do you think I have time to be bored?"

Katarina looked meaningfully at the pocket watch in his hands, preparing to argue the point on principle, but Maxwell intervened. "For some the pleasant green haven is a cage, but for others it's a happy ending. Happy endings are different for different people." He held a hand out to Trevelyan. "Glad to see you in yours. Good luck with it."

Trevelyan clasped the hand briefly. Then he shut the timepiece, set it in Maxwell's palm, and closed Maxwell's fingers around the gleaming gold. "Fix it," he said. "Go tilt against your windmills and mend this enormous problem that drives you to bend time to your will. Then if you can, come back and tell me how the story ends."

"If I possibly can." Maxwell made it a promise. He handed the working timepiece to Katarina, and she bestowed it ceremoniously in her reticule along with the pendant. The tension in Maxwell's shoulders relaxed.

Now that they had a means of locating the second pocket watch, they could not justify an instant's delay in doing just that. They made one attempt to compensate Trevelyan for his services, thanked him sincerely for his aid when he derisively refused to be compensated, and followed the inventor and his wife back through the herd of unruly children and then through the house.

At the front door, Trevelyan stopped Katarina with a touch on her arm. "I should just like to say—you have the most magnificent voice I have ever heard."

She widened her eyes at him, letting a little more Cockney trickle into her tone. "Oh, you wouldn't ever have heard me sing, sir. I'm just a music hall girl. I do impersonations mostly."

"Mm-hm." Trevelyan reached for her hand and kissed it briefly in the Continental manner. "Honored to be of service, Madame."

"Come back before the end of the tale, if you need to," Brenda said quietly to Maxwell. "If you've need of provisions, or safety."

"I'd rather not put you and your family at risk," Maxwell demurred.

"I'd rather you didn't as well, but I can always take the children to Pendoylan if need be. It seems to me the heroes of those tales sometimes need refuge more than once before the story's done. Come back if you need help." She dimpled. "I've no wish to ride with the Wild Hunt, but I don't mind quartering it for a night or two. Good luck to you both."

∽

It was different to wear a functioning timepiece than it had been to wear a broken one. Now Katarina saw some of what Maxwell must have been seeing all along—changes that flickered out of the corner of her eye, settling into normalcy as soon as she turned to look at them. She did not think it was anxiety that made the well-known streets of the East End seem subtly wrong, in a myriad of small ways, from what she remembered. And she could now recall, somehow, simultaneously, the past in which Jacob had been the son of a jeweler and the one in which he had been the son of a pawnbroker.

She and Maxwell spent the morning methodically walking up and down streets of pawnbrokers, waiting for the pendant to vibrate against Katarina's palm. The names on the shop windows no longer had the variety of ethnicities she would have expected—only two or three looked foreign, in an otherwise unbroken sea of solid Germanic-British appellations. The faces on the streets were now also more uniform—many fewer Lascar sailors, Chinese merchants, children born of British mothers and Indian fathers, Jewish peddlers, and gypsy fortune tellers than she knew ought to have been there. And both she and Maxwell kept stumbling over nothing, as though gusts of wind unbalanced them or little breaking waves tugged at their feet.

The pendant began to shiver in Katarina's clenched hand as they turned up the street on which Abramson's Pawnbroker Shop was situated. The street looked dirtier than it had the day before, the shop itself less well-kept. Katarina had time to wonder whether the timepiece might have been brought to Abramson's since the previous day, or whether the shifting of time might mean that it had somehow been there all along—

This wave of changing time seemed to break right over her head. For an endless instant it was as though she was physically tossed within it, as blinded and disoriented as she would have been within any wave of saltwater—and then it subsided, and she was aware of her own body again, and her feet were once more planted on the ground, and she could see and hear the normal sounds of an East End street around her.

Beside her, Abramson's Pawnbroker Shop was a boarded-up, abandoned husk of a building. And she had a new set of memories competing for her attention, and in these, her first love Jacob had never existed.

She turned to find Maxwell bent over, one hand on a grimy brick wall for support, the other pressed to his head. She managed, "Did you see that?"

"I see all of it," he said hollowly. "All the possibilities, all the timelines, all the years, layers upon layers of shifting sand. It's been like this since I became unmoored—but worse this past week. Almost unbearably worse, at times, this past day or so. I can see it all changing."

Her head seemed to be clearing faster than his. Grateful that the character of Colin Ramsey did not require her to conceal her true strength, Katarina gave Maxwell a shoulder to lean on for the few paces until he could collapse on a convenient crate. At least there were now many fewer people present on the street to stare.

She sat on the crate beside him, watching as his color began to slowly improve. "Well," she said at last, "this is suddenly no longer a game."

Maxwell looked up. He appeared to understand, but Katarina nevertheless felt the need to clarify. "I mean to say—it never was a game. But—"

"It affects you personally now. It just became real."

She nodded. "I hadn't had the chance to discuss this with you," she said. "But I had a very odd conversation with Martin Hewitt this morning, and it led me to a realization. I mean to come with you when you leave to fight this war." She hesitated. "It's been my intention for days, in fact. But now I am even more firmly resolved."

Maxwell was silent a moment. "I feel as though I should argue with you. In many ways I wouldn't wish this life on my worst enemy, and you—"

"What are my other options?" Katarina interrupted. "I am *obviously* not safe here." She waved a hand to indicate the altered street. "I can stand still and wait for the wave to crash over me and write me out of existence. Or I suppose I could stand still wearing a timepiece, if you left one with me, and wait for the world to crumble from under my feet while I stayed protected and unchanging. Or I can come with you and meet the crashing wave as it forms and *stop this*. I know which way I'd rather risk death."

"I feel as though I should argue with you," he repeated. "You wanted to be an opera singer—"

"I've been an opera singer."

He exhaled. When he looked up, he was smiling a little. "I should argue," he said. "But all I will say is, 'Now I know we'll win.'"

She smiled at the absurdity of that. "I'd like to keep my engagement to sing tonight," she said. "Assuming we can risk spending another half-day here. I'd like to sing for—for Jacob and my gypsy father, if you can understand that."

"I can," Maxwell said. "And of course, yes, a few hours shouldn't make a difference. We haven't found the timepiece yet in any case."

As if in answer, the pendant vibrated in her palm.

They followed its call to a pawn shop tucked into a corner on a frigidly respectable street, made all the more morally rigid by its proximity to the slums. The overlarge pocket watch, twin to the one tucked into Katarina's waistcoat, was not only present but plainly visible, neatly tagged and hanging on a peg behind the proprietor's shoulder.

This pawnbroker was not, in point of fact, an established fence of stolen goods. Katarina had met too many of those in her previous life to mistake him for one. Oh, he received goods of suspect provenance, to be sure, but that did not mean he knew what to do with them, and a whiff of scandal in so respectable a neighborhood would surely close his doors and drive him to ply his trade in less salubrious areas. He had no desire to truck with the police. Once she established that, it was almost too easy.

The boy who had pawned the item that very morning had looked nothing like the thief's newspaper portrait Katarina still carried. Nor had he looked old enough or wealthy enough to own the item he pawned, a fact that could lead to trouble for the pawnbroker if it were known. The pawnbroker was only too happy to hand the watch to the persuasive young gentleman and his older friend in exchange for a bribe and an agreement not to involve the authorities. And with no more fuss than that, they were back out on the pavement with their prize.

"Done," Maxwell whispered as though he could scarcely believe it. He opened the casing and the fourth face sprang to life. "And it's even working. Katarina, *thank you.*"

"My privilege," Katarina said. Trying to lighten the moment, she added, "I understand this means you may depart whenever you choose—but you had *better* not leave without me."

Maxwell looked up, startled, and their eyes met. He started to smile. Still looking straight into her eyes, he said, "I wouldn't dream of it."

She was the first to look away.

"We won't leave for the battlefield at once in any case," Maxwell added as they began the walk home. "We'll need to recruit a little more help first."

"Trevelyan?" Katarina guessed. "I don't think it would take much to change his mind. I'm fairly sure I could persuade him to join us just for a brief excursion, just long enough to—"

"No," said Maxwell, with surprising sharpness. "He's a family man. He has responsibilities here. A brief excursion can turn into— No. The Trevelyans have more than earned a peaceful civilian retirement."

"Whom do you intend to recruit, then?"

"It's time," Maxwell said, "I took you to meet my parents."

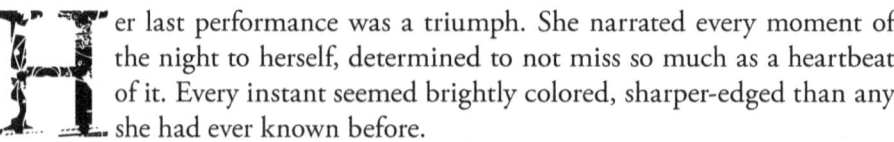

Her last performance was a triumph. She narrated every moment of the night to herself, determined to not miss so much as a heartbeat of it. Every instant seemed brightly colored, sharper-edged than any she had ever known before.

What would the papers say afterward? What would the rumors say, after that? *Madame Rasmirovna's manner on the night of her disappearance seemed exactly as usual. Some say her performance that evening was especially stirring, though others insist this is true only with the veil of hindsight.*

Afterward, she emerged from the theater—for what she alone knew would be the last time—into the usual sea of bouquets and accolades. She glimpsed Martin Hewitt in the crowd, and to her greater surprise, both Mr. and Mrs. Trevelyan. Several men of obviously noble birth clustered closer, with society reporters hovering nearby to see which claimed the honor of escorting the *prima donna*, but— *Madame Rasmirovna ignored them all, choosing instead to take the arm of a white-haired gentleman whose dress and offered bouquet were no more than respectably middle-class. He had never been seen in Madame's orbit before, yet they seemed to know each other, for those nearest in the crowd heard her murmur, "How kind of you to bring flowers, Mr. Maxwell," and heard him reply, "I wanted to do it once."*

The crowd and the society reporters were still trailing them when they reached her hotel. *Madame Rasmirovna promised she would see them all at the usual round of supper clubs, and excused herself, laughing, just for a moment, just to change her dress. Her escort accompanied her into the lift, invited by her to wait in her sitting room. Neither of them were ever seen again.*

Katarina had already packed a small bag. It held Colin's clothing, the fake Cat's Eye, her actual jewelry, and most of her savings, converted that afternoon into gold. Laughing to herself in the bedchamber while Maxwell and Emil waited for her outside, she stripped off her lavish evening gown, left its components in an obvious pile upon the floor, and donned instead her most discreet and sensible walking dress and low-heeled boots. She braided and bound up her hair, looped over her wrist the reticule that carried the pocket watch that would keep her safe, and opened the door to the sitting room.

Maxwell rose as she entered.

"I'm rather sorry to leave the flowers," Katarina told him, and it was true, but they were impractical to carry, and besides which, leaving them here would add so much to the scene she was crafting. When the crowd below grew tired of waiting and dispatched a chambermaid to ask after Madame Rasmirovna's health, the maid would find Madame's magnificent evening gown in a heap on her bedroom floor, a sum of money sufficient to cover her hotel bill upon her sitting-room desk, and no sign at all of her famous emerald or any of her lesser jewels. Very likely Martin Hewitt would be asked to investigate her disappearance. Very likely he would decline. *The vanishing of Madame Katarina Rasmirovna took its place among London's unsolved mysteries, a fitting and dramatic end to a successful and dramatic (and mysterious) career. Madame Rasmirovna's end remained forever after as unknown as her beginnings were obscure.*

"Ready?" Maxwell asked beside her.

Katarina took one final look around the sitting room. "Ready," she said, and Emil struggled to his feet. The three of them spent a moment or two arranging themselves in the most sensible fashion, in physical contact and with the weight of Katarina's small amount of luggage evenly distributed.

Maxwell pulled out his pocket watch with a flourish and set the dials. "It's a shock, the first time," he said. "Hold on tight."

Chapter 24

Katarina Rasmirovna thought she had made peace with the bizarre course her life had taken. She had observed and handled the time-pieces; she had seen the world literally change around her; Maxwell had proven his *bona fides* with a dozen pieces of knowledge both large-scale and intimate. Had there been anyone with whom she could have discussed the last impossible week, she would have said that of course she believed Maxwell's tale of time traveling to be true. She had changed the entire course of her life based on her belief in his veracity, after all.

But when her hotel sitting room dissolved around her, replaced with a shimmer like the sparks of dying fire, Katarina knew that the depths of her heart had not *really* believed it all until that moment.

Now she stood outside a dilapidated little green cottage, gasping with shock and cold in the frigid early morning. If Maxwell had done this magic trick of his correctly, it was the twenty-sixth of December, 1815. The snow lay all about appropriately deep and crisp and even, and England was staring down the maw of the coldest winter in living memory. The coming "year without a summer" would destroy crops and lead to widespread famine, although of course Maxwell's parents and their contemporaries couldn't know that yet. A moment ago, she had been in her hotel sitting room, overlooking turgid September London; now she was standing up to her calves in snow that had fallen eighty years previously, supporting a trembling Emil Schwieger and shivering as the wind hissed under her skirt and chilled her soaked stockings. She wondered what exactly she had been thinking when she had donned feminine clothing for this outing. Why had she assumed they would arrive indoors? Katarina looked about for Maxwell and found him a few feet away, methodically forcing one of the ground-floor windows of his parents' cottage.

"Are you certain that's wise?" Katarina hissed to him. "Didn't you say your father has a pistol?"

Maxwell ignored her, shoving the window sash upward with a thrust of his shoulder, and turning to offer first Emil and then herself a hand over the sill. The skirt of Katarina's gown dragged through the clinging snow, plastering itself wet and clammy against her stockinged legs and hampering her ability to swing said legs even over this low barrier—*why* had she not just costumed as Colin and been done with it?

The sitting room in which Katarina found herself was snug enough, though as badly in need of upkeep as the exterior of the cottage was in need of paint. It was also as cold as a barn, the fire dead in the hearth. Which was, in one sense, a good sign: Maxwell had chosen this day on the assumption that any servants his parents might be able to afford would have taken it as a holiday, and indeed, that seemed to be the case.

Maxwell closed the window, deposited the hamper and Katarina's carpet bag in the corner, and began to build up the fire. Emil, shuddering hard in a way that must have been painful to his still-healing injuries, leaned on the back of an armchair and watched. Katarina felt sensation draining away from, instead of returning to, her icy-cloth-clad legs.

"I mean the question seriously," she said to Maxwell. "Is there some reason we didn't go to the front door like normal people?"

Maxwell still did not reply, giving his full attention to the business of coaxing the spark into flame. That done, he piled a shovelful of coal into the grate. "There," he said at last, rising. "Sit and be comfortable, both of you. I want to have a quick word with them before I introduce you."

An unobserved quick word, Katarina inferred. Which was perhaps the reason for the subterfuge—he wanted to have this conversation with his parents in reasonable privacy, not in front of their guests in the main hall. Still, though—

But there was no opportunity for any further discussion, for at that moment they heard footsteps on the stairs. Katarina turned instinctively toward the sound, and Emil paused in the act of lowering himself into the armchair. Maxwell sighed in exasperation and strode past them to meet the owners of the house. The door leading into the hallway was not completely closed, and though his shoulders blocked most of the view, they did not block it all, so Katarina, without having consciously decided to eavesdrop, saw all that transpired.

The young woman and her husband came down the stairs carelessly, he making some laughing jest, she turning her head to riposte. They were both fully dressed, but something in the way they moved reminded Katarina that they were newly married, and confirmed her deduction that no servant would be underfoot today. Young Mr. and Mrs. Carrington had clearly been expecting to have the downstairs rooms to themselves. And they were even younger than Katarina had imagined after hearing Maxwell's tale—the husband in his early twenties, the wife surely not more than eighteen.

But then young Mr. Carrington's eyes landed on the shadows cast by the flickering firelight, and the laughter dropped from his face. Katarina abruptly remembered his Peninsula experience. He caught at his wife's arm to stop her, but she had already stopped, her eyes also on the moving shadows, her entire attitude as alert and watchful as a deer in a meadow. These two were both older than they looked, in experience if not in years.

Maxwell stepped out from the shadows to face them.

For a long moment, nobody moved. Then William Carrington said, "Oh, thank God," and put his hand on the bannister as though his knees had gone weak.

Elizabeth Carrington let out a breath and ran down the rest of the stairs into Maxwell's awkward embrace, and Katarina realized she had no business at all watching this reunion. She withdrew to join Emil by the hearth, thought about taking the other armchair, glanced down at the soaked hem of her skirt, and decided it would be better to stand. She gave her attention to the bravely burning little fire, letting it warm her numbed fingers and chilled legs, but the room was not very large and the door still ajar, and the conversation taking place in the hall was plainly audible.

"You, er…" Maxwell said. "I take you worked it out."

"You did leave us your locket," his mother said. "But yes, we were most of the way to working it out before we opened it. I'm so glad you're well. We've been so worried."

"We wanted to look for you," added her husband, coming down the stairs to join them, "but it would have been foolish, with all of space and time to search. We've been telling each other for six months that we had to trust you, and you'd be bound to find us instead." A rustle of cloth, and Katarina imagined William's outstretched hand. "Welcome home."

The sincerity of his tone brought a lump to *her* throat, and it wasn't even as though this was her family. But Maxwell said only, "Thank you."

"Did you build up the fire in there?" young Mrs. Carrington asked.

"It seemed the least I could do. I forced a window to get in. There aren't servants we need to elude?"

"Thankfully not," Mr. Carrington said. "An unexpected benefit of your, ah, your grandfather's—?" He said the word as though it tasted unfamiliar. "—your grandfather's obstinacy with regard to Elizabeth's dowry."

"I'll set some tea brewing," his wife said, "and then we have to know: what *happened?* How did you get free of Emil Schwieger, where did he take you—"

"I'll tell you all of it. First, though, I must tell you something else. I, er, brought some friends to spend the Christmas holiday." Katarina thought he was trying for a jesting tone. "Without leave or warning, as a feckless son should."

"Of course," Elizabeth Carrington said. "It's your home too, more or less. I assume they're part of this?"

"Very much so," Maxwell said. "But in one case, I'll have to provide introductions anyhow. There were some things I meant to say in private first, but—well, we may as well do it this way." The sitting room door swung open, and Katarina looked up from the fire as the Carrington family entered.

The resemblance between Maxwell and his father was not overly strong, but with the two of them standing side by side, she could see it. Though completely dissimilar in build—William slim and fine-boned and Maxwell taller and broad-shouldered—their eyes were identical as to shape and color, and the structure of their faces, the pleasant regular features, echoed each other.

Between Maxwell and Elizabeth there was no physical similarity at all; it was apparently only in personality that Maxwell resembled his mother. Katarina turned interested eyes upon the woman who was the center of Maxwell's tales—the fiery, unstoppable, literally legendary Elizabeth Barton Carrington.

She saw bright blue eyes, a tangle of brown curls unconfined by the caps usually worn by married women, a slight boyish figure, and the most startling expression of vivacity Katarina had ever beheld. Elizabeth was not strictly speaking beautiful—"pretty enough," as could be fairly said of most girls her age, but nothing out of the common way—but she was saved from plainness by the energy that radiated from her. She seemed twice as alive as anyone else in the room.

And she was looking upon her guest with absolute unfeigned delight. *"Katarina,"* Elizabeth Carrington said, bounding forward with outstretched hands.

Katarina had known she would be meeting people who in a sense already knew her, but grasping such a concept with her logical mind had not prepared her for this moment. She did not draw away, but the instant's self-control it took to deny the impulse must have been visible. Certainly she was not reaching back with equal enthusiasm—and Elizabeth stopped at once, letting her own hands drop, then took an apologetic step backward. "Of course," she said. "I'm so sorry. You don't know us."

"I…almost feel as though I do," Katarina offered. "I have heard many remarkable stories about you both. It might be more accurate to say I do not know this woman you are greeting."

"May I present Madame Katarina Rasmirovna," Maxwell said, *"prima donna* of Milan's Teatro alla Scala, and toast of London and the Continent. Katarina, my mother and father, Elizabeth and William Carrington."

William bowed and Elizabeth curtseyed, in the old-fashioned formal manner that was of course *a la mode* from their perspective, and Katarina was glad to be spared the more intimate embraces and handclasps for the moment. She gathered the folds of her sodden green skirt and curtseyed in return.

"I am very happy to know you," Elizabeth said.

"As am I," her husband said, more quietly but with equal warmth. "You are very welcome here."

"Thank you," Katarina managed, uncomfortable at their fervency. "I'm— pleased to be here, honored to meet you both."

"Our other visitor you already know—" Maxwell began, then broke off. The Carringtons had clearly already recognized the figure who had risen quietly from the armchair and was standing waiting in the shadows.

Young Mr. Carrington regarded Emil Schwieger without speaking. Emil looked back and said nothing.

Mr. Carrington's left hand had barely twitched with the desire for motion, but Maxwell spoke as though he had drawn back a balled fist. "No, don't! He's injured. Wait until he heals."

Mr. Carrington spared Maxwell a glance. "How did you know what I meant to do?"

"Because the first action your son took, the instant we were alone, was a roundhouse punch," Emil said.

"For striking his mother?" William Carrington interpreted. Katarina had not even heard that story. The four of them had *so much* history she did not know or share— "Good," Mr. Carrington said. "But that's his vengeance and not mine. Since you do indeed seem to be injured, I'll save mine for a more convenient season—but hear me now. You will never again lay a hand on a member of my family."

Emil nodded shortly. He looked past Mr. Carrington, clearing his throat. "Mrs. Carrington, I do beg your pardon."

The color was high in her cheeks, and Katarina thought she too might have been contemplating a roundhouse punch. But Elizabeth Carrington said only, "I accept your apology, Herr Schwieger. At least provisionally. There must be a good reason for Maxwell to bring you here, and certainly I will not allow your presence to mar my joy at seeing my son or the friend I have missed so terribly these six months."

She had missed Katarina terribly for six months? The *five* of them had so much history, and suddenly the fact that Katarina did not know any of it seemed like an unscalable obstacle. It was like being outside Jacob's shop, staggering under the waves of changing time, floundering forward despite knowing nothing of what hammered in the air all around her. The weight of all this Carrington history was like the weight of all that global history. Then the feeling of drowning had come from being the only constant in a sea of change. Now it was due to being the only the one wrong note in a pattern intimately familiar to everyone else involved in it.

Young Mrs. Carrington was watching her with concerned eyes. "This must be—" she began, then stopped and started over. "I know something of how difficult time travel is at first. How dizzying."

"That's the word," Katarina agreed.

"We could start with tea?" Mrs. Carrington said. "That's what you did, when I was the newly-arrived time traveler who knew nothing of the world she'd just stepped into." She dimpled at what appeared to be a shared jest, one that Katarina of course did not share. "We haven't any brandy either. Nor any gin."

"Neither brandy nor gin is necessary," Katarina said. "Tea—yes, thank you, Mrs. Carrington, tea seems like the place to start."

"Please won't you take a seat, then?"

"Oh. Ah—" Katarina glanced guiltily at the soaked flounce of her skirt. She could not stop it drenching the carpet, but so far she had managed to save the armchair. She had grown up in poverty exactly similar to that which the Carringtons now maneuvered their way through, and she was determined not ruin an armchair if she could help it.

"Oh," Mrs. Carrington said, "I'm so sorry, I didn't notice! You must be frozen. In that case, we should start with finding you something to wear that isn't soaked! Come with me."

"Thank you." Katarina stooped to retrieve the carpet bag Maxwell had dropped in the corner. "I did bring something I could change into, but I don't know how appropriate—"

Mrs. Carrington seemed to be having a conversation with her husband, using only her eyebrows. He nodded agreement to whatever she had just proposed, and Mrs. Carrington turned her attention back to Katarina. "I'm sure it's fine, and if not we can find something better. Come upstairs, we'll dry you off and find you some warm clothing—and we can go from there, can't we?"

Her manner was so earnest and so friendly that Katarina could not help but relax a little in the face of it. "Yes," she said again, "thank you"—and followed her hostess both upstairs and into a brave new world.

❧

The air of the stairway was colder than that of the sitting room or downstairs hallway, and the air of the sparsely-furnished upstairs bedroom even colder than that. Katarina found herself shivering again, once more aware of the clammy, icy stockings pressed to her skin. "I'll get you a towel," Elizabeth Carrington said, concerned, "and I could heat up some wash water, if you wanted it?"

Katarina darted a quick glance at the basin on the unsteady-looking corner table. Ice filmed its top—a thin layer, having formed in the short time since her hosts had broken the nighttime ice to wash their own faces. There was no hearth in the little bedroom, so any wash water would have to be hauled up from the kitchen, by her hostess' own hands since there was no servant to do it. It was a situation so intensely familiar from Katarina's own childhood that she could not bear to inflict what might well be perceived as an embarrassment upon the young woman who found herself suddenly presiding over an uninvited house party. "Oh, there's no need, Mrs. Carrington," she said. "Just the towel, please." She wasn't *that* cold. Once changed into dry clothing and seated before the downstairs fire, she would soon be comfortable.

Mrs. Carrington fetched the towel hanging above the basin. "Here, sit down and take off your wet things."

Katarina considered the neatly-made bed, with its brightly-colored unfashionable quilt, and chose instead to lower herself and her soaked skirt onto a little wooden chest. The wet cloth couldn't hurt it; its paint was already faded and peeling. She unbuckled her low boots and stripped off her stockings, once again exasperated with herself for not dressing more sensibly. At least she was only wearing a shirtwaist and skirt, not the full elaborate absurdity of her more formal costumes.

"I feel as though I ought to apologize for the primitive furnishings," Mrs. Carrington said wryly, coming back with the towel. "You probably already know I 'married to displease my family,' as the saying goes, and they were quite a bit more displeased than William and I expected."

"Maxwell did say something of the sort," Katarina agreed, rubbing the feeling back into her legs, "but goodness, you needn't apologize. We're the ones who have shown up without warning. I hope you won't consider it a liberty—" She glanced up to meet Mrs. Carrington's sparkling blue eyes. "—but I convinced your son to bring along a hamper of cold meat and such. I knew the butcher would be closed today, and I thought your servants would have taken the holiday—and all I could think was how my own mother would have reacted to unexpected guests under such circumstances."

Young Mrs. Carrington laughed. "That was very kind of you. No, of course it's not a liberty—*you* couldn't take one if you wanted to. You're always welcome here." She went on, turning to the wardrobe before Katarina could look away in embarrassment, "I don't know what you brought along to wear, but I'm sure William and I between us can supply anything you need." She opened the wardrobe door, gesturing impartially at the frocks hanging on one side and the trousers hanging on the other.

Gesturing impartially at...both.

Katarina said slowly, "Like your son, you appear to know a great deal about me."

"In fact, this is the first time I've ever seen you wear a gown," her hostess said, sitting down on the bed and gathering up the threadbare quilt to use as a shawl. "The other times I've known you, you were always in trousers. It—it quite took my breath away, you know, when we met the first time. I'd never seen a woman wear trousers before. It—it seemed like a symbol, of all the other things I didn't know a woman could do until I saw you do them."

Katarina thought over the phrasing. "You didn't meet me when I was playing at being Colin Ramsey. You met me as Katarina, but wearing men's clothing?"

"No, not wearing men's clothing, just wearing trousers. And a pretty blouse and a tight bodice. All together. You gave me the same outfit to wear, and you took me for a walk through the streets of 1885. It was the most wondrous and the most frightening and honestly the most dangerous place I've ever been. You...made such a difference." Elizabeth Carrington swallowed and looked down. "I can't tell you how much. You said I wasn't helpless. You said I could change things. No one had ever said anything like that to me before. And I *did* change things. *We* did eventually change things. We got it wrong at first, but we did fix Waterloo in the end, just as you wanted me to. You told me I could, and...and you were right."

"That wasn't me," Katarina said.

Mrs. Carrington looked up. "Of course it was. Who else? Even if you can't remember it now—"

Katarina shook her head. "It's more than not being able to remember it. *I* didn't do those things. I'm not the person you've missed for six months. What makes you think I can—" She broke off, took a breath, and tried again. "Listen, Mrs. Carrington—"

"'Elizabeth.'"

"Elizabeth. I want to help. Truly I do. Maxwell's quest matters to me. He hasn't had a chance yet to acquaint you with this new danger, but this enemy he fights threatens my world and my loved ones; I have a personal stake in destroying them. And it's more than that—I truly feel as though I've been waiting for this siren call my whole life. But I haven't the least idea what I'm doing. I listen to the four of you talking, and—" She took another breath. "You already know how to do this. You speak of me as though I know how as well. As though I've only forgotten, as though I've been in an accident and lost my memory and it all will come back in time. And that's a kind conceit, Mrs. Car—Elizabeth, but it's not true. Someone who looks like me did brave and brilliant things, and I'd like to live up to her reputation, but I haven't the slightest idea whether I'm equal to the task."

Elizabeth had listened closely to all this, twice biting her lip in an obvious trick to stop herself from interrupting. Only when it was clear that Katarina had done speaking did she look directly into Katarina's eyes. "Of course you are equal to the task. Very well, you've no experience yet—but you're Katarina Rasmirovna. You couldn't be less than yourself if you wanted to be. We don't *need* you to be anyone other than yourself. And to that end—" Elizabeth gestured toward the wardrobe. "—what clothing would you be most comfortable wearing?"

"Your gowns will be too small for me," Katarina said. "I suppose I could... May I ask how long it will be before your servants return?"

"We only have the one woman, who does for us by day. She'll be by tomorrow."

"It might be easiest if I became Colin Ramsey for the duration, then." Katarina considered it. "It would solve a number of problems. Your guests would seem more respectable if you didn't have to explain a woman traveling in the company of two men to whom she is not related by blood or marriage. Maxwell and Emil and I could all three of us be acquaintances of your husband's from his Army days—two British and one Prussian."

"If you wish to make yourself up as Colin Ramsey," Elizabeth said, "you certainly may, and my husband would be happy to loan you whatever clothing you might need. But that wasn't what I asked."

"You asked what I would be most comfortable wearing." Katarina thought about it. She had never once considered the question that way. "Trousers *and* a fitted bodice, you said?"

"Yes—the sort gypsy women wear, or peasant women on the Continent." Elizabeth mimed front lacings.

"I haven't anything like that," Katarina said. Slowly she began to smile. "Yet." She considered it again. "Well, perhaps—just for today—I might try the rest of it."

It might actually have been the most daring thing she had ever done, and given her past that was saying something, to draw on Colin Ramsey's trousers and sensible sturdy boots, but pair them with her frilly, puffed-sleeve shirtwaist blouse buttoned over her unbound chest. She surveyed herself in the streaky cracked glass hung beside the wardrobe. The outfit was indeed most comfortable, in the physical sense and in some other unspoken sense as well. Still— She sought Elizabeth's eyes in the reflection. "Are you *certain* this won't cause you problems?"

"Of course I am. Costume as you must for Mrs. Brewer, but for us? Wear your own clothing and do your hair how you like."

It *was* her own clothing, all of it. She had just never combined it this way. She tried to imagine adding a bodice such as Elizabeth had described to the ensemble, and found it an attractive image. At some point in the—ah—in the future, she would have to go looking for such a thing.

Do your hair as you like. She hesitated, then slowly reached up to loosen the thick braided and coiled mass. She had not worn her hair loose in public since running away to London at the age of sixteen. Nor did she think she would do it often after today, for loose hair would be most inconvenient while trying to execute any active maneuver—but if all they meant to do today was sit around the fire, she might as well try it. Just this once. Unbound, it fell past her waist.

Elizabeth gathered up the wet green skirt. "We'll can hang this to dry in the kitchen. I don't think it will need washing; these stains are only water. Which is very fortunate, as I was never taught how to get mud out of anything." Katarina followed her back down the stairs, and the temperature seemed to increase a welcome degree with every step. "I find the education I received in my father's house to be utterly inadequate for the life I now live," Elizabeth said. "I wouldn't change a bit of the life, however my husband may worry, but I do wish I could go back and get myself a better education. By the time I've learned everything I need to know, I'll have turned twenty-one and it won't be so urgent to know it."

"Ah," Katarina said, remembering. "Your father's 'obstinacy with regard to your dowry' is a temporary problem?"

"Yes, thankfully. It's not his money, you see. My mother's father left it to me in my own name, to be received when I attained my majority or married with my parents' consent. We did not obtain their consent before we went to Gretna Green, but I assumed they'd give it afterward, to avoid the scandal. Instead, they forwarded my belongings and forbade me from darkening their door." She sighed, but in annoyance rather than grief. "So we're living on William's half-pay for the moment. And I *don't care.* He says he wouldn't blame me for thinking I'd made a bad bargain, but I *don't.* I'd do it all over again. I'd just…learn plain cooking and mending first."

In the kitchen, Elizabeth hung the green skirt to dry, then set about slicing bread and making tea. The cups she set out on the tray were a motley assortment, the Carringtons understandably not possessing a matched set of wedding china. Elizabeth grinned a little and said something about unmatched teacups being traditional, which was obviously another jest she had shared with some other Katarina. Katarina tried not to mind.

Well, she would just have to ask Elizabeth about it, wouldn't she? Later; they had more important matters to discuss first.

She followed Elizabeth back into the sitting room, bearing the tray with bread and butter while Elizabeth managed the one with tea and teacups. Katarina was watching for everyone's reaction as she crossed the threshold, back braced for disapproval or derision, but not one of the three men even looked twice at her combination of unbound hair and trousers. She was almost disappointed.

"Ah, there you are," young Mr. Carrington said, looking over at her with a fond smile. "Now you're here, we can begin."

Chapter 25

The early winter sunset was truly the most magnificent he had ever seen. A band of emerald green encircled the horizon, fading smoothly upward into pale blue, then dark blue, then indigo. It was impossible for the naked eye to determine at what point exactly it became black.

Down in the village, the church clock began to chime four. Maxwell felt in his breast pocket for another of the cigarettes he had inadvertently brought with him from the Victorian era, and lit it with a matchstick he shouldn't have brought to the Regency either. An exhalation of tobacco smoke obscured the clear cold sky, but only briefly.

Behind him, the kitchen door opened. He glanced over his shoulder to see Katarina, outlined in a dim red glow only fractionally brighter than the evening light outside, a kettle in one hand.

"All right?" she asked.

"Yes," Maxwell said. "Yes, fine."

It was true enough, if incomplete. He had no idea how to even begin the rest of it, so it was just as well that she accepted his answer and closed the door against the winter chill. She must have merely happened to glimpse him through the window on her way to refill the kettle, and no sensible person would choose to stand out here without first bundling up against the frigid air. He congratulated himself on having escaped a difficult conversation.

The door opened again, and Katarina, now without the kettle and with a patchwork quilt draped over her shoulders, stepped out onto the porch to join him.

"It will take some time to boil," she said in explanation, closing the door behind her. She came to stand beside him, looking out and up into the indigo-blackness. "Oh, my. *Green* in a sunset. Everything I've heard about this year is true."

"Schwieger says the sunsets, like the weather, have something to do with a volcano on the other side of the world," Maxwell explained. It wasn't what he wanted to say.

"Oh, do they?" Katarina rested her elbow on the rail.

"Apparently they do." There was a little silence. "You know you'll catch your death out here, dressed only in that." That wasn't what he wanted to say either.

Katarina didn't seem in a hurry to retreat back to the warm kitchen. "No need to worry. I never catch cold."

"Would you like a cigarette?" And what on earth had possessed him to make that offer? That was *definitely* not what he wanted to say.

Katarina looked back at him in frank astonishment. "Um, no. Thank you." After a moment she added, "Many of the fine ladies of the Continent partake—or I suppose I should say will partake—but I can't think of anything that makes less sense than an opera singer who coats her throat with smoke."

"An excellent choice on your part," Maxwell said. "Even if you've paused the opera singing life for now." He saw the opening then. "I am beginning to appreciate your philosophical quandary."

Katarina turned this over in her mind, then smiled a little. "What one does after one gets what one wants?"

"That precisely." Maxwell let out a mouthful of smoke. "If this story began with a child watching a Christmas party through the bannister railings—well, here is the story's conclusion." He waved to indicate the cottage behind them, with the world's strangest Christmas party assembled in the parlor. "Not only is it nothing like what I expected, by this point it's many course changes removed from relevant. What does one do after one gets what one spent quite a long time wanting?"

"I suppose," Katarina said with a slight smile, "one might begin by spending Christmas with one's parents."

"Talking time travel mechanics and the tactics appropriate for prying the grip of the Nazi Empire off the throat of humanity," Maxwell said. "Because my life never will be a normal one." He sighed a breath, almost a laugh, because it was all too absurd not to laugh at. "Living or dead, I'm the revenant of my past. I got what I once wanted, but it doesn't make up for not having it then, when it mattered. I'm living my entire life out of sequence."

"More people do that than you'd think."

He glanced at her sidelong. "I imagine you do not mean literally."

"Well, we don't know how many time travelers there are, do we?" Katarina said. "So perhaps literally, who knows. But no, I meant metaphorically." She looked back out at the sunset. "I meant, the more I see of the world, the fewer examples I see of 'everyday normal life.' That one we're all meant to live, the one it looks like everyone else lives, the one with the accomplishments of youth and maturity and age neatly sorted. I think more people live in a jumble than would care to admit it." She paused, turning her head back toward him. "So may I suggest an alternate perspective on this situation?"

"Please."

Katarina laid chilly fingers on his wrist. "You are time traveling."

For a moment the world lurched around him. For a moment he could see this cottage overlaid with another, a burning *doppelganger*, shouts and alarums as Schwieger smoked out the Frankenstein papers—

But Katarina was still smiling a small smile, unaware of his momentary hallucination. "We are *all* time traveling," she said. "You only get one chance to live each day, no matter the order in which you live them. This is the only

Christmas of 1815 you'll ever have. One day between morning and midnight, at the top of the precipice, before whatever is about to happen comes upon us." She smiled at him again. "Therefore, would you not say you owe today your full attention?"

He had to smile back at that. "You always have been a wise woman."

The frosty kitchen greeted them with a blast of what felt, in comparison to the outdoors, like summer air. The kettle was bubbling merrily by this time, and Katarina used it to refill the teapot, moving as deftly as though the kitchen were well-lit, or perhaps as though it were intimately familiar. Maxwell followed her through the cool eddying air of the corridor and back into the actual warmth of the sitting room, where Elizabeth, William, and Schwieger all clustered close to the fire. A single rush light illuminated the table, casting odd shadows over the half-empty platter of cold meats and the scattered mismatched teacups.

"As little as I like this fact, it has to be you," Schwieger was saying to William. "Maxwell and I have spoiled our chance to affect Vermok. We can't go back."

"I do understand that's why you came here," Elizabeth said. "As little as you liked the necessity." Her lip curled at that, but then she looked at Maxwell in the doorway with more sympathy. "Or you either, I expect."

Maxwell took a moment to steel himself, then plunged back into the room and into the conversation. "I dislike exceedingly the notion of sending you into danger," he said, "but there's no choice about it now. The stakes are intolerably high, and Schwieger and I can't be in the Vermok high-concentration cell room twice. It's not a matter of pocket watch rules and mechanics any longer; it's a matter of sanity and common sense." He dropped into the armchair Schwieger was not occupying. "I'd just as soon let you handle it in any case," he told Elizabeth. "You're rather gifted at this art. You fixed Waterloo, after all." He smiled a little, but could taste bitterness in his mouth. "And it took you something under a week to divine the trick of affecting the past, which compares favorably to the fifteen years it took me. I always thought history resisted my attempts to change it because I wasn't forcing it hard enough or tricking it successfully enough, and then you solve the Waterloo problem by showing Viktor Frankenstein where his actions would lead and offering him the chance to be the best version of himself." Maxwell stared into the fire, seeing the Pendoylan duck pond. "A tactic that literally never occurred to me."

William shifted abruptly in his chair, and Maxwell looked over to surprise a rare look of anger on his face. "That's a more telling statement than you know," William said. "I've half a mind to call my brother out."

Maxwell could not immediately piece that together.

But it seemed Elizabeth could. "George and Anne haven't done anything yet, love," she pointed out.

"Nor will they be given the chance to." William spoke with grim resolve. He took his wife's hand, but looked over her head at his son. "We intend to take appropriate precautions. No child of ours will be left to their guardianship."

"And so the future changes," Elizabeth said. "We are shown the shadows of things that may be only, and we change the course that foreshadows the end."

Katarina looked up from her teacup, startled. "Are you...actually quoting...?"

Elizabeth smiled at her. "You, as it happens."

"Ah." Katarina leaned back. "The idea that I was quoting Dickens to you in some lost timeline is less distressing than the idea that you spontaneously came up with his words. Sorry, carry on. You were speaking of the past being resistant to change...?"

"It's more than resistant," William said. "As near as we can tell, it is *impervious* to change enacted upon it by an outsider. By a time traveler who does not belong there, in other words. The only people who succeed in changing their timelines are the people who live in them."

"Which means," Elizabeth said, "a time traveler can only change history by changing the mind of the person making it. Force doesn't work. Trickery doesn't work." She addressed Maxwell. "You told your patron Katarina the truth. You told your student Katarina the truth. We told Viktor Frankenstein the truth. And all three times, history changed."

"Wait a bit." Katarina rubbed at her forehead—and then looked up, seeming quite disconcerted by the way they all obediently paused the conversation to allow her the time she needed to find the words. She shook her head a little, but did not comment upon it. "It can't be true that trickery never works," she said instead. "It worked for us, for Maxwell and me. We executed a beautifully-crafted chess game against the firm of Bastion and Bastion, using Bill Ellis as a pawn. I similarly fooled a consulting detective. The tactics we used to get the timepiece back were nearly all trickery."

"I venture to suppose they were all your tactics?" William said.

Katarina thought it over. "Certainly all the tricks were."

"You belonged to that timeline," Elizabeth explained. "The tactics of the person local to the timeline do not matter. The *choice* of the person local to the timeline matters. Once the choice to change the future is freely made, the one living in a straight line may act upon the world however she or he likes."

Katarina thought about it. "So does that mean...to undo the Nazi campaign to rewrite history, does that mean we need to persuade a thousand good men to act differently at a moment of truth? And a thousand mediocre men to follow their better instincts rather than their baser ones? Over and over again, everywhere your Nazis travel, follow them and persuade those who live there to undo the damage? That's the work of a lifetime, but...but it's the sort of work that would mean a life well spent. I would help with that in any way I could."

"So would I," William said. "If that's what we must do, and it may prove necessary to do exactly that."

"But we ought to try to reverse that one moment first," Elizabeth said. "Tactically speaking, it would be far preferable to prevent the evil empire from getting the timepiece in the first place. That's why Maxwell came to us, the hope that we could change that one moment."

"So whose mind is it that must be changed?" Katarina asked. "Stanislaus Lis?"

"I wonder…" Maxwell said slowly. "I wonder if we couldn't… Just this once, just this one last time, I wonder if we couldn't manage something better. The Vermok gorge *can* be climbed, Lis proved that. Perhaps it's the leader of the Norwegian sabotage team whose mind must be changed. Perhaps we could persuade him to dispense with the orders from London and climb the gorge." He remembered. "I mean to say, perhaps you could. I can't be there twice."

Elizabeth looked interested, but Schwieger cut her off before she could speak. "It's not that simple," he said. "The bridge was only half their problem. Persuading them to climb the gorge does nothing about the defensive measures they'll meet once inside. There's still a very real chance of failure, and failure that night means the Nazi war machine is supplied with the atomic bomb, and Stanislaus Lis grows up in Warsaw's nuclear winter, and all the dominos come tumbling down just as before."

"Fine." Katarina got up and started to pace, to the shadows at the end of the cramped room and back. "It's a two-pronged strategy, then. Those are the best sort in any case. How do we sabotage the inner defenses before we send the Norwegians into the gorge?"

"I'm not sure a loveless childhood is entirely to blame for Maxwell's approach to the world," Elizabeth said to William. "This mode of thinking he must have learned from the Spider. Katarina, we just went through this. Sabotage won't work, trickery won't work."

"I didn't say we'd enact the sabotage ourselves," Katarina said impatiently. "We *did* just go through this, and you said sabotage and trickery *would* work if they were the chosen tactics of someone belonging to the timeline. Very well, then, we need an emissary who belongs to that timeline. Someone who will rise to the right kind of prominence to lessen the defenses and can be persuaded to do so. How do we go about finding an ally within the Nazi regime?"

Very quietly, Emil Schwieger said, "You already have."

The sudden silence was so profound that the fire's crackling sounded like drumming horse's hooves.

"I'm from there," Schwieger said. "I'm from then. I may have traveled in time, but I'm free now to go back and live in a straight line if I choose…and I do choose. Rosamund convinced me to rise above my upbringing, and Stach convinced me that the world he had been born into could not be allowed to exist, and you've just convinced me that this tactic is worth trying. Suppose I go home. I live in a straight line. I soften the resistance ahead of Operation Gunnerside. And then you persuade them to climb the gorge."

"The work of a lifetime," Katarina said slowly.

Schwieger smiled at her. "A lifetime well-spent might be enough to finally atone for…for all of it. You never know, I might even be able to mitigate some other horrors along the way."

"What year would you return to?" William said it slowly, clearly thinking out all the implications.

"I don't look thirteen any longer, so it can't be 1921." Schwieger frowned. "It's been ten years, more or less, but 1931 doesn't give me enough time. 1926? I'd be eighteen, old enough to enlist, and that gives me twelve years to do all the subtle damage I can. I'll say I ran away from home and lived rough, to account for me looking a bit older than my age. I think twelve years might be enough time to get into position to weaken Vermok's defenses."

"It's also enough time to get caught," Katarina said quietly. "Or killed."

"But we could correct for that," Maxwell said, seeing the possibilities opening before him. "Act as guardian angels. That's something I *could* do. The years between 1926 and 1943 are open to me, and I could rescue Schwieger from death however many times is required. Not through force or trickery, just by bringing the information needed to avoid the wrong choice of the moment." He looked at Schwieger. "For that to work, you'll have to give me coordinates for your headquarters."

"I would have had to in any case," Schwieger said. "New guardians are needed."

"Slow and careful, to position Emil," Elizabeth said. "Subtle, to weaken Vermok's defenses. And then straight truth to the Norwegians, the direct approach." She looked at William with a smile. "I approve of the direct approach."

"That is not new information," he told her, but he was smiling also. "Very well, then—" he looked around the room to make sure of it "—it would seem we have a plan."

Maxwell started to get up from his chair.

"But there is no need for anyone to go haring off today," William said, and Maxwell abashedly settled back "A direct approach—even a swift approach—does not require haste on this end. We are not running for our lives, and as long as we each wear a timepiece we are safe from history being rewritten from under our feet. We are damned well spending at least a day planning this mission and collecting the tools we need."

It took, in the end, much longer than a day. Time was required to change some of Katarina's gold to local currency. Time—and a journey to London, made immeasurably more difficult by the snow and lack of steam-trains—was required to acquire something close to the right kind of cloth for Schwieger's 1943 clothing. Time was required to make the clothing. A journey to headquarters was required for detailed military studies of the conflict into which the young Prussian proposed to insert himself. Schwieger took William and Elizabeth with him on this jaunt, but Maxwell and Katarina had to stay behind.

"A time traveler can always return to the time from which he or she started," Maxwell explained to her, "but cannot count on being able to return to any other time, after having left it. Except headquarters, apparently."

"You can go home whenever you like," Katarina interpreted, "but you may only be able visit other times and places once."

"Exactly."

This meant, of course, that William and Elizabeth had to bring Schwieger to 1926, leaving Maxwell and Katarina with nothing to do but await their return. And it meant, Maxwell realized sickly in the moment after they vanished, that when it was time to impact Vermok, he would be left behind alone. He would send Elizabeth, William, and Katarina into danger, and await their return in the cottage, *alone.*

Of course you'll be sending them into danger, he berated himself, pacing the little sitting room. *You came here with the specific intention of sending them into danger.* But it hadn't felt real until now. Katarina watched him from the side of the room, arms folded. If there was sympathy in her eyes, he did not turn his head to see.

A minute and a half later, William and Elizabeth reappeared. Maxwell unclenched his fists, seated himself outside the circle of firelight, and there perused a history of Vermok with the candle held between himself and the paper so that no one could see his face.

He had expected the next stretch of time to be peppered with frequent trips to headquarters and minute course corrections of Schwieger's life, but in fact the first journey to check in on their emissary's personal history led to the conclusion that he had survived until 1943 with no assistance needed. Suddenly the time before the trio could embark upon their attempt to change Vermok shrank from unknown frustrating weeks to "as soon as possible," and Maxwell found himself incapable of either sleep or deep breaths. The three travelers tarried a few days more anyhow, to be sure of provisions and of proficiency with the various weapons they had collected—William's large and cumbersome pistol, Katarina's little revolver, and the assortment of even smaller and sleeker hand weapons acquired from headquarters.

And then the day was upon them, and there was nothing more for Maxwell to do but see them off.

If circles of hell could be custom-designed for their occupants, surely he stood inside his own now, watching at one helpless remove as the three people he cared for most adjusted their costuming and rucksacks and weapons.

At least he would not have a long wait before they returned.

If they returned. What would he do if they did not return?

"We'll be back before you have time to worry," Katarina told him cheerfully.

Maxwell managed a twisted smile at that. "You may underestimate my capacity."

She tossed her head, feigning insult. "I believe you underestimate our capability."

"Never." Maxwell closed the distance between them in two resolute strides, then reached out to deliberately shake her hand, then Elizabeth's, then William's. "The future could be entrusted to no one better."

Elizabeth and William exchanged glances. They both looked anxious, and no wonder. Maxwell rather thought it was his place as a senior time traveling mentor to say something further by way of encouragement. Nothing came immediately to mind. What *was* he to do if five minutes went by, or ten—or a day or a week—and they did not return?

"Very well," William said. They had agreed to use his timepiece, and he held it up now. "Are we all prepared? All in contact?" Elizabeth took hold of his right arm and Katarina laid a hand on his left shoulder.

Maxwell stepped back from the three of them, by sheer force of will keeping his jaw set, his posture straight, and his hands unclenched.

"One," William said, depressing the side button. "Two—" He depressed it again.

"Good-bye," Maxwell said, in a completely steady voice.

"—Elizabeth—" William said, but he needn't have bothered. She was already reaching her free hand to grab Maxwell's sleeve as the universe dissolved into sparkles around them.

Chapter 26

"That was stupid," Maxwell managed after long moments of coughing and retching. His breath puffed white in the frigid Norwegian cabin. "That was truly, deeply, unquestionably—" He choked and bent over the bucket again.

He had barely made it to the fortunately-placed pail in the corner of the cabin before evacuating the entire contents of his stomach, and his head was pounding like a steam-engine. He had felt this sick exactly twice before in his life, the first time when his reckless mother had seized his arm and tricked him into bringing her to Waterloo. He remembered vividly the seeming endlessness of the journey, as the two timepieces each tried to pull him in a different direction. He had arrived in the Forest of Soignes so dizzy he could barely tell which way was down, ears ringing and head pounding. He had suffered similarly unpleasant effects when forcing his timepiece to bring Schwieger along to their first attempt to fix Vermok.

This third experience was worse than either of the previous two, perhaps because *he* was the one violating the rules of time travel. The pain in his head was so sharp he would not have been overly surprised to find an ice pick protruding from his temple, and the tiny Spartan Vidda cabin whirled about him like a carousel. "Here," Elizabeth said, offering him a dampened handkerchief.

He glared at her. "That was *unbelievably* stupid. I am already here! Schwieger and I are a mile away awaiting our chance to—"

"You're not," William said. "Quite yet."

"Does that sound like the point I am making? You've just broken a timepiece and risked who knows what else, and for no better reason than to—"

"Bring you with us," his father finished. He made eye contact for just a moment. Maxwell was silenced.

"The timepiece can be fixed," his mother added airily. "That's been proven. Katarina can always pop back home and visit Mr. Trevelyan, even if it turns out the rest of us can't get back there."

For another moment, he could not find any way to reply. Then, grasping for the old curmudgeonly manner, he grumbled, "Reckless," and hauled himself to his feet. Elizabeth rolled her eyes fondly.

Katarina had watched this family drama play out from a few feet away. She looked drawn and pale as well, but she did not appear to be having difficulty keeping upright, an ability Maxwell found himself envying. "Glad to have you along," she said with a smile. And then, more sharply, "Maxwell. Sit down."

It was good advice, so he took it, dropping his head between his knees and waiting for the room to stop its spinning. After a few minutes, the dizziness, though not completely abated, had at least eased enough that he was able to look up and take stock of where they were.

The place known as the Fjøsbudalen cabin was whitewashed, neat, and barren. Built as a holiday retreat for Norwegians of happier earlier days, it featured little beyond table, chairs, bed, and stove. Outside, the Vidda stretched endlessly, equally white, equally lifeless. The men of Operation Grouse had already spent four months living in a place just like this, surviving on reindeer and some kind of moss. Maxwell could not imagine how. Claus Helberg, scouting ahead of Operation Gunnerside to discover the best way to Vermok, would rejoin the rest of his team here the following day. Before that, Stanislaus Lis would pause to rest before continuing his headlong journey into hell.

The room refused to stop spinning. It was like standing on the pavement outside Abramson's shop / the place where Abramson's shop should have been. Like standing knee-deep in a shallow sea with waves approaching from all directions and colliding.

"Hey," Katarina said. Somehow she was kneeling in front of him.

Maxwell tried to clear his head. "Sorry."

"Don't be ridiculous," she said. "I feel it too. Many possibilities died and came into being and died again, right here. Many people tried to stop Lis." She studied him. "I feel it. So do your parents. There must be some reason why it's so much worse for you."

At that moment, the door was flung open. William already had a pistol out, Katarina was turning sharply while drawing her own—but there was no immediate need. The man framed in the doorway had a wild look in his ice-blue eyes, but held no weapon.

"Stanislaus Lis?" Elizabeth stepped forward, hands raised to show she intended no harm. "Rosamund and Emil sent us—"

"I know!" Lis snapped. "I can tell! What the *hell* are you doing?" Snow swirled around him as he entered the cabin, slamming the door behind him. His eyes zeroed in on Maxwell. "You, specifically—what are you doing? The universe is shredding around you, as though you— Are you already *here*?"

"Yes." Maxwell hauled himself to his feet. "About a mile away, trying to stop you the first time. It doesn't go well—"

"How did you even manage to get here a second time? You shouldn't be able to—"

"One *can* cross one's own timeline," Elizabeth explained brightly. "If one sacrifices a timepiece."

Lis swung to glare at her. "I know you *can*. Do you know why you shouldn't?"

"No." Katarina locked eyes with him, her stance and voice equally calm. "By the time we got involved in this, there was no one left alive at your headquarters to teach us any of the regulations."

Lis stopped at that.

"It doesn't go well, this attempt you're about to make," Maxwell repeated. "Welcome to the most noble fraternity of We Who Do Not Look Before We Leap." He glanced sidelong at Elizabeth. "It's a Barton family trait. Carringtons are more cautious."

Katarina said, "It would more accurately be titled the most noble fraternity of Missing The Target Because You're In Too Much Pain To See. I understand why you're doing this," she said to Lis, still quietly. "I'm on your side of this battle. I didn't grow up in their world, but I have a personal stake nonetheless."

Lis looked at least somewhat interested. *Half statements are more valuable than whole statements. Pique their interest.* "And your personal stake is—?"

"I'm half Romani and my first lover was Jewish." Katarina paused to allow this to sink in. "He no longer exists. I was there at the moment he stopped existing. Can you guess why?"

Lis shook his head slowly—not, Maxwell thought, because he could not think of a reason, but because he could not risk believing it.

"What's the only thing worse than Nazis with atomic weapons?" Katarina asked.

Lis sat down suddenly in the nearest available chair and let his head drop into his hands. "Oh...God."

"You fail in your sabotage and you and your timepiece are captured," William said quietly. "From our perspective, it has already happened. My son has already tried to stop you once."

Lis looked up at Maxwell. "You really shouldn't—you really can't be here."

Maxwell shook his head, trying to dislodge the migraine. "Then let us resolve this matter quickly, so that I may leave."

Lis looked around at the others. "You *really* must not ever play with time like this again."

"Noted," Katarina said. *Grant concessions that do not matter.* "We can promise to never do so again. But desperate times..."

"Lis," William said quietly, but in a tone of finality, "*you* really cannot go through with your plan. It will only make things worse."

Lis didn't argue, only pressed the heels of his hands against his eyes. "But this can't be allowed to stand. We must do something—"

"We thought of another approach," Elizabeth said. She drew up the chair beside him. "Shall we explain?"

Lis listened with some interest if without any great appearance of conviction. "I suppose it's worth trying," he said. "I suppose you could be right about change enacted from the outside...All right. It's worth trying." He fingered the timepiece hung around his neck, and for some reason chose to speak to Maxwell. "I'm willing to delay my frontal assault. I'm willing to try to influence

Helberg." With some ceremony, he pulled the watch over his head and passed it to Maxwell. "I'm your canary. If Gunnerside gets the job done, my timeline disappears and I along with it. If I survive tomorrow night, then we keep hacking at keystones—at—you called them something else—at junctions—until we bring the Nazi Empire down."

"But you don't have to do that," Elizabeth protested. "You needn't give your life in such a way. If you kept the timepiece and survived, surely you could make a life for yourself afterward—"

Lis looked at her with bleak, haunted eyes. "For what imaginable reason would I want to do that?" he said, and Elizabeth was silenced.

And so they sat, waiting for Helberg. The room around Maxwell dipped and spun, flickering between different furnishings from one minute to the next. "You really should not be here," Lis said to him.

Maxwell resisted the urge to press a hand to his head. "I heard you the first three times."

"But even so, you're having an unusually severe reaction." Lis studied him, starting with the top of his head and slowly working downward until his eyes stopped, arrested, at the pocket watch Maxwell wore stretched across his waistcoat. Lis looked from it to the one Elizabeth cradled in her hands. "Is that the same timepiece?"

"More or less." Maxwell drew a deep breath past the nausea. "I found this version of it in a garret, in a timeline in which my parents died young. My mother received her version of it in the post, apparently from me."

"Apparently? Because you haven't sent it yet?" Lis interpreted. "Well, there's your problem. You're living in the future that results from an action you haven't taken yet. Until you give her the watch, you'll be fractured like this."

"I thought this was the side effect of surviving a dead timeline," Maxwell said.

Lis shook his head. "Survive a timeline and you'll always be a little light-headed, but you can learn to live with it, or so I'm told. It's survivable. What you're doing isn't."

"Noted," Maxwell said. "I'll address that situation next. One problem at a time."

"Yes." Katarina looked over from the window. "I believe that's your Claus Helberg approaching."

∽

Afterward, Claus Helberg said only that while he was returning from his reconnaissance mission, he "suddenly got the idea" that it would be possible for Gunnerside to climb the gorge and avoid shooting the guards on the bridge. He allowed his comrades-in-arms to believe his conversation with Rolf Sørlie had led him to this conclusion, since Rønneberg had, after all, sent him to Sørlie in the hope of receiving the most up-to-date information as to the defenses the Nazis had built around Vermok. As Sørlie remembered the conversation years later, neither man spent any time discussing the idea of climbing the gorge—yet somehow, on Helberg's journey home, "the impression suddenly came to him" that this was the correct course of action.

Claiming a sudden idea was easier than telling his companions of the strange visitors who had come to him at the unoccupied Fjösbudalen cabin, just as he was trying to decide whether he was hungry enough to ignore the ants that had drowned in the improperly-sealed tin of syrup he had hoped to eat. When he attempted to convince the rest of Gunnerside that the gorge was climbable, he said nothing about pocket watches, about visions of the future, or about the intense Pole with the burning eyes and the stories he told. There were things it was just impossible to explain, even to brothers-in-arms with whom he starved for months on the Vidda.

He rationalized to himself that the visitors might indeed have been only a hallucination brought on by cold and hunger. In that case, their advice was even more valuable, for in that case it came from his subconscious, the mind that had been debating with his fellows and listening to Sørlie and turning the matter over and over in his head as he skied: Which was more dangerous, the gorge or the bridge? Certainly by the time his Gunnerside companions joined him in the empty cabin, the conviction was his own, and how he had gotten there was surely unimportant.

"London wants us to use the bridge," he began, "but if the guards can alert their fellow in the guardhouse, he will raise the alarm with the press of one button. If the alarm is raised, floodlights will illuminate the entire area, from the penstocks to the suspension bridge to the roads leading away from the bridge. The Nazis in the barracks will be alerted, and the entire garrison in Rjukan will be right behind them. The gorge has none of these drawbacks. It is not guarded or mined, Rolf was sure of that. We can cross beneath the bridge, avoid the sentries entirely, and follow the railway tracks right into the Vermok yard."

"The gorge is not guarded because the Germans know it is unclimbable," Rønneberg said.

"The Germans *believe* it is unclimbable," Helberg corrected. He did not mention that Rolf believed that as well, and that Helberg himself, native of Rjukan, had too embraced this belief as truth until the Polish time traveler with the burning eyes convinced him otherwise.

Kasper Idland looked at the aerial photographs Rønneberg had scattered over the dining table and shook his head. "They believe that because it is true. Look at it! The suspension bridge carries risk, true, but it's still the best of the choices. We can silence the guards before they can raise the alarm, and from there we'll go up this steep slope here to the railway and follow the railway tracks. Your informant said the railway is not guarded, correct? So that is the weak point we can leverage."

Helberg shook his head. "It is the one weak point in the defense system, but we will reach it by climbing the gorge. We will never be able to cross the bridge without alerting the third guard—"

"—and that means alerting every German from here to Rjukan," Poulsson agreed.

"Shooting the guards is a stupid risk if we have another alternative," Haukelid said. "If we once land in the middle of a firefight, we've lost. We don't have enough men for a frontal assault."

Rønneberg stared down at the aerial photographs.

"Where trees can grow, a man can climb," Helberg said.

Rønneberg looked up. "Trees grow there in summer, but this is winter."

"It can be done," Helberg insisted, wondering if there was a way to tell them of Stanislaus Lis' past and future feat, without telling them of Stanislaus Lis.

Rønneberg was silent another long moment. "Prove it," he said at last. "Tomorrow morning, get on your skies and find out once and for all if it is possible."

Helberg let out a long sigh. "Fair," he said, and the party bedded down to get what sleep they could.

❧

Helberg set out early the following morning under a cloudless sky. He would have preferred clouds, as the sun glinted painfully off the snow, half-blinding him. Finally he reached the gorge and found a place to leave his skis. He and his comrades could leave their skies and equipment in the same place that night.

For a time he stood staring down the six hundred foot drop. It certainly did not look like a safe descent. But Lis had said—

There was nothing to be done but prove it by experiment.

The surface of the snow was hard and crusted, and seemed capable of supporting his weight, but all at once he slipped. Then he was sliding, uncontrolled, terrified, grabbing desperately at a juniper bush to slow down.

He waited long enough to recover his breath, and tried again.

He slipped again. And slid again. And recovered again. Without the bushes to clutch at, he would have been dead a dozen times over.

Finally he reached the bottom and stopped once more to breathe.

The wind that whipped along the top of the gorge could not reach down here. The ice of the Mana River seemed to be turning to slush under an early thaw. The suspension bridge was perhaps a quarter mile away, and there was no sign the patrolling guards noticed him in his white snowsuit.

He walked away from the suspension bridge, looking for a better path of descent. He finally found one with a less steep incline and with a few more straggling spruces and pines to grab onto. The other side of the gorge offered similar handholds, which was something, at least. It would still be a hellish climb, in the dark with heavy equipment weighing them down—but the gorge was climbable. Stanislaus Lis had assured him that any risk was less suicidal than alerting the guards on the bridge.

Now all Helberg had to do was convince his comrades.

Chapter 27

Knut Haukelid could feel the repetitive thud of the turbine as a dull throb in his breastbone. At first it had been hard to pick out the sound over the swirl of the wind and the roar of the waterfall, but now it filled the air, overwhelming, inescapable, signaling the journey's end. Vermok lay before him, shining in the moonlight, on the other side of a gorge said by everyone except Claus Helberg to be steep to climb.

Tonight, he and his companions would attempt to climb it.

They had decided, the matter put by Rønneberg to the others in a democratic vote, to disobey London's order. They would avoid the suspension bridge and climb the gorge. Helberg had done all he could to supplement their knowledge of the Nazi defenses, but the intelligence still remained sketchier than Haukelid liked. The tracks were *probably* not guarded. They were *probably* not mined.

It was not an inspiring degree of certainty.

But even dissatisfied as he was by the rigor of the intelligence, Haukelid regarded the gorge with a sense of relief. In their planning sessions, he and Poulsson had maintained it would be impossible to get across the bridge without alerting the Nazis, and argued that the last thing Gunnerside wanted to do was attempt the sabotage in the middle of a firefight. It was a great relief to have Helberg, a local boy like Poulsson, ranging himself on that side of the argument.

If they succeeded, London would forgive them disobeying orders. If they failed—well, it was unlikely any of them would make it out alive to face the wrath of the London planners.

The nine saboteurs divested themselves of skies, ski poles, and white camouflage suits. Haukelid looked his comrades over. They all wore British uniforms now, in the hope that no reprisals would be visited on the locals for the night's work.

"You have your set of charges?" Rønneberg said to Strømsheim—calmly, as though discussing theater tickets. "Good, and I have mine."

Tonight Rønneberg would be in command of the demolition team, while Haukelid led the covering party. Haukelid had absolutely no doubt of the demolition party's ability to execute its mission; they had been training for months. Every one of them could have found his way around the plant blindfolded, and could have planted the explosives and set the charges nearly in his sleep. Rønneberg and the demolition party would have no difficulty in doing their part once inside. And Haukelid's team, armed with Tommy guns, grenades, and pistols, would get them there.

Rønneberg nodded to Helberg, who took point. Haukelid preferred to be the man in front, from which position he could most easily guarantee his comrades' safety, but Helberg was the local expert. So he gave way as Helberg guided them to the gorge—and down.

It was not unlike descending into hell—the frozen rather than the fiery kind. The branches and shrubs Haukelid clung to seemed inadequate to support his compact weight; his feet slipped on the slick steep snow-covered rocks, sending miniature avalanches ahead of him to trumpet his presence to anyone who might be watching. And getting down, he thought sourly, was the easy part.

The bottom of the gorge was treacherous in its own right. An unexpected thaw was causing an early melt of the Mana River, and for a moment Helberg hesitated in the lead. *He can't see a way across,* Haukelid had time to think, but then Helberg was moving again. The ice bridge he found seemed to Haukelid to be in imminent danger of melting. There was no guarantee it would still be there in two hours. But then, there was no guarantee any of them would live long enough to need it.

The thought did not depress him. As long as they lived long enough to get the job done, it hardly mattered what happened next.

Haukelid looked up. The mountainside soared above him, an almost sheer face disappearing into darkness. But spruce and pine grew out of crevices in the rock face, and where trees could grow, a man could climb. Helberg had called it climbable, and Helberg should know.

To call the ascent a nightmare was to underrate nightmares. Haukelid found that he must count himself lucky to have one handhold and one foot support, and sometimes, more terrifyingly, he was forced to manage with only supports for his feet, sliding his hands up the slick slippery surface that might or might not actually have a higher handhold to offer him. Every time he stopped to breathe, he could hear the whisper of melting snow sliding down the cliff around him.

At one point he thought himself lost. He found a firm handhold for his right hand, but then could not find another for his left. He dangled in mid-air while desperately patting the sheer rock face and finding nothing.

Don't panic, he told himself firmly. *Try again.*

With infinite care, he wriggled his right-hand fingers from the crevice and wriggled his left-hand fingers in their place. Then he reached with his right hand out into the empty darkness.

The tips of his fingers just barely brushed a tangle of vine.

Right. Good. He was not without options. He merely needed to discover how to use them. He reached out again, swinging his body as it dangled from his one handhold, trying to get a grip on the vine. Again his fingers brushed it, but he swung back before he could close them around the vegetation.

Try again.

He swung back once, twice. He could not secure a grip. The last of the strength was draining from his numb left hand. His options were closing off fast. He had to survive this damned climb, or leave his comrades without his protection inside Vermok's gates.

With no other options, with no feeling left in his left hand, with nothing left to lose, he swung himself to the right and let go of his handhold.

For a terrifying moment he fell through black space.

Then his right hand clamped over the vine.

And he was safe, for one more moment. You couldn't plan more than one moment ahead, hovering between earth and sky like this.

He was out of breath from more than just exertion. He clung hard to his tangle of brush, trying to slow his heart, trying to recover his nerve. A sudden gust of wind sprang up, and he redoubled his grasp only just in time.

If that gust had come a minute sooner, I'd be at the bottom of the gorge.

But it had not, and he was not, and they were counting on him.

Haukelid unclenched the fingers of his left hand, shook and flexed them to restore what circulation he could, and reached out into blackness to find his next handhold.

∽

Finally, every muscle trembling, Haukelid hauled himself onto solid ground. Beneath his shivering belly was the rock ledge on which the railway ran. Once more the sound of turbines filled the air, as though they had paused during his laborious ascent.

He had to take a moment to breathe. To breathe, and to savor the victory. Where trees could grow, a man could climb.

"All right," Rønneberg was saying over his head. "Let's get closer. The covering party leads the way."

He meant Haukelid, as the commander of the covering party. Haukelid was once more to resume his role as the man in front.

Right. Right. Up. He would not let himself visibly shake as he hauled himself to his feet.

The railway tracks were *probably* not mined.

Haukelid stepped out into the snow, the man in front.

∽

S tep by careful step, he led the others down the railway line, keeping to the frozen gravel to avoid leaving footprints, keeping to the shadows to avoid being seen. The roar of the turbines howled in his ears, beat in his bloodstream.

Ah—there before him was a path trodden in the snow beside the tracks. Trodden by a person who had not, it would appear, been blown up by a mine. Haukelid placed his feet in the footsteps of this unknown guide, and the straggling line of saboteurs behind him did likewise, one after the other.

They rounded a bend, and now he had a clear view of the suspension bridge below, gleaming in the fitful moonlight. The silhouettes of the two guards were clearly visible. Straight ahead was the gate that would lead into Vermok's yard. About five hundred yards before the gate was a small snow-covered shed, and he led the others to it. There, they could crouch out of the wind and await their moment. He arranged himself where he could clearly see the guards on that deadly suspension bridge. Shift change was supposed to occur at midnight.

It actually occurred a few minutes after the hour, as though the replacement guards had been unwilling to venture out into the cold, or perhaps had needed some extra time to properly wrap up against the wind. Haukelid watched them plod down the hillside to the bridge with a faint stirring of hope, for they were no testament to Nazi discipline. Their caps were pulled so low down over their ears that their peripheral vision must surely be compromised, and even their posture within the great bulky coats suggested bored complacency. They took up a rather listless attention on the far side of the bridge. Their replacements trudged up the hill to the barracks, equally listless, weapons held loosely.

Haukelid began to wonder if his brothers-in-arms might survive this night's work after all.

He watched the bored guards on the bridge. Rønneberg's planned half hour delay had been intended to allow the guards time to relax and become complacent, and it almost seemed unnecessary. It was as though these men did not understand the value of what they guarded. One was tall, the other shorter and stockier, and the former seemed to be doing all the talking, intent on convincing the latter of something. Was this the famed Nazi discipline?

Ronneberg spent the half hour reiterating the plan, and although each of the other eight could have recited it with him, they all paid close attention. "If we are detected and the alarm is sounded," Rønneberg said in conclusion, "the covering team will attack the Germans immediately. The demolition team must prioritize its own survival long enough to get into the plant. However." He had not raised his voice, but he held everyone's attention. "If the demolition party is killed before the plant is reached, everyone is to act on his own initiative to complete the operation." He looked at each man in turn. "One of us at least *must* arrive at the objective to do the job. Do you all understand?"

Everyone understood.

"Very well, then." Rønneberg looked at his watch. "Half past twelve. Remember—what we do in the next hour will be a chapter in history for a hundred years to come. Together we will make it a worthy one." He nodded to Haukelid.

Haukelid stepped out into the snow, Kjelstrup close behind him. The seven others came single-file—first the rest of the covering team, then the demolition team.

The gate that led into Vermok's yard was intended to be easily opened, to allow the train to enter without undue obstacle, and was consequently secured only with a padlock. The chain was trivially easy to cut, as long as one had the upper body strength required, and Kjelstrup did. The padlock broke off with the sound of a dry stick snapping, somehow audible to Haukelid's ears above the turbine roar, and Haukelid unthreaded the chain and pushed open the gate. Behind him, the rest of Operation Gunnerside came single-file.

And Vermok was taken.

⌀

ønneberg watched out of the corner of his eye as his men fanned out into their prearranged positions. Storhaug covered the road that led to the suspension bridge, lest the two guards awake to their duty. Kjelstrup kept his eyes on the sentry patrolling the penstocks high above. Helberg positioned himself to cover the retreat. Haukelid and Poulsson took up position behind two large steel storage tanks that gave them a view of the barracks. In the event that an alarm was raised and the soldiers ran from the barracks, the two sharpshooters would prevent at least some of them from interfering with the demolition party.

Rønneberg paused to look all around, straining his ears for sounds above the roaring of the turbines and the roaring of the water.

The hydrogen plant and the power station loomed before him, eight stories high, the German guard barracks nestled between the two enormous buildings. With Kaysar guarding Rønneberg and Idland guarding Strømsheim, the demolition team crept across the open yard and around the eastern wall of the hydrogen plant.

Rønneberg tried the basement door. It was locked. Kaysar ran lightly up the stairwell and returned shaking his head. The first floor door was locked as well.

They had brought along explosives sufficient to blow a door off its hinges, but now, at the moment of truth, Rønneberg hesitated. The guard barracks were *right there*. He did not dare an explosion that might rouse the guards, might position them to stop the explosion that mattered. He was astonished that Operation Gunnerside stood in Vermok's yard, right before the plant and not a stone's throw from the barracks, and had not yet encountered a single guard or watchman.

Strømsheim touched his arm. Rønneberg turned, and the other man tilted his head, silently indicating that he and his guard Idland were leaving to look for another way in. Rønneberg sent him off with a nod.

Rønneberg circled the building in the other direction, Kayser at his side. If he had to blow the door open, he would, but...

The shadowed snow under his feet was marred with little specks of light. Rønneberg looked for their source and saw a ground level window. It had been blacked out with paint, but crudely—did *any* aspect of Vermok security live up to its reputation?—allowing some light to escape.

And allowing an operative such as himself to see in. Rønneberg put his eye to one of the gaps as to a keyhole.

He could have melted with relief at the sight. Six feet below sat two sets of heavy water cells. In the middle of the room, a man in overalls hunched over a desk, writing something in a book. Overalls, not uniform—a Norwegian workman, not a Nazi guard.

Kayser raised a fist to smash the glass. Rønneberg stopped him with a sharp gesture. If they broke the window, light would pour into the yard, signaling plainly to any Nazi soldier that mischief was afoot. Kayser frowned at him, his thoughts as clear as if he had said them aloud: *It's risky, yes, but less risky than an explosion.*

Rønneberg shook his head again, holding up a hand with three fingers showing. "Third option," he whispered.

Back in Scotland, Gunnerside's overseer Leif Tronstad had taken Rønneberg aside to discuss entry points into the plant. Tronstad had been concerned that the explosion deemed necessary to blast open the outer door would bring down upon Gunnerside a flood of Nazis from the adjoining barracks. If at all possible, Tronstad had told Rønneberg, he was to effect a silent entry.

Tronstad was hoping for a door left unlocked, but acknowledged the small chance of such a gift. If there was no unlocked door, he advised Rønneberg to seek out a narrow tunnel filled with pipes and cables that ran along the basement ceiling. It predated the Nazi occupation by enough that they might not even know about it, might not have sealed it over or posted guards around it. It was a chance, at least. Now Rønneberg motioned Kayser to follow him.

Around the corner of the building, a ladder led from snowbank to roof, smothered in snow. Rønneberg set his hands on the ice-coated steel. It never occurred to him to do anything except lead from the front; one did not send one's men to do what one dared not do oneself. And it was nowhere near as bad as climbing the gorge had been.

Fifteen feet up was the tunnel entrance, disguised by snow, happily not blocked over. Rønneberg squeezed himself inside. Kayser followed. There was barely enough room for them to push themselves along with their hands, back and belly pressed against the cold concrete of the tunnel ceiling and floor, listening all the time for the sound of pursuit or ambush.

Where were Strømsheim and Idland? In one sense, it hardly mattered. Even if their companions had encountered a Nazi patrol, even if the Nazis were now closing in, the only thing to do was move forward, as swiftly and silently as possible. Every few minutes Rønneberg swept the space ahead with his small flashlight and moved aside any cable or pipe that might make noise when crawled over.

At last a hole opened before them. Peering around the water pipes that ran through it, Rønneberg spotted the room with the high concentration cells and the Norwegian workman. They had nearly made it.

The sharp clank of metal behind him froze the blood in his veins. He squirmed around enough to see Kayser grasping desperately after the pistol that had fallen from his shoulder holster. It was attached by a long string to his body, so he did not lose it entirely, but it struck pipe after pipe as the string uncoiled, rattling and clanking against the maze of metal with a sound loud enough to wake the dead. Kayser gave Rønneberg an appalled, despairing look. They were done.

What now? Hold still, and hope the inevitable running feet did not find them and the mission could still be carried out? Throw caution to the wind and prioritize speed over stealth, in the hope they could get their job done before they were captured? Rønneberg had to decide now, but fear held him frozen.

He was motionless for long enough to realize no pounding footfalls had followed that appalling clanking racket. Had the background roar of Vermok smothered it? Were the Nazis simply inured to the plant making strange noises? He could hardly hear at all over the turbines and his thundering heart, but it gradually became evident that no one was coming.

Forward.

After another twenty yards, they came upon an opening large enough for a man to fit through. It led downward into a large antechamber—and just beyond was the door to the high concentration cell room. Rønneberg checked for guards, then dropped fifteen feet into a roll on the concrete floor. Kayser was right behind him. Kayser drew his retrieved pistol, Rønneberg drew his own, and they kicked open the doors.

The man in overalls leapt around to face them, but Kayser already had the pistol pointed at his chest. "Put your hands up," he said in Norwegian, and the man obeyed instantly. "Good," Kayser told him. "What's your name?"

"Gustav Johansen," the man stammered.

Rønneberg relaxed minutely. A Norwegian, as they had hoped. "Nothing will happen to you if you do as you're told," he told Johansen. "We're British soldiers." To Kayser, he said, "Cover him." Then he went and locked the door. Then he got to work.

There was something—meditative? Could that possibly be the right word?—about the task. The concentration cells before him were identical to the replicas on which he had been practicing for months in Scotland. The explosives were beyond familiar in his hands. The detonator fuses could be trimmed to allow for different burning times. A full-length fuse took two minutes, time enough for a saboteur to flee. He couldn't think about flight yet. His hands worked automatically through motions so familiar he might have executed them in his sleep.

He had just finished fastening the ninth explosive to its assigned cell when glass shattered behind him. He grabbed for his gun and whirled to the window.

☙

aukelid's eyes flicked ceaselessly from side to side, but he otherwise stayed motionless. He would not fidget even so much as to shift from foot to foot. He *thought* he and Poulsson were positioned where they cast no shadow, but mistakes that small had damned missions like this before now. They had seen nothing—no guards, no dogs—but that did not mean they could relax.

It felt as though hours had passed since he took up this guard stance. He wondered if Rønneberg's team had made it inside. He wondered if Strømsheim's had. He had heard no explosion of a door being blown from its hinges. Perhaps they had found a quieter way?

Or perhaps they had already been captured. At literally any moment, a watchful Nazi soldier could notice something unusual and raise the alarm, and then it would be searchlights and sirens and baying dogs and—if they were very, very lucky—death rather than capture.

A shiver ran up his spine. A goose walking over his grave, one of his British comrades would have called it. For a moment he swore he could see the blinding flash of floodlights, hear the stutter of machine-gun fire, feel the icy ground connect with his cheek as he fell. For a moment, it was as though it had already happened.

Then he pulled himself together and recommenced the constant shifting watchfulness. He looked at the barracks. The guard patrol. Every shadow that might hide a threat. It did no one any good if he wasted attention speculating on scenarios that had not yet happened. Or wasted energy wondering what on earth could be taking the demolition team so long.

☙

torhaug, positioned where he could see the suspension bridge, was at least having a less stressful time of it. He could both see and hear the Nazi guards who stood at its end. The taller was still trying to convince the shorter of something, both of them talking in easy, casual, carrying voices. They clearly suspected nothing of what was going on in the plant.

Or, at least, what Storhaug hoped was going on. It seemed to him too as though years had passed. What the hell was taking the demolition team so long?

☙

t that precise moment, the demolition team was engaged in a furious whispered altercation.

"You idiot," Rønneberg gasped to Strømsheim. "First of all we could have killed you, and second of all…"

"How were we to know you'd made it inside?" Strømsheim hissed back, clearing the broken glass from the window with the butt of his gun.

Rønneberg cut his hand on the glass and bit back an oath. "Get in here," he said to Strømsheim, but lifted his bleeding hand to forestall Idland. "You stay there and block the window. If the guards see the light, they'll be on us in droves." How many more mishaps could the mission survive? They had already somehow failed to alert the guards with the banging of the dropped pistol on the pipes…

Rønneberg was slowed by his bleeding hand, but Strømsheim worked so quickly beside him that it didn't matter. When all the explosives were attached to the cells, Strømsheim looked between the two-minute fuses and the thirty-second fuses. "The thirty-second is the better bet," he said. "Less time to run, but less of a chance any of the bastards will discover and disable it."

Rønneberg had to agree. "Set the two-minute first and see that it works. Then we'll set the thirty-second and run."

But as they attached the thirty-second fuse, Johansen looked over from beyond Kaysar's shoulder in alarm. "Wait! Sir! My eyeglasses!"

"Your *what*?" Rønneberg repeated, hands frozen over the fuses. It might have been considered a moment of comedic relief, except this situation was too dire for comedy.

"My eyeglasses," Johansen pleaded. "I need them for my job. They're impossible to replace these days. Because of the war!"

"Fine!" Rønneberg paused in his task and darted across the room. In the mess of papers on table, he found the glasses case.

"Tusan takk," Johansen said. But then, as Rønneberg bent over the fuses again, "No, wait! The glasses are not in the case!"

Rønneberg's usual self-command was badly shredded by this time. "Where the hell are they, then?"

"I don't know—they were on the desk when you came in—"

Rønneberg grimly crossed the room again, imagining alarms and sirens and floodlights and dogs. How long could his people stand guard out there and not be spotted? Idland could not possibly be blocking every speck of light; how long before someone noticed that? The glasses were tucked into the logbook like a bookmark. He grabbed them, thrust them at their owner, irritably waved off Johansen's thanks, and finished his work.

"Go open the basement door so we have an escape route," Rønneberg told Strømsheim. "Kayser, take Johansen out of here, clear of the blast."

And then, to his horror, he heard footsteps on the stairs.

Footsteps on the stair could only mean a Nazi guard. Alerted by a pattern of light flecks on the snow, or on a routine patrol? Did it matter? Should Rønneberg light the thirty-second fuse now, or wait until they had killed the guard? What if they did not manage to kill the guard? Or what if the exchange of fire summoned more guards? Might the Nazis even now win this night?

Strømsheim and Kayser were looking to him for leadership. He dared not hesitate. Rønneberg blew out the match and leveled his own pistol at the door.

For the second time that night he found himself within an instant of killing an ally. The man who entered wore a coverall like Johansen's, not a Nazi uniform, and at the sight of the three armed intruders, he gasped and flung up his hands. Strømsheim herded him over to stand with Johansen, under Kayser's guard, and Rønneberg for the third time went to light the fuses.

"How can this be?" the second Norwegian babbled. "British soldiers inside Vermok? Vermok! This is the most important room to the Germans in all of Norway, there are guards all about the plant, mines on the hills, I've heard no shooting—" Rønneberg ignored him and kept on working, scattering the British parachute badge and other paraphernalia they had brought to ensure the Nazis took no reprisals against the local population.

"Go open the door," he ordered Strømsheim again. Then he struck a match.

The two-minute fuses appeared to be burning correctly. He lit the thirty-second one, signaled Idland to get clear, and ordered the two Norwegians up the stairs. "Lie down and keep your mouths open," he said, "or the sound will blow out your eardrums." The Norwegians ran.

Strømsheim already had the steel basement door open. Rønneberg and Kayser sprinted through it, out into the snow. Idland joined them as they pounded away from the plant.

A muffled *boom* barely shook the air. Rønneberg looked back and saw flames escape the broken basement window. "Done," he breathed. He could scarcely believe it.

❀

At their guard post, Haukelid looked over at Poulsson. "Is that…it?"

Poulsson indicated the light that now streamed through the broken basement windows of the plant. *Something* had obviously happened, but could so small a sound really signal so huge a victory?

A motion caught the corner of Haukelid's vision, and he stiffened.

The door of the Nazi barracks opened.

A single, unarmed, bareheaded soldier appeared in the doorway, light streaming out all around him.

Haukelid could almost hear the sirens again, could almost taste blood in his mouth.

But the soldier only looked left, then right. He crossed the fifty yards between the barracks and the plant with no urgency. At this angle he could not see the light from the broken basement window, nor did he walk around the building to a vantage point from which it could be seen. He tried the basement door and found it locked. Then he returned to the barracks and closed the door behind him.

So much for the famed Nazi training.

Haukelid slowly relaxed his finger from the trigger of his Tommy gun.

⌒

aukelid led the way back to the railway track, feeling a little stunned. He had to restrain himself from continually looking over his shoulder at the marvelous lack of response from the Nazis. They had accomplished their mission without a single shot being fired, and their enemy still seemed unaware of how the Reich had been checkmated.

The entire complement of Gunnerside met back at the railway line, and Haukelid saw no worse injury among them than a bleeding hand Rønneberg insisted was nothing. Haukelid therefore herded his comrades at a run back down the railway line.

They had nearly reached the gorge when the first siren split the air behind them.

The men of Gunnerside hurled themselves back down the rock face. Even with a head start, their situation could still be dire. Dogs would doubtless pick up their scent. Troops would be called in from Rjukan. One the floodlights were turned on, they would be immediately visible, and machine guns could pick them off as they clung to the walls of the gorge. Why, Haukelid wondered as he desperately lowered himself into the darkness, were the floodlights not turned on already?

His boots touched the valley floor. Water from the melting ice sloshed up his legs, frigid and soaking, but the ice bridges had not quite disappeared yet. Helberg found a safe crossing, and the others followed.

Haukelid's hands grasped the first of the handholds that would guide him back up the gorge, and the floodlights still were not on. Craning for one look back, he saw specks of light moving along the railway line, identifiable after a moment as the electric torches of a search party. The broken chain of the railway gate must have been discovered. But it hardly mattered—the floodlights were still off, there was no baying of dogs mixed with the shriek of the sirens—it seemed as though the Gunnerside saboteurs might actually make their escape.

And even if they did not, that hardly mattered either. Their sabotage had succeeded.

⌒

 p on the hilltop, Stanislaus Lis let out a long breath. He touched Maxwell's arm with fingers that felt curiously insubstantial, as though muffled through far more layers of clothing than they were actually wearing. "Don't," he said precisely, "let anyone else do this."

"I promise," Maxwell said, but it was unclear if Lis could hear him. Lis was already transparent, and as Maxwell watched, he faded from sight like a ghost. He was smiling as he did.

Chapter 28

Katarina was glad of her layered warm clothing as Maxwell grandly bowed her through the doorway that looked like flickering flame. Nor did she mind his air of exaggerated showmanship; she was the only one of the four of them who hadn't yet visited the mysterious headquarters.

"Right, then." Elizabeth looked at the row of darkened windows with a lifted chin, as though in answer to a challenge. "It's time to see what we have wrought."

Maxwell raised his voice. "Scheherazade?"

"Yes?" The response seemed to come from all corners of the room, amplified as though by an opera house's acoustics.

Katarina raised her eyebrows in an attempt to show no more surprise that that.

"Scheherazade," Maxwell said, "this is Katarina Rasmirovna. She will be joining us."

"Welcome, Katarina Rasmirovna."

"Um," Katarina said. "Thank you?"

"Scheherazade can state the information aloud," Maxwell said, "or display it so that we can read it." He made a gesture of deference toward Katarina, indicating that it was her choice.

Katarina considered this. "I suppose reading would be more familiar, and therefore easier?"

And so, sitting upon a remarkably comfortable chair that nevertheless succeeded in being upright, hands resting upon a remarkably uncomfortable desk whose strange shiny material seemed designed to suck the warmth straight out of her skin, Katarina perused the historical accounts of the Operation Gunnerside raid. William leaned over the back of her chair, reading along with her. He fumbled with the little buttons that controlled the windows, but to Katarina they were not quite so alien—she had, after all, seen a typewriter or two before leaving the Victorian era. They took turns shuffling through the information and reading it out to the excited Elizabeth and nervously pacing Maxwell.

"Brilliant," William murmured. "Oh, they did Norway and Britain proud. See here, von Faulkenhorst himself said the sabotage was the finest *coup* he saw in the whole course of the war."

"Von Faulkenhorst…?" Elizabeth asked.

"Military commander of occupied Norway," Katarina said. "It was an uncommonly effective blow, that's certain. Not only were all of the high-concentration cells completely drained of their heavy water, but the facility itself had been undergoing improvements and expansions. The Nazis were poised to reach a quarter-again improvement in production within the month—and Gunnerside utterly destroyed that. It took most of a year to clear away the damage, repair the cells, and start over from scratch, and by then the Nazi high command was no longer focusing so intently upon this heavy water as a weapon. It sounds as though at that point a great many different government overseers were attempting to manage the project, and we all know how *that* goes. Gunnerside could hardly have picked a better moment to destroy their enemy's advantage."

"What about Schwieger?" Maxwell asked, not ceasing his restless movement. "Any news of him?"

Katarina shook her head. "He disappears into history. Which is…about right, when you consider it, since that's precisely what he intended to do. Vanish into the crowd from which he came, use the privilege of invisibility to climb to where he could do some good, and quietly weaken the fortifications from there."

"And he did that," William noted with a chuckle. "Or someone did that, at least; we'll assume it's his hand we see. If it was his, he earned his redemption. Goodness, what a *mess.*"

"Do tell." Elizabeth arranged herself on one of the other strangely comfortable cup-like chairs.

"For a location of such overwhelming strategic importance," William said, paraphrasing from the information hovering on the window before them, "Vermok's guards were remarkably poorly trained. The Gunnerside team faced little opposition going in, and even the Nazi guards who heard the explosion did not respond in any useful manner—like that fellow who poked his head out of the barracks, saw nothing, and went straight back to his card game. Gunnerside not only got in and did the deed, they managed to get out."

"Was no search made?" Maxwell wanted to know.

"Oh, to be sure, but not an effective one. The Nazis wasted all sorts of time searching within the complex—balconies, stairwells, closets, sheds—because they were convinced the saboteurs must still be there. No one had crossed the suspension bridge, after all; no one had climbed the penstocks; the gorge was *known* to be impassable—" William grinned. "So Gunnerside got clean away."

"But what about the rest of it? The dogs, the floodlights, the soldiers in Rjukan—?"

"The horseless carriages conveying the Rjukan soldiers passed along the road while the Gunnerside team was climbing up to the Vidda on foot," Katarina read. "Neither the dogs nor the floodlights were used that night."

Elizabeth sat up straighter. "Whyever not?"

"Oh, that's the best part," William said. Katarina had never seen him smile so much. It seemed a well-executed military coup was to his taste. "Right, so the Nazis at Vermok sent a message—a *telegraph,* must be like a semaphore, I wish we'd had those back on the Peninsula—and the Nazi high command in Oslo came immediately. The horseless carriage appears to go quite swiftly; they reached Vermok early the morning of the twenty-eighth of February, so mere hours after Gunnerside escaped. Von Faulkenhorst was absolutely furious with the commandant of Vermok, so much so that he dressed him down in front of Norwegian bystanders, which is why we have such a delightful record of the conversation.

"Von Faulkenhorst had all the same questions you just did—how could the guards have been so complaisant, why were the dogs not used, why was the floodlight not turned on? We can only speculate who caused the Nazi guards to be so badly trained—I'd place my money on Schwieger, but we'll never know for certain—but the commandant told von Faulkenhorst that the guard dogs had not been used on patrol the previous night because of the severity of the weather."

"It wasn't warm by any sensible person's standard," Katarina added, thinking wistfully of the Mediterranean and moving her cold arms off the desk to rub some warmth into them, "but it was on the warm side for a Norwegian night, so the dogs must never have seen much action at all."

"The commandant tried to defend himself against von Faulkenhorst by reciting all that had been done to fortify Vermok after the Operation Freshman disaster," William went on, "all the same improvements we've heard so much about. Landmines along the penstocks, plans for landmines along the railway track, a barbed-wire fence around the plant, Gatling guns on the roof, floodlights. He would have done better to keep quiet, because he gave von Faulkenhorst the opening to probe into each inadequate defense. Obviously the barbed-wire fence was inadequate; Gunnerside had cut through it. Obviously the mines had not yet been laid along the railway track; why not? The commandant said he hadn't the men to do the work. Von Faulkenhorst asked why he had not hired women, as apparently was done in Russia and America during this war, and the commandant had no answer. Dogs were no good if they were not taken on patrol; men were no good if they were not properly trained; Gatling guns were of no use without light to see by. And why exactly had those lights not been turned on? The commandant had no answer for that either, but von Faulkenhorst proved the reason by experiment. He had the commandant send a guard to turn on the famous floodlights, and then he and the commandant waited. And waited."

"Had the lights been sabotaged ahead of time?" Maxwell guessed.

"Better than that," William chortled. "The guards were so badly trained that the one the commandant chose for the errand could not find the switch!"

Elizabeth clapped her hands. "This conversation could not have ended well for the commandant or the guards."

"No," Katarina said. "Von Faulkenhorst re-assigned the commandant to serve on the Russian front—which I can only infer from context must have been a particularly dreadful assignment—and then issued orders to improve Vermok's fortifications. For one thing, he forbade the guards to wear bulky warm clothing on duty, or to turn up their collars or pull down their caps, since they were cutting off their lines of sight and muffling their hearing. For another, he ordered that there should be guards not only patrolling the bridge and penstocks, but also guarding the railway gate and standing inside the room with the heavy-water machinery."

"The quotation is delightful," William added. "'When you have a chest of jewels, you don't walk around it! You plant yourself on the lid with a weapon in your hand!' He'd ordered the right sorts of changes, and no doubt he also ordered drills and so forth to improve the training of the men carrying them out, but by then it was much too late. The damage was done, and the Nazis could not recover the advantage. Their Empire lost the war, never again to rise."

"At least," Maxwell said, ceasing his pacing at last, "not until another of those bastards finds one of the five lost timepieces." He dropped into the bowl-shaped chair beside Elizabeth, resting his elbows on his knees and his face in his hands. After a moment, he scrubbed his palms over his face and looked up. "I promised Stanislaus Lis I would never let this happen again."

"So that's what we do next," Katarina said. "We find those five timepieces, we bring them back here and keep them under lock and key, and that way we see to it no one else can use them for evil ends."

"There may well be more than five," Elizabeth pointed out. "They survive their timeline, so one can become two, at least for a time. Like ours, Maxwell, mine and yours."

Maxwell groaned agreement. "There could be any number, anywhere in space and time. How are we even to begin?"

William looked around the room. "Well, with surveillance from here. I think we could learn to see—what was it Miss Holborn called them? Ripples? Indications of time out of joint. And then once we had a year and a place, Trevelyan's dowsing rod ought to be able to find the timepiece in question."

"That's the work of a lifetime," Maxwell said, but Katarina thought he sounded hopeful rather than oppressed by the thought. He glanced over at her.

She smiled at him. "I didn't have anything else planned."

❧

Much later that night—or what felt like late at night, at least, though there was no sun or moon to indicate the time—Maxwell dreamed about the Spider.

She was sitting by the fire in her drafty kitchen, her ubiquitous knitting forgotten on her lap as she looked past him at something he could not see. She moved slightly, and her ball of yarn dropped from her lap. It rolled away, end over end, unraveling itself, until it disappeared into a heavily-shadowed corner. Maxwell sought it out, located it by touch, and brought it back to her. And woke, blinking, in his strange new bedchamber at headquarters.

If there was a message in that dream, he was damned if he could see what it was.

He tried to interpret it as approval of the plan to hunt the timepieces, and then as disapproval of the same plan, but it wouldn't quite fit either mold.

He wondered if he would spend the rest of his life measuring his actions by trying to determine what she would have wanted.

He thought of Emil Schwieger and Rosamund Holborn, and realized the answer was probably yes. Well, there were worse measurements.

Too fully awake now for any additional sleep, he left his bed for a wander through the echoing gray corridors. He poked his head into laboratories whose function he could not guess at; examined what put him in mind of a steamship's engine room, of which he could say little except he was certain it did not run on coal; glanced from the doorways at cabins containing the personal possessions of time travelers who had never existed. At last he turned his steps to the library, thinking it likely Scheherazade would be able to offer some form of entertainment to while away the hours until the others awoke. Music, perhaps? Or, hell, it was a library. She had to have some novel he could read.

He arrived at the top of the steps to find he was not the only one awake. Katarina sat on the far side of the room, lit only by the glow of the screen before her, which apparently displayed some information that held her full interest.

She was facing him but looking at something else. The blanket draped around her shoulders pooled its excess into her lap like a forgotten piece of knitting. The screen at which she gazed threw a ghostly light up onto her face, hollowing her cheekbones and eye sockets and elongating her shadow on the wall behind. Except for the straightness of her posture, she looked *exactly* like the Spider of his dream.

Was that the message? "Stop worrying about what she will or would have wanted; she's here now to tell you herself"?

"Good evening," Katarina said. "Can't sleep?"

Maxwell shrugged acknowledgement. "Can't you?"

"I never sleep well the first night in a strange bed," she made excuse. "And…well, there was something I needed to know."

Maxwell realized a moment later. "Jacob Abramson."

"Scheherazade found his obituary for me," Katarina said. "Ninety-two, of natural causes. Survived by children and grandchildren. I couldn't have wished better for him." She adjusted the blanket around her shoulders, and her shadow arched its exaggerated arms in a movement like knitting.

The ball of yarn had rolled away from her and he had put it back into her hands…

Oh.

Katarina was watching him with her head to one side. He supposed his expression must have looked rather odd. "What is it?" she asked curiously. "Have I said something strange?"

Maxwell seated himself on the top step and told her the truth. "Not at all. You only reminded me that I was dreaming about you just now."

She raised interested eyebrows.

"I should say," he amended, "I was dreaming of an old woman I used to know, who deftly remade the tapestry of her world while she lay dying of the black lung." *And sent me back to hand the ball of yarn to her younger self.* "I suppose some of those stories in Scheherazade's library must be about people who have as literally saved themselves…but I doubt there's one in which the saving was done in quite so unconventional or so dramatic a fashion. And…that's about right. Both halves of it. That's you."

Katarina laughed a little. "It's a pretty compliment. But can I really deserve the praise if I can't remember the action? It's not really my action, is it?"

"You can't remember the action because it succeeded," Maxwell said. "It's as real as it's possible for something to be."

And then—it wasn't a trick of the light, it was an actual overlaying of images—he saw her in triplicate. Katarina leaning back from the screen, the Spider leaning back in her rocking chair, Seward's second leaning back against the wall and looking up from her volume of Dickens.

Damn.

Katarina got quickly to her feet. "Are you all right?"

"Yes." But the word came out on an unsteady breath. Maxwell rubbed at his forehead, holding up his other hand to ward her off. He ducked his head between his knees for five long inhalations, then straightened and tried the reply again, this time attempting to pair it with a smile. "Yes, fine."

She stood looking down at him. "How many timelines did you see just then?"

"Three," he had to admit. "But it's all right. I've been navigating this for a while now, Katarina, it really is all right." He could tell he was not convincing her. "There are worse fates," he tried again, and then attempted to make a jest of it. "I've lived through a few of them."

"Isn't that the truth," she agreed. She managed a smile through the concern in her eyes. "But this won't get better on its own, will it?" She looped the trailing edge of her blanket over her arm and came to sit on the step beside him, and Maxwell slid over quite unselfconsciously to make room for her. She was warm against his side in the uncomfortably chilly air.

In the morning, they would really have to learn the local equivalent of putting another shovelful of coal on the fire…

"Max, are you listening to me?"

He blinked. "I'm sorry," he said. "My thoughts wandered."

"I said," Katarina repeated, "this won't get better on its own. If Lis is to be believed, and I see no reason why he shouldn't be believed, it will only get worse. And the only way to fix it is to close the circle. So perhaps we ought to go and do that first thing tomorrow morning."

Maxwell didn't say anything.

"By which I mean," Katarina said, "I'll go with you to Hartwich of 1815 and bring you home after you give that Elizabeth the pocket watch. Or if you prefer you can simply take two and return here under your own power."

"I can handle the hallucinations," Maxwell said. "I've gotten good at it. I can do it a long time yet. I am in no rush to close the circle." He leaned back in an effort to see more of her face. "There are plenty of adventures I mean to have first."

She looked exasperated. "Is there some reason you don't wish to resolve your illness by the most expedient possible means?"

Somewhere along the line he had gotten into the habit of being honest with her. "Yes," he said. "I'm afraid I might get it wrong."

She looked confused.

"None of us know what we're doing," he tried to explain. "I know Elizabeth received the package by post, not from, for instance, an oddly familiar mysterious old man in the wood. So that means the package has to go by post. And *so many things* can go wrong in the time it takes a package to travel post from anywhere to anywhere in 1815. What happens if I don't do whatever it is I'm supposed to do, or I do it too late or too early, and the post overturns or is robbed or delayed by a few hours and her parents see the parcel before she does—"

Now the look on Katarina's face was stricken understanding.

"What if I get it wrong," he repeated, "and I undo what we have now?"

"But your parents would be here, at headquarters," Katarina objected slowly, thinking it out. "If they're here, wearing timepieces, they'd surely survive any alteration to their timeline—"

"'Surely,'" Maxwell said, "has gotten me into trouble before now. 'Surely' is an opinion, not a fact. None of us know how this all works, not truly—and there's no one left alive to ask. We can only learn what we need to know by trial and error…and historically speaking, most of my trials are errors. I don't want to risk losing…all this." Now he couldn't meet her gaze. He sought something over her head to look at. "I think *this, here,* is what I wanted all along without realizing it. I want to have it for a while, before I—I—use it as a wager." There was nothing interesting to look at in the shadows. He dropped his eyes back down to her face. "I can handle the hallucinations. For a long time yet."

Katarina nodded slowly.

"Don't tell them."

"I wouldn't dream of it."

He nodded once in gratitude.

"So we'll have some adventures," she continued, as though lightly. "We'll have many of them, for a long time, before there's any need for you to risk losing anything. We'll start in the morning." She smiled at him. "In that case, we should both try for some sleep. We'll want to be well-rested if we mean to start hunting timepieces tomorrow."

Epilogue

cross the Channel, the forces of two Empires were drawing into battle formation, cannons primed and men tense with anticipation, poised for a duel to the death that must be won by fair meals or foul—but no one would ever know it looking at the streets of Hartwich.

Bees drowsed in the apple blossoms of the Carrington orchard. Within the house, a young soldier stared incuriously out the window while the conversation of his relations droned behind him. Across the orchard, a girl chopped the heads off perfectly healthy roses and bemoaned the hedgerows that restricted her view.

It was still the time considered by most Hartwich inhabitants to be the dinner hour, and so no one happened to be present in the village street to observe the old man descend stiffly from the post-chaise. No one had been present to observe him appear out of thin air in London the day before, either—though that, he reflected, was no more than statistical inevitability. Somehow, there never did seem to be a local present to observe the moment of what Rosamund's journals had termed "materialization." He wondered how the timepieces knew. There was so much he still didn't know about them.

The thought of the timepieces stung. The emptiness of his left-hand pocket was like an ache.

But he had put off the moment as long as he could. He leaned his weight on his stick and considered the village inn—aware, as he always was, of the possibilities that flickered in the air around him. He had spent so long with competing timelines clamoring for his attention that he had become quite adept at navigating through them, guessing correctly moment to moment which of the available colors and shapes were being shared by the people nearby. But the guess required an unavoidable pause for thought, which tended to give other people the impression that he was not attending to them, even when he was. It made him wonder about other men and women, particularly inventors, who had been labelled "vague" and "distracted" by their contemporaries. He had suggested to William that a review of such historical figures might yield leads for the remaining missing timepieces. It had been his last communication with his father before embarking upon this final journey.

It was a journey he had really put off too long. The vividness of the hallucinations had steadily increased over time until, despite practice and even with longer and longer pauses for guessing, it had become almost impossible for him to tell the current timeline from its opposite numbers. It was past time he sent Elizabeth Barton a timepiece, past time he allowed that story to begin. They had all wanted to come with them, but he had insisted upon doing this alone.

And so here he was. Back in Hartwich. The Carrington estate was just up the hill there, and inside (a young soldier stared incuriously out of window) (a boy would stare through the bannisters at his aunt's Christmas party). Down the street and around the corner lay the woodlands where (Georgie and his brothers would ambush their cousin one infamous day) (Christopher Palmer would lead an armed insurrection against the French invaders). He could see even the things he had not been there to see, stories layered over stories.

The old man waited for the postilion to carry his valise into the inn. It held very little, only those few things he knew he would want at his side. He explained to the innkeeper his decision to break his journey for an afternoon and evening before continuing on tomorrow's post-chaise. He was able to commandeer the best of the inn's rooms, the one facing the street. Step by painful step, he dragged himself up the stairs.

The timing of this maneuver had given new meaning to the word "delicate." He had not dared arrive in Hartwich too soon, for everything would be news in so small a village, and he would attract unwanted attention as a mysterious old man inexplicably staying in the inn. And yet he'd had to allow enough time for this to work. Enough time to correct course if the first attempt failed, because it *had* to work. (Across the Channel, the shadowy figures of a girl and a boy and a man plotted a mad scheme in a barn.) (Across the Channel, the shadowy figures of Wellington's monsters paced within their pens.) (Across the Channel, the Prussians marched to England's aid.) He could see them all, overlaid contradictory ghosts. It was all balanced on a knife's edge between two manners of victory and one manner of defeat, and whether he got this part right would decide which track the train took.

Not that there were trains, in 1815. It was the worst part of having spent most of one's life doing this sort of thing—the metaphors that occurred to one were often ill-matched to one's current time period. If there *had* been trains, this ticklish maneuver would have been rather easier to execute.

But he had been restricted to the post-chaise. He had arrived in London the previous day, taken a room in a shoddy inn, and then posted the parcel with his own hands. It had to arrive by post, because it had arrived by post, but it was with a feeling of almost physical sickness that he let the pocket watch out of his sight. He had taken care with the packaging: velvet bag, sturdy box, brown wrapping paper, name written in a clear bold hand, exactly as she had reported receiving it. No note, though every fiber of his being screamed to leave a note, because this wouldn't work, none of this would ever work, monsters would run screaming onto the field at Waterloo and Brenda Trevelyan would die under their claws and Katarina Rasmirovna would cough her lungs out, if Elizabeth did not have free choice over what happened next.

He had forced himself to pry his fingers off the package, and arranged for it to be sent in the morning mail.

Then he had booked himself a seat on the same post-chaise, because he was damned if he'd leave anything more to chance than he had to.

Now he dragged himself step by step up the staircase of the village inn, to a room from which he could observe the Hartwich post office.

The postilions unloaded the parcels, shouting to each other and making jests. He watched the box containing the pocket watch pass from hand to hand. (Elizabeth's head rotted on a pike, Elizabeth grabbed his sleeve and forced him to take her to Waterloo, Elizabeth shouted at him about pawns and chessboards, Elizabeth grabbed his sleeve and brought him to Vermok.)

The postmistress came to receive the letters and parcels. He watched her fingers close over the one parcel in which he was interested. (William dragged himself off to die in the woods, William delivered the note to Placenoit, William greeted Christopher Palmer after an absence of seven weeks and seventy years, William faced Stanislaus Lis in a cabin on the Vidda and spoke in a low persuasive tone.)

He watched the street for a long, long time, hoping for the sight of a Westerfield servant come to collect the family's letters. (Katarina looked up at him from the rocking chair from which she wove her web, Katarina fell in a hail of bullets, Katarina stole a timepiece and ran off into the night, Katarina spread arms white-gloved from hand to elbow and entranced an opera house with her voice.)

It felt as though years had passed when the Westerfield's lad finally walked down the street, hands in pockets and whistling as though this were just another day. (Across the Channel two armies waited, the Carrington family plotted a mad scheme in a barn, the monsters paced with in their pens, the British pinned their hopes on Prussian aid—) The boy pulled off his cap, entered the post office, and a few minutes later emerged, cap back on his head, brown-paper-wrapped parcel under his arm. The old man watched the serving lad and the parcel disappear down the street, up the hill, through the Carrington orchard, out of sight.

He followed the lad's steps in his mind. He knew that orchard well enough, since he had spent / would spend / would never spend most of his childhood climbing its trees. He pictured the boy entering the Westerfield kitchen, which he did not know at all from personal experience but could imagine. He pictured Bronson taking charge of the parcel, he pictured the butler's progress into the garden inhabited by an impatient young lady whose hand deserved a better tool than pruning shears—

The shadowy images that flickered at the edge of his vision suddenly vanished, like a lamp blown out. Maxwell rocked with the impact of it, and the little inn bedchamber spun dizzily around him. He held tight to the window sill and squeezed his eyes shut until the spinning sensation vanished.

When he opened his eyes, it was to one world.

He could no longer see layered images of all the things that might happen—and because of that, he knew what would. She would steal out after dinner to the Carrington orchard to investigate her prize. William would encounter her there and they would explore it together. Perhaps two hours' subjective time from now, a white-haired curmudgeon would rescue them from a construct on a London street. And they would follow the path, up and down a variety of roads, in and out the Eagle and more than one timeline, to an ending where Frankenstein never made his monsters, the British held until the Prussians reached them, no constructs imprisoned Britain thereafter, no genocidal empire spread its poison over the globe, and Maxwell Carrington wound up here, in this place at this moment. He was finally and forever unmoored from the timeline that had birthed him, kept from disintegrating with it only by the second timepiece he had tucked into his right-hand pocket.

All around him stretched rich blue sky, rich brown road, rich green grass. Bees buzzed in and around the flowers of the trellis just outside his window, and roses bloomed in the hedgerows across the way. It was the finest sort of spring afternoon. He hadn't noticed that before.

And for the first time since his hollow youth, he was free to do whatever he liked.

Which meant, come morning, he would make tracks back to London.

∞

The inn dated from the Tudor era, and there was no evidence that it had enjoyed any sort of repair or maintenance in the two hundred years since that era's end. This might not be the worst quarter of London, but it was far from the best—as vouchsafed by the drunkards swilling gin in the middle of the morning and the raucous bets being placed on the cockfight behind the stables. The polished youth decked out in frock coat, buckskins, Hessian boots with tassels, and stovepipe hat pulled down over glossy black hair could not have possibly been more out of place—but so great a level of confidence did this figure project that none of the loiters or gamblers seemed inclined to offer a challenge. The youth rapped smartly upon the inn's front door and was greeted by a slovenly-dressed innkeeper's wife, who initially seemed reluctant to engage in conversation but was eventually persuaded by the glint of silver in her visitor's gloved hand.

Two minutes later, the youth was being conducted up the stairs by a disheveled and exhausted-looking maid-of-all-work, who knocked upon the first floor bedchamber door but did not wait for an answer before pushing it open.

Within, an old man dressed in laborer's clothing that better suited the surroundings was staring rather vacantly out of the tiny window that looked onto the stables and the cockfight. His entire attitude was one of exhaustion, and he looked over at the opening door without any particular surprise or interest, as might a man numbed by drink or age.

"Ah, yes," the youth said. "This is my uncle. I'm glad I've found you, sir."

The old man did not reply.

"Thank you," the youth said to the servant, and bestowed upon her a coin of the same value he had given her mistress. "I need to speak privately with this gentleman, if you please." The servant was more than willing to leave them to it.

As the maid undertook the trudging journey back down the stairs, the door began the process of whining shut, taking its time about the matter and complaining shrilly each instant. The youth reached with an impatient boot heel to hasten the progression to its end; the door clicked shut; and Katarina Rasmirovna and Maxwell Carrington looked at each other.

"What are you doing here?" he greeted her.

She raised her eyebrows at him under the stovepipe hat. "Looking for you, and you didn't make it easy." She took off her hat, a symbolic divestment of disguise—but removing it seemed to strip off her armor of detachment as well, and she was unable to hide the worry that had been swelling in volume within her for months. "So? Did it—?"

"Yes," Maxwell said. "It worked."

Katarina let out a hard breath. "Then you're—"

"Yes." He smiled at her. "Yes, fine."

"Oh," Katarina said. "Oh, that's good." She suddenly found herself urgently needing a better view of the men throwing dice below, so she went to the window to peer down at them.

"You're frankly lucky I found you at all, you know," she commented a few moments later, eyes still on the stable yard. "I almost passed on, thinking I'd come once again to the wrong place. The innkeeper's wife seemed to think you were a much older man."

Behind her, she heard Maxwell get up from his chair, stretching out to his full height and rolling his powerful shoulders within his coat. "Age is all in how you move," he said, a smile in his voice as though he shared a jest with someone not present.

She could guess who. "Is it? Well, don't drop the disguise quite yet. We still have to leave the premises. As efficiently as possible, by preference; I've never seen a room that depressed me more."

"Leave the premises?" he repeated. "I can't yet. I mean to stay until the news from Waterloo reaches London—"

"Of course you do!" Katarina said, turning, exasperated. "But you needn't stay and wait in this flea-ridden hovel. I've acquired for you a far better viewing platform for the festivities." She retrieved her hat from the table. "Your mother and father can't attend, of course, having unfortunately already spent the twenty-first of June eighteen hundred and fifteen doing something else—but we can. You deserve to be there, after everything you've done to bring it about."

"I deserve to be where?"

Katarina set the hat on her head. "Where do you think?"

He stared, honestly shocked. "How in the world did you manage to wrangle an invitation?"

Katarina gave him a smile. "I invested a bit of time building this persona. And in answer to your next question—yes, I do in fact think tonight is that important."

∽

The air outside was warm and light. Within the Boehm household, packed as it was with candles and warm bodies, the temperature had already reached "sweltering"—but none of Mrs. Boehm's guests would have wished themselves elsewhere. They were, after all, among the honored comparatively few who had received an invitation to dine and dance with the Prince Regent.

The fashion for gauzy dresses with high waists and low bodices was unkind to all but the slimmest of women, and Katarina knew perfectly well it did not show her to best advantage. But fashions that accentuated the waist were not due to arrive in London for more than a decade, and at least she was allowed the rich colors befitting a mature woman. She had chosen a dark red silk ideally suited to her coloring. And at least she might dress her hair with a jeweled comb, having mercifully avoided by a couple of years on one side and a couple of years on the other the need to wear a turban or feathers. She would have worn the damned feathers if it had been the only way to blend into this crowd, but the comb made her feel at least a little like herself.

At her side, Maxwell was similarly clothed in a fashion that did not suit him: tightly-fitted breeches, high boots, double-breasted blue frock coat with tails. He was a man born for the looser trousers and waistcoats that would replace breeches and tail coats in fifteen years' time and linger in one form or another for more than a hundred years thereafter; though she had gotten the measurements right and the clothing he wore fit him, he still looked like a man wearing a costume. And it suddenly occurred to her to wonder whether he even knew the steps of these dances.

They had arrived at the Boehm household just a smidgeon later than fashionably late, entering the ballroom to find the musicians were a measure or two into the first dance. At the top of the room, His Royal Highness was officially opening the ball by dancing with his hostess. Katarina and her escort need to do nothing for the moment but watch.

Katarina's eye traced the patterns that formed and broke and reformed as the dancers wound around each other. Occasionally her thoughts strayed to the larger matter, but she resolutely forced them back. Concentrating on the cotillion was all that enabled her to keep from fidgeting while she waited for the news.

She was not worried. She was *not*. Maxwell believed he had successfully delivered the watch to Elizabeth Barton; the abatement of Maxwell's symptoms would seem to confirm successful delivery; there was no reason to think some loose-cannon madman with one of the unrecovered pocket watches would have undone the victory at Waterloo.

But then, there never *was* any reason to suspect such a thing until the threads of history fell into disarray at one's feet.

Katarina was *not* worried, but she *had* been mentally following the chess moves—on the battlefield and off of it—for the last five days. Maxwell had posted a watch on the sixteenth of June. On the seventeenth, Elizabeth had received it. On the eighteenth, Wellington had sent Freemantle for Prussians rather than for monsters, and on the following morning he had sat down to write his dispatch. Just after midday on the nineteenth of June, Major Percy had left for London with the report, still clad in the bloodied uniform he had worn on the battlefield, clutching the captured Imperial Eagles to prove his claim of victory.

Katarina knew the history: it had taken Percy more than forty-eight maddening hours to cross land and Channel and land again. She had followed every step in her mind while hunting Maxwell through inn after disreputable inn. If the history books were accurate, if Maxwell had in fact managed to get the watch to Elizabeth, if no unknown actor with a timepiece had undone their work, if, if, if—if all had gone as it should, Percy ought to have embarked upon the road for London a few hours before, with the Eagles sticking out the window of his post-chaise. He was very likely in the city now, perhaps even at the Prime Minister's house already, and surely therefore it could not be much longer—

Katarina became suddenly aware that at her side, Maxwell was watching the musicians and the swirling couples with quite an odd expression upon his face. She opened her fan with a flourish to give the two of them a screen behind which they might speak. "All well?"

"Oh, yes. I was just…reminded of something." The eyes he turned toward her were clear, not narrowed in an attempt to select between competing sets of images, and his expression was rueful rather than bitter. "Looking through the bannister at the ball is a metaphor for the time traveler's life, isn't it? The unmoored traveler, at least. After all this wandering, I've deliberately chosen a life in which I will always be watching this sort of thing from the outside."

"Yes," Katarina said. "But you will not be watching it alone."

He smiled a little. "Very true. And of course we can always join in briefly, when we have a mind to."

She chose to take the statement literally. "Do you know how to dance a cotillion?"

"I know how to dance a quadrille. More or less the same thing, I believe?"

Katarina pursed her lips. "Well, more when compared to a salsa or a hula, but…rather less when in a room of cotillion experts." She gestured with her fan at the room. "Quadrilles don't arrive in London until next year. This step is slightly different."

"Ah, well," he said, still smiling slightly, and as the music came to an end, raised his gloved hands to applaud along with the other onlookers.

The musicians struck up another tune. "This is a waltz," Maxwell said in surprise. "Are waltzes the done thing? I thought in 1815 they were still considered most shockingly modern and improper."

Katarina grinned, quickly hiding the unguarded expression behind her fan. "They are indeed so considered by most mammas of marriageable daughters. And by the patronesses of Almack's, who will only grant permission to waltz to girls whose deportment is considered 'impeccable.'"

"I don't believe I know any such girls."

"I don't believe you do, no. Certainly you're not related to any. But the waltz became fashionable among the aristocracy sometime last year, during the premature first round of Napoleonic victory celebrations—so yes, it is the done thing in, let us say, *avant-garde* circles."

"By which you mean, it *is* considered risqué and improper," Maxwell interpreted, "but those of a certain temperament dance it anyhow?"

Katarina kept her fan up to hide the broadness of her grin. "That is precisely what I mean."

Maxwell looked out over the ballroom, that same odd smile on his lips, as though carefully contemplating what she had told him. Then he took a deep breath, drew himself up to his full height, and turned back to her with a gloved hand outstretched.

"Madame Rasmirovna, may I have this dance?"

Katarina let her fan close in her hand. "My dear Mr. Maxwell," she replied, "I thought you would never ask."

The musicians were playing a rather fast tempo, and if Katarina had been able to plan, she would not have selected this for a first dance with a new partner. Unlike a cotillion or a quadrille, a waltz was an interpretation, a blend of the steps and the personality of the man or woman who danced them. One had to know how one's partner moved, what grace or nimbleness or caution ran through the lines of their body, how the cues for movement were to be given and acknowledged, and one might be forgiven for wanting to discover such things slowly, with plenty of time to adjust and correct. One might expect that having a quick waltz as a couple's first dance would lead to an awkward, stumbling experience—an experience that both parties might laugh at with painful affection in years to come, but one which they would first have to endure.

But she and Maxwell found the rhythm of the dance as though they had done it a hundred times before. After the first three steps she did not have to think about her feet at all. She knew from the slightest pressure of his hand what he meant to do next, and he took her subtler cues as readily as if she had shouted them, matching his steps to hers without any apparent effort. They whirled in and out of the whirling couples, no patterns to follow here except what they chose to make, or what naturally evolved as they threaded their way through all the twirling spinning-top obstacles—each of which was also intent on making patterns of its own—a dazzling tumbling component of a beautiful multicolored chaos. In and out the Needle, wasn't that the expression? Or it would be someday.

Over the music rose the sound of shouting.

Katarina's heart had not been racing from the dancing, but now it thumped hard beneath the unflattering red silk. The shouts outside—were they cheers or were they something more ominous?—swelled to a volume no one could ignore. All around her on the dance floor, steps were missed as heads began to turn. The musicians stumbled to a squawking silence; the spinning couples fell out of the waltz step and stumbled in their turn to an ungraceful halt. Half the guests were rushing for the windows. The other half stood still, waiting. At the top of the room, the Prince Regent seemed to be holding his breath.

A gaunt, grim-faced man appeared in the doorway. He looked like a ghost, white with fatigue, heavy bags under his eyes, his uniform stained with the mud and blood of the battlefield. Something long and lean was wrapped in canvas and cradled in his arms. At the sight of him, all remaining speculative whispering stopped. The ballroom was all at once utterly, eerily silent.

The soldier's eyes searched the room—found the Prince Regent—and his exhausted face broke into a smile.

"Victory, Sire!"

The room seemed to release a collective held breath. The glittering *ton* parted before Major Percy as he strode across the ballroom, fell to one knee, and presented the Regent with the captured Imperial Eagles.

Then it was as though the sound had been switched back on. From the street outside came increasingly wild cheering and the sound of ringing church bells. Beside Katarina, Maxwell let out a breath as though setting down a load. He really did look decades younger when he smiled like that.

All around them on the dance floor, the other guests exclaimed with relief and joy. Questions were shouted. Toasts were proposed. Cheers rose, uncoordinated, overlapping, deafening. In the midst of such happy chaos, it was quite easy for the man and woman who ought never to have been there in the first place to slip away.

As she and Maxwell made their unobtrusive way through the hallway, past the dining room where was spread a sumptuous supper that no one would now be interested in eating, Katarina heard the irritated voice of her hostess. "All this trouble and expense utterly thrown away! Of course one is very glad to know one has beaten those horrid French, and all that sort of thing, but surely Henry Percy could have waited quietly until morning, instead of bursting in upon us in such indecent haste! Such an unkempt figure, too, and those nasty dirty Eagles—" Katarina had to bite her lip hard to keep from bursting into laughter, and she didn't dare catch Maxwell's eye.

Katarina led the way into the cozy first floor library of the house she had taken for the Season, stripping off her elbow-length dancing gloves as she walked. She dropped them on sideboard holding a collection of bottles and snifters, and continued without pausing to the polished wood desk in the corner. "Brandy?" she asked over her shoulder as she crouched down beside the desk. The fabric of her gown strained and something gave with a soft ripping sound, and Katarina swore and repositioned herself.

"No, thank you." Maxwell watched with interest as she detached a false panel from the desk, revealing within a strongbox, a portmanteau, and a very familiar rucksack. From the strongbox she took a quantity of envelopes, checking the contents within each and the names inscribed on the front of each before stacking them on the desk. "For the servants," she explained to Maxwell, looking up to catch his gaze. "A month's wages and a character reference for all of them. This—" She lifted from the strongbox a bag that clinked suggestively. "—goes with us."

Maxwell came to claim his rucksack. "May I infer you intend to vanish from within your locked house?"

"Why not? We couldn't find a quiet street corner out there anyhow—I believe the whole of London is running about celebrating Napoleon's defeat. Leaving a bit of a mystery by vanishing from here seems preferable to drawing attention out there." She opened the portmanteau and rummaged inside it, shifting aside journals and costuming bits, until she unearthed the trousers, blouse, and bodice that were her preferred clothing when she was not dressing a part. She pulled the comb from her hair, tucked it carefully within the portmanteau, and began pulling the rest of the pins out of the shining black coil. "If you wish to change your clothing, you're welcome to go behind that door."

Maxwell took his own default outfit from the rucksack and went behind the door to strip off the irritatingly constrictive Regency garb. When he returned, wearing the suit that had proven close enough to the fashion of the Victorian and many other eras, Katarina was dressed in her familiar trousers, boots, and blouse, and was just threading the last bodice lacing. *Her* ensemble did not blend well with the fashion of any nearby era of which Maxwell was aware, but Katarina never seemed to consider that factor worth considering. Her thick black hair swung loose, a sure sign that she anticipated no combat in the near future.

At her feet, the red silk dress lay in an artistic heap. He was reminded of—but did not actually see, thank heavens—the opera gown left abandoned in 1895. He nodded to the pool of silk. "Again? Do you mean this to be your signature?"

"Something like that." She looked up from fastening the bodice lacing, and their eyes met.

He swallowed hard. She had always been beautiful in candlelight.

He had stood this close to her before. Often. He had stood closer when holding her in his arms for the waltz.

She did not move away.

After a moment, he did, stepping back and clearing his throat. "So. Where are we going next?"

Katarina smiled a little, but answered readily. "We are next due to meet your parents in May of 2014, in a city a short ways outside Boston, in Massachuessets. Your father believes he has a lead on a timepiece there."

"The Colonies, two hundred years from now?" Maxwell said, allowing himself to be distracted by this genuine surprise. "I can't imagine they'll still be wearing this." He touched a hand to his chest, then indicated her bodice. "And I'm fairly certain they won't be wearing that. Will we not attract all sorts of undue attention?"

"No," Katarina said, now also distracted by it, eyes sparkling with the promise of a new adventure, "that's the glorious part of it. The city holds a faire to celebrate olden times, *this* time, or at least what they imagine this time to be like, and we'll fit right in. I even more than you, if you can believe it. No, I am *absolutely* serious. Just you wait and see. It'll be a right puzzle to sort a real abandoned timepiece from all the replicas for sale, but I've no doubt we'll manage it in the end."

Maxwell took up one of the candles and held it aloft, checking that nothing had fallen out of his rucksack that would need to be repacked. He had been overly careful about such things since the history book that recorded Elizabeth Barton's martyrdom had been abandoned and made it the printers in a timeline that did not include her death. That thought led to another, and he asked, "How's the Frankenstein situation, in 2014?"

"Firmly categorized as fiction. Ready to go?"

"Yes—" He started to blow the candle out, then stopped. "No." *If not now, when?* "Katarina."

At his change in tone, she stilled completely. It was as though the universe stilled around them. All the universes, all the timelines, all the possibilities, collapsed into one unmarked path forward. Katarina looked at him steadily out of very serious dark eyes. "Yes?"

"We...will not actually keep them waiting at the dinner-table, if we go somewhere else between here and 2014 in Boston."

"That's true," Katarina agreed, her eyes not leaving his. "Where do you wish to go?"

"Well—to begin with—to begin with, I believe you agreed to dance a waltz with me, and by my estimate we barely danced half of one before Percy interrupted. I should like—" He held out one hand to her, aping the manners of the ballroom. "—to claim the second half of our dance."

She laid her hand in his, eyes crinkling in the beginning of a smile. "I should like that as well."

He pulled her closer with an arm around her waist, essaying a step or two though there were no musicians here to provide the tempo. "And then there are musical performances we might attend? Vienna in the late eighteenth century, let us say." She was moving with him in this strange playful pretense of a waltz, the little smile widening. "Or the theatre? One of Shakespeare's plays performed at the Globe before the Great Fire?" He led her into a turn, and she glided with him as though she had anticipated it. "Or...walks through green meadows, if green meadows appeal to you." At the end of the turn he stopped her, so they could see each other's faces. "I think I just erased any house and fortune I may have once had in 1848, but we could visit anyhow if you'd like to explore the era. The fashion would be closer to what you're accustomed to, and I did once know that version of London rather well. I could show you about. We could have a pleasant time. We could even go during the Christmas season and seek out one of Mr. Dickens' performances, in which he reads from that wretched book."

She laughed at that. "Yes," she said. "I like all these ideas very much. Mr. Maxwell, I thought you would never ask."

He exhaled. "I've been at the point of it before now, but we had business to attend to first." He reached for her hand again, and she automatically stretched out her own to meet it. He touched his lips to her knuckles. He had begun seductions that way before; he knew how to begin seductions.

What he did not know, he found, was how to begin something more complex. After holding her hand for a moment in a silence that threatened to be awkward, he admitted it. "I don't have a script for this part. This is the part in the romance novel where the marriage proposal takes place, but..."

Katarina paused. "Are you proposing marriage?"

"No."

"Good."

"Good?"

"Well, we hardly know each other well enough yet, do we? I couldn't say at this point whether or not I might someday wish to marry you. I *do* wish to do all the things you suggested just now. I wish to do some other things you did not suggest but I think were in your mind. And who's to say what either of us will wish for, after that? I can't see that far ahead. Can you?"

"Not any longer," he said. "And what a relief that is."

"Then let us go listen to Mozart, and dance waltzes, and walk through green meadows, and I think I shall accept your gentlemanly offer of a Dickensian Christmas, thank you. And then...we'll see where we are. And let us by all means do these things, or some of them at least, before we meet your parents in 2014. As you say, it's not as though we'll be keeping them waiting."

"In fact," Maxwell said, deliberately choosing to make the stupid jest, "we have all—"

"—the time in the world," Katarina finished. Because she did, actually, know him that well.

With one hand he smoothed back her hair. With the other he encircled her waist and drew her closer. He kissed her for the first time while outside the crazed city of London celebrated its victory over foreign conquest, rewritten history, and rampaging monsters. When his lips touched hers, the world went rainbowy and dark and bright.

༄ THE END ༄

Author's Note

n February 27, 1943, nine incredibly brave Norwegians, four of whom had been starving on the Vidda since Operation Grouse dropped them there four months before, infiltrated the mountain fortress that was the Vermok Hydroelectric Plant and destroyed the heavy water production that was about to fuel the Nazi atomic bomb. They were stalwart in the face of enormous bodily deprivation and despite the likelihood of capture and torture; they executed a sabotage so neat the furious Gestapo commander was forced to admit it "a most splendid coup"; and they needed no one's help. I didn't have the arrogance to insert my time travelers into their story.

But it is true that the resistance they encountered was much softer than what they had been led to expect. They went in prepared to face mines, machine guns, dogs, floodlights, and potentially the entire German garrison in nearby Rjukan. What they encountered, according to what I've read in more than one work based on their personal recollections, was surprisingly unprofessional. I didn't invent either the Nazi who barely looked up from his card game or the one who couldn't find the light switch.

Wondering *what the hell?* about discrepancies like this is where alternate universe time travel stories come from. The mistakes made by the Nazi guardsmen that night were so egregious that it makes one (it made me, at least) wonder about internal sabotage. It wouldn't have been the only internal sabotage going on at that time, after all; while the Allies were planning Operation Gunnerside, a number of (also incredibly brave) Norwegian plant workers were, on their own initiative, surreptitiously adding castor oil to the heavy water, trying to slow the Nazis down as much as they could.

I like it as a metaphor. We can't all parachute onto the Vidda, survive a climb, or set the charges. Nor is everyone in a position to sabotage enemy training. But most of us can find some castor oil somewhere. That's how you fix the future when you're living in a straight line.

⌒

y deepest and sincerest apologies to Kayser Idland, whose terrifying account of the climb up the gorge I gave to Knut Haukelid. My deepest gratitude to Neal Bascomb, author of *The Winter Fortress,* and to Thomas Gallagher, author of *Assault in Norway,* both of which I relied upon extensively for accounts of the Gunnerside raid. Any errors introduced are of course my own.

Thanks and apologies are also owed to Arthur Morrision (because I let Katarina pull the wool over the eyes of his detective Martin Hewitt), to Verna Tilley (because I let Katarina borrow some of her act), and to the Watch City Steampunk Festival (where the Carrington family was certainly not searching for a real timepiece amid a sea of replicas in May of 2014). And finally, my deepest gratitude to Rocco and Claire Albano, Jennifer Regan, and Ron Streeper, the "Mary Shelley"-level Kickstarter backers who named Stanislaus Lis, Rosamund Holborn, and Arcturus Bastion.

About the Author

HEATHER ALBANO is a storyteller, history geek, and lover of both time-travel tropes and re-imaginings of older stories. In addition to novels, she writes interactive fiction. She finds the line between the two getting fuzzier all the time. Heather lives in Massachusetts with her husband, two cats, a tankful of fish, and an excessive amount of tea. Learn more about her various projects at **heatheralbano.com**.

Read more from
Stillpoint Digital Press!

Exploring the seams where humanity and technology, society and individuality intersect, Nebula- and Sturgeon-nominated author Kenneth Schneyer presents thirteen mind-bending, thought-provoking tales of near and far futures that will amuse, amaze, and unsettle. The law will change, and the heart will change, and the heart will change the law. These stories confront the question of just what makes and keeps us human.

Samurai, assassins, warlords…and a girl who likes to climb.

Though Japan has been devastated by a century of civil war, Risuko just wants to climb trees. Growing up far from the battlefields and court intrigues, the fatherless girl finds herself pulled into a plot that may reunite Japan -- or may destroy it. She is torn from her home and what is left of her family, but finds new friends at a school that may not be what it seems.

Magical but historical, Risuko follows her along the first dangerous steps to discovering who she truly is.

STILLPOINTDIGITALPRESS.COM